GAY LONGWORTH

Born in 1970, Gay Longworth trained as an oil trader after graduating from university. It was during this time that the idea for her first novel, *Bimba*, came to her. Eventually she took courage, left the job, and moved to Cornwall to write. *Bimba* was published in 1998, and her second novel, *Wicked Peace*, came out two years later.

During that time Gay had too many jobs to mention, though donning fishnets for Club Med was probably a low point. Thankfully she is now a full-time writer.

Dead Alone is the first in a series of Jessie Driver novels, and she is currently working on the second. Gay lives in London with her husband, theatre producer Adam Spiegel, and their daughter.

By the same author

Bimba
Wicked Peace

GAY LONGWORTH

DEAD ALONE

HarperCollins*Publishers*

HarperCollins*Publishers*
77–85 Fulham Palace Road, London W6 8JB

www.fireandwater.com

This paperback edition 2003

3 5 7 9 10 8 6 4

First published in Great Britain by
HarperCollins*Publishers* 2002

ISBN 0 00 713956 X

Typeset in Sabon by Palimpsest Book Production Limited,
Polmont, Stirlingshire

Printed and bound in Great Britain by
Clays Ltd, St Ives plc

To my mother
A hard act to follow

ACKNOWLEDGEMENTS

Becoming a thriller writer is a daunting prospect and I could not have done it without the help of Paul Dockley, retired Detective Chief Superintendent of Hertfordshire Constabulary. Many pints were sunk for the sake of accuracy.

For reading, advice, soundboards and shoulders to cry on I'd like to thank Stephanie Pavlik, Joanna Longworth, Thalia Murray, Dee Poku, Juliet Dominguez, Felicity Gillespie, Angelina Davy and my mother. For chai made to exacting standards I'd like to thank Sophie.

A special mention to those who shall remain nameless who lifted the lid on celebrity and let me take a peek inside.

To my fantastic agents Stephanie Cabot and Eugenie Furniss at William Morris Agency whose influence and assistance go far, far beyond the limits of literature. Thank you also to Marie Baron and Tracy Fisher in the WMA in New York for giving this London-based book an international audience.

At HarperCollins I'd like to thank everyone involved in the impressive production of *Dead Alone*. A special mention to Anne O'Brien, a brilliant copy editor who turned a usually painful process into a joy.

Most importantly, my sincere gratitude to Julia Wisdom, for her faith, expertise and insight; thank you.

Lastly, but most heartfelt, my love and thanks to my husband Adam – it just gets better.

Everyone sees himself as a star today. This is both a cliché and a profound truth. Thousands of young men and women have the looks, the clothes, the hairstyling, the drugs, the personal magnetism, the self-confidence, and the history of conquest that proclaims a star. The one thing they lack – talent – is precisely what is most lacking in those other, nearly identical, young people whom the world has acclaimed as stars. Never in the history of show biz has the gap between amateur and professional been so small. And never in the history of the world has there been such a rage for exhibitionism. The question is, therefore, what are we going to do with all these beautiful show-offs?

Albert Goldman. *Disco.*

PROLOGUE

Jessie Driver had her thighs clamped round the leg of a man she hadn't been introduced to. Hanging upside down, she could feel the sweat running through her short spiky hair. From the corner of her eye she watched two men shake hands. The small envelope of folded lottery paper passed from one palm to another. Jessie was pulled back up and spun around. It was time to leave this club. Local boys from the nearby estate were eclipsing the dance aficionados and the atmosphere was becoming increasingly hostile. Jessie couldn't relax any more. She ran her hand down the perfectly smooth biceps of the man she'd been dancing with, squeezed his hand reluctantly and left. Her flatmate, Maggie Hall, was signing a flurry of autographs by the bar. All men, Jessie mused as she approached.

'Jesus, you're soaking,' said Maggie, looking at Jessie in disgust.

'Properly purged.' Jessie leant closer. 'Can we go?'

Maggie nodded, flashed an 'if only' smile to the admirer she would instantly forget and walked with Jessie to the coat check. Maggie was a presenter; with ruthless ambition she had come up through the highly competitive ranks to become a household name. It was strange watching an old friend gain in fame. Of course, at thirty, it hadn't come soon enough for Maggie. People asked Jessie whether Maggie had changed. The answer was no. She'd always been ambitious.

They had reached the motorbike bay when Jessie heard the sound of a van backfiring. Twice. In quick succession. She turned abruptly towards the noise. Like a solitary clap in a crowded room, the sound silenced the world around them. For a second. And then people started to scream. A man ran across the road and climbed into a waiting car. From the narrow doorway and two fire-exits people spilled out into the street. Jessie threw her helmet at Maggie.

'No, Jessie!' shouted Maggie. But Jessie didn't hear her. She ran straight into the sea of oncoming frightened faces. Ducking, side-stepping, shouldering against the outpour. She battled against the tide down the narrow staircase. At the bottom, a young man lay on the ground. He'd been shot. Twice. Two girls stood next to him screaming and jumping up and down intermittently. She threw her phone at one of them.

'Call the police and ambulance service,' barked Jessie. Her commanding voice silenced them as swiftly as the gunshot had set them off. 'And someone turn that music off!'

Only the man made a noise now. He wasn't dead. But he was bleeding profusely.

'What's your name?' asked Jessie.

'Carl,' he whimpered.

'Carl,' she said, 'the ambulance is on the way. Meantime, I've got to try and stop this bleeding. You stay focused, concentrate on me.'

Jessie ripped his trousers and T-shirt and examined the singed, bloody holes.

'Perhaps you should think about a change of career,' said Jessie. 'Small-time dealing on someone else's patch is a sure-fire way to get yourself killed.' She smiled at him. 'And I think that would be a waste. Good-looking boy like you.' One bullet had embedded itself in his right thigh. The other had passed through his left flank. Jessie guessed he must have spun round from the impact of the first bullet and been hit by the second in the leg. Better aim and the boy would have died instantly.

'Well, Carl, seems it was your lucky day,' said Jessie.

The boy continued to blink at her, mesmerised. The girls stepped forward to get a better look. Jessie pulled a couple of super-sized tampons from her bag, ripped the plastic off with her teeth, and inserted one gently into the bullet wound in the boy's leg. It was soon plump with blood. Carl clenched his jaw and shuddered. Jessie inserted the second into the boy's fleshy side.

'Carl,' said Jessie, 'you still with me?'

'Man,' said one of the girls, 'she just stuck a Lil-let in your leg.'

Carl groaned and passed out.

The sight of two uniformed officers careering down the stairs made the girls jump.

'Step away from the body,' shouted one of the officers.

'Show your hands, slowly,' shouted the other.

Jessie turned around. 'Everyone calm down. Where is the ambulance?'

'Move aside,' ordered the police officer.

Jessie did.

They stared down at the gunshot wounds. 'What the hell is this?'

'Don't worry, they're sterile. Thought it best, given the length of time ambulances take to get to shootings in this part of town.'

The coppers didn't appreciate the snide comment. 'And who are you – Florence Nightingale?'

Jessie reached into the back pocket of her tight blue jeans and held up a leather wallet. 'I'm Detective Inspector Driver from West End Central CID, and if you want to know who shot this man, he is five foot eight, medium build, mixed race, wearing a red Polo running top. He left in a dark blue Audi 80, number plate T33 X9R.' Jessie looked over to the girls. 'Sound familiar?' she asked.

Neither of them spoke.

'Thought so,' said Jessie, standing up.

Two paramedics arrived. Jessie stepped away. The uniformed officers stared at her as she began to mount the stairs.

'You know where to find me,' she said to their fixed expressions.

The paramedic looked up at her. 'Thanks for bridging the gap,' he said, folding out a stretcher.

'My pleasure,' said Jessie, and left.

Out on the street, Maggie stood holding both helmets. She smiled at Jessie.

'All right, Mad Max. You done with your life-saving antics?'

'Yes thank you, Anne Robinson, I am.'

'Sure? No burning buildings to run into? No pile-ups to attend?'

Jessie swung her leg across the leather seat of the chrome-and-black Virago and started the engine.

'Finished?' Jessie asked, backing out of the parking bay.

'Yes.'

'Then get on.'

Maggie smiled. 'I love it when you get all masterful.'

'Kebab?' asked Jessie.

'No,' said Maggie. 'I'm off to Istanbul, that means bikini and camera crew in close quarters, that means no kebab.'

'I'm hungry,' complained Jessie, revving the bike.

'You're weird. Now, take me home, Arnie. And don't blast that music in your ears, it makes me nervous. You have precious cargo on board.'

Dutifully placing her minidisk player back in her pocket, Jessie pressed the bike into gear. It heaved forward. Jessie turned out of the cul-de-sac and raced down Goldhawk Road just as police reinforcements arrived.

West End Central was an old-fashioned, York stone building in the heart of Mayfair. Jessie had recently been assigned to the Detective Chief Inspector there, a man called Jones, a legendary police officer who had her hanging off his every softly spoken word. His Area Major Investigating Team were responsible for a large portion of Central London, and with around two hundred murders in London a year, they were kept reasonably busy.

She loved this new posting. She loved being back in London after four years in the regionals doing exam after exam to gain the necessary qualifications to make her the youngest DI on the team. Though her brothers, parents and friends were proud, there were others who did not appreciate her achievement. Jessie draped her leather jacket over the back of her chair and sat at her desk. A large box of Tampax had been placed in the middle of her blotting pad. The subtlety was not lost on her. She rested her chin in her cupped hand and stared at it. She could see the humour, really – if it had been left by anyone other than Mark Ward. Her professional equal. Her personal opposite.

A small, curvaceous girl was pacing the corridor outside her open doorway. Jessie watched the vaguely familiar creature wiggle, swivel and sigh dramatically. Puppy fat on heels.

'Can I help you?' Jessie enquired politely.

The girl stopped in the doorway, weighed up Jessie's role and decided on secretary. 'I'm waiting for Mr Ward. He's a friend of my father's. Can you check his diary, he should be here.'

'What are you seeing him about?'

'Someone is out to kill me.'

'Oh.' Jessie nodded in a manner she hoped looked sympathetic. 'Your name is . . . ?'

'Jami,' she shrieked. 'With an "i". I'm a singer. Some man has been sending me these letters.'

'How do you know it's a man?'

'It always is.'

Jessie took the 'death threats' from her just as Mark Ward appeared. The forty-eight-year-old glanced downwards, unable to resist the gravitational pull of the well-mounted chest on display. Jessie could hear the saliva in his throat when he spoke.

'Sorry to keep you waiting. You must be feeling terrible.' He snatched the letters back from Jessie and gave her a warning look before leading the girl away. Jessie gave it a few minutes before following them across the corridor. The great divide.

'Thought you might want to take a DNA swab,' said Jessie, leaning into the room. 'The person sending these threatening letters may already have acquired personal items belonging to Jami.'

'We don't need your help, thank you,' said Mark bitterly.

'No, that sounds good. People will want to know what you're doing to protect me,' said Jami.

'We can also compare it to the saliva on the envelope,' said Jessie. The young performer held the smile until she fully comprehended Jessie's words. 'Then we'll know when we've found the person responsible,' she continued.

'Excuse me, Driver,' said Mark furiously. 'I'm in charge of this.'

'I'm sorry. I was only trying to help. I've brought a couple of swabs –' She showed Jami the white spatula in its grey plastic case. 'We'll just scrape the inside of your cheek, and that's it.'

'I . . .' Jami looked around the room for an exit. 'I can't have any foreign objects in my mouth. It could damage my vocal cords. I'm a singer!'

'They are completely sterile,' assured Jessie as she took a big step towards the shrinking girl.

Jami started backing out of the room, reached the door and picked up speed. 'I need to talk to my manager about this. I'll come back.' Her six-inch heels clicked like castanets as she made her getaway.

Jessie turned back to Mark, smiling.

'What the hell do you think you are doing?!'

'Come on, you didn't –'

'Go away, Driver. Why don't you do us all a favour and fast-track your tight arse back to the classroom, eh? Leave the real jobs to the real policemen. And stop sticking your oar and any other pussy paraphernalia where it's not wanted, needed or desired.'

Ah, thought Jessie, that was the line he'd been working on. Quite inventive, *pussy paraphernalia*; quite a poetic ring about it. She flashed him a smile. 'Tell me, Mark, do you play with yourself as much as you amuse yourself?'

Mark picked up the phone. 'I need to call the press office, tell them they won't be getting their photo op.'

'*Their* photo op. Right.'

He raised his eyebrows. 'Yes, actually, their photo op.' He paused dramatically. 'Imagine that, Driver, you don't know everything, after all.'

Coming out of Mark's office, Jessie bumped into their boss, DCI Jones. He was an unassuming man with grey eyes that matched his suits. As far as Jessie could tell, his only mistake was thinking that she and Mark Ward could learn from each other. Ward had been in the Force nearly thirty years, starting on the beat and working his way up until he was made a detective twelve years ago. He'd dragged bodies from burning cars, rivers and ditches, picked bomb victims' remains off buildings, and dismembered bodies off railway lines – a hard-drinking, notebook-carrying copper who was being phased out. She was thirty-three, same rank, and all her experience was two-dimensional. They were vastly different species occupying the same ecosystem; it couldn't last.

'Jessie! Perfect. I'd like you to come with me,' said Jones.

'I've got to go to the press office.'

'Not that bunch of interfering old bags.'

'I've made a –'

'This is important. You can read the file on the way.' Jones suddenly tensed.

'You all right, sir?'

'Old age. I'll meet you downstairs.'

When she went to retrieve her jacket from her chair, Mark appeared in her doorway.

'Managed to wiggle your way out of trouble again?'

She didn't bother looking at him. 'Fuck off, Mark.'

'Thought you lot were supposed to use long words.'

Jessie zipped her leather jacket and stood back. 'I'm sorry I got in the way of your voyeurism. Had I known it was the closest you'd get to the female form, I'd have left you to it.'

Mark watched from his office window as Jones and Jessie crossed the car park. When they'd pulled out of the gate, he called the duty officer.

11

'Who's doing the next few shifts?'

'I'm on double,' said the man. 'Getting married, need the overtime.'

'Next duff DOA you get in, give it to DI Driver. The duffer the better. I want to teach that little upstart a lesson in good policing.'

'Yes, sir.'

'When you go off duty, pass the message on to whoever comes on.'

'Yes, sir.'

'I'll get a pot going, for your wedding.'

'Thanks, sir. Much appreciated.'

'This is between us.'

'Of course.'

Mark put down the phone and prayed for a fly-infested OAP.

∼

Jessie stood alongside Jones as he knocked sharply on the door twice. The flat was on the third floor of a council block that overlooked a poorly maintained central courtyard deep in the heart of Bethnal Green. The square mile's adjunct; as poor as its closest relation was rich. Robed women pushed prams, men stood in groups on street corners and bored kids kicked a deflated football against a wall. Jessie felt the resolute atmosphere of foiled expectation all around her. They heard the unmistakable scrape of a chain and a large brown eye peered out at them. Jones held up his badge. Clare Mills, the woman they had come to see, drew the door back. She was a thin woman, tall, and very lined. She had a thick crease etched between her eyebrows. A permanent worry line. Her light brown hair was short, thinning, and Jessie could see strands of wiry grey in amongst it. This woman looked as though she'd been worrying all her life and, according to Jones' story, she obviously had.

Twenty-four years ago an innocent passer-by was shot during a robbery. That man was Clare's father, Trevor Mills. He'd been on his way home from a job interview. Carrying an innocuous brown paper bag. Sweets for his kids – he'd got the job. The stray bullet had been fired by a man called Raymond Giles, a notorious gangster of his time. At first the police thought Giles had fled to Spain, but after an anonymous tip-off he was found hiding out at a hotel in Southend. Eventually Raymond Giles was sentenced to sixteen years for manslaughter. The tariff was high because, although the prosecution could not prove intent, the judge knew men like Raymond Giles. Intent to harm was not specific. It was innate. His arrest was a coup for all concerned.

But for Clare Mills it was only the beginning of the nightmare. Her large brown eyes were suspicious, she blinked nervously, continuously. The torn skin around her nails was bitten back to the knuckle on her long, thin fingers. Jessie followed Clare through to the surprisingly light, bright

13

yellow kitchen and tried to break the ice as she made tea. 'I don't sleep much,' was the answer she gave to most questions. Hardly surprising, thought Jessie as they returned to the small sitting room. The day Clare saw her father lowered into the grave was the day her mother committed suicide. She was eight when she found her mother hanging from the back of the wardrobe, the mascara-stained tear tracks barely dry on her cheeks. Even that was not the worst thing that was to happen to Clare Mills.

Jessie tried again. How did she manage to do so many shifts at work and look after the elderly lady next door? How did she find time to draw and paint? The answer always came back the same. 'I don't sleep much.'

It was different when they started talking about Frank.

'My little brother. Five years younger than me. Their miracle child, Mum and Dad used to say. They were so happy. We were. He was a gorgeous kid, simply gorgeous. I played with him every day, every day until . . .' Clare turned away from them and stared out of the rectangular window. The day after their mother died a car came to take the children into care. Except that two cars came. One took Clare and one took Frank. It was the last time she saw him.

Clare's pleas had gone unheard for years. Until she had begun chaining herself to the gates of Woolwich Cemetery, where her mother was buried.

14

It had become a PR nightmare. The search for Frank had at last become a matter for the AMIT team, and Jones had been given the case. Now he was talking, apologising, trying to find the right words.

'. . . and whatever happens, we'll find out what happened to Frank and we'll make those responsible for what has happened pay –'

'There is only one, and you've let him out.' Clare spat out the words. 'The man who shot Dad. That thieving bastard, swanning about –'

Jones leant forward. 'He spent a long time in prison, Clare. He did his time. Let's concentrate on Frank and the people who were supposed to be looking after him. And you.'

'Mum and Dad were supposed to be looking after us.'

'Clare . . .' pleaded Jones.

Clare turned to Jessie. 'My mother sat by my dad's hospital bed for three weeks. She didn't sleep, she didn't eat, she just sat there and waited for him to wake up. He fought, I've seen the records, I've spoken to one of the nurses who was there, she remembered my mum, sitting there, praying for him. Mum refused to leave, she wouldn't let anyone in neither, except her friend Irene, of course. They remember Dad fighting to stay alive. He fought so hard he came round a few times, just to tell Mum he loved her, and us, but it was a losing battle. Stray bullet? Stray? Tell me, how does a stray bullet hit a man point-blank in the heart?'

'We can't change the law,' said Jones. 'He served nine years behind bars. That's a long time.'

So, thought Jessie, the man who ruined Clare's life was out. A free man again. Jessie believed in repaying one's debt to society. She believed time served meant a slate wiped clean. She actively dissuaded her team from reaching for the con-list every time a body appeared. But she could see in Clare Mills' saucer-sized eyes that she would never be free of this crime. Her sentence meant life.

'Not long enough for three murders.' She was shaking now. 'No, make that four.'

Clare had no other family. Her father's parents had died before she was born. Clare's mother, Veronica, hadn't spoken to her family in years. Clare had never met them, her mother had never talked about them. All the information Clare had came from Veronica's best friend, Irene. A hairdresser who had never left the area.

'They changed my name. Those people in care. Care! Don't make me laugh. I knew I wasn't Samantha Griffin, I was Clare. I kept telling them, "I'm Clare."' She paused. 'I was punished for lying.' Clare closed her eyes for a brief moment. The nervous energy was eating her alive.

Jessie and Jones exchanged knowing glances. The seventies were not childcare's proudest era. 'We'll start with his birth date and the day he was taken into care. I don't know who has tried to help you with this, but the truth is that you've been misdirected at every turn, and for that I am truly sorry. You have my word,' said Jones, 'we'll find him.'

Clare seemed to retract into herself. 'Dead or alive?'

Jones nodded. 'Dead or alive.'

The timer on the video switched itself on to record. Clare stared wide-eyed at the empty television screen. 'I'm not normally here in the daytime,' she said, sounding far away again. 'There are certain programmes I can't miss.'

Jessie wondered which daytime host held Clare's attention. Kilroy. Oprah. Trisha. Vanessa. Ricki. Springer. Pick a card. Any card. 'I'm surprised you ever get time to watch television,' she said.

Clare bit at her forefinger. 'I don't sleep much.'

~

'Pull. Pull. Pull. Three, straighten up.' The tip of the boat cut through the deep cold water, parting the mist. 'Three, are you listening?' Oars collided. A whistle blew long and loud. The boat started to drift out of line, carried along by the rush of the tide. The muddy brown water slapped heavily against the fibreglass hull. Cold spray covered the girls' bare pink thighs, mottled with exertion. 'What on earth is going on?'

'I thought I saw something on the shoreline. I'm sorry, it looked like . . .' the girl paused, her fellow rowers peered to where she was pointing, '. . . bones.'

17

'Oh God,' said the cox. 'Any excuse for a break! It's pathetic – get rowing.'

'No, I swear. I think we should turn around.'

They rowed the boat round and backed towards the muddy stretch of bank. The tide was rushing out, they had to fight it to stay still. The five girls stared over the water. Patches of mist clung to the river, reluctant to leave.

'There!' shouted the girl.

There was something lying on the thick, black, slimy surface. Strange outstretched fingers, poking out of the mud like the relic of a wooden hull.

'It's just wood,' said the cox.

'White wood?'

'Yes. Let's go.'

The girl at the back of the boat was closest. 'I think I can make out a pelvis and legs.'

The girls began to row away from the bank. They didn't want to get closer. They didn't want to get a better look.

'What do we do?' asked a shaky voice from the back of the boat.

'Row. We'll call the police from the boathouse. Get a marking so that we can tell them where it is.'

'It's right below the nature reserve. We'd better hurry, it'll be open soon.'

'Oh shit. Okay, okay . . . um, pull, pull – fuck it, you know what to do . . .'

~

A fully decomposed skeleton had been found in the mud on the bank of the Thames. No skull. No extremities. Probably a forgotten suicide. A local PC was on site. It warranted nothing more from CID than a detective constable. It was perfect. Jessie was early to work, as usual, and when she asked what was in, as usual, all he had to do was obey.

'Headless body on a towpath,' said the duty officer, crossing his fingers. Her leather-coated arse didn't even touch the seat.

～

Jessie parked her motorbike on Ferry Road in south-west London. Here, secreted between a man-made nature reserve and a primary school, was a little-known cut-through to the Thames. As pavement gave way to mud and puddles, and buildings became trees and brambles, Jessie had the distinct impression of being drawn back in time, to Dickensian London. She feared the worst. A young woman, sexually assaulted on this heavily wooded, unlit, desolate path, strangled and then dumped. Decapitated.

She marched on through the puddles, the swirling Thames far below her. She saw DC Fry up ahead, sipping coffee from a Starbucks cup. He was chatting to five women all wearing matching tracksuits. Jessie assumed he had his back to the body. His eye on the girls.

'Good morning,' she said loudly.

Fry turned and looked at Jessie.

'Morning, ma'am. What are you doing here?'

Another police constable she didn't know hovered nearby. Jessie beckoned Fry over. 'Where is the body on the towpath?'

'There's another body?' he asked, excited. Bones in the Thames were too run of the mill to be inspiring.

'What do you mean, another one? Where's the first?'

He pointed over the edge of the wall. 'Careful, it's slippery,' said Fry. Jessie left the path, crossed the few yards of brambles and low-growing branches, and stepped on to the stone wall. It was covered in a film of algae, as frictionless as ice. She felt the soles of her boots slip. Jessie grabbed a branch and looked over the edge. It was a twenty-foot drop to the mud. Down a steeply angled slope of greenish stone. Leading away from the base of the wall was a beach. A fool's beach. The tide had gone out, leaving a wide expanse of deep, dangerous mud. Gulls criss-crossed it with their weight-bearing webbed feet, searching for titbits, leeches, worms, tiny spineless organisms on which to dine. By the look of the algae-coated wall, Jessie guessed the tide often reached as high as where she now stood. She looked back at the glistening mud. A semi-submerged ribcage jutted out of it. Was this her headless body on the towpath?

'Is this it?' she called back to Fry. He nodded.

The DOA had been exaggerated. Grossly exaggerated. 'Who are the girls?'

'Rowers. They spotted the bones and called it in.'

'And the PC?'

'First bobby on the scene, local boy.'

'His name?' asked Jessie, getting impatient.

Fry shrugged. 'So, is there another body?'

'No,' she said. 'I have been —' son-of-a-bitch '— misinformed.' She turned back to face the river, then looked down. 'So what have we got here, Fry?'

DC Fry walked over to join her on the river wall. 'I'm surprised fewer people fall in. This stuff is lethal,' he said, sliding his foot over the slime.

'Would you mind taking this a little more seriously?'

'Aren't we just waiting for the undertaker to arrive and scoop this thing up?'

'You been down there?'

'Are you joking? Have you seen that mud?' Fry yawned.

'You haven't even been down there?'

He handed her a small pair of binoculars. 'I can see from here that it's a fully decomposed skeleton, no doubt been there for years. Search the records and we'll probably find it was some drunken fool who fell off a boat New Year's Eve ten years ago and lost his head to a propeller.'

Jessie looked at the perfectly formed skeleton, its grey-white bones the same colour as the grey-white sky. 'Possibly,' she said. She scanned the bank through the binoculars, across the water and over to the opposite side. A cyclist had stopped among eight tall larches. There was a depot of some kind. No visible signs of activity. To her right was the beginning of the small island known as the Richmond Eyot. The curve in the river restricted any long view of the beach below her feet. She'd have to get down there. She returned her sights to the opposite bank; the cyclist was already moving away. She lowered the binoculars and turned to Fry.

'Then again, possibly not.'

'There's nothing here for you, ma'am. You can return to the station, I'll deal with this.'

'No. I will.' If Mark was going to send her out on false pretences, she was going to call everyone else out on false pretences. 'Right, got any wellies?'

'No.'

She looked down at DC Fry's nice-boy leather lace-ups. 'Shame.'

'Oh, come on . . .'

She took the coffee from Fry's hand. 'Cordon off an area around the body. Get that PC to keep an eye on it. I want all entries and exits to the site logged. Get the scenes of crime officers down here now and a pathologist, if you can lay your hands on one. I want them to see the body *in situ*. After that, you can follow me round and take notes. And tell forensics to bring a video. The tide will be coming back in, we don't have long.'

Fry's frown deepened between his eyebrows. 'You're calling in the cavalry for *that*?'

'This is a suspicious death, it will be treated like a suspicious death.' He looked as if he thought she might be joking. She glared at him. 'What are you doing still standing here?'

'How the hell do I get down there? That's a thirty-foot drop.'

'Men and their inches,' said Jessie. 'Always exaggerating.'

Fry was furious, but Jessie was his superior. No doubt he'd vent his spleen in the pub later, telling everyone what a bitch she was.

'There are some steps in the wall about a hundred yards back.'

Fry peered over. In some places the water reached the wall. 'But . . .'

'Be careful of the run-off channels. We wouldn't want to lose you to a sudden gush of effluent.'

'You can't be serious, guv?'

Jessie narrowed her eyes against the sun's low-lying sharp reflection. 'Deadly.'

Fry flounced off. Mark Ward, that bastard. Well, he picked the wrong girl to start a war with. She'd make him sorry he hadn't simply put a bucket of water over an open door and been done with it. Jessie got on the phone to the riverboat police, the underwater team and the helicopter unit, then she went over to the first officer on the scene. 'Hi, I'm Detective Inspector Driver, West End Central CID.'

'PC Niaz Ahmet.' He was lanky, with heavy hands that flapped like paddles at his sides. His narrow head was perched on a long neck, but his eyes were bright and alert.

'Were there any markings when you got here? Tyre tracks, footprints?'

'Indeterminate number of markings on the path. But the mud was flat as it is now. Except for where the water runs off the bank. Rivulets, I think they're called.' Jessie immediately warmed to the man. 'Definitely no footprints, or tyre tracks down there.'

'Anything resembling a skull?' asked Jessie.

'Not that I could see. But, like Detective Constable Fry, I haven't been down there. Didn't want to disturb the scene.'

Jessie blew on her hands and rubbed them together. 'Anything else?'

'No. Few bits of debris, broken bottle, bit of metal pipe, trolley wheel, a dead jellyfish. But no footprints. I noted that especially.'

'Follow me. I want you to take statements from the girls. And anyone else who turns up.'

'Yes, ma'am.'

She walked along the footpath to where the rowers still stood, huddled over cold coffee, exhaling clouds of expectant breath. Gold letters adorned the navy-blue tracksuits: CLRC. Jessie introduced herself and began her routine questions.

Jessie climbed the frost-covered grass embankment on the other side of the pathway and peered over the iron railings. The so-called nature reserve looked like a filled-in chalkpit or a disused water reservoir. Steep banks surrounded the rectangular expanse of water. It seemed a desolate place, offering none of the comforts the name suggested. She turned away and walked back down the path after Fry to the stone steps. Like the wall, they were covered in algae. The river's mucus. Fry was f-ing and blinding as he fought through the mud. It was almost worth the humiliation to see him pick his way like a girl in Jimmy Choos. Jessie took a step down on to the slippery tread. The slightest pressure on her heel and she'd lose what little grip she had. There was nothing to hold on to and the stairs were very steep. If these remains had been brought to the river, they hadn't come this way. Above her was a canopy of branches, stretching low and wide over her head. There was no lighting on the path above, nothing opposite and no residential buildings for a quarter of a mile. For central London, this was an extraordinarily deserted spot. Perfect. Suspiciously perfect.

She rounded the wall and saw a tunnel entrance. No run-off channel emerged from the black mouth of the tunnel, but there was a silt fan. Did that mean the tunnel was active, or was the silt backwash from high tide? Jessie pulled a slim black torch out of her rucksack and pointed it into the darkness. Disturbed pigeons flapped past her. On the right was a raised stone walkway. Jessie mounted the slimy steps, stooped to the arc of the airless tunnel, and began to walk uphill away from the daylight. Below her on the gravel and silt floor were the beached whales of the river's lifeless catch. A shopping trolley. A rusting bicycle frame. Two heavy-duty plastic sacks. There was something that looked like clothing caught under a plank of wood. Jessie jumped off the four-foot ridge and landed squarely on the solid ground. The cloth was a woman's coat. She slipped on a plastic glove and took hold of the coat, gently tugging it free. She stared into the never-ending darkness ahead of her. Where would such a steep, dry tunnel lead?

'Ma'am,' shouted Fry. She could make out the silhouette of the lower half of his body at the tunnel entrance. He sounded anxious. 'Ma'am, what are you doing in there?'

She walked back down the tunnel. It got softer underfoot the lower she got. Jessie passed Fry the coat without saying anything, then picked a high ridge and walked down the sloping bank to the skeleton. The ground was still getting softer with every step. She stood over the bones. Slowly sinking. Thinking. What had bothered her about the bones when she'd studied them through the binoculars bothered her even more now. She looked back to the gaping archway of the tunnel, staring at her like a one-eyed monster. Dormant. But dangerous. Her eyes returned to the skeleton. It wasn't what Jessie expected a river to regurgitate. Bodies pulled from the Thames were the worst kind. Like leaves left in water, the skin formed a translucent film over flooded veins. Bloated with river water, corpses would burst at the touch, emptying their contents like a fisherman's catch. There was something about the whiteness of this ribcage, rising out of the brown-black mud like a giant clam, that made her think the river had not claimed this body. Human hands had put it there. Nature was never that neat.

The forensic team arrived eventually. With no sense of urgency, they ambled along the sliver of countryside towards her, laughing and joking, in a pack. Shift workers all. Bodies had a habit of turning up at odd times; theirs was not a nine-to-five existence. They looked confused when they saw the bag of bones they'd been called out for.

'I want everything picked up inside the area. Film it, photograph it, then bag it up. I've called the River Police. Low tide is in fifty minutes, then the tide will be racing back in. Take mud samples, water samples and get the temperature of the water and air.'

They looked at her the same way as DC Fry had. *What? For this?*

She felt unsure in front of these men. They knew more about the nature of death than she ever would. She tried to keep the nerves out of her voice. 'The head, hands and feet are missing. Keep an eye out,' she said.

'They'd have fallen off during decomposition. The head is probably in Calais by now.'

'Exactly,' said Jessie. 'So why isn't the rest of this poor soul in Calais too? The tide is too strong. This skeleton should be completely broken up, not sitting neatly in the mud like that.'

'What are you thinking?' said one of them, softening immediately.

'I don't know yet. But bones don't emerge clean and white from years of being buried in the mud, without a billion micro-organisms making them their home. Just because it's a skeleton, doesn't mean it's old news.'

She left them standing in the mud.

'This is a wind-up,' said one.

'Sounds like she knows what she's talking about,' said another.

'Trust me,' said the first. 'I heard it from a mate at her AMIT. She's being taken down a peg or two.'

DC Fry looked up into the sky. 'Bloody Nora, you got the flying squad out!'

Jessie didn't look up.

'They are filming the foreshore and surrounding area. On my orders.' Was she mad? She should never have risen to the bait. Jones would go ballistic.

'Ma'am, that isn't our lot up there, that's the press.' PC Ahmet pointed as he walked, his long frame almost reaching the sky.

'What?' She looked up. A helicopter hovered above. She could feel the telephoto lens aimed at them.

28

'Like sharks, they have a great nose for blood,' said the sombre PC.

'Get that skeleton covered,' she screamed at the scenes of crime officers. 'Now! Jesus Christ, how do they know so quickly?' she said. 'The body was only reported to me an hour ago.'

'Their technology is more advanced and they are permanently tuned in to police scramblers.'

This young constable continued to surprise her.

'Right,' said Jessie, trawling her memory for correct procedure. 'Fry, get on to Heathrow, get an exclusion order and get that thing out of here.'

'On what grounds?'

'On the grounds that its propellers are disturbing a murder scene!'

'With all due respect, *ma'am*, you don't know that it is a murder scene –'

'And you don't know that it isn't.' She faced Fry full on and lowered her voice to a whisper. 'Unless there is something you aren't telling me?'

He shook his head. She smelled a rat, but there was nothing she could do about it now.

Jessie watched the helicopter withdraw to the limits of the exclusion order. The tide was rising, and she'd been denied a Home Office pathologist. News was out about the circus she was whipping up on the banks of the Thames. Mark was probably somewhere watching her hang herself and Jones was nowhere to be found.

'Ma'am, the pathologist has arrived,' said DC Fry. Her reluctant shadow.

A smart, auburn-haired woman held out her hand. She looked almost too delicate for the job, but her handshake was firm and her boots were caked in mud from previous grisly expeditions. 'Sally Grimes,' said the pathologist.

Jessie turned back to DC Fry. 'I want those rowers filling out PDFs.'

Fry looked horrified at the amount of paperwork Jessie was accruing, but kept his mouth shut. The two women walked out to the skeleton. The water level was rising. 'PDFs?' queried Sally Grimes.

'Personal description forms,' Jessie said, ducking under the tarpaulin. 'They describe themselves on it for the Holmes database back at the station.'

'I know what they are. I was wondering why you were using them.'

'Because I haven't got a clue who this person is, or why they ended up here, and I've got to start somewhere.'

'Bodies from the river are usually just picked up and matched to missing persons.'

Jessie studied the pale-skinned woman. 'I was told you weren't an investigative pathologist?'

'I'm not. Yet. So what do you think you've got here?'

'No idea, to be honest. I suspect I've been set up with a dud call by my fellow DI, who thinks I need bringing down several pegs. I thought I'd get him back by going by the book, give them the classroom detective they are waiting for.'

The police helicopter made another pass, its shadow gliding over the milky-white tarpaulin. It was getting hot under the plastic.

'With bells on,' said Sally.

Jessie shrugged. She wouldn't admit she was wrong to call out the police helicopter. Not yet.

'So they sent me and not a Home Office pathologist, because they don't think you have anything,' said Sally.

'Like I said, I've been set up. Thing is, while I've been here, something about this skeleton has been bugging me.'

Sally smiled conspiratorially at Jessie. 'Well, let's see if we can find something to wipe the smile off your fellow DIs' faces. What's been bugging you?'

'The smell.'

'It is aromatic, I agree.'

'I don't mean the river smell. There's something else. I only noticed it when the tarpaulin went up. It isn't organic. In fact, it's almost like bleach.'

Sally got down on her knees in the mud and smelled the bones. Jessie made a mental note to buy the woman a drink. The pathologist repeated the action at two more locations on the skeleton, nodded quietly to herself, and stood up. From her bag she took a swab and ran it along the exposed clavicle, then another down the fibula.

'I'm not touching this until I've sent these to the lab.'

31

'What is it?'

'This corpse is too clean and too intact to have been here for years, and too decomposed to have died recently, unless someone has taken a cleaning fluid to it. How far would your DI go to make you look a fool?'

Jessie couldn't answer that. She was too new on the scene to know. 'He doesn't like me.'

'Would he get a freshly preserved lab skeleton, place it here and call you out to get you fired?'

Jessie's face collapsed in panic. 'A lab skeleton?'

Sally nodded. 'I'm pretty sure these bones have been treated.' They emerged from the tent. Sally arched backwards, stretching her spine. Jessie was too distraught to speak. 'The undertakers are here. Let them bring the remains to the hospital. We'll wait for the results on these swabs, see what we've got. If your DI has borrowed this from a medical college, we've got him. If he didn't, then we'll do a PM tomorrow and find out what we are dealing with. Okay?'

No, she was not okay. She had danced right into Mark Ward's trap.

'Tell all the undertakers to wear protective clothing,' said Sally.

Jessie lifted her head. 'Why protective clothing?'

'The smell could be a cleaning agent mixed with formaldehyde, but it could be worse. We don't know and it isn't worth taking the risk. Plastic gloves will protect them from germs, not acids.'

'Acid?'

'It's possible. Acid is still used as a way to make people disappear. No skull means no dental records. These bones are virtually unidentifiable.' Sally touched Jessie's arm. 'For what it's worth, I think you did the right thing. Leaving it to the undertakers to pick up without examining it first could have got someone hurt.'

'You think so?'

'Yes. Something is not right here. Stick to your guns, Detective. Whoever this dead woman is, she did not end up here by accident.'

'So it's a woman?'

'Yes. But that's all we know.'

The two women made their way laboriously up the bank. The mud sucked at their boots. Jessie looked back at the staked-out area. Already the furthest two poles were being licked by the rising water.

'We going?' said DC Fry hopefully.

'Once you've checked that lot have picked up everything and photographed everything. I'm making you exhibits officer, don't let me down.'

'Come on, ma'am. You're not still going through with this?'

'Through with *what*, Fry?'

He did not answer her. Not directly. 'It's just . . . I thought you were doing something special with DCI Jones.'

There was no point in saying anything. Jessie left him smirking. Fry sat so neatly in Mark Ward's pocket she kept forgetting he was there.

PC Ahmet was still taking the rowers' statements. 'Can you stay here, guard the site until it is completely covered in water, then be back here when the tide falls?' said Jessie.

'Would overtime commence at the appropriate time?'

'Of course.'

'Then I accept your request.'

'Thanks. Here's my card – if anything strange happens or anyone comes asking questions, take their details, get a PDF and call me. Only me. Got it?'

'Yes, ma'am.'

'Thanks, PC Ahmet. You've been great.'

~

Clare Mills stood at her father's grave and listened to the belching buses trundle by. Cars hooted, mopeds buzzed and boys swore loudly. Not a very peaceful resting place, Whitechapel. She knelt down and swept away dead leaves. *Here lies Trevor Mills. Loving husband and father. Born May 13th, 1933. Died April 27th, 1978. RIP.* When Clare had first found the plot, she'd been angry that it didn't say murdered. 'Died' implied that her father had something to do with his own death. He'd had a bad heart, weak genes, hadn't eaten his greens, or had fallen at work. Drowned. Clare watched a drunk urinate against a once majestic headstone.

The angel's head was missing. Vandalism was a great leveller.

She looked back at the small flat square of stone under which her father's bones lay. 'Good news, Dad,' she said quietly to herself. 'The police are finally taking us seriously. I'm going to find Frank.' Her mother was in Woolwich burial ground. Another almighty disaster in a life coloured by other people's mistakes. Even in death, they couldn't be together. Clare always felt bad that she visited her father more often than her mother. She felt guilty whenever she walked into Woolwich and saw the fresh yellow roses that Irene had dutifully brought. Irene had been her Mum's best friend. It was Irene's family who took Veronica in when her mother had run off. In a way, Irene was Clare's only real friend too, if she thought about it. Irene never said she left the flowers. Clare knew that it still hurt her to talk about it. Irene missed her friend as much as Clare missed her mother, they were united by that common denominator. It was their foundation. Irene had been with her all through the search for Frank. Given her valuable clues and held her when, again, they came to nothing.

A man stood by the bench behind her. She glanced at her watch. Trawling time again. She was due at work. She blew a silent kiss to the ground and turned away. Two men were emerging from behind an ivy-clad tree. One was rolling up a rug, the other was struggling with his flies. It made her sick what went on in the graveyard, but she'd never seen anyone do anything near her father's grave. No grip on a small flat stone. The tombs were the worst off. Illicit sex: another of life's levellers. Judges or bricklayers, they all looked the same with their trousers down.

Clare took the bus to work, changed into overalls for the morning shift and began to sweep. She liked autumn. Red leaves made a welcome change from fag butts and beer cans.

~

In the police station's yard Jessie rinsed the mud off her boots, watching the dirty water mingle with the soapsuds that bubbled in the drain. Above her was the shower-room window, where the washing men's words billowed out into the yard, enveloped with steam and the smell of expensive soap. Jessie wished she smoked; she needed more time to think about how she would handle Mark. The men were talking football. Something about transfer rules. Then she heard something that made her concentrate.

'That was gross, wasn't it?'

'This fucking job is bad enough without rotting jellyfish pouring out all over us.'

'Insides is one thing, jellyfish have always given me the willies.'

Jessie catapulted herself into a run.

'Do you think it was part of the joke?'

'What, some metaphor about a stinking fish?'

They laughed.

'Fucking hell, ma'am!'

'What jellyfish?' demanded Jessie.

The scene of crime boys slipped around on the wet tiles, frantically trying to protect their modesty.

'Jesus Christ –'

'Do you mind –'

'This is the *men*'s locker room.'

'What fucking jellyfish?'

A ballsy lad put his hand on his hips. Jessie's eyes did not leave his.

'The one that fell out of the skeleton's torso.' He gave her a challenging half-smile.

'Did you bring it in?'

'No way.'

Jessie turned to leave. They could tell she was pissed off.

'It was just a rotting piece of fish. It was nothing.'

'One jellyfish maybe, but not two, not in the Thames.' She hurried to the evidence room, where the booty from the morning's crime scene was being examined and labelled by DC Fry. 'Where's the jellyfish?'

'What?' he said, looking up.

'I asked you to bag everything around the body. There was a jellyfish. Where is it?'

'I didn't think you meant that. It was dead, slimy, it wasn't anywhere near the thing.'

'When I said everything, I meant everything.'

'Sorry.'

'What about the one that fell out of the body?' He looked at her blankly. 'You did stay until the others had finished, like I asked you?'

He looked around the room nervously.

'Fuck!' She glanced at her watch. 'The tide will be back up by now. We didn't have a second chance.'

'Sorry.'

She ignored the tone in the guy's voice. If he didn't like taking criticism from someone his own age, he shouldn't get things wrong in the first place.

Jessie put on a pair of waders and some long rubber gloves. The tide had turned and was lapping at the area where the body had been found. Smaller bits of the river's cargo moved in rhythm with the tide: a condom, a small plastic bottle, a recently devoured packet of cheese-and-onion crisps. A pole had been sunk into the mud to mark the crime scene. She couldn't risk taking the steps and wading a hundred yards back through water. It had been bad enough when the tide was fully out. She was scared that if she attempted it now she might step into a run-off channel, lose her footing and be dragged out by the current.

As she removed the rope from her backpack, Jessie was glad of the hours she'd spent being dragged up mountains by her brothers. She wrapped the rope around a tree trunk and tied a slipknot. She pulled against it and, when satisfied, threw the length of rope over the side of the river wall. Waders did not make good rock-climbing boots. Her arms had to take all the weight as she slid down the wall on the base of her boots and landed in a few inches of water that disappeared as quickly as it reappeared. She'd had no idea the Thames was so mighty. Every time she looked back, the water seemed to be reaching higher up the wall.

Sinking deeper with each step, Jessie waded through the mud until she got to the pole. As each wave receded, she put her hands flat and felt around the area where she thought the chest cavity would have been. It was no use. Everything felt the same through the thick rubber. Reluctantly, she peeled off one glove and bent forward again. The glistening top layer of mud felt like thick, viral mucus. She withdrew her hand and waited for the water to be sucked back by the weight of the Thames. Then she dug her nails and fingers in deeper and found purchase on the more compact riverbed below. It was no use with one hand, the water was coming in too fast. She took off the other glove and began to dig. She stepped into the hole left behind by the search for the skull, but still nothing.

Jessie stood up and looked around her. More condoms, more crisp packets and Coke cans. Further down the bank, she thought she saw something move in the water. She trudged towards it as quickly as she could, knowing she was getting dangerously deep. Many anglers drowned in shallow stretches of water, held down by water-filled boots. She felt the cold water push against the rubber. She saw it again. A semi-suspended jellyfish. She watched it ebb and flow with the rest of the flotsam. Her hands reached out for the slippery lump. Resisting the urge to pull away, she made a cage with her fingers and held on to it as an incoming wave rushed between her forearms. The water was now above her knees and the mud had sucked her into a vacuum. One boot was stuck. Jessie looked up to the bank. Even if someone had been on the path, they wouldn't have been able to see her unless they were standing on the wall. This was not a spectator sport. If she got sucked under, no one would know until she rose to the surface two weeks later, bloated with river water and methane.

She tried to pull her leg out of the mud again, but it was only making the other foot sink deeper. Jessie took a deep breath, exhaled, fixed her vision on the post and, once she'd found her balance, slowly lifted one leg fully out of the boot. The tide nearly toppled her, but she threw the bare foot out behind her and her arms in front, with the jellyfish oozing between her fingers, and somehow she managed to stay upright. The mud squelched between her toes as she retraced her steps.

The area PC Ahmet had shown her earlier was under two foot of water, the saturated mud was even more dangerous. If she fell, she would be dragged under and carried downstream within seconds. She had one jellyfish. It had to be enough. Water was rushing in and out of the tunnel. It was too dangerous to stay down there any longer. With stinking, itchy, cold arms and a filthy, numb foot, Jessie carried the jellyfish back to the wall. She shrugged off her rucksack and placed the jellyfish in the container she had brought. Then, flinging the bag back over her shoulder, she grabbed the rope. It had got wet lying against the sodden brick-work. The first few times her hand simply slipped straight off it. She was getting very cold. Jessie rubbed her hands together, kicked the other boot off, peeled off her wet socks, wrung them out and wrapped one round each palm. The looped cotton absorbed the damp and gave her something to hold on with. She lifted herself out of the mud and, with burning biceps and frozen feet, worked her way back up the slimy wall. At the lip she dug her knee into a small ridge and hauled herself over the top. Lying face down on the wall, breathing heavily, she looked back to where she'd found the jellyfish. The wader had already been claimed as the river's own.

~

Jessie placed her helmet on the wooden boards by the door and prayed her bleeper wouldn't go off. The flat housed two women too busy to buy anything. There was nothing on the walls except the previous inhabitants' choice of paint; the floors were bare and the rooms blessedly uncluttered. Maggie's only possessions were clothes and make-up, most of which she had purloined from the make-up rooms and wardrobes of television centres around the country. This, she assured Jessie, was normal.

The lights were on, but the flat was silent. Jessie knew the signs. Maggie had had bad news. She pushed the door to the sitting room open and saw Maggie sitting cross-legged on the floor. She did not look up. Instead she held out a piece of newspaper.

'Bastard,' she whispered.

Jessie took the newspaper and began to read.

Dear Lord. Give me strength. Is it too much to ask for – an intelligent female presenter of an intelligent show? Clearly it is. Bar the rare exception, TV has become the vessel of the inane, mundane and vain. The saturation of the saccharine blonde was distressing enough, but now they come at us with banal brunettes who I presume by their hair colour are supposed to at least *look* intelligent. Don't be fooled. These women are in fact lower down the evolutionary scale than their pitiful predecessors. These are the new blondes. Faux blondes. Blondeabees. And they are springing up like weeds. Chickweed, to be precise. An abundant plant which is known to be particularly troublesome on rich soil. I write this as a warning to all those impressionable producers, pop stars and players. They, like the blondes before them, will suck your AmEx dry.

I could name them all but fear the heavy hand of the ever-watchful lawyers. There is, however, one I feel I must pick on. I couldn't live with myself if I let this pass without comment. Shown last week, 'The Olive Oil Revolution' was a programme about the changing eating habits of the British population. A reasonably interesting subject matter, you would have thought. Wrongly, as it turns out. It was utterly and spectacularly unchallenging. The presenter, I admit, was working with some pretty dire material, but even so she managed to lower the tone. Maggie Hall shook her equine mane, beating all the L'Oreal girls in an instant, and declared that we eat Italian food because it is 'yummy'. Come back, Anthea – all is forgiven.

Jessie looked at her flatmate, who shook her head mournfully. There was no point telling her it didn't matter, that no one read such columns, that the paper it was printed on would be polishing shoes and wrapping up broken glass tomorrow; she'd tried before and words didn't work.

'It gets worse,' said Maggie, as Jessie leant down beside her and gave her a hug. 'He was on some chat show yesterday.'

'Who?'

'Joshua Cadell, the creep who writes this shit.'

'Slagging you off?'

Maggie shook her head. 'Just increasing his sphere of influence by a few thousand miles. They watch him on telly, they'll sure as shit read his column.'

'I've never heard of him,' said Jessie.

Maggie didn't have to respond to Jessie's declaration. Ask Jessie how long it would take a six-foot man weighing fourteen stone to bleed to death and she could tell you without hesitation. Put a gun to her head and ask her who was Number One in the charts and she would have to say 'pull'.

'You may not have heard of him, but you'll have heard of his mother. Dame Henrietta Cadell.'

'The author?'

'Queen of the literati, the doyenne of all historical biographers. He is her son.'

'So?'

'That makes him famous by proxy. Even if people only read his column to slag him off, they still read it.'

'Listen, Maggie, you said yourself the script was poor. He's taken the "yummy" comment out of context –'

'I know that. Doesn't make it read any better though, does it?'

Jessie stood up. 'Want a drink?'

'There's a bottle open,' said Maggie.

There always was.

'At least there was some good news today,' said Maggie when Jessie returned to the room, boots off, glass in hand. 'I got my first bit of obsessed stalker mail. Now that *is* a good sign.'

Jessie hoped Maggie was being sarcastic. She didn't want to put her flatmate in the same bracket as the desperate Jami Talbot.

Maggie threw her the envelope. 'Not the most stunning bit of prose you've ever read, but it beats the signed-photograph hunters with all their gushing.'

'It wasn't so long ago that you loved every last gush.'

Maggie shrugged.

Jessie looked at the solitary page of cheap blue writing paper. '*I know you want me as much as I want you, I'm waiting for you in our special place.*' Jessie looked up. 'That's not funny. Do you know who sent this?'

'Course I don't.'

'What "special place"?'

Maggie shrugged again.

'Do you want me to get it checked out?'

'God no, it's only some nutter. Everyone needs a stalker.'

'Maggie, you should take this seriously –'

Jessie felt a cushion land on the side of her face.

'I'm joking!' exclaimed Maggie. 'God, I worry about you sometimes.'

Ditto, thought Jessie.

'Come on, Miss Marple, let's watch this video and see if the bastard nails me.'

Maggie put the video in and they watched the clock tick down the seconds. It was a pre-recorded show; a friend in the edit suite had copied it for Maggie. *Today with Ray.*

'This is just a shit cable channel,' said Jessie. 'I wouldn't worry about this.'

'People watch this.'

'Who? Who watches it?'

'People,' said Maggie belligerently.

There was no point trying to reason with Maggie while she was like this. Relativity and ambition didn't go hand in hand. Jessie watched a man with pale blue eyes fill the screen. His hair was white and cropped short, his face was lined but he carried it well, like Clint Eastwood. His scalp was tanned where the hair had thinned. He wore an open-necked shirt – blue, to match his insipid eyes. A small gold cross was embedded in the white hairs on his chest. It matched the cap on his incisor.

'Who is this con?' said Jessie. 'He's got HMP written all over him.'

'Shh,' said Maggie, increasing the volume. 'There's Joshua Cadell and his mother.'

Jessie stared at the robed woman walking on to the set. She was about five foot eleven and was carrying at least four stone too many. She had wiry amber hair that enveloped her head and shoulders. Her jewellery matched her hair and the design matched her shape. 'She's huge –'

'Shh, listen.'

'. . . and so to the bloodthirsty world of four-teenth-century Britain. For this week's "Mother'n'-Son" we have here in the studio Dame Henrietta

Cadell, author of *Isabella of France*, which is out this week, and her son Joshua, author of the weekly satirical column, "The Mallard". Henrietta, I've flicked through all your biographies and was quite shocked by the violent nature of most of them . . .'

'Bastard,' said Maggie again. 'Satirical fucking column.'

'. . . do you think the violent nature of your books has helped you corner the market in mediaeval biography?'

The majestic woman laughed behind a bejewelled hand, smiled for the camera and began to talk.

'People are interested in history. They should be. You cannot predict the future, but you can understand the past. Insight. It's all anyone really needs. And insight comes from history. I think that is why all my books are so successful. Everyone can find something in the past that they can empathise with, take consolation from –'

'Like infidelity.'

The smile remained fixed on the author's heavily made-up mouth, but her eyes told another story. Dame Henrietta Cadell clearly thought herself far too classy for this outfit. 'Absolutely. The list is endless; it's about betrayal, loss, love, war – even murder, Mr St Giles.'

'Yes. You describe Edward II's death quite flamboyantly.'

'Mr St Giles, don't tell me you are squeamish

about violence.' Henrietta Cadell smiled malevolently at the interviewer. 'I would have thought hot pokers were right up your street.'

The corner of St Giles' mouth flickered upwards, and he turned towards Joshua. The columnist was tall like his mother, but very thin and pasty. He had none of Dame Henrietta's colouring, none of her pizzazz. He wore a plain black suit and his black hair was pulled tightly off his face. His cheeks looked hollow under the overhead studio lights. Joshua Cadell was a pale imitation of his mother.

'It must have been very alarming, growing up around blood and guts, Joshua?' asked the blue-eyed interviewer.

'I grew up around history, as my mother has already said, learning the repetitive nature of mankind. Blood and guts have nothing to do with it.'

'Still, you didn't want to write yourself?'

'I do write.'

'Yes, but not books . . .'

'Who is this guy?' interrupted Maggie. 'I love him, he's ripping the arsehole apart.'

'Ray St Giles,' said Jessie quietly before standing up. Keeping one eye on the screen, she backed out of the room to fetch her heavily laden backpack from the hall.

'I've read your column – quite the executioner's style,' continued St Giles.

Maggie swore loudly.

'If you can't stand up and be counted,' said Joshua Cadell, not looking into the camera, 'don't stand up at all.'

'Fair enough. But don't you think people who criticise others should at least have achieved something themselves?'

Maggie clapped her hands. 'Bloody hell, this guy's evil. Mark my words, he'll have a cult following before you can say "Whoops, there goes Jerry."'

'Evil,' repeated Jessie, removing a manila file from the backpack. The camera zoomed in to the presenter's face. Jessie looked up from the open file and pressed pause.

'Hey, I'm enjoying this.'

The television flickered. Raymond Giles. Ray St Giles. The ex-con who had orphaned Clare Mills. The studio lights reflected in his pale blue eyes. He was smiling, his crooked, capped tooth the only evidence of his criminal past.

'When was this on?' Jessie asked.

'Three in the afternoon yesterday. Why?'

Just the time Clare Mills' video recorder had automatically switched on. Jessie recalled the array of video cassettes that had adorned Clare's shelves where books should have been. Ray St Giles, Clare's nemesis, a chat-show host. No wonder the poor woman didn't sleep much.

~

Jessie pushed open the door to Jones' office. She was too excited to notice the black circles under his eyes, the papery look to his skin, the slight yellow tinge to his fingers. Her jellyfish was back from the lab and her suspicions were confirmed. Her mud bath had been rewarded.

'Great, you're back. Can I show you something?'

Jones pushed himself up from his desk without a word and followed Jessie down the corridor to an evidence room. He was lagging behind.

'What's the hurry, Detective?'

Jessie turned back. 'It's about the bones we found on the Thames. I think I can identify them.'

'What bones?'

'Didn't you hear about the . . .' Jones was frowning at her. 'Are you feeling okay, sir?'

'How?'

'What?'

'How can you identify these bones?'

'Oh,' Jessie smiled, extremely pleased with herself. 'I found a jellyfish. Let's just say it didn't look indigenous to the sullied waters of London. Turns out I was right.'

Jessie led Jones to one of the tables where her jellyfish lay, oozing over a square glass plate. A borrowed microscope stood close by. Jessie got the equipment in place, then stood back.

'Have a look.'

Jones came up shaking his head. 'I hate to tell you this, but that is no jellyfish.'

'I know.'

'What is it then?'

Jessie stepped back and crossed her arms. 'A partially dissolved silicone implant.'

'Breasts?' he said incredulously.

'One breast, to be accurate. And, being pedantic, a fake.'

Jones closed one eye and lowered his head back down to the microscope. 'What are the letters and numbers on it?'

'Part of a security barcode. It's an American brand. A very recent model. Cosmetic surgeons started coding silicone implants several years ago after too many went missing. Can you imagine – a black market in fake boobs? Anyway, to have got to its current skeletal state, the body this belonged to would have had to start decomposing eighteen months before this type of implant was even invented. This is not a typical river DOA.'

Jones frowned.

'At first the pathologist thought the body had been cleaned, or preserved. Possibly even left as a joke.'

'Joke?' asked Jones suspiciously.

'By med students,' said Jessie quickly. She was no snitch. 'Now I am convinced it was acid we could smell. It explains the disfigured implant and the fact that the bones were so clean. This is a serious crime.' She handed Jones the preliminary photos. He held one up. It was an aerial view taken from the helicopter. The white arch of the ribcage rising up from the mud, the dirtier leg bones splayed wide, covered in silt.

'But you didn't know that when the body was called in. What were you doing on the river, Jessie? Hardly a stiff for the murder squad, was it?'

The pause was a fraction longer than a second. Too long. 'I had nothing else to do,' said Jessie. 'Thought I needed to accumulate some field experience.'

'Nothing to do? What about the Mills case?'

'I thought that's what you were doing. I couldn't reach you all day.'

Jones involuntarily rubbed his hand over his chin, feeling for bristles. Jessie had never seen him with anything resembling a five-o'clock shadow. He was the closest-shaved copper she knew. He was studying her. Closely.

'So this,' he said, waving the photo in the air, 'has nothing to do with the five calls from Mark Ward yesterday?'

She retrieved the photos and put them back in her file. 'I thought you said you didn't speak to anyone.'

'I didn't.'

'Oh, well then, no, I doubt it.'

He nodded in that all-seeing all-knowing way of his. Jessie held her ground.

'So what now?' he asked.

'See what the lab results tell us, then try and match the part of the code that hasn't been destroyed with the manufacturer. They will know the surgery it went to, and we can take it from there.'

Jones looked exhausted. 'What about the Mills case?'

'I'm on that too, sir. Did you know that Raymond Giles has a cable show?'

He nodded. Jessie was put out.

'We concentrate on Frank,' said Jones sternly. 'Not Raymond. He's done his time. Am I clear?'

'Yes, sir.'

The door to the evidence room opened. It was the PC from the river. 'Morning, ma'am, sir. I thought you might want these before I resume my post on the river.' PC Ahmet passed her the Personal Description Forms. 'I think this will turn out to be more helpful, however –' He held out a Tupperware container. 'I put it in my sandwich box.'

'What?' asked Jessie.

'The jellyfish I saw. Those SOCOs didn't pick it up, so I thought I would. Call me particular, but since when did you find jellyfish in the Thames? They are saltwater creatures – medusoid coelenterate, to be precise.'

Jessie smiled at Jones, took the box from Niaz, emptied the deformed implant on to another glass plate and brought the magnifying glass over it. Finally she looked up, smiling.

'You are brilliant, Niaz.'

'So it isn't a jellyfish?'

'No. It's one of a pair of silicone implants. With

the two, I think we now have the full barcode.' She took a pen from her back pocket and wrote out the number from the first and then added the one from the second. The middle three numbers overlapped. She stood back. 'We'll soon know who she is.' She glanced at her watch. 'How behind is LA?'

Jessie's mobile rang. It was Sally Grimes, the pathologist. 'Sulphuric acid. The bones were drenched in it.'

'Jesus.'

'Will that wipe the smile off your DI's face?'

'Yes.'

'Congratulations, Detective Inspector.'

'Thank you. One more thing, Sally – would sulphuric acid dissolve silicone?'

'Depends how long it was exposed to the acid.'

'Same length of time as the body.'

'Partially probably. Maybe totally, depending on the make. No doubt you'll be wanting a *proper* Home Office pathologist to do the tests at the postmortem.'

'Will you assist?'

'If you insist.'

'I insist.'

'Leave it to me then.'

Jessie looked at Jones. 'Acid.'

'I gathered. But does that necessarily mean the bones and the implants belong to the same person?'

'One of them fell out of the chest cavity.'

He weighed it up in his mind. Jessie needed this one to cut her teeth on. And silence those doubting Toms. 'Well, they belong to someone, let's find out who.' Jessie was watching him, her large hazel eyes full of concentration and excitement. Jones continued: 'I've a friend in the LAPD, you can start there.'

Jessie smiled. 'Thanks, boss.'

'You'd better start taking notes, Detective Inspector. Looks like you have a murder investigation on your hands.'

'PC Ahmet, would you do it? I'll get you a temporary transfer.'

'It would be an honour.' He smiled broadly.

'Right then, follow me.'

~

For the second time that morning Jessie burst into Jones' office without knocking. 'You are not going to believe this.' Again, she didn't notice Jones straighten himself up. 'The implants belong to Verity Shore.'

'Who?'

'Verity Shore.'

'I said who, not what.'

'Sorry. She's an actress. Well, actually, not really – you know, she's married to that pop star, um . . . Oh God, I'm crap with names. He's had three huge hits, used to play with that band Spunk, went solo and is now enormous . . . P. J. Dean. You know?'

'No.'

'She stripped for a tyre ad and got into trouble doing pregnant nude poses for *Playboy*.'

'Hardly narrows the field.'

'She wore a see-through piece of gauze to a film premiere. You couldn't have missed that!'

He shrugged.

'You're hopeless. Where's Trudi?'

'On an errand.'

Jessie raided Jones' long-suffering assistant's desk drawer and retrieved a dog-eared copy of *Hello!* 'She's in here all the time. I don't think she can help herself.' She quickly flicked through it. 'Here we go, "At Home with Verity", following her stay in a health farm.' She looked up at Jones. 'She'd been suffering from exhaustion,' she said, handing Jones the article.

'A lot of that going about,' he noted drily.

'You've got to feel sorry for the woman: all those parties, all those photo ops, it's bound to exhaust the girl.'

Jones studied the photo. A leggy blonde languished on a white sofa. A bedraggled man stood in the background, blurred. 'Not any more.'

'The thing is, sir, she hasn't been reported missing. I don't really want to turn up and scare everyone, only to find out she's asleep upstairs and LA haven't quite got their filing system in order. She's got kids. Two, I think. Not by him – two other guys.'

'Nice.'

'She has a habit of leaving one when a more famous other comes along.'

'And the kids?'

Jessie shrugged. 'She got custody in both cases, though I don't know if the respective fathers fought that hard, if you know what I mean.'

'You think he'd kill his wife?'

'P. J. Dean?' Jessie shook her head. 'I don't think so. He's very well respected, though of course you never know what's true and what isn't these days.' Jessie held up a photograph. 'But if this is Verity Shore, she was decapitated and dipped in acid. That is not the same as picking up a bread knife in the middle of a drunken domestic.'

'So what do you want to do?' asked Jones.

'Pay P. J. Dean a visit. See if his wife is missing and whether they are trying to keep it quiet. They live in a modern house in Richmond.' Jessie held out the magazine. 'According to this, anyway.' The conversation was taking on surreal proportions.

'Okay.' He stood up. 'Let's go.'

She appreciated that. It meant he would come with her. Lending her the weight of his far superior badge. After all, bones were one thing, P. J. Dean was another.

~

Jessie pulled up to a solid wood gate, twelve foot high. It was painted green. Quite a bright green. Not a very rock'n'roll green. Above and either side of her were security cameras. Jessie leant out of the window and pressed the buzzer.

'The Dean Residence.'

'Detective Inspector Driver and Detective Chief Inspector Jones from West End Central Police Station. We'd like to speak to Mr Dean.'

'Have you got an appointment?'

'No.'

'Well then . . .'

'We're not asking.'

'I see. Could you show me your badge?'

Jessie frowned.

'Just hold it in front of the box. You can't be too careful.'

'Quite,' said Jessie, holding it up. A few seconds later the gate buzzed and slowly began to slide open. The black granite driveway said it all. Jones and Jessie exchanged glances. The driveway was edged with a raised white wooden border brimming with white winter roses, beyond which lay perfectly mowed lawns. She spotted a couple of five-a-side football goals. A gardener was walking around replacing divots. The atmosphere was relaxed, thought Jessie, not the house of a missing person. Perhaps this was more of an elaborate hoax than she had given Mark Ward credit for.

Jessie eased the car slowly up the granite drive as it curved round to the left. The house was a modern building, three storeys, lowering to two then one. An architectural wedding cake. The walls were white, the woodwork was black. To her right, the single-storey block housed one enormous garage. Jessie had read about P.J. and his cars. A tall sandy-haired boy was polishing a Ferrari. He watched them drive by, hands on his hips, full of judgement and testosterone. Big-boy bravado; she'd seen it a hundred times in the faces of her brothers' friends. The façade was a prerequisite of puberty, and this one looked like a loose covering. Jessie pressed her police badge to the window and watched the boy take an invisible punch to the solar plexus. When he'd recovered, he pushed himself from pillar to pillar of the garage, matching the speed of the car with wide paces and wide, worried eyes. He clutched the last pillar with both hands; it was doing more than holding up the flat roof, it was holding up the boy. Jessie could only assume that this boy knew something the gardener did not.

'What an amazing collection of automobiles,' said Jones.

'P. J. Dean has a reputation for fast cars,' said Jessie.

'And loose women.'

'I think a poor taste in women. Girlfriends were endlessly going to the press, some from years ago, with pictures of him at about eighteen and stories of him being bad in bed, that sort of thing.'

'I doubt many teenagers would fare better.'

'Don't remind me. Can you imagine, getting famous then all those little mistakes you've brushed under the carpet come screaming back at you from the front page of the *News of the World* or some other gossip-fuelled mag?'

'I didn't have you down as the trashy-mag type.'

'Even I go to the hairdressers, sir.'

'Not that you'd notice.'

Jones saw the expression on Jessie's face as she involuntarily ran her hand through her short hair. Three weeks before joining Jones' team, she had cut ten inches off and had it styled into the spiky bob she thought more fitting for a DI. Although she wished she'd had the guts to do it years ago, she still missed the weight of it, like an amputee. Every morning she woke up surprised it was gone.

'Stop fiddling,' said Jones. 'For a detective, that's a compliment.'

Jessie parked outside the black double doors. 'I'll have to take your word for it, sir.'

A modern-day manservant opened the door. Tall and thin and bald, he looked at them with steely eyes, studying their badges again before admitting them into the house.

'Danny Knight,' he said. Jessie wondered if he fancied himself as a bit of a Richard O'Brien. The black tiles continued throughout the ground floor; the furniture in the main hallway was white, but that was the extent of the monochrome look. The walls were painted blood-red and the ceiling was gold leaf.

A young-looking woman peered out from a black side-door, but disappeared just as quickly when Jessie caught her eye. P. J. Dean had a lot of staff. And a lot of expensive 'art'. Mounted on the red walls Jessie recognised an Eve Wirrel, the bad girl of contemporary art. It was part of a series called 'The Wirrel Week', the contents of which had almost become as famous as that shark. Jessie took a closer look at the two and a half condoms lying in a Perspex box. They'd been used. It was titled 'An Average Week'. Next to it was a black-and-white nude study of Verity Shore. Exhibitionists unite, thought Jessie, then remembered the skeleton in the morgue. The actress-turned-model-turned-serial-celebrity-wife was not so photogenic now.

Danny Knight showed them through another high black door, this one flanked by gold pillars, and led them into a gigantic games room. A screen was pulled down over one wall, DVDs covered another, from the ceiling was suspended a digital projector. A curved seven-seater sofa had been placed behind squashy Ottomans for perfect viewing comfort. Jessie felt the first twinge of envy. A bar in the corner suddenly swivelled, revealing a descending staircase.

'Very Agatha Christie,' whispered Jones as the manservant beckoned them to follow. 'I'll go first.'

'Age before beauty.'

'Charming.'

'Just getting you back for the hairdresser comment.'

'Actually, we may be dealing with a madman.

Who's to say he didn't dip his wife in sulphuric acid?'

'Too much to lose.'

'Or a man who has taken his role of modern deity to such heights that he believes himself above the law.'

The walls were covered with framed headlines and publicity photos of Verity.

'Of course, we could be dealing with an extremely elaborate publicity stunt,' said Jessie.

Danny Knight reappeared. 'Please, keep up.'

'I don't like dungeons, they make me nervous,' said Jones as they followed the manservant's shiny pate. The corridor was lined with fake flame lanterns. Looking at the pieces of material flicker in the heat of the bulb, Jessie didn't think Jones had anything to worry about. Acid-dipping homicidal maniacs didn't shop at Christopher Wray.

The manservant knocked on a door, a voice answered, and in they went. To a bowling alley. Jessie let out a shocked laugh. P. J. Dean looked up.

She had known she was coming to P. J. Dean's house, and she had known what P. J. Dean looked like. She could recall his face in her mind easier than her own. He was billboard big. She had known exactly what to expect – except her own reaction.

Dean's dark hair was cropped to his head. Not too fiercely – Jessie guessed a number three. His eyes were sea green, each the size of a two-pound coin and outlined by thick black eyelashes. Jessie and Jones walked slowly towards him and the two small boys by his side. The taller one was fair, the younger had dark hair. Both of them wore pyjamas. Neither of them had their mother's colouring. Bleach blonde. Peroxide blonde. Ammonia blonde. Jessie pushed the smell to the back of her memory. She was about to orphan these children.

'You go on playing, kids,' P.J. said, ruffling their hair. The older one looked at Jessie and tried to flatten his hair back down.

Jesus, thought Jessie, that voice. P. J. Dean was also wearing pyjamas. Bottoms only. And an old fraying dressing gown that hung open over his shoulders, chest and stomach. Jessie couldn't help it. She looked down. Then sideways. Then at her feet. She had spent hours in the gym Thai-boxing, running and doing yoga, and in all that time she had never seen a stomach like it. It was a *Fight Club* stomach, disappearing into a taut V that pointed indecently to his low-slung pyjamas. As he came forward to meet them he pulled the dressing gown together and tied the cord around his waist. Only when the knot was secure did Jessie look up.

'Sorry about my appearance.' He held out a hand to each in turn. 'P.J.,' he said simply.

'Detective Inspector Driver and Detective Chief Inspector Jones,' said Danny Knight, pointing to each.

'Chief Inspector, eh?' P.J.'s eyes narrowed. 'Danny, watch the kids a while. We'll be in the studio.'

Another corridor led to his recording studio. Among other things it was soundproof. One window looked back out to the bowling alley, another looked on to a padded recording room. Dean pulled over some chairs then pressed a button on a phone panel and spoke into it. 'Bernie, can we have fresh coffee, orange juice and croissants.'

The telephone replied: 'On its way.'

Panels of mixing decks stretched away from them, a million sliders, buttons, lights, dials, switches, plugs, meters, like a giant cockpit.

'What has she done?'

'Excuse me?' said Jessie, who'd been studying her unusual surroundings.

'Verity. I presume that's why you're here. It can't be something I've done. I pay my taxes, I certainly haven't been kerb-crawling recently, and hotels are too minimal these days to smash up. Which leaves Verity. My wife.' He spat the last word out, but seemed exhausted by his own venom. He sighed heavily before looking out towards the bowling alley. He waved. The kids waved back.

'Is she here?' Jessie asked.

He looked at her. 'No. It's a big house, but I don't think so. You'd know if she were here – the bell never stops ringing.'

'Has she many visitors?'

'Not that bell. She has a staff bell, and she seems to be eternally in need of something.'

These were definitely not the words of a loving

husband. 'When did you last see her?' asked Jessie, sitting forward.

'Just tell me what she's done. I'll sort it out, pay, whatever. You haven't arrested her, have you? She doesn't need that sort of publicity right now.'

'No. The thing is, Mr Dean . . .'

'Mr Dean?' he looked from Jessie to Jones. 'Oh shit. It's serious, isn't it?'

Jessie didn't know what to say.

'Someone is dead,' he said slowly. Then added angrily, 'I fucking knew this was going to happen.'

'Did your wife ever have cosmetic surgery?'

'What?'

'Please answer the question.'

'No one's dead? Thank God.'

'Please, answer the question.'

'Absolutely not –'

'The truth please, not the spin.'

P. J. Dean's shoulders dropped. He rubbed his forehead and wrestled with the truth. 'Where do you want me to start? Lips, hips, eyes, tits. Course, she denied it all and plugged her diet books and exercise videos. What has all that got to do with anything?'

'I'm sorry to have to tell you this, but a body was found on the bank of the Thames. We traced the silicone implants to your wife.'

He stared back at her. He didn't move. He didn't blink. He didn't breathe.

Jessie persevered. 'I'm sorry, I know this is difficult, but when did you last see your wife?'

Very slowly, P. J. Dean lowered his head. 'You said no one was . . . Is she . . . ? Oh my god, you think you've got Verity.'

'Please answer the question,' said Jessie.

'Um, I was in Germany last Wednesday, got back late on Thursday, she wasn't here, and now it's um, Wednesday. So, just under a week.'

Jessie looked over to Jones.

'That's bad, isn't it?' said P.J. 'I don't understand what you're saying. You've found her silicone implants, what does that mean?'

'We found a body, sir. We're trying to identify who it is. Has anyone in the household spoken to her – the kids, for instance?'

P.J. stood up and knocked on the window. Jessie noticed he was shaking. The bald man came to join them. 'Danny, when was Verity last home – and don't cover for her, this is serious.'

Danny looked at the police officers. 'She went out on Thursday night. We haven't seen her since. She called during the day on Friday, wanting to talk to the boys, but she was incoherent. I'm afraid I wouldn't put them on.' He turned back to P.J. 'Actually, she fired me, I've been meaning to mention it to you.'

P.J. waved a hand, dismissing the idea of his wife firing the man. Jessie wondered whether Verity Shore had a point. Knight seemed a bit shifty to her, a bit in a hurry to go somewhere and yet a little too eager to stay. She gave him a long hard look. 'So you haven't seen or heard from her since Friday, when she called you, obviously distressed?'

P.J. came to Danny Knight's defence. 'It's not like that. Her disappearing for a few days isn't particularly unusual. Verity likes to party, I like to spend the weekend at home with the boys. We had a rule: she couldn't bring anyone back here. I don't mean lovers, I mean . . . well, shit, you probably know already – the liggers, the party people, the coke-heads. I . . . well, you know, it was hard keeping track of her. I've sort of given up trying.'

It didn't sound very impressive.

'Danny, could you take the boys upstairs. I think I need to go to the police station.'

'Actually, Mr Dean –' P.J. put his hand up. Danny didn't move. Eventually Danny got the hint and left.

'Call me old-fashioned,' said P.J. 'I trust him as much as is possible, but most people have a price.' He stood abruptly. 'Do you need me to make a formal identification?'

'Please sit down, Mr Dean,' said Jessie.

'P.J., please.'

'This thing is, the body is not in a good condition. To be honest, there isn't much to identify.'

'What do you mean? What happened to her?'

'We don't even know at this stage that it is her.'

There was a brief knock and the young woman from the entrance hall pushed the door open with her foot and carried in a large tray weighed down with coffee and pastries. P.J. was up in a second to take the tray from her. She pulled a fold-away table from behind the door and P.J. lowered the tray. He sat back down while the young woman began to pour the coffee. She was short with dirty blonde hair tied back in a ponytail. A good figure, Jessie noted, under the sweatshirt and jeans. She looked about twenty-eight. Young for a housekeeper. Young and pretty, if a little unkempt. Her eyes kept watch on P.J. as she poured by instinct.

'What's going on?' she asked.

In keeping with P.J.'s previous instructions, Jessie and Jones remained mute.

'I don't know,' said P.J. 'The police were just telling me.' He looked at Jessie. 'Go on . . .'

Jessie nodded towards the woman pouring coffee for Jones. 'Perhaps we should wait.'

'Oh God, carry on. You can say anything you want to now; previous comments do not apply.'

'Are you sure? This is quite delicate.'

'What's happened?' asked the woman. 'Is Verity all right?'

'We found the body of a woman on the bank of the Thames yesterday morning,' said Jones.

The woman dropped the spoon she was using to ladle sugar into P.J.'s coffee. She put her hand over her mouth and stared at P.J.

'At this point,' continued Jessie, 'we don't know the cause of death. There will be an autopsy at four p.m. today, and you are welcome to be there for the results.'

'Oh my God, P.J., the boys.' P.J. took the

woman's hand. She stood up, still clutching his hand. 'I've got to go and see –'

'Keep this to yourself for the moment. They don't know that it is Verity.' He turned back to Jessie. 'Do you?'

'Not absolutely, no. Though I'm sorry to hear that no one has spoken to her since Friday.'

'Tell them about the letters,' said the young woman. 'Tell them about the letters . . .'

'What letters?' asked Jones.

'It was nothing.'

'But, P.J. . . .' The woman put her hand on his shoulder.

'I think you should go and see the boys,' he said sternly.

'But –'

P.J. turned to Jessie. 'The police have been here before. The boys aren't stupid, they'll know it's something to do with their mother. It always is.'

'Yes, sorry. Excuse me, I've got to, um . . .' The woman was frowning and backing out of the room. 'Sorry . . .' Again, she didn't finish her sentence, she simply bolted.

'Who was that?' asked Jessie.

P.J. watched the woman run through the bowling alley and back up the steps that they had come down.

'When you say the body is not in a good condition, what exactly do you mean?' asked P.J., ignoring Jessie's question.

Jessie repeated the question. 'Who was that woman, Mr Dean?'

'Call me P.J. My father is Mr Dean. And I am not him.'

'About the girl?'

'Girl?'

'The woman who brought in the coffee?'

'Excuse me! You've just told me that my wife might be dead, I'd like a few more details, please. I want to know what happened to Verity. I want to know whether I have to tell those boys that their mother is dead!'

She let it go. For the time being. 'Do you know why your wife would have been in Barnes? Do you have friends on the river?'

'Define "friends".' He sounded angry. 'It was drugs, wasn't it? She was fucked and fell in, was that it? Was she hit by a boat? Is that why she's in such a mess? I can handle it, just tell me.'

'What sort of drugs did she take?'

'I don't know. She was clean for a lot of the time, then suddenly she would binge, go off the rails. I don't know who she was with or where she went. I have done everything in my power to stop her, but she wouldn't. Not for me, not even for the kids. She was unstoppable.' P. J. Dean fiddled with his dressing-gown cord for a while. Jones and Jessie remained quiet. It was always a good idea to let the next of kin talk. People often talked when they were in shock. It was probably the truest insight they would have of P. J. Dean and Verity

70

Shore, before the others got involved. The advisers. Press managers. Image consultants. Lawyers. Producers. Staff.

'I always thought it would end like this,' he said quietly. 'I just didn't know when. She couldn't cause herself any harm here, you see. I banned all drink and drugs from the house. No sharp objects. No deliveries went unchecked. She'd stay in bed for a few days after the binge, put herself through some sort of mini cold-turkey, then she was good for a few weeks. Played with the boys. Talked to me. Then she'd begin to feel housebound, she'd call up "friends", photographers. It always started with the shopping. More and more parcels would arrive, then the drinking and then, well, she'd disappear for a few days. I couldn't keep her under lock and key, like I do the beer in the studio. I even do stock checks so I'd know if she was stealing vodka. But she wouldn't have jumped into the river, I'm sure of that. It would have been an accident.'

He went quiet for a while.

'P.J., we're pretty sure that whoever died did not do so by accident.'

'Trust me, she was too selfish to kill herself. Whatever it may look like, it was an accident.'

'What about these letters?'

P.J. sighed loudly. 'Just the normal trappings of celebrity. Hate mail, death threats, pig's blood.'

'Sent to you?'

'Well, us. Look, they don't mean anything. They

come from bored, sad, disappointed people who feel angry at anyone who's succeeded where they failed. There are plenty out there. They're not serious. I wouldn't put it past Verity to send a few to herself.'

'Have you kept them?'

'Don't be ridiculous,' said P.J. impatiently.

'Well,' said Jessie, 'perhaps you should have taken them seriously.'

P.J. stared back at her. Iridescent eyes. Signature eyes. 'Just fucking tell me, will you?'

She nodded briefly. 'There was no head with the body.'

P.J. put his hand over his mouth, his cheeks blew out, he swallowed hard.

'I'm sorry,' said Jessie.

'I . . .' He struggled for breath. Jessie watched. Waited. He stood up, walked around the high-tech room then sat back down. 'Jesus, what am I going to tell them?' He looked out to the bowling alley even though the boys had been taken upstairs. 'You know, they're great kids. Paul is very sensitive and Ty, he –'

'Don't tell them anything for the moment. Until we know more. Here's my card, it's got my mobile number on it. If she comes hòme, call me. If she calls, call me. If she doesn't, we are going to have to question everyone in the house. So now will you tell me who lives here?'

'Me, the boys, Verity . . .' He lowered his head. 'Bernie, she's been with me for twelve years. She has a son, Craig. He's seventeen.'

'And the young woman who brought in the tray?'

'That's Bernie.'

Jessie was startled. The woman looked considerably younger than her. '*She* has a seventeen-year-old son? That boy I saw in the garage?'

'She looks young for her age,' said P.J., standing up again.

'How old is she?' asked Jessie, suspicious.

'This has nothing to do with Verity,' said P.J., sounding pissed off again.

'How old, Mr Dean?' asked Jones in his slow, deliberate way.

'Thirty-two. Do the maths yourself. She is a very good woman, and a great friend. Her private life has got nothing to do with Verity. Do you understand?'

No. Jessie didn't understand. She didn't understand why P. J. Dean was more concerned with his housekeeper than the death of his wife.

'We'll have to question you too, Mr Dean,' said Jones.

'Fine. Give me a time of death, I'll give you an alibi.'

'Who said anything about alibis?' said Jessie quickly.

'Don't insult my intelligence. I know where you look first. That's fine, do your job. I certainly had a motive. I won't hide it, I'd begun to detest Verity. She was a monster, entirely self-centred; whatever she had she wanted more – more attention, more

73

money, more fame, more handbags, more drugs, whatever. But I didn't kill her, and I'll give you an alibi to prove it.'

'How can you be so sure?' asked Jones.

'Trust me, in this business, you are rarely on your own.'

'P.J., is there anything you know about Verity that could help identify her? An old injury . . . ?'

'She has a tattoo, on her –'

'I'm afraid that won't help.'

'Jesus. What did happen to her?'

'We really don't know yet.'

'Um, confidential?'

'Absolutely.'

'She had six toes. On her right foot. She'd had the extra one removed, it left a small scar. I'm sure an expert would know.'

Jessie looked at Jones, who shook his head. It was a fraction of a movement. P. J. Dean had enough information for his imagination to play havoc with, he didn't need to know his wife's feet were missing too.

∽

The door of the Portakabin burst open. 'Well? Anything to say to me?'

Tarek paused. 'That was a great show, Ray,' he said timidly.

'Bollocks. It was crap, another fat bird bleating on about why her skinny boyfriend shagged her best friend. All you have to do is look at the best friend to know why. And as for that hooker whose pimp was her dad – Jesus, can't you get me some fucking decent guests?'

Tarek chewed his biro. 'You had Dame Henrietta Cadell.'

'Whoop fucking whoop. Intellectual snobs, the pair of them. No idea about real life. No wonder her old man sticks his dick in everything; you'd need a ladder to mount her. These are not the sort of people who are going to endear me to the masses. Elitist bollocks, I want celebrities.'

'Nothing very proletariat about celebrities,' said Tarek.

'That's only because you haven't met any.' Ray was staring at himself in the shaving mirror he kept on his desk. He adjusted his gold cross.

'Listen, Tarek, if we are going to have authors on this show, I want it to be Andy fucking McNab, got it!'

Not very likely, thought Tarek.

'What are you looking at?'

'Nothing. Your agent called, Trevor MacDonald is doing a Yardie special, needs an expert, was wondering if you'd do it.'

'Course I'll fucking do it, it's got that Carol Vorderman on it. Now, she looks like she needs a good –'

'And there is someone holding on line one.' There was only a line one, but Ray liked the sound of that. 'He wouldn't give his name.'

75

'Carol Vorderman, now that's more like it. I'll show her the joys of long multiplication.' He picked up the phone and listened. 'Hang on a second. Tarek, go and get me some coffee, will you? Not that instant shit either – the one from the machine. Put it in a proper mug with a bit –'

'Yeah, I know.' It was always the same when Ray wanted to speak to one of his – Tarek searched for a word – associates. Associate was a good word. Hood was another. He opened the door and stepped down the aluminium steps into a potholed and heavily weeded car park. Walking towards him was Ray's research assistant. Associate. Hood. He was a strange bloke. Somewhere in his thirties, Tarek thought, though it was difficult to tell. He was short and thin, but there was nothing weedy about Alistair Gunner. He was built like a featherweight fighter and showed no fear of the man everyone else shied away from. He didn't talk much, had no friends and seemed to shadow St Giles. Tarek and Alistair eyed each other. He wasn't sure who was more suspicious of whom. All Tarek did know was that Alistair had an ability to discover things about people which would make the *News of the World* weep.

'Morning, Alistair,' said Tarek.

'Ray in?'

'On the phone.'

As always he just pushed the door open and walked in. No knock. No waiting for the summons. Bold as brass, walked on in.

'Face down in the mud, eh?' said Ray before Alistair closed the door on him. Tarek walked round the interconnecting Portakabins to the main studio and office building. Alistair Gunner had appeared one day from nowhere; he had no c.v., no experience in TV and no qualifications. But Ray St Giles had given him a job anyway. Just like that. Gunner had so much information on other people, Tarek found himself wondering whether he'd got something on the main man himself. They were close without being close, like a couple in an arranged marriage. Very occasionally, Tarek caught Ray staring at Alistair with a look of apprehension. It was as if he needed him around but didn't trust him. Ray St Giles probably didn't trust anyone.

In the shoddy reception area there was a coffee machine. Tarek put his own money into the slot and waited for it to regurgitate the pale, foamy drink. Somewhere inside the studio real programmes were being made. But not by him and not by the cable company that had put their trust in Ray St Giles and his shadow. Tarek carried the drink back and knocked on the door. Ray and Alistair were leaning over an open file. He'd seen the type of file before. Marked 'Cadell'. In it, Tarek had glimpsed a photograph of a man in a pinstripe suit checking into a hotel with a young blonde. Shortly afterwards Henrietta Cadell's agent had rung up out of the blue and offered her for the 'Mother'n'Son' slot. Whatever he might say, Henrietta Cadell was the sort of guest Ray would pay good money for. Looking at Alistair's shiny new leather jacket, Tarek guessed he had.

'Tarek, get my agent on the line, tell her yes to the Yardie special, and tell her no more fucking supermarkets and cancel my talk at the young offenders' unit. I've had enough of that shit. We are changing gear.'

'Ray, you've got to –'

'Just do it, Tarek. Who is paying your salary?'

Tarek picked up the phone. 'This shitty cable company,' he whispered.

'What?'

'Nothing.'

Alistair Gunner was staring at him with his cold eyes. Tarek needed another job. This one was killing him.

~

Jessie, Jones and P.J. emerged from the underground playground and walked back out into the hall.

'Do you mind if I check her room?' asked Jessie.

'Whose?'

Was he being deliberately obstreperous, or just downright stupid? Unless he thought she meant Bernie's room. 'Your wife's room,' she said deliberately.

'Sorry,' said P. J. Dean. 'It's up the stairs, on the right.'

'Would you mind accompanying me?'

'Oh, okay. This way.'

'I'll wait in the car,' said Jones, already reaching for the front door.

Jessie followed the billowing dressing gown up the stairs. At a half-landing the stairs split in two directions. A tall window reached up to the ceiling, giving an incredible view of their hundred-foot garden. The stone wall at the end backed directly on to Richmond Park.

'The boys and I watch for deer,' said P.J., pointing to the three pairs of binoculars on the table below the window. 'You can usually find them in the vicinity of the Isabella Plantation. See, the clump of oaks over there on the left?' P.J. was pointing out of the window now.

Jessie looked at her watch. 'If you don't mind . . .'

'Shit! Sorry, I keep forgetting why you're here.' He shook his head. 'Does that seem weird to you?' His green eyes were staring into hers.

'It's probably shock,' she said quietly.

'You don't really think that, do you? You probably think I'm a law unto myself, that my marriage was a farce and I screwed every backing singer that walked through my door.'

'I'd like to see the room now,' said Jessie.

'I'm a good father to those boys.'

Jessie didn't know what to say. He turned away from her and took the right-hand staircase two steps at a time. Jessie followed him along a galleried landing until they reached a corridor, at the end of which was a set of double doors. There was a key in the lock. P.J. pushed both doors open wide and stood back. Jessie walked into the forty-foot bedroom.

'My room is down the other end,' said P.J., before Jessie could ask.

There was an awful lot of space for one small, insecure woman. Too much space. Immaculate. Soulless, like a hotel room. Huge white pillows were puffed up on a huge white bed, white sheets, white duvet, white bedspread. Thick white curtains were draped over an old boat mast; too long for the window, the material cascaded on to the white carpet. Jessie couldn't decide whether it was virginal, marital or sacrificial. Whatever it was, this white, sunlit room was now a mausoleum. Verity Shore was dead, Jessie knew it, from the hairs on the back of her neck to the chill in her bones.

The walk-in wardrobe was the size of Jessie's bedroom and bathroom combined. Row upon row of designer labels and stacks upon stacks of shoe boxes. Jessie was momentarily awestruck. Maggie would have wept at this sartorial altar. The sickly sweet aroma of Estée Lauder's White Mischief emanated from the clothes.

'Obscene, isn't it?' said P.J. 'Half this shit, she never even wore. The arguments we've had about that.'

Jessie turned to him. He was walking slowly towards her, his eyes on his wife's clothes. 'I think she did it to shock me. The price tags. They all came up on my credit card, of course. How can anyone spend twelve grand on a top?' Jessie watched him close in on her and said nothing. 'Where I come from, that could practically buy a house. I swear those shops saw her coming and licked their greedy lips. Talk about the emperor's new clothes.' He stopped walking, but continued to talk to his hanging hundreds and thousands. 'Eventually I had to put a limit on any individual spend. Anything over a thousand and the bank rang me to verify it.' He turned to look at Jessie. Those piercing green eyes a few centimetres from hers. 'She didn't like that one bit.'

'Are you telling me your marriage was over?'

'Not over, poisoned.'

'By Verity?'

'By everything, I suppose. My own stupidity, for thinking that she would change.' He pinched the bridge of his nose with his finger and thumb and bent his head forward. 'My own stupidity for believing that women like her married men like me for anything other than money and position.' He laughed drily. 'The oldest profession in the book.'

'Talking like this is not going to give people like me a very good impression.'

He looked up. 'But it's the correct impression.'

'P.J., you just called your wife a whore.'

'No Detective Inspector Driver. I called myself a sucker.' He turned to leave. 'Do you mind? I can't stand the smell.'

*   *   *

81

Jessie carried on through the dressing room to the bathroom. There were enough mirrors in that room to give anyone a complex. There was no hiding from self-scrutiny. Along one wall was a mirrored dressing table the size of a pool table. More cupboards lined either side of it. All mirrored, of course. Jessie ran her finger along the mirrored surface then looked at it. Not a speck of dust. This room was exceptionally clean. Suspiciously clean. Gleaming bottles of serum, scrub, toners and tonics lined up like an army. A fight against age. To the death. She approached the bath. It stood alone on a pedestal and it smelt of bleach. On the edge of the tub were more goodies. A family of Paul Mitchell bottles. Did women like Verity Shore wash their own hair? Jessie picked up a bottle and shook it. She unscrewed the lid and sniffed. Obviously not. For a second she pictured Verity Shore, an unhappy, over-indulged woman, lying amongst expensive bubbles in her big white pedestal bathtub, sipping from a shampoo bottle.

She put the shampoo bottle back with the others and returned to the bedroom. A large sash window on the far wall looked directly on to the flat roof of the garage. One big step up. Made easier by the presence of a conveniently positioned window box. The window pushed up easily. Silently. Jessie looked at the window box. No flowers. Well-trodden soil. Apparently P. J. Dean had less control of his wife than he thought. She took a digital camera from her bag and photographed the footprints. Someone had been sneaking out after bedtime.

Jessie and Jones left the rock star standing at the doorway to his exorbitant mansion. Somehow the building did not reflect the man. He was still wearing his dressing gown. The boys had appeared either side of him. He put an arm around each. Jessie didn't envy P.J. telling them.

'Do you think he is involved?' asked Jones once they were outside.

'Instinctively, I'd say no, it seems too vicious for a normal man. But then I don't suppose there is anything very normal about P. J. Dean.'

'He has a lot of money, he could have paid someone,' said Jones.

'A simple overdose would've been more sensible.'

Jessie could see Bernie in a first-floor window, her arm around her tall son. Her shoulder came to his waist. How did such small women produce such enormous sons? He was as tall, maybe taller than P.J. and as well-built. Even the gardener watched them pull away. 'P.J. was very candid about Verity, but clammed up about Bernie, that's what sets my alarm bells ringing. I think there might be something going on between Bernie and P.J. The question is, has it got anything to do with Verity's death?'

Jones rested his head on the headrest. 'We still don't know for sure that it is her.'

'If we did, I'd have people all over that house.'

The gates opened automatically, Jessie looked up at the CCTV camera and resisted the temptation to wave. Then she remembered the window box and stopped the car. She climbed out and ran back up the drive. Barefoot, P.J. came to meet her.

'The security tapes? Can I have them?' said Jessie.

P.J. shrugged. 'Sure.' He turned round, saw Bernie and Craig in the window and pointed to one of the cameras. Bernie opened the window.

'What?'

'The tapes, can you get them for the inspector.'

'As far back as they go please,' said Jessie.

Bernie seemed hesitant. She looked at her son. Craig said something. Jessie couldn't catch it, but whatever it was made Bernie relax. She looked back to P.J., gave him a brief smile and disappeared.

Jessie turned to P.J. 'You say Bernie has worked for you for twelve years. How did you find her?'

P.J. scratched his short dark hair. 'I heard she needed a job.'

'How?'

He shrugged. 'I can't remember now. Look, do you mind?' he pointed at his feet. They were blue. 'My feet are about to fall off.'

'Fine. I'll wait for the tapes, but you'll have to answer all my questions eventually.'

'If it's Verity.'

'Do *you* think it is?' asked Jessie.

He didn't answer her but his body language did. He ran his hands through his dark hair, gathered his dressing gown around him and crossed his arms. Then he turned away and walked back to the house. A few minutes later Bernie came out with the tapes. Twenty of them. The handover was a silent one.

Jessie returned to the car.

'What about a crazed fan?' said Jones as Jessie climbed back in. 'They've been getting letters.'

'*If* they've been getting letters.'

'You think that was a set-up?' asked Jones.

Jessie hoped not. 'Crazed fans kill with guns and knives. This is too planned, and very hateful. We were supposed to find her the way she was. Indistinguishable. The legs spread. The implants. What does it say about her?'

'Not a great deal.'

'Exactly.' Jessie left the well-protected mansion in her rear-view mirror, the green gate sliding closed behind them. 'Someone is making a brutal point.'

'What happened to the boys' real fathers? If she left them and took their kids, that's a motive.'

'I'll check them out as soon as the ID is verified.'

'Too busy being the has-beens of the future to look after their own offspring,' said Jones.

'A perfect sound bite. You should remember that for the press office.'

Jones started to laugh, it was an unfamiliar sound. 'Wasn't that surreal?' he said, through the giggles. 'And as for that bowling alley – God, how the other half live.'

Jessie joined in with the laughter. The tension from the previous hour erupting in a wave of hysterical giggles. Jones was clutching his stomach, gasping for air.

'P. J. Dean in his pyjamas!' exclaimed Jessie before another bout of giggling grabbed her. Jones was still clutching his stomach, gasping for air. Jessie looked at him. Jones wasn't laughing any more.

'Sir?'

He didn't reply. He was bent double, hyperventilating, his neck quickly turning the colour of beetroot.

'Hold on!' Jessie put the sirens on, her headlights flashing blue and white. She put her foot on the accelerator and began to weave through the traffic. Jones' breathing had slowed. He lifted his head and looked at her.

'What are you doing?' He groaned as he spoke.

'One of the perks of the job. Ever noticed how patrol cars never get stuck in traffic? Don't talk, just breathe. You've gone a very odd colour.'

'You win. I'm sorry about the hairdresser comment.'

'No, I mean it, you really have gone a very strange colour.'

Pain clamped around his stomach and Jones doubled up again. Jessie sped on to the nearest hospital she knew. She didn't radio ahead. She didn't think Jones would like anyone to know a senior officer was being admitted; news travelled fast.

When they arrived, she half carried him through

to A&E and at the desk quietly informed the nurse who he was. She filled in as much detail as she could. He'd been off-colour for some time, she suspected, but he never rested. Recently it had been getting worse and he had actually spent a day at home. As far as she knew it was stomach cramps, possibly appendicitis. A doctor came straight away. It was clear to everyone that Jones was now feeling worse. The hot, angry colour of purple had drained away, leaving his lips a pale grey and his skin bone-white. She left the doctor to it and took a seat in the waiting room.

Like most people, Jessie had an aversion to hospitals, so when a nurse offered her their tea-break room she gladly accepted. A pile of magazines was offered to her and hot tea with digestive biscuits. The simple things in life. She accepted them all. Research, she told herself as she began to read up on the lives of the rich and famous. Anything to keep her mind off the colour of Jones' lips and P. J. Dean's eyes.

∽

Jessie walked along the corridor to her office carrying the twenty video tapes. PC Ahmet was sitting on a chair outside Jones' door. She was about to ask him what he was doing there when Trudi came out of her office. She looked distraught.

'He's not going to die, is he?' she asked, breathless and upset.

'Oh, Trudi, no of course not. I've just left him. He asked if you would go and see him – only you, he can't face anyone else.'

Trudi picked up her bag and coat, then put them down again. 'What shall I do about . . . ?'

'Don't worry, we'll get a PC in here to answer your phone. You go, I'll see to it.'

'Thanks, DI Driver.'

'Please, call me Jessie.'

Trudi backed out of the room. 'Oh, DI Driver, there's a woman to see you. She's in Jones' office.'

'But –' Jessie looked down at the video tapes. The autopsy was in an hour.

'I know, but this is important. It's Clare Mills.'

'Perhaps you'd like to dispense with those,' said Niaz, holding out his giant hands to receive the stack of tapes.

Clare was standing at the window, looking out. She was taller and thinner than Jessie remembered. It seemed like months ago that she and Jones had gone to Elmfield House to meet her. Poor Clare. Despite the promises, they'd already let her down. Jessie couldn't explain why, either; murder was like that. Clare turned. She looked haunted.

'Sorry to disturb you at work, I just wanted to give you this.' Clare handed over a black-and-white photocopy of a newspaper article. 'It's amazing what these machines can do with old photos and stuff.'

It was a child. The face of a child. Blurred like

an ultrasound scan, but distinguishable nonethe-less.

'Frank?' asked Jessie gently.

'I found it a while ago. It's from an old local rag, God knows why they were interested in Dad's funeral, but I don't care, at least I have this.'

'Look, Clare, I –'

Clare straightened up. 'I know, you're busy, you'll let me know. I just wanted to give you that and explain something about Mum . . .' Clare hesitated.

'Go on . . .'

'She didn't mean to kill herself. Not really. Have you ever stayed awake for three weeks, not eating, nothing but hope to keep you going?'

Jessie shook her head.

'I have. Another great fuck-up in a history of almighty fuck-ups.'

'Sorry, I'm not with you,' said Jessie.

'I was told they'd found a boy called Frank in care. Obviously, he was a man by then. He had no recollection of his family, but he was the right age, came from the right area. I thought maybe it was him, maybe he'd remembered his name even when everything else around him changed. I did. This Frank was in a mental hospital, which figured. It took three weeks for the paperwork to come through so I could go and see him. I didn't eat or sleep; I sat and prayed it was my Frank. Finally I went to the hospital to meet my brother . . .' She paused. Jessie swallowed nervously. 'He was black.

The boy they thought could be my brother was black. Oh, social services were sorry, somehow my colour had been overlooked. If I'd had the strength, I would have killed myself that day. I would have killed myself even though all I want to do in this pitiful life of mine is look my brother in the eye and tell him I'm sorry. I'm sorry I let them take him away. I'm sorry I didn't protect him from those grown-ups who told me they knew best. I'm sorry that he doesn't know what amazing parents he had, who loved each other, and who loved us. And more than that I'm sorry I didn't go up and check on Mum sooner.'

Suddenly Verity Shore's self-obsessed, insecure, drug-taking antics didn't seem so pressing. Jessie folded the picture of the boy and put it in her wallet then walked Clare to the canteen. Despite Jones' request, Jessie confessed to seeing Ray St Giles on the telly. They agreed it was a sorry world that took known hooligans and criminals and made them into celebrities. Even if they were reformed, which Clare clearly doubted was the case for Raymond Giles, the hard-man angle was the linchpin of their marketability. There was no point denying their past. That past was the only reason they were on television. Clare told Jessie that Raymond Giles also frequented the news studios. Appearing on *London Today* any time a 'gang'-style shooting took place so he could give his 'expert' opinion.

She was so quiet, so unassuming most of the

time, but when Clare talked about Ray St Giles, the anger blazed from her.

Niaz was still sitting in the corridor when Jessie returned.

'What are you doing, Niaz? Haven't we got enough on our hands?'

'DI Ward told me to leave.'

'Did he now? Why?'

'Because I am "a useless piece of pedestrian shite who is good for nothing except beating off". By which I believe he was referring to the act of masturbation and trying to tie it in with the redundant term of beat officer and thereby be humorous and rude at the same time. He failed on both counts.'

'Did you tell him I'd transferred you?'

'Yes.'

'Does he know about the implants?'

'No.'

'Verity Shore?'

'No.'

Jessie smiled. 'And the medical records?'

'They're on their way. DC Burrows organised it.'

'Good. Get their bank details too.' Niaz nodded. 'Now, follow me.'

'Yes, ma'am.'

She opened the door of the CID room. It suddenly went very quiet. DC Fry had clearly been enjoying centre stage. Some of them had the decency to look embarrassed. Not Ward, he just threw himself straight in.

'What the bloody hell have you been doing? Helicopters, divers, the River Police – do you know how many suspicious deaths we deal with here? We haven't got the resources to play Sherlock Holmes with every sad fucker who washes up on the banks of the Thames. Jesus, we probably pull out two a month. It could have come from anywhere. I hear you even got the SOCOs down there. A body can wash up fifty miles from the crime scene, if that is what it is.'

Jessie looked at her watch.

'And what the fuck is he still doing here?' Ward jabbed a finger in Niaz's direction.

She had planned to do this privately. But to hell with him.

'Initial tests on the bones reveal that they have been soaked in a sulphuric acid. Two silicone implants that survived the acid bath were found in the vicinity of the body. They belonged to Verity Shore.'

'Shit! The jellyfish.'

'Yes, Fry, the jellyfish.' Jessie turned back to Mark. 'This morning DCI Jones and myself went to P. J. Dean's house, where we were told by Mr Dean that his wife has been missing for five days. There is to be a full postmortem in an hour at Charing Cross Hospital, which I, as acting Senior Investigating Officer will be attending –'

'Hang on, you're the SIO? What about the guv'nor?'

Jessie continued talking over him. She'd stuff

his insubordination right down his fat throat. 'DCI Jones has been admitted to hospital with a burst stomach ulcer. He has put me in charge. I've written my team down here. Please have an incident, evidence and briefing room set up for when I return from the postmortem, which I am hoping will give us absolute confirmation that the remains are indeed Verity Shore.'

Silence.

'PC Ahmet will shadow me and DC Burrows will be my second-in-command. Both will be accompanying me to the hospital now. Thank you.'

'What about me?' asked Fry. This was a big one, he wanted to be there.

'Oh yes, DC Fry, thanks for reminding me. Niaz, give those tapes to DC Fry so he can start watching. These are the security tapes from the Dean residence. You see someone leaving, clock it; arriving, clock it; any deliveries clock it, number it, and show me when I get back.'

'But –'

'Okay, Niaz, Burrows, you're with me.'

'Yes, ma'am,' they said in unison.

Jessie returned to the corridor. It was the first time she could ever remember shaking on the job.

'Where are those medical records, Burrows?'

'On their way by bike.'

'Is that safe?' asked Jessie as she marched down the corridor.

'They're experienced drivers.'

'Yes, but how are they with large offers of cash?'

Her breathing was returning to normal with every step she took away from Mark Ward. She glanced quickly behind her, didn't see the press officer spring from a side office, and accidentally sent her flying. Kay Akosa fell back and skidded a few yards on her well-rounded rump before coming to a stop.

'God, I'm so sorry.' Jessie helped her up.

'Don't you look where you're going? Didn't anyone tell you not to run in the corridors?'

'Yes, at school, when I was twelve.'

Kay Akosa withdrew her hand and brushed it against her other one. Kay had a reputation for being a tyrant, reducing nervous new recruits to tears over their expressions when caught on camera policing a picket line. She'd call them in over their hairstyle, acne, facial hair, weight. Verity Shore wasn't the only one expected to be image-conscious. These coppers barely had enough money for a beer and a packet of pork scratchings, let alone trendy hairdressers, beauty salons, facials. When Jessie had first appeared at West End Central they needed someone to do a piece to camera outside the building. She could recall Kay Akosa's fateful words: 'You're pretty, you'll do.' It wasn't even a matter for the murder squad. Jessie had refused. She and Mrs Akosa had not shared a canteen experience since.

'We've had every major paper in the country calling about unconfirmed reports that Verity Shore has drowned. What do I tell them?'

'Nothing.'

'And one paper knows you were at P. J. Dean's house this morning.'

'Shit!'

'So?'

'I have nothing to tell you.'

'I can't tell them nothing. Nothing won't do.'

'We don't know who we have in the morgue. So no comment.'

'They already know a body was found.'

'Fine. So they know as much as we do.'

'But –'

'I'll come to the press office as soon as I know more.'

The woman leant back on her heels and crossed her arms. 'Where's Jones?'

Jessie ignored her. She, Niaz and Burrows walked away.

'Don't think I've forgotten about the debacle with Jami Talbot,' Kay called out after them. No one turned around.

'Have you ever been to a postmortem, Niaz?' asked Jessie when they reached the car park.

'No.'

'Well, you're in luck. My first was a woman who'd been raped and then strangled and left in a ditch for two weeks. This will be a breeze. Sally said they'd been busy, so there will probably be bodies piled on top of each other on the surrounding tables. It's cold in there, but I don't think we'll be long, so you should be okay. They'll give

you a mask, shoe covers and a green surgical coat.'
She turned to him. 'You all right with this?'

'Yes, ma'am.'

'Right. Let's go.'

The bones lay on the convex stainless steel table, tilted slightly to where the feet should have been. It allowed the running water to drain away with all the excess mud and silt that the departing tide had left. It was the cleanest PM she had ever seen. The photographer clicked. The pathologist listed what was missing. A few small bones that had been found in the nearby mud were brought in from the evidence room. Most had been matched to the skeleton. One had not.

'Cause of death, unknown. Hairline crack in cerebral vertebrae, recent, could have been caused by being hit over the head. Then again, the body could have been dropped after death. Impossible to say. Female, yes, age between thirty and forty. Early signs of osteoporosis and calcium deficiency. Childhood fracture on the upper arm, almost invisible, nearly missed it. The most interesting thing about this case is the acid test my colleague Sally Grimes did early this morning. She was on site with DI Driver, neither of whom would accept that this was some old drowning victim. The tests are very revealing. Sally, would you like to explain?'

Sally stepped forward.

'Good afternoon, everyone. The initial test showed that sulphuric acid dissolved the flesh and internal organs, but secondary tests picked up traces of ammonia. Although ammonia could not have done the damage that the sulphuric acid did, it is the reason why the bones are so white. It bleached them.'

'Like peroxide,' said Jessie.

'Peroxide is a much weaker form of ammonia, but yes, in principle they're the same.'

Jessie looked at the remains of the bottle-blonde with big tits. The implants were in a jar. If Niaz hadn't found the other implant, they would have had a difficult job on their hands narrowing the field. Verity Shore was not alone. There were many like her. It didn't need to have been her specifically. It could have been anyone.

'Do you know who it is?' asked the pathologist.

DC Burrows' pager bleeped. He looked at Jessie. 'Those records are here.'

'Go.'

She looked back at the pathologist. 'If the records show a childhood break, then that is Verity Shore. If no break, then someone wants us to think that it is Verity Shore. It could be either.'

It suddenly dawned on the pathologist. 'Verity Shore, that blonde who is always taking her clothes off? The one with the big knockers?'

'Dyed blonde and breast enlargements. She was alive last Thursday.'

'Good God,' he said, looking back at the bleached bones lying on a plain of running water.

That was the worst-case scenario. 'What's the best you can hope for?' he asked.

'That these are old bones and Verity Shore is headline hunting.'

'Nobody would go this far,' said Sally Grimes. 'Would they?'

No one replied. The publicity stunts by headline-hungry celebrities were becoming increasingly desperate. Getting pregnant didn't do it. Getting pregnant, taking coke and throwing oneself down the stairs did. So it wasn't impossible. Verity Shore might just be a more ambitious version of Jami Talbot. The door swung open. Burrows stood with the file in his hand. He was reading from it as he walked. 'Twelve – fell off horse, broke arm.'

The pathologist took the file. Read it, flicked through some more pages, returned to the body. He looked up. 'Verity Shore will get all the headlines she dreamt of. It's her.'

Jessie was already out of the door. 'Burrows, call Jones. Tell him.' She peeled her green mortuary coat off as she walked, 'Niaz, get two officers to P. J. Dean's house now – whoever is nearest.' Jessie hopped from one foot to the other as she removed her shoe covers.

'You'd better call the press office,' said Burrows.

'Shit.' She pulled her phone out and dialled a number. 'This is DI Driver. If you're listening, P.J., please pick up the phone. I was at your house –'

'Hello.'

'P.J.?'

'The phone has started to ring – journalists. What's going on?'

'Get out of the house, take the kids somewhere safe. The press know we came to see you this morning, all hell is about to break loose.'

'Shit!'

'We may have been followed.'

'Bullshit.' Then he shouted. 'There's a fucking SNITCH IN MY HOUSE!'

'I gave you my mobile number. Call me when you are out of the house.'

'So it is her?'

'P.J., call me when you are out of the house.'

'You think my phone is bugged?'

'I'm thinking of the boys.'

'Okay, okay, shit, I'll call you back.'

Jessie slipped the phone back into her pocket. Burrows was watching her. 'What?'

'You know you may be protecting a guilty man,' said Burrows.

'Perhaps. But perhaps he's innocent. And those kids certainly are. You know what the press are like.'

'What if they do a runner?'

She tossed this possibility in her head. Niaz was already on his radio. She turned back to Burrows. 'The press are already on to him. In five minutes' time, that man won't be able to take a shit without the world knowing about it. He won't be going anywhere. Call Kay Akosa. We release a short statement: Verity Shore was found dead on the bank of the River Thames at 06.05 on Tuesday morning. Her family have been informed and an investigation is underway to determine cause of death.'

'That's it?'

'What does she want, gory details?'

'Ahmet and you finding the jellyfish?'

'No.'

'It's good stuff, boss.'

'Do you want those kids knowing their mother was dipped in acid?'

'They won't read the papers.'

'Come on, Burrows, those boys go to school, their classmates' parents will talk about it, kids'll overhear it, headlines glare at them at eye-level . . . What the fuck do you think they're going to do, come to a mutual agreement not to discuss the case in their presence? The oldest is seven, he'll be in the playground with much older boys and girls, who know full well they are Verity's kids, that they're rich. You think they'll keep it to themselves? Get an injunction, whatever it takes – this information stays with us. If anyone goes to the press they lose their job, their pension, their fffu—' She clenched her fists.

'You can't control this,' said Burrows.

'I can try.'

'Boss, Verity Shore was dipped in acid and was ID'd by the fake tits she claimed she never had – you're already out of control.'

Jessie didn't want to hear it.

'Don't take on the press, boss. You'll lose.'

She turned round. 'What do I do, then?'

'Throw them titbits, that way they'll stay hungry for the story but not so hungry that they go looking for blood elsewhere.'

She stood her ground, but Jessie knew he was making sense.

'It is a media-ruled world we live in. The tabloid press is judge and jury, you want them onside. Give them the tits, keep the rest, and tell P. J. Dean to keep his trap shut.'

'It's a fucking circus,' said Jessie angrily.

'No doubt about it. Just make sure you're the one with the whip.'

She smiled at him gratefully. 'Thanks, Burrows.'

'No sweat, boss.'

'Okay, tell Kay about the implants. But I want to see that press release before it goes out.'

'What do you want me to do?' asked Niaz.

'Get on to the water board. I want those sewage tunnels searched. I'm going to P. J. Dean's house, find out what's been going on in paradise.'

'So you *do* think P. J. Dean is involved,' announced Burrows.

'I didn't say that.'

~

Jessie stood in Verity Shore's bedroom and stared at the window box. Chrysanthemums. Freshly planted. Hours old. Too new. Once again she lifted her camera to her eye and took a photo, then she beckoned to one of the guys in plastic overalls. It was the guy from the shower. The ballsy guy. 'Bring the window box in,' said Jessie. 'And make sure you get prints from all round this window, outside and inside.'

'Sure.'

She turned to look at him. 'What, no snide comments, defiant gestures?'

'Actually, the lads and I were wondering if you'd join us for a drink after. Our way of saying sorry for being such twats.'

Jessie raised an eyebrow.

'Dicks then.'

'You buying?'

'With all this overtime you're earning us, we thought it would be rude not to.'

'In which case, I accept your offer.'

He turned round and made a thumbs-up to the three men systematically working their way through Verity Shore's private life.

'Don't forget the window box,' said Jessie. 'And check the drains for remnants of large quantities of blood.'

He put a hand to his heart. 'Your wish is my command,' he said, performing a slight bow.

'Settle.'

He smiled. 'Sorry.' Stuck out his hand. 'My name's Ed.'

'Ma'am,' shouted someone from the bathroom. 'Think you had better come and have a look at this.' Jessie walked through the wardrobe, back to the hall of mirrors. Two of the white-suited men were leaning over the tiled surround. Their presence only enhanced the bathroom's tomb-like quality. One of them had prised off a tile. 'I noticed it was loose when I knelt on it. Looks like someone has been stashing pills.'

Jessie peered inside. P. J. Dean had said all pills and booze were banned. Which meant Verity had resorted to subterfuge. Jessie had found the booze hidden in the shampoo bottles. And now they'd found the pills. She took a pair of tweezers from the cabinet and picked one out.

'Looks like some bathwater got in. These are all partially dissolved,' said the guy holding the removed tile. Jessie peered back in the man-made hole. 'Wouldn't they have dissolved into one big lump?' she said. 'Bag them all up, take them to the lab and have them tested.'

'What do you think they are?'

'Could be anything – amphetamines, antidepressants, painkillers, Ecstasy. P. J. Dean said she often took to her room, maybe this was what kept her entertained.'

'I think we're done here.'

'What about the wardrobe?' said Jessie. 'Someone has to go through every single shoe box.'

'Why?'

'Why? Because they make good hiding places and it looks like Verity Shore had a lot to hide. Then we'll go to the pub. And not a word of this outside this building.' They all gave their word, Jessie wondered how much it was worth. As P. J. Dean said, you could only trust people so far, everybody has a price.

Jessie left the house and walked round the back of the garage. There was a thick rainwater pipe, with two offshoots at different heights. And bins at the bottom. If there had been any footprints before, they'd been wiped away. Someone had been doing some tidying as well as some gardening. Jessie put a foot on the sturdiest-looking bin, grabbed the pipe, put another foot on a windowsill and grabbed the first offshoot with her left hand. A redundant nail gave her the third secure step, an over-spill pipe her fourth. Within ten seconds she was on the roof. She walked across the flat, sun-warmed asphalt to Verity's window. The window box had been taken away, leaving two sturdy brackets. It was a big step up, but it wasn't impossible. If needs must. She turned and leant back on the white wall, pulled out her phone and dialled a number.

'Fry, it's Driver here. What news on those video tapes?'

'Bugger all.'

She nodded to herself. 'Good.'

'Good? I've been watching hours of the same image and you think that's good?'

'Yes. Didn't want to tax you with anything too complicated.'

'Look, ma'am I'm sorry about the –'

'Forget it. Keep watching the tapes.'

'What are you expecting me to find?'

'Nothing.'

She snapped her phone shut, retraced her steps across the roof of the garage, and peered out over the garden. To the right of the house there was a building that looked like a pool house. Pools meant chemicals. Chlorine. Bleach. It all came from the same family. It also meant sun-loungers. Privacy. By easing herself backwards off the roof and clinging to the over-spill pipe, she could climb down with relative ease, even in the dying light. She felt for the nail. Perhaps not so redundant after all. The windowsill. The bin. The ground. Escape. But not to the outside world. Cameras would have caught her. No, Verity Shore found escape in-house. Provided, perhaps, by the adoring arms of a seventeen-year-old.

This house held secrets. Jessie could feel it. She walked across the clipped lawn, past the football goals to the pool house. The smell of chlorine got stronger as she drew closer. There was no key to this room. It was a big pool, but Jessie could have walked from one end to the other with ease. Not because it was a steady shallow depth, but because it was empty. Drained. Jessie called the forensic team. And the reaping began again.

~

'Mark, thanks for coming to see me in this Godawful place.'

'It's all right, guv. I've been wanting a word with you anyway. That Jessie Driver, she gets –' Jones put his hand up. 'She's running the department like a despot, circumnavigating the press office, she's –'

'A different sort of detective to you and me, Mark, that's all, but that doesn't mean she isn't, in her own way, as good. I need you in charge in my absence, not whipping up a battleground. I've got something important for you to do.'

'Police a pensioners' march?'

'Mark, come on, I'm too ill for your shit. You are a good man, don't make me have to convince her of that.'

Ward shook his head. This pep talk touched the surface of years of booze, boys' club, marital break-ups, bodies. He'd given the Force too much to be passed over for a girl half his age with none of his experience. 'Whatever.'

'Please?'

'What was this important case?'

Jones passed over the file. 'Find Frank Mills. Use whatever means, do whatever you have to, but find him.'

'Thought you put Miss Open University on the job.'

'It was a mistake.'

Mark opened the file. 'Well, well, well, your old friend Raymond Giles.'

'Exactly.'

'I remember him going down.'

106

'Exactly.'

'And coming out.'

'Exactly.'

'He shot this boy's dad, and the boy disappears?'

'Exactly.'

'He'd be how old by now . . . ?'

'Exactly.' Jones closed his eyes. When he opened them, Mark Ward had gone. He'd slept for four hours.

~

Jessie let herself into the flat, put her helmet on the wooden floor and walked through to the kitchen. There was a bottle of wine open on the table and singing coming from the bathroom. Jessie poured herself a glass and walked to the bathroom, with her foot she eased the door open. Maggie was lying in bubbles up to her ears, smoking a fag, singing to Heart FM and sipping from a half-empty wine glass.

She stopped singing and looked at Jessie. 'Hey, Morse.'

'Hey, Anthea.'

'Ouch. You're late.'

Jessie put the seat down and sat on the loo. 'Yup.'

'Boy or body?'

'Latter, sadly.'

'Anything you can tell me about?'

The sigh was uncontrolled and came from deep inside her. Jessie shook her head.

'Then can I rant?' said Maggie.

Jessie took a slug of wine. 'Rant away.'

'Firstly, I want to kill everybody.'

'Okay, but it'll take some doing,' said Jessie, smiling.

'I have had it up to –' she had no free hand, so kicked a leg out of the bath and promptly slipped – 'here!' Maggie was gurgling.

Jessie wondered if Maggie was already on her second bottle of wine. 'What's happened?'

'You know that job I was up for – the Istanbul thing?'

Jessie crossed the proverbial fingers and waited.

'The fucking Titled Tart got it. I am inconsolable. I am mad with rage.'

'Who?'

'That awful blonde, skinny posh bird who writes, ha, ha, for the *Mail on Sunday*. Lady Cosima Broome. She was at school with my sister, you know. Thick as pigshit. Just because she's a size eight and her father owns most of Oxfordshire, she gets my job. Honestly, Jessie, I want to kill her. I hate them all. But I particularly hate her. I'm good at my job, despite what that bastard Cadell wrote.'

Jessie opened her mouth to respond. But she wasn't quick enough.

'We live in a mad, celebrity-obsessed, media-run, PR-polluted world. I went to college to learn how to present, produce and write pieces to camera. And I was fucking good, too. We went to

Trinity, Jessie. Trinity! Doesn't that count for anything? Just when I think I have a chance of a boost, some fucking pseudo-celeb comes and pinches my spot. Jessie, I'm telling you they *all* do holidays. Some soap star has a new single out and the bright sparks at the PR company send them our way – and the precious little mite ain't going to do Skegness. Journalists, It-girls, models, singers, actors, actresses, ex-*Blue Peter* presenters, anyone who wants a little career lift, comes calling. You know when they are going down for the count of ten when our producers pass on them and they end up on *Ready Steady Cook*. Jesus, it's depressing. Why can't journalists stay journalists, why do they suddenly want to be novelists, food critics and presenters? What's with all this multi-tasking bollocks? I trained hard to be a presenter, what the fuck do they know? I mean, please, the Titled Tart? It is so insulting!'

'Feeling better?' said Jessie.

'I need a celebrity shag.'

'So you keep saying.'

'I know what I should do. Go on a miracle diet, pose naked for *FHM*, get engaged to Robbie Williams for five minutes and discover my father is really Jeffrey Archer. That should give me enough print to get on *The Big Breakfast*. Oh, and did I mention sleep with the producer?'

'Several times.' Jessie poured more wine into her flatmate's glass. 'But luckily you have more self-respect than all those dolly birds put together.

You're good at your job, Maggie. I wouldn't say so if you weren't. You just have to persevere.'

Maggie gave Jessie an impenetrable look then sank lower in the bubbles.

Jessie thought about Verity Shore and her picture-perfect life. The camera lied. 'Do you really care? Do you really want it that much?'

'Yes. And so do you, otherwise you wouldn't put up with the shit those boys in blue send your way. Ambition is what ambition is. Don't kid yourself that you haven't got it in body-bags.'

The door to Jessie's bedroom creaked open. Maggie was pink from too hot a bath and too generous a drink.

'Hey, Rebus,' she said.

'Hey, Fergie,' said Jessie, looking up from the pages of *Hello!*.

'Oh, that's harsh.'

'You deserve it.'

'Sorry. I really should stop venting my anger on you, shouldn't I?'

'I'd appreciate it.'

Maggie threw herself on to Jessie's super-king-size bed. 'You love me really. Listen, Bill called earlier, wants to know whether you've got any time off. He's in Egypt, right?' Jessie nodded. Her brother moved around the world with Médecins Sans Frontières; he was a picture-book hero in her mind, one that made Indiana Jones look old and tired. 'I think he has some plan to take a canoe down the Nile. I said that's exactly the sort of relaxing holiday you'd like after examining dead bodies. Perhaps I should pitch the idea of following him with a camera,' said Maggie. Jessie shook her head.

'Everyone wants to be on TV, even if they don't admit it.'

'Not Bill,' said Jessie proudly. 'He'd hate it.'

Maggie pouted. 'Even if it was me . . . ?'

Jessie smiled but said nothing. Bill found Maggie too pushy for his liking. Her lack of subtlety grated, and she always flirted with him. Jessie told Bill not to take it personally, Maggie flirted with everyone. She missed him when he was away.

Maggie picked up the magazines fanned out around Jessie. 'You little closet!'

'Research,' said Jessie.

'Like fuck it is. These are old, I've got the latest issues in my room.'

Jessie lowered the magazine. 'It's amazing you don't swear on air.'

'I'm a pro, honey. So what are you looking at?'

'Nothing.'

'Oh my God, you're on the Verity Shore case! Jessie, that is brilliant! Why didn't you tell me? Stupid question, I know, you can't tell me anything. Does that mean you get to meet – oh my God, P. J. Dean! He is so sexy. He must be in one of these somewhere.'

Jessie pulled the magazine away.

'Okay, I get the message. Just tell me one thing – is he as sexy in real life?'

Jessie smiled.

'I knew it. Right, I'm going to some film party, you want to come? You don't even have to change out of your fatigues, the lipstick lesbian look is in at the moment. Very *Matrix*.'

'I can't. But thanks for the compliment.'

'Well, if you change your mind, here's a spare invite. You can spy on the celebrities.'

Jessie stared at the picture of Verity Shore and her second husband. They were in a pool. The same pool that experts had been crawling all over that afternoon, looking for Verity's remains. 'I've got to work.'

Maggie leant over and gave Jessie a kiss. 'Suit yourself.'

Jessie's mobile phone rang. Maggie grabbed it.

'No, Maggie!'

'Please, let me say it, just once.'

'No.' Jessie took the phone. 'Detective Inspector Driver.'

'Hi. It's P.J.'

She pointed to the door and Maggie retreated grudgingly. Jessie swallowed. 'Where the hell are you? I've been dragged over hot coals for letting you out of my sight. You said you'd phone me straight back.'

'Sorry. Had to get the kids away. Took a bit of time.'

'You are still in London, aren't you?'

'I take it that it was Verity.'

'Yes. I'm very sorry, Mr Dean. I wish you'd phoned me back sooner.'

'It's P.J., for fuck's sake.' There was a long pause. 'Can you tell me what happened?'

'I'd rather not tell you over the phone.'

'Are you still worried about being listened to?'

'Actually, I'm more worried about you, your family, and what I have to tell you.'

She heard a long sigh down the phone.

'It wasn't an accident then?'

'Absolutely not.'

'Can you meet me now?'

Jessie glanced at her watch. It was nine o'clock. 'Yes. Where?'

'The middle of Hammersmith Bridge in half an hour. I'll be on foot,' he said.

It wasn't until she saw the swirling mass of the Thames under the sickly orange haze that the location struck Jessie as odd.

~

Ray span a pencil through his fingers. Tarek listened to it click against Ray's thick gold ring. Tarek couldn't look at Ray's hands without wondering whose neck they had been around. He'd done his homework on Raymond Giles. His name was associated with the death of at least two women who worked in his clubs. Hostesses. Prostitutes. Whatever the nomenclature, like

113

associates and hoods, Tarek was sure Ray was involved. You only had to look into the eyes. And the way he kissed that cross, like a man desperate to keep his demons at bay. It was typical, wasn't it, that a crook like St Giles should be superstitious. Tarek believed it was because only the truly evil believed in hell, like only the truly good believed in God. Everyone else floated in between, dipping in and out when it suited them.

The shanty office was gradually being heated by light bulb, Tarek's hard work and Ray's nervous energy. They were attempting to put an unscheduled programme through in three days. Ray was trying to keep the guest under wraps, but Tarek was beginning to get savvy. The more he knew, the more danger he was in, but the more in control he felt.

Alistair entered the room without knocking, as usual. He didn't walk, he slunk, watching Ray with large eyes that made him look as if he'd spent his childhood in the dark. Tarek wondered if Ray had found him inside, in the nick, doing bird. He had an imprisoned look about him, a mixture of fear and arrogance. It would explain their rather peculiar relationship.

Ray asked Tarek to go and fetch coffee when Alistair came through the door. Another custom that Tarek was getting around. If he ran to the coffee machine he could programme it and return to the open window to listen. Nine times out of ten, Ray didn't even drink the stuff.

'Coffee,' barked Ray. 'It's going to be an all-nighter.'

Tarek started running.

~

Jessie sat astride her bike and watched P. J. Dean approach. He wore a grey woolly hat pulled down to his eyebrows. His jacket collar was turned up and, although it wasn't too cold, he had wrapped a scarf around his jawline. His hands were thrust deep into his pockets and he walked with a slight hunch. He glanced briefly at Jessie then away to the other side of the bridge.

'P.J.?' Jessie called, removing her helmet.

He stepped back. 'Sorry, you've got the –'

'It's me. DI Driver.'

He scratched his stubble and peered at her. 'Course it is. Sorry, you look a little different.' Jessie swung her leg off the bike and they moved to the railings. 'I love the bike. Triumph?'

'Virago.'

'Had it long?'

'Five years, but don't get me started. I have a tendency to become a petrol-head if encouraged.'

'I used to nick bikes in Manchester, race them around the streets and dump them where they ran out of petrol. We couldn't afford more petrol and we were too young to think of selling them on.'

'How young?'

'Ten.' He paused. 'I got lucky, I guess.'

'Very.' Jessie knew what happened to kids like that. If they were fortunate, someone they looked up to guided them away from the inevitable. For most of them it was glue, petty theft, young offenders' units, hard drugs, real crime and then prison. Prison made them into absent fathers and the whole sorry tale would begin again.

'Why did you want to meet here?' asked Jessie.

'I love the bridges. I love the view. I'm not a big fan of water, but I don't seem to mind it from up here. I come here at night, when I know I won't be mobbed.'

'That constant, is it?'

He nodded. 'I know I can't complain. I'm the lucky one, right? But once in a while it would be nice to sit in a coffee shop, chat to a mate, have a laugh and not have to wonder who is watching and what your mate's motive is.' He leant on the freshly painted green-and-gold balustrade. A River Police launch honked from somewhere up river. Netting bodies. Night after night.

'What was Verity's motive?'

'The worst, I'm afraid. But I didn't kill her, Detective Inspector.'

'You seem remarkably sanguine about your wife's death.'

He shrugged. 'I knew a long time ago that she wasn't going to make it. The drink was going to kill her.'

'Drink didn't kill her.'

He turned and stared at her, then looked back at the water. 'You'd better tell me.'

'We don't know exactly how your wife died, but we do know that at some point her body was submerged in industrial-strength sulphuric acid until only her bones remained. We can only hope that she was not alive when this happened.' Jessie watched P. J. Dean take in the information. He didn't move for a few minutes. He stood, hunched over the railings, staring at the water as it buffeted the bridge's foundations. The eyelashes on his upper lid almost touched his cheek when he looked down.

'They say drowning is the nicest way to die. Do you think that is true?' he said quietly.

'No,' said Jessie.

'No. Nor me.'

'Did you hear what I said, about Verity?'

He turned to face her. 'Nothing would surprise me. We are capable of such terrible things. Children are forced to drink bleach, they are raped and sodomised, cut up and burnt, starved and tortured, and that's just in this wealthy middle-class country of ours. So, no, nothing would surprise me.'

'Do you know anyone who would want to hurt Verity, get rid of her?'

'Well, she didn't have a lot of friends, but off the top of my head I don't know anyone who would dip her in acid. Then again, people like that don't wear signs.'

'How would you describe Bernie and Verity's relationship?'

P.J. sighed. 'Exhausted. Verity exhausted us all. You can't help a person unless they want to help themselves. The first rule of the addict. It didn't matter that she had two great kids who worshipped her, it didn't matter that I loved her, it didn't matter that she had everything money could buy. It can go two ways, either you hate them for not changing or you hate yourself for not being good enough for them to want to change.'

'Is that why you let her go out, even though you knew she'd get into trouble?'

'We couldn't stop her. How do you stop someone who is hellbent on self-destruction?'

'We are going to have to question everyone in the household, find out everyone's movements.'

'Give me a couple of days, I need to tell the boys that their mother isn't coming home this time. Paul asked me which hospital she was in. Isn't that depressing? You think you can hide these things from kids, but you can't. Do you have family – brothers and sisters?'

'Three older brothers.'

He smiled knowingly. 'It wasn't enough at home, you had to take on the oldest bastion of the dominant male?'

Jessie took a step away from him. 'I have wanted to be a murder investigator since a headless woman was found in a field near my parents' house. That was twenty years ago. They still don't know who she was, how she died, or who killed her. My choice of career had nothing to do with my brothers;

118

it had everything to do with that woman in the field. And one day, I'll solve that case. Meanwhile, I'm going to find out who killed your wife, how, where and why, and I shall stop at nothing until I do, because the only person who's important in this is Verity, despite the person you say she had become. The only right left to a murder victim is to have their murderer caught. I'll give you till the morning. Then I'm coming to question everyone, and that includes Craig.'

'Craig? Why him?'

'Why did you empty your pool?'

P.J. frowned. 'I didn't know it was empty.'

'You have a pool that you don't even know is empty?'

'I told you, I'm not a fan of water. It's probably being cleaned.'

'Who used it, then?'

'An amazing thing about Verity, it didn't matter how shit she felt, she'd still do a hundred lengths. Even when she was drunk, she'd swim, up and down, up and down. That kind of vanity is hideous.'

He really hated his wife. 'Mr Dean, do not under any circumstances speak to the press, leave the country, or be seen out on the town with some model.'

He started to protest.

'There are only two reasons why you wouldn't help me find your wife's murderer: you did it, or you want to protect the person who did. The moment I come up against any obstacles, any PR bullshit, or prima donna antics, that is what I will think. Do we understand each other?'

'My name is P.J.'

'Do we understand each other?'

He nodded once.

She put the helmet back on and returned to the bike. Comments about her brothers hit a nerve. She may have spent her life keeping up with them, but not in her career. Her career was all hers, she was in it alone because she alone wanted to be in it. She had no contemporaries on the inside and no one she could completely confide in on the outside. She was in this for the victims and the families who needed to know why. P. J. Dean turned his back on her and began to walk away. And when there was no grief-stricken family, she was in this for the dead alone.

P.J. quickly merged with the night gloom. He had discovered a way he could move through the world as an ordinary man. It was simple. All he had to do was dress like an ordinary man, walk like an ordinary man, stoop like an ordinary man. Getting noticed, that was the hard part.

~

Jessie left her helmet and jacket with one coat attendant, while another was being harassed by a couple of fourteen-year-olds. The two precocious, overly made-up teenagers were standing with their hands on their undeveloped hips, clutching their 'freebie' bags, demanding the poor French cloakroom girl find their belongings. Apparently some glittery evening bag was missing. These were the people Maggie partied with.

As she looked around the room, for the first time in three months Jessie was glad of her choice of career. It was tough and there were people out to get you, but at least you knew who your enemies were. If you were good at your job, you got results, and if you got results you got promoted. The battlefield was ugly, but open. Here, she felt as though she was standing on a tropical beach. Beneath the fine white sand was a minefield. One wrong step and boom!

Just as she was about to give the girls a piece of her mind, a tall, handsome, dark-haired man brushed through the onlookers and spoke softly in French to the girl behind the pile of coats. The attendant laughed, glanced over to the two teenagers and laughed again. The tall man said something else and the girl nodded, replied, then pointed at the designer coat that the child-woman was holding.

'It's in your pocket,' said the man.

The girl searched it, found her bag, huffed and turned away.

'I think an apology is in order, don't you?'

The girls looked horrified. How dare anyone speak to them like that? Unsure what to do, they turned their backs on him.

'And a simple thank you to me will do, considering I saved you from making more of a spectacle of yourself than you were already.'

'She lost my purse,' said the girl, pointing at the coat attendant.

'No, you misplaced your purse. Now you owe everyone an apology.'

'Do you know who I am?'

'A spoilt precocious child, which is only marginally less attractive than the spoilt precocious adult you are soon to become. I'm afraid you've just embarrassed yourself in front of people who have long memories. Apologise, then go away.'

Now the girls looked terrified, but still would not relent. 'I'm going to tell my mother about you.'

The man laughed. 'She'll be hearing from me before I hear from her.'

Too cryptic for the children; they departed. But Jessie knew what he meant. She knew who he was. Joshua Cadell, the hack who'd done a hatchet job on Maggie. She needed to find her flatmate immediately.

Maggie was with a group of people, enthusing wildly, all hands and hair. Jessie waved frantically. Maggie waved back happily and beckoned her over. Maggie had no idea that Joshua Cadell was fast descending on the group of people she was with. Jessie half walked, half ran across the room, grabbed Maggie and swung her around in midsentence.

'Two o'clock. The enemy approaches,' said Jessie in a hoarse whisper.

'Enemy?' enquired a robust voice next to her.

'Jessie? I'm so glad you came. Let me introduce you to Dame Henrietta Cadell,' said Maggie, pinching Jessie's arm hard. Jessie stared at the heavily made-up face of the historical novelist. Boom. Where were the bomb disposal squad when you needed them?

'Darling, I must know, who is the enemy?' gushed Henrietta Cadell.

'Jessie's ex,' said Maggie swiftly, looking at Joshua then Jessie. 'It's okay, I think I saw him go to the bar.' She winked at Jessie. Jessie did not wink back.

'I'm so sorry. Love is a violent pastime, is it not?' Henrietta turned back to Maggie. 'Go on, dear, you were telling me about your next big job. You'll be focusing on the Loire Valley, you say. Marvellous. Do you have a good producer? It is imperative. You seem to be a class act, you need a good team behind you.'

Maggie beamed. Jessie took a step back.

'Ouch. Big boots, thin leather brogues. You win.'

Jessie turned and looked up into the boyish face of Joshua Cadell. He had looked so angular and pale on the television, yet up close his dark blue eyes weren't remotely threatening and his hair that had looked so sinister now fell in curls over his eyes. He seemed to be smiling at her. But she wasn't going to let that put her off.

'I'm sorry I wasn't wearing stilettos.'

She watched Joshua do a double-take, then nod. 'It was you by the coat check. I saw you watching. I'm sorry, you obviously don't approve of my parenting skills.'

'Oh no, they deserved it.'

He was confused by her hostility.

'Have we met before . . . ?'

'No,' said Jessie.

He frowned again. 'I'm Josh.' He held out a hand.

'Joshua, darling, come and meet my darling new friend. Maggie . . .' Henrietta turned back to Maggie.

Jessie smiled in anticipation of the banshee. But the banshee didn't appear. Instead, Maggie stuck out her hand, her breasts and her lips, and pulled Joshua towards her. '. . . Hall,' she said sweetly. 'Maggie Hall. I don't think we've met.'

Jessie's mouth dropped open. Joshua was shaking Maggie's hand but he was looking at her.

'Do you two know each other?'

'Oh yes,' said Henrietta. 'This young lady's ex is here somewhere. We're shielding her. Broken hearts are more painful than the rack, my dear. Joshua wouldn't know, of course, lucky for him.'

'Actually –' Jessie began to protest.

'Jessie's over it,' said Maggie.

Jessie was too angry with Maggie to speak.

'Why don't we go and get a drink?' said Maggie.

'It was lovely to meet you. I really am loving your book.'

Joshua looked at Jessie. 'I'm going to the bar. What would you like?'

Jessie remained stubbornly mute. This was Maggie's fault, she could deal with it.

'No, we'll get you something. What do you want?' asked Maggie, still pouting.

'I'll come with you,' said Joshua.

'No sweetie, stay with me. My publisher has just arrived and you know how she adores you.' Henrietta took Joshua's hand and pulled him towards her. 'And there are some more important people for you to meet. Another adoring fan sent over a bottle of champagne, so you may as well drink that.'

Maggie dragged Jessie to the ladies loo. Jessie turned on her flatmate. 'You lying little toad! You're not reading her book. And as for being so nice to –'

'Shut up, Jessie. Until we're alone.'

Maggie waited for two girls to leave the room before speaking. Jessie was seething with indignation. She didn't mind Maggie using her as a date at difficult parties until a suitable and more masculine other came along to relieve her of her duties as prop. But this, this was too much. The door closed.

'I can't believe you –'

'Look, Jessie, I don't like them but, trust me,

these people are better if they're on your side.'

'Sure, but you wouldn't catch me prostrating myself at Mark Ward's feet and letting him walk all over me. Where is the self-respect in that? She's patronising you and you take it, then she tells you that you aren't important enough for her treasured son and you take that too, and that's forgetting the whole shitty article he wrote. It's embarrassing.' Jessie realised she had gone too far when Maggie began to slide down the wall and sit on the floor. 'Get up, Maggie.' She didn't move. 'I'm sorry. That was unnecessary.' She grabbed Maggie's hands and pulled her up. 'I was shocked.'

'I've got to play the game, Jessie. You know that.'

'I know.'

'She is very well connected. I've got to make them like me.'

Jessie wanted to tell her that it wasn't worth it, the loss of face was too high a price, but she didn't. She relented. 'Joshua looks quite sexy in real life.'

'You don't fancy him, do you?'

'Me? After what he did to you? That would be breaking the code of sisterhood. I'll hate him until my dying day,' said Jessie.

'I wish I had that luxury.'

'Come on, Cilla, don't think about it. Let's go and get that drink. Seeing as it's free.'

Maggie nodded. 'I've got to pee. I'll catch you up in a minute. And, Jess – be nice to him, I know that tongue of yours can draw blood, but keep it curled up tonight, please?' Jessie frowned. 'For me?'

'If you say so.'

By the cigarette machine, Jessie passed a man who was leaning heavily against a girl. At first she thought they were kissing, but the girl was in fact trying to push the man away.

'Don't make a scene,' said the man, just loud enough for Jessie to hear. She couldn't help herself, she walked up to him and tapped him on the shoulder. Jessie could now see that the girl was younger than the man, much younger and very frightened.

'Everything all right here?' she asked, looking at the girl.

'Oh, Christ,' moaned the man. 'What do you want?'

'I think you've had a bit too much to drink, sir.'

'Too much? You obviously don't know who I am.'

'No. And I don't want to. Now, perhaps you should call it a night.'

He laughed. 'Very good, you almost sound official.'

'Actually,' said Jessie, holding open her wallet, 'I am. So perhaps you wouldn't mind removing your hand from the lady's shoulder and taking yourself off home before I have to make you, whoever you are.'

He stepped away from the girl, who quickly scampered into the safety of the ladies. The man sneered at Jessie then straightened out his pinstripe suit and walked over-cautiously back out into the party. No sooner had Jessie replaced her wallet than Maggie came out of the loo, wiping her hand in front of her nose. 'You don't have to wait for me. I'm a big girl now, you know.'

'I was just –'

Maggie grabbed her hand. 'Come on, let's show those Cadells how truly fabulous I am!'

Conjuring up an image of a long stretch of river, bulrushes, blue sky, Jessie followed Maggie back out into the fray. She watched Maggie return to the Cadell group and slip in with ease. She thought about following, but couldn't bring herself to. She simply wasn't interested in listening to an overweight historian holding court to a gathering of sycophants. If she snuck off now, Maggie wouldn't even notice. She glanced back and saw Maggie accept a glass of champagne. Maggie was in her element, at the centre of things, letting a little stardust rub off on her. No wonder she looked so attentive, so alert.

Jessie had almost made it to the exit when a hand landed on her shoulder. It was Joshua.

'You're leaving already?'

'Early start,' said Jessie, stepping back.

'Shame to go so soon.'

Jessie looked over to Henrietta. 'Not a great deal to keep me here.'

Joshua laughed. 'Most people can't get enough of my mother.'

'I was always better at geography,' said Jessie.

'Me too. Of course I was made to do history anyway.'

'What did you get?'

He smiled ruefully. 'Don't ask, it's a big family secret.'

They looked at each other for a moment until Jessie got embarrassed. 'Good night, Joshua.'

'Can I walk you to a taxi rank?' She held up her helmet. 'Your bike, then?'

'Will you be able to get back in? They're like the Gestapo on the door.'

'No problem. I'm Henrietta Cadell's son. Practically royalty.'

'Even here?'

'She wrote the film.'

'Oh! Sorry, I didn't realise.'

'You didn't see it?'

Jessie shook her head, embarrassed.

'Don't worry, most people just come to the party, say something about the costumes and try and get their photograph taken with Mother.'

'And what about you? What do you do?'

'I bask in her reflected glory, accept the perks and get laid frequently by women who would like the Dame as a mother-in-law.' He smiled. 'It could be worse.'

'Could it?'

'Much. I might have wanted to be a historian myself. The world does not look kindly on the off-spring of celebrities who go in search of their own merit. That is a true curse.'

'But you write. Don't you?'

They arrived at the parking bay. 'Let me explain something about that piece.'

'What piece?'

'The thing I wrote about Maggie. The reason why you're so hostile.'

'Don't take it personally. I'm often hostile.'

'I don't believe that. You think I stitched up your friend. It's the pressure I get from the editor. They want the dirt – dirt sells.'

Jessie looked at him. 'It was a bit brutal.'

'It's what the editors want. Stitch them up or get another job. I could just go home and spend my allowance, but I don't want to. Everyone is under the same pressure; people like to read abuse, it doesn't mean I think it.'

'Good to know British journalism is in such good hands.'

'It's what people want to read.'

'So you keep saying.'

'Your friend doesn't seem to mind. She knows the game, she didn't take it personally.'

Not in front of you, no. But behind closed doors, with a bottle of wine and a destructive helping of self-doubt . . . 'You know, it's late, I'm tired . . . Thanks for escorting me to the bike but –'

'You've got to go home,' said Joshua, bowing his head slightly.

'Yes. Goodnight.' She pulled her helmet over her head, pushed the bike out of its slot and started the engine.

'Don't you ever compromise yourself in your job?' asked Joshua.

Jessie tapped the side of the helmet. 'Can't hear, sorry.'

'Never mind,' shouted Joshua. Good, thought Jessie. She hated telling people what she did. They either shunned her or launched into a tale about their trouble with the neighbours.

~

The earth blew warm air out into the dawn's cold face. Deer snorted, shifted and regrouped. Trees appeared to float in the distance as the sun eked over the horizon. The runner increased his pace, parting the whispering mist, disturbing the peace. He inhaled deeply, the cold air stinging his nostrils. Birds evacuated the trees above him. They squawked. He spat. Up ahead, his dog barked, but his pace did not falter. The dog often barked. Usually at the deer.

He turned right and ran between the four giant oaks that marked the beginning of the end of that day's endurance test. His pace quickened. Like a well-ridden horse, he was spurred on by the thought of home and a hot shower. He was looking forward to it. Not down. Suddenly the ground was higher than it was supposed to be. His unsuspecting ankle turned, he heard the tell-tale crunch of bone and lurched forward. He lay in the damp mulch and breathed in the smell of decay, waiting for his ankle to protest, but all he felt was a dull throb. It didn't feel like a break. The dog was barking louder now. The runner turned to see what had made him fall. The grey-white flesh of a naked corpse glowed at him from under the damp, auburn leaves. He began to scream.

~

Jessie was outside P. J. Dean's house, clutching a double espresso, when she heard the call. Royal Parks Constabulary had found a stiff in Richmond Park. Some poor jogger had put his foot right through the sternum of a corpse. A possible identification had been made, but the Parks police didn't want to commit yet. Jessie knew why. Foxes. Lean time of year. Easy pickings made identification difficult.

She tapped in the security code to open the gate. P.J. had sent all the auxiliary staff home, but the house was teeming with people. Her people. They were going over every inch of the house, the garden and the pool. She watched the green gate slide back, half thinking about Verity Shore and half listening to the crackle of the police radio.

'. . . spread-eagled in the mud between four large oaks in the Isabella Plantation. Royal Parks Constabulary asking for back-up on this.'

Isabella Plantation. Mud. Spread-eagled. Jessie picked up the radio.

'DI Driver and PC Ahmet on location,' she

barked, waving for Niaz to get in and throwing the car into reverse. 'ETA seven minutes.'

~

Jessie and Niaz followed the sergeant through the crisp, cold grass, away from the body. She took a quick look at the corpse. Bile rose and fell. She stepped away. Glad of her empty stomach. Patches of hoarfrost clung to the areas of ground not yet warmed by the rising sun. Elsewhere, dewdrops hung from every available surface. It would have been a beautiful morning. She almost envied the jogger. The SOCOs had done a fine job; the area was taped off, a PC stood at the entrance, a man was taking photos of each tree trunk. One of the guys in white suits walked up to her. He was smiling. It was Ed.

'Another boring day in the office?' said Jessie.

'When we heard you were on your way, we thought we'd better make it look good.'

So, thought Jessie, I'm still in favour.

'Great outfit,' said Ed.

Jessie looked from her leather trousers to his all-in-one plastic suit with matching hood.

'I'm sorry I can't return the compliment.'

He shrugged. 'I'm sorry I haven't seen you stark bollock naked in the showers, but we can't have everything.'

'Well then, I have the advantage, and you have a head to bag.'

He looked down.

'Not that head,' she said, and pointed to the body. He squinted at her. The sun, low in the sky, picked out the yellow flecks in his eyes.

'More's the pity.'

'Jessie?'

She turned. Sally Grimes was making her way through the trees, bag in hand, head in hat and feet in sensible shoes.

'Sally, thanks for coming.' They shook hands warmly.

'Is it true? Is it Eve Wirrel?' asked the pathologist.

News travels fast. Gossip even faster. 'That is unconfirmed speculation. But she's wearing a necklace with the name Eve on it, so . . .'

'I'll have a look. You coming?'

Not yet. Jessie wasn't quite ready to go back. 'I just want to look at these trees. Go with Ed, he's about to bag the head, hands and feet.'

'But not the woman,' Ed said, looking at Jessie.

'No,' said Sally, unaware. 'Give me a few moments first, then we'll bag her up.'

Jessie walked over to the photographer. SOCOs were known for their warped sense of normality. Obviously spent too much time with stiffs. She smiled. Dear God, it was catching. She introduced herself to the photographer. The man showed her the markings on the trunk: D.E.C.

'But it's October. Perhaps it's a boy's name . . .'

Jessie was thinking out loud.

'There's more.' The photographer indicated for her to follow him to the next tree.

'"o.m.p." What does that mean?'

'Wait.'

They continued their walk along the periphery of the site. Jessie kept one eye on Sally Grimes. The pathologist had put a mask over her mouth. She was kneeling over the body, taking temperatures.

'Look at that –' said the photographer. Three more letters, same height, this time in capitals: O.S.I. Jessie closed her eyes.

'Follow me,' said the photographer.

'It's okay,' said Jessie. 'I've got the point.'

'No, you have to look.'

'Tio – t.i.o.'

The photographer stopped. 'How did you know?' Jessie didn't say anything. 'It's brilliant, isn't it? I mean, she was always over the top, but this really is something else. I mean, fuck, to be here – good thing I brought so much film.'

'How can you be so sure it's Eve Wirrel?'

'We were at art school together.'

'You recognised her?' *That*.

'The jewellery and the hair gave it away.'

'And you don't mind?'

'Mind! Eve's last piece. Titled even.' He was smiling. 'It's a gift.'

'Look, I don't think you should –'

'Don't put a bag on her head!' The photographer screamed into Jessie's eardrum.

Ed and Sally looked up. Everyone else stopped what they were doing.

'He has to,' said Jessie, waiting for the ringing in her ear to stop.

'Jesus,' said the photographer, marching back to the entrance of the cordoned area. 'This is art, that's the whole point. Once they've cleared the leaves, we need to photograph her, as she intended.'

'You need to, you mean,' said Jessie.

'I am a photographer.'

Jessie nodded slowly. 'I think you had better leave.'

'What! I've been taking photos all morning.'

'Yes, and I'd like all the film now.'

'Don't be ridiculous. I always develop all police work myself.'

'Not this time. I'm sorry. This is not a career opportunity. You are employed by the police to take photos of crime scenes. Those films are our property.'

'I don't fucking believe this.'

'Well, you'd better. Fry, make sure he hands over all the film. And the Polaroid camera in his left pocket. I'd like the Polaroids of the trees, please.' She held out her hand. 'The ones in your breast pocket.'

'Bitch.'

'Yeah, yeah, whatever.'

He handed them to Jessie.

'Unbelievable,' said Jessie as she watched Fry lead the man away. 'Get those bags on.' She turned

136

to Niaz. 'Find Mr and Mrs Wirrel – use Interpol if you have to, but find them. Get hold of her agent or gallery or whatever and find out where she lived, where she worked. I want a media blackout on this until we find them. No one speaks to the press.'

'Jessie,' called Sally, taking a step back from the body. 'I think you should come and have a look at this.'

Jessie approached. The smell got stronger as she drew nearer. Sally was holding a pair of medical tweezers, hanging from which was a pair of knickers. Soiled knickers.

'Where did you find those?'

'Her mouth,' said Sally. What the foxes had left of it. 'And the femoral artery has been cut. One long incision.'

'And nature isn't that neat,' said Jessie.

Sally shook her head. 'Not in my experience.' She waited for Ed to finish bagging the feet then rolled the corpse to one side. Excrement poured out from the body's defunct bowel. Jessie tried not to gag. There was an area of ground stained with blood. Eve Wirrel had bled to death in the middle of the Isabella Plantation. Where the deer were. Jessie looked up. She couldn't see the house clearly, but with good binoculars . . .

The rising sun was spreading warmth through the earth but the cloud cover was not burning off. The upward drift of air was minimal. The high-pressure cell seemed to intensify the closer you were to the body, the sky above did not want this methane-laden, ammonia-reeking air to join it. It was holding it here, low on the ground, to cling to the back of the throat, seep by osmosis into the skin, the subconscious. 'I don't think this is a suicide, Jessie,' said Sally. 'Died Blonde. Dead Art. The knickers are a cosmetic touch, just like the bleach.'

'Look at this.' Jessie fanned out the Polaroid photos in the correct order: D.E.C. o.m.p. O.S.I. t.i.o. 'Decomposition.'

'Where's the N?'

Jessie pointed to the corpse. 'Eve is the N. Nude. Nubile. Narcissistic. Nasty. Needless. Take your pick. It depends on whose point of view you are looking from.'

'You agree with the photographer? You think this is a composition? Even following on the heels of Verity Shore's murder?'

'There are no immediate signs of a struggle, she wasn't bound . . .'

'No sign of a camera either. If dying was a process undergone for art, wouldn't Eve Wirrel have filmed it?'

'Not necessarily. She wouldn't have known she'd end up looking like this. Perhaps she was relying on people like that photographer. Maybe that was the point.'

'Let me get her to the lab. I'll do the full blood-works – we should get the results in time for the postmortem. We'll soon know if she came here under duress. If she did, this may be victim number two.'

~

Jessie stood in the nondescript doorway with Niaz Ahmet by her side, carrying some items that P.J. had requested. A female constable stood behind her. Everyone was instructed not to mention Eve Wirrel. When P.J. opened the door, he was wearing old 501s and a black V-neck T-shirt; the stubble he'd had when she met him on the bridge was fast becoming a beard. Jessie saw the WPC's eyes widen as they hurried inside. The boys snaked around P.J.'s legs, looking wary and getting trodden on as everyone sorted themselves out, until P.J. stroked the elder boy's hair and said, 'Take your brother to the kitchen and ask Bernie to make these nice people some tea. Paul likes baking. Just wait till you see what he's made for tea.' Paul smiled, took his younger half-brother by the hand and left.

'Paul cooks when he's upset. Bernie can't get him out of the kitchen at the moment,' said P.J. quietly as he showed them through to a small sitting room. A significant step down.

'Why do you call him Paul?' asked Jessie. She'd been reading up on Verity's very public life, sifting through countless magazines, photo shoots, shopping sprees, drying-out sprees, endless gossip about Verity's lovers, rumours about lovers, photos of alleged lovers, more shopping sprees and finally the biggest headline grabber of all, her death. An explosion of tabloid activity. Verity Shore had never been so famous.

'Yeah, well, Apollo is a nonce's name. Poor lad was getting grief at school. He chose it. I was flattered. It's my first name. Not very rock'n'roll, mind.'

'What about Paul Young . . . ?'

'Ouch. I'm going to try and forget you said that.'

Jessie smiled. She tried not to. 'How are they?'

'Fine. Considering. I got the lawyers on to Danny Knight. Bastard. He must have called the *Daily Mail* before you'd even left the house.'

'I thought he looked a bit shifty.'

'Yeah, well, that's me to a T, always the last one to know. Anyway, the boys are being amazing, but that's probably because it hasn't sunk in. All this running about is exciting for them. Couldn't do without Bernie. Listen, thanks for meeting me last night, I'm sure it was beyond the call of duty. And thanks for, you know, telling me what had happened to her.'

'I usually spare families that sort of detail.'

'We're not a normal family though, are we?'

There was no denying that. On average, a piece about them appeared in the press every other day. Usually centred around Verity. Though, it had to be said, in his heyday, P.J. had given the tabloid press a run for their money. The hotel rooms. The endless models. The coke. The no-speaks with his father.

The death of his mother and his non-attendance at the funeral. The typical rock'n'roll stuff. Then Verity and the boys arrive on the scene and he becomes the model parent of someone else's children. The question Jessie wanted to ask was, could it all be too good to be true?

Niaz sat unobtrusively in the corner, a pencil poised over his pad. Jessie hoped P.J. would forget he was there. The WPC was standing outside the door.

'I've written everything out, like you asked. All the machinery in the studio is clocked and timed – makes billing the record companies easier. The names and phone numbers of the people who came and went are there, and you can cross-check that with the house security system,' said P.J., proffering a list.

Jessie took it. 'Do you alarm the house at night?'

'Yes.'

'We'll need those records.'

'I'll get Bernie on it.'

'It should be you.'

His expression changed abruptly. 'What do you mean by that? Bernie is a named keyholder.'

'You trust Bernie then?'

'Implicitly.'

'Why? When you don't trust anybody else?'

'I've told you. Because she is trustworthy.' He said it in a voice that implied he wished to change the subject.

'What makes you so sure?'

He folded his arms in front of his chest. 'Is this about Verity or Bernie? Because when I last checked, Bernie was in the kitchen and Verity was in the morgue.'

Jessie knew when to pull back, but she wondered what Verity Shore had felt about the trust her husband so clearly put in his young, attractive housekeeper.

'Let's talk about Verity then.'

He sat down without complaint. 'Good.'

'Why did you keep her under lock and key?'

'What?' He reacted calmly, given the question. Too calmly. More calmly than he had when she'd asked him about Bernie.

'You locked Verity in her own room at night. Why?'

'I . . . She locked her door, quite a lot.'

'You sure about that? The key is on the outside.'

'The doctors told us to do it.' At least he wasn't going to persist in denying it. That would have undone all the progress they'd been making. Police work was all about trust. It was often the most personal details, the ones people were loath to tell, that led to the conviction of the right person.

'Us?'

'Sorry, me.'

'Why?'

P.J. pushed his palms against his thighs, stretched, then, seemingly exhausted by his actions, collapsed back into the sofa. 'It was to protect her. She was erratic after her binges.'

'But she always came home?'

'Yes.'

'Or did you have to go and find her and bring her back?'

'Sometimes. Jesus, I didn't know what else to do.'

'P.J., you told me she put herself through a mini cold-turkey every time she came home, implying some sort of control over her drug-taking. Is that really what happened?' Jessie looked at him. This time she didn't shy away from those big, famous green eyes. They didn't seem so big and famous any more. He was just another man with a bad marriage and unusual domestic arrangements.

'We thought we were helping her.'

'We, P.J.? Always "we". One husband, two wardens.'

'It wasn't like that.'

'Then tell me what it was like.'

'Okay, shit, so Bernie helped me with her, so what? I couldn't do it on my own.'

'Do what?'

'Stop her from killing herself.'

'But you said she wasn't the suicidal type. And, according to you, she had her drugs under control.'

'She wouldn't have done it on purpose.'

'I'm sorry to tell you this, P.J., but you locked her in with her drugs. We found a quantity of heroin and cocaine in a shoe box, she kept vodka in her shampoo bottles, and instead of taking the Antibuse and Zyban you gave her to wean her off her addictions, she hid the partially sucked pills behind a loose tile in the bathroom. She was on something all the time. The problems with your wife only started when she ran out. That was when the shopping sprees happened. You said hundred of bags came home, thousands of pounds' worth of clothes. Well, I don't suppose you searched the contents of those bags: the clothes, the pockets, the toiletry bottles, the shoe boxes?'

'You worked all this out from one visit to my house?'

'Two. That's my job. Now, you have taken enough drugs in your life to recognise when someone is in an altered state. I have, and I'm not a rock star. So, explain to me, how come you didn't recognise it in your own wife?'

P.J. remained quiet.

Jessie could feel the heat. She was warm. Close. 'You knew about the drugs, didn't you?'

'I suspected.'

'Do you know where she got them from?'

'No.'

'How she got them?'

'No.'

'And you still trust Bernie?'

'You can't possibly think Bernie was getting drugs for Verity.'

'I'm asking you.'

'Bernie didn't know about it. I knew but kept

144

quiet. It made life easier. Verity spent a bit of time with the boys, the boys liked it and I kept an eye out. Jesus, alcoholics do it all the time – hold down a job, families. I thought it was okay.'

'Until she keeled over and died.'

P.J. walked across to the fireplace. 'I meant to get her back into rehab, but, Jesus, I couldn't keep telling the same old exhaustion story. The woman didn't bloody work, what the fuck was she exhausted from, shopping? Most of the rehab places wouldn't have her back because of the disruption she caused. Sleeping with the suicidal, arranging drug drops and escape plans. She could be very persuasive, that one. You don't become a something from nothing without one unique selling point.'

'What was Verity's?'

'She wanted it so much she could get even the hardened cynics to believe she deserved it. People in the limelight don't just find themselves in the right place at the right time. They put themselves there. Time and time again. At the expense of everything – family weddings, friends, funerals, Christmases. All with one goal in mind: fame. At any cost.'

'Is that what you did?'

'I was in a successful band. It went with the territory.'

'What about the drugs?'

'That too goes with the territory, and anyone who tells you otherwise is lying.' P.J. paced the room.

'And the pig's blood, the death threats – they too go with the territory?'

'Absolutely.'

'Can you remember what they said?'

'They were long tortured letters written by some loon telling Verity to leave me alone or she would die.'

'So they were sent to her. Not you.'

P.J. pulled back the netted curtain for a second then let it fall. 'God, this place is claustrophobic.'

'What did Verity think of these letters?'

'She didn't know about them.'

'But they were sent to her, weren't they?'

He picked up a china dog from the mantelpiece, looked underneath it, then replaced it. 'Like I said, everything that came in the house was checked.'

'Even her post?'

'Especially her post.'

'For drugs?'

'What else, if not drugs?'

Jessie let the question hang in the air. 'Are you sure you weren't checking up on your wife? I've seen the press-cuttings, P.J. All those alleged lovers, are you sure they were nothing more than rumours?'

'Yes. All manufactured by Verity. She didn't have lovers. Trust me, she wasn't a sexual person. Sex was just another way of getting attention and causing havoc.'

She'd have to take his word for it, for now.

'Look, what if Verity simply took too much

146

coke and had a heart attack? It happens more often than you think. The people she was with might have panicked and tried to disguise the body. That's the only rational explanation I can think of,' said P.J.

Jessie had thought about that. Trouble was, they had done a test on the silicone. Sulphuric acid would have eaten through the implant as fast as it would have the liver, heart and lungs. Each silicone implant had been purposely removed, kept to one side, then replaced in the ribcage where they were supposed to be found. Somewhere, someone had created an awful lot of mess. Jessie thought about the smell of bleach in Verity's bathroom, the locked door, the secret exit over the garage, the drained pool. That kind of mess would have taken a great deal of expert tidying.

She stood up. 'Perhaps now would be a good time to talk to Bernie.'

P.J. walked over to her. He was only inches away now. Jessie could see the individual hairs of the long stubble on his face, the line of slightly chapped skin on his lip where he'd been chewing it, eyelashes the thickness of Diana Dors', eyes the colour of sea-smoothed glass. Is he magnetic because of who he is, she thought, or is he who he is because he is magnetic?

'You think I was a terrible husband, don't you? I can see it in your face.'

'This isn't about what I think,' said Jessie, staring back.

'Get to know me, I'm not the person you think I am,' he said softly.

Jessie wondered if this was the technique he used to get women into bed: *I'm not the star you think I am, I'm an ordinary man . . .* Well, she wasn't for bedding.

'I have no opinion of you, Mr Dean. As I said to you last night, all I'm trying to do is establish what happened to your wife.'

P.J. stepped away from her. He didn't like that, Jessie could see it in his body language. 'I did what I thought was best,' he said.

'If you knew she was on drugs and you knew she wasn't bringing them in, who did you think was? Assuming that it wasn't you.'

His eyes narrowed. He opened his mouth to say something but changed his mind. He turned away from her. Seduction over.

'One more thing, do you know Eve Wirrel?'

'The artist?'

'Yes. Do you know her, personally?'

'No. I'll get Bernie for you,' he said, and strode out.

Jessie was beginning to lose patience with P.J. and his little housewife. Locking Verity Shore in her room, opening her post, watching her every move. No one could cope with that level of scrutiny. Jessie's sympathy for Verity Shore was taking an unexpected turn.

Bernie came in a few minutes later. Jessie knew

immediately that something was up. Bernie reminded her of Clare Mills. Too tightly wound for one slight woman. She sat down on the edge of the sofa. Her dirty blonde hair was washed and fluffy, she wore tracksuit bottoms and a thick knitted polo-neck. Not your model mistress, thought Jessie, but she couldn't think of another explanation for P.J.'s loyalty to the woman and Bernie's complicity in holding Verity prisoner in her own home.

'Must be fun working for P. J. Dean. Like living in the pages of *Hello!*'

'I don't read *Hello!*,' she said bluntly.

'How long have you worked for P.J.?'

'Twelve years.'

'Before he married Verity?'

'Yes.'

She reminded Jessie of Clare again. Guarded. Monosyllabic. 'Did you like her, your boss?'

Bernie eye's locked on Jessie for a brief moment, then slid sideways to their resting place over Jessie's shoulder. 'I tried to. But I failed.'

'But you like P.J.?'

She grew with the long inhalation, then shrank again. 'Yes.'

'How did you get the job?' asked Jessie.

'He offered it to me.'

'Where were you on Friday?'

Her back stiffened. 'I did the weekend shop in the morning at Waitrose on the High Street, collected some cleaning, then came home and made some lunch for P.J. and three or four others in the studio. Picked up the boys; P.J. came and did homework with Paul, then they all watched *Aladdin* while I made supper. We usually eat early in the kitchen with the boys.'

'Sounds like domestic bliss.'

Bernie said nothing.

'Does Craig eat with you too?'

'Yes.'

'On Friday?'

She looked to the door. The way out. Exit. Escape. It was a subconscious gesture. A tell. And Jessie had seen it.

'No.'

'No? Where was he?'

'After-school club. He's training to be a mechanic, spends his life in the garage.' The fondness for her son was evident. 'He's usually back by ten.'

'Usually?'

'He had a puncture.'

'Is that so?'

The weekend had continued in much the same vein. Bernie looking after P.J. and the boys, Craig largely absent, and Verity wholly absent. Bernie got up to leave.

'Does Craig see his father?'

She stared at the door again. Took a deep breath. 'No.'

'One more thing, Bernie. Why did you lock Verity in her room?'

Bernie stood stock-still. There was that minefield again. One wrong step. Boom! It's all over.

'Acting on the boss's orders, were you?'

'It wasn't like that.'

'Really?' said Jessie. 'What was it like?'

'She was sick, we tried to take care of her.'

'So you both keep saying. Okay, that will be all. For the moment.'

The door closed behind her. She didn't hear footsteps for a while, but when she did they were firm and purposeful. From the noise erupting in the kitchen, the boys were glad to have her back. All three of them.

'She is lying,' said Niaz firmly, surprising Jessie. He'd been taking notes so quietly even she had forgotten he was there.

'I don't know about lying, but she is nervous about something. What about P.J.?' she asked.

'Simple. He wants you to like him,' said Niaz.

'I think Mr Dean wants everyone to like him,' said Jessie, slightly unnerved by Niaz's comment.

'That is what I expected you to say, ma'am.' He smiled in that enigmatic way that made him look as though he held all the secrets of the world under his thick head of hair. The door swung open, and Jessie turned away from Niaz. An anxious-looking P.J. carried in a tray, followed by an equally anxious-looking Paul. Jam tarts. How very surreal, she thought, looking at P.J. He smiled at her. Back on the charm offensive.

'I hope you like them,' said Paul.

'They look fantastic,' she said, examining the

151

plate, then Paul. He was a beautiful child, all private thought and earnest word.

'Paul is a monster cook. You should taste his cheese on toast. We'll have to get you round for a Paul special.' P.J. had a habit of making her want to forget her reason for being there, sink into the sofa with tea and tarts and play Trivial Pursuit with the family. She had to bring back the image of those bleached bones lying on a stainless steel tray and remember that only a week ago this boy's mother had been living and breathing. She may not have been happy, but she was alive.

These poor fucking kids, thought Jessie. The seven-year-old watched solemnly as she picked up the sticky concoction. She couldn't, wouldn't play this game.

'I'd like to talk to Craig now,' she said, still holding the jam tart.

P.J. pulled back again. 'Right. I'll go and get him,' said P.J. Paul looked torn, Jessie felt terrible. None of this was his fault. She bit enthusiastically into the tart and chewed.

'Wow,' she said, 'these are really good.'

'Bernie helped,' said Paul. 'But I did the rolling-pin bit.' He smiled, looked up at P.J., took his hand and followed him out. It left her feeling slightly odd. Such mixed feelings made for poor detection.

'Little Paul has the bone structure of his mother. Strong genes,' said Niaz.

'Stronger hopefully,' said Jessie. 'Niaz, could

you leave us, please. I'd like to do this next interview alone.'

Craig was thin like his mother, but tall, almost as tall as P.J. He had sandy blond hair that lay flat against his forehead, covering the remnants of poor pubescent skin. His large, pale brown eyes darted between her and the floor. He'd been crying. His thick, dark eyelashes stuck together in mini triangles. His upper eyelids were swollen and pink. She could see salty tear-tracks on his cheeks. He was the first person she'd seen who was mourning the death of Verity Shore. Perhaps anywhere.

'Craig, I need to ask you some questions, so we can find out what happened to Verity. These things are never easy. Take as much time as you like, don't worry about being brave. Not everyone can be brave all the time.'

He nodded his understanding.

'You ready?'

He nodded again.

'When did you last see Verity?'

'Thursday.'

'Where?'

'She was getting ready to go out.'

'You were in her room?'

'Mum was with the boys. Ty – he's the youngest – had fallen over.'

'Did you often help with Verity?'

'She wasn't like normal people, she needed a lot of looking after.'

'What was wrong with her, Craig?'

Craig thought about this for a while. 'She was . . . sad.'

Jessie noticed the tears rise in his eyes.

'She had the boys, though,' said Jessie.

'Mum was always with them. All because of one silly accident.'

'What accident, Craig?'

'It wasn't her fault.'

'Your mum's?'

'Nooo,' he wailed, frustrated. 'It wasn't Verity's fault. She didn't realise they were play-ing in the shed, that's all. She didn't realise. After that, they wouldn't let the boys near her unless someone was there. It made her sad. That's all I'm saying.'

'She had you.'

He couldn't reply. Or didn't want to.

'Are you going to miss her?'

A thick tear dropped over his lower lid. He didn't wipe it away.

'No. Yes. I don't know.'

'Do you know where she might have gone?'

His chin dimpled. He shook his head. 'No.' The tears kept coming, he still didn't wipe them away.

'Did she love you?'

'Some . . .' His breathing became more ragged. 'Sometimes.'

'When you climbed into her room?'

His head jolted like a charge of electricity had been shot through him. He looked terrified.

'It's okay, Craig. I'm not going to tell anyone. This is between you and me.'

He bit down on his lip and nodded.

'And what about the pool house? Did you meet there, too?'

He was visibly trembling.

'It's okay, Craig, no one else knows. And as long as you want it that way, it will stay that way. But I think you should tell them how you feel. This is too much for you to carry alone.'

He stared at Jessie blankly.

'When didn't Verity love you?'

He sniffed loudly. 'When she wasn't herself.'

Jessie lowered her voice to a whisper. 'When P.J. and Bernie gave her pills, is that when?'

He looked at her again, wide-eyed.

'I know about the pills, Craig. We found the hiding place. Do you know what they were?'

'Sleeping pills, to make her ill and drowsy and sick.'

'Is that what Verity told you?'

The boy nodded. 'If they'd just left her alone, she'd have been fine.'

Jessie shook her head. 'No, Craig, she was ill. The pills your mother and P.J. gave her were to wean her off her addictions. That's why she was sick, because she was still drinking.'

Craig nodded. A trickle of comprehension making its way through the guilt, pity and sorrow.

'Then she found a way of not taking them, didn't she?'

Craig nodded again.

'Why did she hide them? Why didn't she flush them down the loo or throw them away?'

His eyes darted towards the door.

'They checked?' she said quietly.

He nodded.

'Even the loo?'

'They listened,' he whispered. 'She had to get away from them. That's why she disappeared. I didn't want her to, I worried about her when she left the house. I tried to stop her, but she said it was like living in a prison. She needed help.'

'You helped her, didn't you?'

'Yeessss,' he sobbed.

'It's okay, Craig. You were just helping your friend.'

'I had toooo.' He continued rocking. 'No one else wooould. I had to, she neeeeeeded me.'

'You brought things to her room at night, didn't you?'

'Yeeeessss.'

'Vodka?'

'Yeeeessss.'

'Where did she go, Craig? When she left you on your own, where did she go?'

'Baaarrrrrrrrnes . . .' It was a long, low-pitched howl. 'It was horrible . . .'

Bernie opened the door. Craig didn't look up. Jessie signalled to the WPC to keep Bernie where she was.

'A house in Barnes?'

He nodded.

'What's the address, Craig?'

'P.J.!' shouted Bernie.

'I don't knooooow.' He wailed. Sobbing into his hands.

'Think.'

'I can't.'

'He says he doesn't know.' It was Bernie. Craig looked at her. 'He is a minor. You're upsetting him. P.J.!'

'Craig, this is important. Where is the house?'

P.J. tried to get past the WPC. 'What house? What fucking house?' P.J. heard a noise behind him, he turned. 'Upstairs, boys. Now.' He looked back at Craig, who was beginning to rock backwards and forwards, and then over to Jessie. 'What the hell is going on, Inspector?'

Jessie ignored him. She leant closer to Craig. 'Please tell me where the house is,' she said softly.

'He doesn't know,' shouted Bernie.

'What house? I want you all to leave. You're upsetting Craig.'

Jessie turned abruptly. 'No. *You've* been upsetting Craig. You kept Verity a prisoner in that house. Who did you think she was going to ask for help? Her sons? You didn't let her near her sons!' She took Craig's hand. 'It's all right, Craig, you have done *nothing* wrong. Just tell me where she went. It's important.'

'Leave. Now!' shouted P.J.

'He doesn't know anything,' said Bernie angrily.

Jessie walked towards Bernie and P.J. 'What, like you don't know anything? Because I tell you, I've had enough of your little charade.'

'Get off me,' Bernie screamed at the WPC.

'How dare you talk to Bernie like that!'

'Something has been going on behind that security gate of yours and I want to know what.'

'SHUT UP! ALL OF YOU! You don't care, none of you care. She's dead. Dead. Dead!'

Jessie went to him. 'I'm sorry, Craig. It's okay to be upset.'

He sobbed for a while, then turned to her. 'I don't know the address,' he said. She believed him. 'But I can show you.'

'No!' shouted Bernie. But it was too late to silence her son.

~

Ray felt the stage lights burn above him, and he basked in the heat. All eyes were on him. Hanging off his every word. Smiling at the swooping camera. The easily pleased eager to please. Ray turned back to Danny Knight, his pate was shining in the spotlight, his eyes were gleaming. The arsehole had been waiting for this moment all his life. At last he was in the limelight. However his fifteen minutes were up.

'You have described a living nightmare. Looking after Verity must have been hell,' said Ray. Danny

158

was nodding enthusiastically. 'I suppose we have to ask you why you stayed? If Verity Shore was as dreadful as you say, why put up with it?'

The audience shouted 'yeah' and 'you tell him'. No one liked a sneak, even if they loved the tales they were telling.

'The perks were good,' said Danny. 'And they paid a high price for . . .' he paused, the caked-on smile cracked.

'Your discretion?' asked Ray softly.

'Um.'

'Loyalty?'

Ray could feel the collective mood swing away from the bald man. They were his. And only his.

'It seems to me that while Verity Shore may have been a pitiful character, while she may not have stood up to any close inspection, while she may have been injecting and smoking anything she could lay her hands on, she was also being ruthlessly exploited herself – and not only by those in her employment. Do you think that is true?' Ray knelt down by the magazine editor. The one who had used Verity's image on three hundred and seventy-two separate occasions.

'No. She knew what she was doing.'

'She obviously didn't. Everyone has done stupid things when under the influence.'

'She wasn't inebriated during all those photo shoots. She didn't have to take her clothes off, no one made her. She chose to.'

'What do you think of her now, personally?'

159

'Sorry for her, I suppose. She was a mess, wasn't she?'

'But you used her as a role model for the readers, the very young readers, of your magazine. Aren't you, too, guilty of exploitation?'

'As I said, we were not aware of the drinking and drugs when we used her. She was a perfect role model: she'd had a dream of being rich and famous, and her dream came true. We had no reason not to believe what her press people were telling us.'

'Are you sure about that? I have statements from several freelance photographers claiming she was always half-cut on photo shoots, that everyone knew to supply miniature vodka bottles whenever Ms Shore was being photographed.'

The woman blustered. 'I'd never heard that.'

'You are in charge of the magazine *Gimme Girl*, aren't you?'

'Yes, but I can't be at all the shoots.'

'Sure, but I knew about it, and I wasn't there.'

The editor had the good sense to say nothing, there was nothing she could say. Ray looked at the camera. 'It seems that everyone has taken their slice of Verity Shore. You could almost, *almost*, feel sorry for her. Then again . . .' Images of the Caribbean photo shoots, the shopping sprees, the backless glittering designer dresses appeared on the screen. 'Maybe not.' The audience cheered. 'Well, I'm afraid that's all we have time for. Thanks to the audience, thank you to our guests – Danny

160

Knight; *Sun* gossip columnist Raffi; ex-wild child Amanda; James, paparazzi photographer; and, lastly, the editor of *Gimme Girl* magazine, Tiggy Bleeker. I'd like to leave you with images of the last photo shoot Verity Shore did for *OK*: "At home with Verity".' Each shot was such an obvious product placement that the audience started calling out the brand names as the images changed.

'Playstation!'

'Gucci!'

'Fisher-Price!'

The clapping rose in a crescendo.

From the control room Tarek watched the three sign men jab their placards at the audience. PLAYSTATION. GUCCI. FISHER-PRICE. They flipped the boards over, dramatically, in unison: APPLAUSE. APPLAUSE. APPLAUSE. The audience obeyed enthusiastically. They stopped chanting and started clapping. St Giles waved and smiled. The megalomaniac freak had signed his own death warrant with that little performance. Finally he'd been outdone by his own ambition. He'd be lucky if he got digital after this, no one was going to touch him with a bargepole. He would disappear to the sound of complaints. Tarek said a silent prayer of thanks, then glanced over his shoulder. Behind him, Alistair was standing silently with his back to the wall with a strange, sly smile on his face.

Ray came bounding into the office. 'Watch the

master at work, Tarekey boy, watch and learn.' He lit a fag and inhaled deeply, then removed the gold cross he habitually wore under his brightly coloured button-down and kissed it. 'We fucking did it! This is it, I can feel it. What did it look like from the edit suite?'

'Perfect,' said Alistair.

'Tarek?'

That amused Tarek. Ray always wanted his judgement on the show. Alistair's didn't seem to count for much.

'They'll never air it,' said Tarek. 'Never.'

Ray grinned at him. 'Course they won't – if they know. But we aren't going to tell them. Are we?'

'What are you going to show them then? What are you going to say you recorded?'

'Don't you worry your little turban about that. Oh, don't look at me that way. Think like a Portakabin, you'll stay in a Portakabin. I'm coming up in the world. You want to stick with me son, or I might not take you with me to the big fat world of Four. Right, where's that make-up girl? By the way, Tarek, everyone else is on for this. Everyone. Aren't they, Alistair?' Alistair nodded. 'All paid-up members. Anyone blabs, and I'll know it was you, Tarek. Now, I like you, we've come quite far together and I wouldn't want any harm to come to you. So keep your head down, and stay safe.' Ray grinned maniacally. 'This is it. What a bit of luck that bint turned up on the bank of the Thames, eh, Alistair?'

Alistair grunted his agreement.

'I've always said it: One man's trash is another man's treasure.' Ray patted Alistair's shoulder. 'Eh, Alistair?'

This time Alistair didn't respond.

～

Jessie re-read the plaque on the wall as she tugged the plastic suit over her leathers and zipped it up. Craig and P. J. Dean had been removed from the site and she had called in the experts. The house in Barnes had already earned its place in history long before Verity Shore inhabited it. It had been used back in the late 1700s by smugglers who would bring barrels of newly taxed brandy from the Thames via a network of tunnels that emerged right under the house. There were several of these houses, their secret history long concreted over and forgotten. But not by everyone.

Someone handed her a mask and she followed the forensic scientist into the building. She could smell the decay through the furry white cardboard. It wasn't the now familiar smell of decomposition, of rotten flesh; it was the smell of corruption. Rotten life.

Craig had told her on the way to the house that Verity had become deeply paranoid. She wouldn't open the windows, she wouldn't let anyone in to tidy the place and when she was there she was in no fit state to do it herself. She was terrified that someone would go through her rubbish, check when she flushed the loo, just like at home. So she had piled bursting black bin liners one on top of the other in a corner of the room. The mountain of silage now took up a third of the floor space. The smell was as thick as treacle. In the empty adjacent corner the walls were stained with a high brown watermark and the carpet was filthy. Jessie looked from the black bin liners to the empty corner. In a house where no one bothered to stub out a cigarette, someone had taken the trouble to move the pile of rubbish from one corner to another.

'Start shifting those bin liners,' said Jessie to a policeman nearby.

'You interested in what's in them?'

'Yes, but I'm more interested in what's underneath them.'

Jessie looked in the downstairs loo. As Craig had hinted, it hadn't been flushed for months. That explained the urine stains and piles of dry human faeces dotted around the house. This was not the same old story of a star sinking into drugs and depression; this was no average cocaine binge in a hotel suite. This had gone further, deeper, darker than that. Cigarettes had been left to burn where they fell. It looked like black slugs were consuming what was left of the carpet. It was only thanks to the damp that the house hadn't burnt down. Evidence of a miserable existence lay all around her. Vomit stains. Bent, blackened spoons. Rust-coloured syringes. Eve Wirrel could not have portrayed the underbelly of modern celebrity better.

Jessie followed the man upstairs. Drugs' bedfellows: sadistic sex, self-loathing. The tools were displayed and tagged, waiting to be taken away by the SOCOs. Jessie was beginning to wonder if P. J. Dean knew his wife at all.

The Thames sidled up to the wall at the bottom of the garden every few moments, then coyly retreated into itself. A floating jetty clacked and bounced with the tide, rising and falling twice a day, every day. There was a chair in the middle of the lawn. Like the grass below it, it was stained brown-black with dried blood. Verity Shore's blood, Jessie was sure. The pattern on the ground was in keeping with massive blood loss from a major artery. Looking at the position of the chair and that of the stain, she could determine which artery. The femoral. Sliced open like the artist's. Eve Wirrel did not die for art. Verity Shore was not killed by her husband. More eerie than the empty chair was the iron bath, denuded of almost all its enamel. She could still smell the sulphuric acid and ammonia. It had been drained on to the ground, leaving a patch of scorched earth. These were Verity's remains.

'Dig up that turf,' said Jessie. 'In the end it can be buried with the bones.' She left the garden wondering if anyone other than Craig would mourn Verity Shore when and if that day arrived. 'Tell the team at Dean's place that they can stop looking for her remains in the pool house. Verity died here.'

The bin bags were being passed down the line to a waiting truck. Jessie watched the diminishing pile of waste and waited. And waited. The first truck filled, the second arrived. The bags at the bottom had almost all split under the weight. Half-eaten cans of food spilled out. Fat, slow flies crawled over the warm, rotting rubbish. Eventually they had to clear it with spades. The smell was poisonous.

'Pull it up,' said Jessie, pointing to the carpet. It ripped away easily from the metal teeth. The SOCOs folded it back. Jessie walked over and stared at the ground beneath. Concrete. Solid concrete.

'Get a drill in here. Dig up this whole floor and the garden if you have to, but find the old tunnel entrance.'

~

Jessie straightened her skirt, and ran her fingers through her dark hair. She looked fine. She pulled her jacket on and buttoned it. It was fitted. Very fitted. It would make a change from the paunchy, red-faced officers who usually took press calls. She left the ladies loo and walked towards the conference room. The press were waiting. She took the notes from Trudi. Burrows joined them.

'We found Eve Wirrel's parents. Sir Edward and Lady Fitz-Williams.' Jessie was surprised. 'Wirrel was a pseudonym,' continued Burrows. 'She wasn't in contact with them.'

'So they wouldn't have heard from her anyway.'

'No, but she still hasn't turned up at home.'

'The listed church she converted – thanks, Burrows, I read your preliminary notes.'

'Her parents are flying back to London as we speak.'

Jessie deflated. 'We'll go straight to the morgue after this, then.'

Burrows nodded. 'They'll meet us there.'

'It is her, isn't it?' said Jessie.

Burrows nodded.

'They're waiting,' said Trudi, pushing her gently towards the door. Jessie entered the stuffy room accompanied by Burrows and a couple of other officers. They were just there for show.

'Thank you all for coming.' Her throat suddenly felt very dry. It was hot under the TV lights. 'As you know, a body was found by the Thames on Tuesday. It was confirmed to be Verity Shore, who disappeared from her house the previous Thursday. We would ask you to respect the privacy of her husband and children at this difficult time.' She paused. 'I know you have a lot of questions, so please, one by one . . .'

'Why has it taken you so long to identify the body if she'd been alive a few days before?'

'Yes, I read that interview with Danny Knight.

Very fast work, I'm sure Mr Dean appreciated that.' She looked away from the *Daily Mail* journalist. 'To answer the question, the body was not in a good condition, making visual identification impossible.'

'What about dental records?'

Jessie knew they had heard about the missing head.

'They wouldn't have helped.'

'Can you confirm the rumours that the body was headless?'

'Please understand, for the sake of her children, we want details to be kept to a minimum. I can say that she did not die of natural causes and that the body had been tampered with.'

'Sexually?'

'We don't know.'

'How did she die?'

'A compression in the upper vertebrae implies she was hit over the head.'

'So you are looking for a murderer?'

'Yes.'

'And a head?'

She ignored that.

'Any leads?'

'We are following a number of avenues at this time.'

'How did you find the house in Barnes?'

She paused. 'We found relevant paperwork at her lawyer's.' It was a half-truth. Verity's solicitors had confirmed the ownership of the house. It belonged to Ty and Paul; Verity's mother had put it into trust for them, a trust Verity – knowing how much it was worth and needing the money – had been in the process of trying to break. But all this information had come after Craig had led them to the house. P.J. had begged her to keep Bernie and Craig out of the press. It was a big favour. And she wasn't quite sure why she was granting it.

'The house is currently being examined for forensic evidence,' she continued. 'I have to say it was in a mess, so don't expect miracles.' Thankfully, she had prevented P.J. or Craig from following her in.

'What about P.J.? Did he know about her den of iniquity?'

'It is nothing more than an old cottage, and no, he didn't. He has been questioned and eliminated from our enquiries at this time. I would like to make that absolutely clear. P. J. Dean was at home all weekend with Verity's children; numerous witnesses have come forward to confirm this. He was with his new band in the recording studio both nights. He didn't leave the house. Security-camera footage backs this up.'

'Is he going to keep the kids?'

'I have no idea. That does not concern the police.'

'Why would someone kill Verity Shore?'

There was a brief ripple of laughter from the journalists. Sympathy was not running high for the 'actress'.

169

'I don't know. We'd like to make an appeal to anyone who uses the footpath along the river in the early hours of the morning. I'm especially interested in hearing from people who visit the nature reserve adjacent to the bank where the remains were found, and any members of an art class that have been seen setting up their easels at that spot during the two weeks prior to the discovery of the body. Any more questions?'

A woman journalist put up her hand. 'Has Verity Shore's death got anything to do with the disappearance of Eve Wirrel?'

Jessie put her pen down. They bloody knew. A blackout meant nothing these days. It was stupid of her not to have prepared a convincing response.

'You are investigating that as well, aren't you, Detective Inspector Driver?'

'We are making no connection between those cases at the moment.' Jessie thought about the discoloured grass. The severed artery. The 'Average Week'.

'Why not? They were rumoured to be . . .' the journalist smiled suggestively '. . . close. Why don't you ask Mr Dean about that?'

'That'll be all, thank you.' Jessie held up her hand, then lowered it. She was shaking.

'What evidence did you find in the house?'

'Was Verity on drugs?'

She was losing control. Jessie remembered Burrows' words. Throw them titbits. Keep the animals happy. 'Could you turn any recording machinery off, please. I'd like to say a few words, off the record.'

That shut them up. There was a shift in the atmosphere. Jessie waited.

'The reason identification was so difficult, as I'm sure you all know, is because there was no skull. What you may not know is that the body had been submerged in an acid compound that dissolved most of her flesh, soft tissue and vital organs. It did not attack the bones and therefore would not have attacked the teeth. After numerous searches of the bank at low tide we have found no skull. Personally, I don't believe it is there. We were never meant to find the head. Her silicone implants, however, did survive the acid and it was the coding on these that led to her identification. If I tell you that peroxide was a component of the acid, you may begin to see that whoever did this seems to have been making a point. Which leads me to conclude that whoever did this had a plan. This wasn't an accident, a sex game gone wrong, a tragic end to a domestic with a lover. This was as premeditated as murder gets. And, yes, this is doubly pertinent since the disappearance of Eve Wirrel. We do have a body in the morgue and I am going presently to find out whether it is in fact the artist. Her parents are meeting me there. This is real, this is about real people. Verity had sons. Eve has parents. I need you to be particularly careful with what is printed. I don't want panic on my hands. It is going to be hard enough to find the culprit without you lot setting off a witch-hunt that could later be used as part of someone's defence. Equally, if you discover anything or know anything about Verity Shore's other life – and Eve Wirrel's, if it turns out like that – please, in confidence obviously, come and see me or DCI Jones when he is back, which I hope will be very shortly.'

'Like lesbian smut?' said a journalist.

She ignored the comment. 'Thank you for your co-operation.' Jessie got up and left the room. She had to meet Eve Wirrel's parents and watch them identify a rotten corpse as their flesh and blood.

~

Mark Ward pulled up outside Elmfield House and stopped the car. He locked and alarmed it, before setting off to find stairwell C. He could hear the television before he reached the door. He could hear something else. Crying. Mark sighed heavily and knocked on the door. Great, he thought, Jones had given him a hysterical young woman to deal with, while Jessie got lights, camera, action. The joys of age. He knocked again. The door opened a crack. A large, red-rimmed eye looked out.

'Detective Inspector Ward – I'm here as DI Driver's replacement.'

'I just saw her on the telly,' said Clare.

'Yeah, well, she seems to have got herself a bit busy. So here I am.'

'Where's Jones?'

'Hospital. Did no one tell you?'

She stared at him blankly. 'So what, you're not going to help me? I wait all this time and now you turn up and tell me you're not going to help –'

'We are, it's only . . .'

Clare started to cry.

'Look, I'm sorry,' said Mark. 'I didn't mean to bring more bad news.'

'Fuck off then. I don't need your pity.'

Mark could feel the frustration radiating off her and it made his antagonism melt away. 'Why don't you let me come in? We'll have a chat – I remember Raymond Giles going down, you know.'

She looked at him. Enormous brown eyes.

'Right bastard, he was. It was a sad day when that man got let out.'

Clare unchained the door. 'Come in. You should watch this.' Clare almost ran back down the short corridor, picked up the remote control and pressed 'play'. 'I recorded it this afternoon.' She barely looked at Mark.

Ray St Giles stared at Clare and Mark from the television set. Mark saw Clare shiver.

'Verity Shore is dead. The celebrity world is in shock. Many have come forward to talk about Verity, what a great friend and person she was. Another side to Verity was provided by Danny Knight, who gave an interview to the *Daily Mail*. He is with us today.' The camera panned out to include a bald-headed man sitting on a chair.

'Welcome, Danny. Tell me, were you surprised to find out about Verity's death?'

'Not really.'

'Oh?'

Mark and Clare both sat down. Glued to the set. The spectacular.

'She had been living an increasingly bizarre life. She was bedridden at home, only getting it together to do press calls – she was on the phone to her publicist day and night, demanding more and more. But interest in her was waning. She looked pretty terrible. Over-exposure, I think they call it. She hated that.'

'What do you think killed her?'

He pretended to pause. Act unscripted. 'Celebrity. Celebrity killed her.'

'P. J. Dean's celebrity?'

'I can't talk about him. Confidentiality agreement.'

'Okay. Was Verity happily married?'

'No.'

'Why didn't she leave?'

'Then she'd have had nothing.'

'Alimony?'

'Nope. P.J. and Verity had no kids together. Without a baby, she gets diddly squat. What was she going to do? Get a job?' The audience laughed. 'I doubt anyone would fall for her tricks and marry her a fourth time. Let's face it, she was beginning to look a bit lived-in.'

Pictures appeared on the screen.

'Airbrushed,' said Danny. 'I have a recent one of her here —' He pulled a photo out of his pocket.

'Can we get a camera on this?'

The audience gasped. Verity looked like a hag. 'That was after another of her disappearing acts.'

'Wow.' Ray was acting out the startled presenter bit to perfection. He turned to the camera. 'She certainly doesn't look like she used to.' A giant picture of him filled the screen for a moment before breaking up into hundreds of squares and fading away to reveal a dark-haired, fresh-faced girl in a cereal advert. It vaguely resembled Verity Shore. Then came 'glamour' pictures, then topless and finally nude. Doctored for daytime television. Somewhere along the way, Verity turned blonde. Now the footage of the marriages began to roll:

'I have found my soul mate. Tommy and I are one, aren't we, babe?'

'Yeah.'

'So how long have you two actually known each other?'

'Two months in this life. But we were married to each other in a former life, so really we've known each other for ages.'

'Literally,' says the presenter.

'Yeah,' says Tommy.

Paparazzi video of a drunk and pregnant Verity falling out of a limousine was followed by a montage commemorating her first stay at the Priory for 'exhaustion'. Then the celebrity baby shots began. Endless images of Verity and child in matching designer outfits. But, bored with her new toy, she soon embarked on a worldwide tour promoting her own scent, inspirationally called 'Verity'.

'Do you all remember this?' Ray waves a video cover in front of camera 2. 'Her exercise video to help women get in shape after pregnancy.' He puts the tape into a VCR and Verity appears on a huge TV screen beside him, bouncing up and down in a trendy black boob-tube and micro-shorts. Ray freeze-frames the image and points to her chest: 'Is it only me, or have these suddenly got bigger?' He presses play. 'The great thing about breast-feeding is how it firms everything up,' says Verity. All Ray has to do is raise an eyebrow and the audience laugh. They are putty in his hands.

'And then this . . .' DIET COKE FOR VERITY reads the headline on St Giles' screen. 'The nanny said Verity was taking coke every day, and that was the reason for her weight loss, but Verity counter-attacked by claiming the nanny had slept with her husband.' Press-cuttings fill the screen as Ray's voice continues: 'She got good advice from her PR agent. This time she won the sympathy vote. But it wasn't long before she was caught in the Bahamas with her pants down. Enter Will Reeves, a drummer from the highly successful band, Tonkers.'

More video, this time of Verity and Reeves. 'We are true soul mates. I loved my husband, but a star-crossed union like this one could not be ignored just because of a piece of paper. Will is my love, my life, the air that I breathe.' Reeves drums out a beat on the table while she talks, but squeezes her arse affectionately when she is finished. 'Another baby, Ty, another spell of exhaustion, another violent split and messy divorce. Then P. J. Dean . . .'

Dean's voice fades in. Deep and low. Kind. Sexy. 'Verity has not had an easy time, she knows she has sunk as low as a human being can. Me and the kids are taking a bit of time out to help her get back on her feet. We love each other very much. I would appreciate some privacy for my family now.'

'Didn't happen, though,' says St Giles to camera. 'Poor sod. His quiet wedding day became a press fiasco. Behind his back, she had sold to the highest bidder the rights to photograph the wedding. When the photographers turned up, P.J. tried to punch one – until they showed him the contract his new wife had signed. Worse than that, she'd been paid a large sum of money by an alcopop company to be seen drinking from the bottle. P.J. refused. Verity obliged. You'll all remember this shot –' Verity, in white, swigging from a pink bottle. 'Very bridal,' says Ray sarcastically. 'After that, P.J. banned all press. Big mistake. He should have known his wife better. Here in the audience, we have James Rolher. He was the journalist she called to her house while her husband was away promoting his new single. James, tell us what happened.'

'At first I thought it was joke, a wind-up. When I got to the house, I was let in and she was waiting for me in her bedroom, stripped to bra and knickers, demanding why I hadn't brought a photographer. We did an interview, but she was incoherent. The paper ran a small story that she was back on the booze. The Dean machinery denied it. She was very well protected by him. She's been courting the press for years, though. I know for a fact that it was her who called the papers when she was in the Bahamas with Will Reeves. Danny's right about her being over-exposed. People were bored of her. But the more it slipped away, the more desperate she became to court the press.'

'Thanks, James. After the break, we'll be talking to Raffi from the *Sun*, and a paparazzi photographer with his own insights of Verity Shore, who died, sadly and mysteriously, some time over the weekend.'

Clare switched the video off. She couldn't take any more.

'Bloody hell,' said Mark. 'I can't believe stuff like that is allowed. Doesn't anyone know who he is?'

Clare shrugged.

'That's disgusting,' said Mark. 'Do you know he used to crack people's heads with a baseball bat on behalf of the money-lending fraternity?'

'He did a lot of things,' said Clare.

She stood up, went to a cabinet and took out

a bottle of whiskey. She held it up to Mark. He nodded. A few minutes later, she returned with two mugs of sweet tea. Mark could smell the whiskey in the steam.

'My dad used to drink tea like this when he got back from work. Mum made it for him.'

'They were happy then?'

Clare smiled. It was big, wide smile. It didn't last long. 'Yeah. They were always messing around together. I'd often come home from school and they'd be here, messing about in their bedroom.'

Mark smiled. 'That's a rarity.'

Clare smiled again. 'Yeah.'

'Why don't you tell me everything you can remember?'

'Okay,' said Clare, a youthful animation suddenly filling her voice. She pulled her legs up under her, took a sip of tea and began to talk.

'I remember when they brought Frank back from hospital. Dad was over the moon. I think they'd been trying, you know, for quite some time. Mum couldn't stop crying, she was so happy. He had a mop of dark hair like Dad's, deep blue eyes – he was so sweet. A real smiley baby. I'll show you some pictures, if you like.' Mark nodded and she pulled a well-thumbed photo album from under the sofa. 'Here's Mum and Irene, dressed up for a Saturday night. That was before Frank was born. Look at those short dresses, so sixties,' she said gleefully. 'Don't they look great?'

Both women had dyed blonde hair backcombed into a beehive. Beneath short fur coats they wore mini-dresses and kinky boots. Both were undeniably attractive, but Veronica was the real beauty. Statuesque, slim and intelligent-looking. 'Who's Irene?' asked Mark.

'Mum's best mate. She owns a hair salon on the High Street. Hasn't missed a day's work in her life. She never got over Mum dying. They were like sisters.' Clare suddenly looked lost again.

'So they let you keep your own stuff when you were in the home?'

'God no. The album is Irene's, she gave it to me when I came back. They knew everything about each other, those two. Like twins, they were. You know, she leaves yellow roses on Mum's grave every month, without fail.'

~

As the mortuary attendant finished severing what the jogger's foot had started, Jessie thanked God that they had found Eve Wirrel's parents so quickly. Upper-class folk. Unprepared for what their daughter had turned into and how she had died. They confirmed the jewellery was hers. Remnants of a tattoo matched. DNA would prove the rest. The bagged hand showed no signs of a struggle. The blood revealed why: Rohypnol.

What was left of the stomach was removed. The contents would tell them when she had last eaten, hopefully give them an accurate time of death. The mortuary attendant then pierced Eve Wirrel's bladder and stale urine spurted out. Missed the attendant's cup and covered his arm. It happened occasionally. As in life ... Jessie thought of the artist's installation, 'A Particularly Heavy Week'. It had made headline news. Seven pairs of her soiled knickers. Each displayed on a podium. No glass case. This was in your face. Odour was an important aspect, Eve Wirrel had said in interviews. Jessie glanced quickly at Niaz. His cedarwood skin had paled to sycamore, but he was standing firm. Vomit and bleach. The smell of death. She wondered what Eve would have thought of this.

The mortuary attendant began to cut the skin off what was left of the face. This was the worst bit. The skinning ...

~

Jessie dialled P.J.'s mobile number then waited several seconds before pressing the call button. She listened to it ring in her ear.

'Jessie! I was just about to ring you.'

'Why?'

'Just wanted, um, to thank you really, for keeping the boy out of the press, and to see if you wanted to come –'

'You have an Eve Wirrel installation in your hall at home.'

'Oh. Yes. Obscene thing. How are you?'

'Not your taste then?'

'You think I want reminding how below average I've become in my old age?'

P.J. was trying to do that thing again. Reel her in. Speak softly to her. His voice was supposed to make her stretch out on a comfy chair, tuck her hands behind her back, the phone under her chin and have a good old-fashioned gossip. It wasn't working any more.

'Where did you get it?'

'Eve Wirrel gave it to Verity.'

'You told me you didn't know her personally.'

'I didn't. She isn't a friend of mine. What's the big deal?' He sounded defensive. Too defensive.

'The big deal, P.J., is that Verity was sleeping with Eve. I would have thought that was personal.' She was raising her voice.

Silence. Breathing. Silence. A door closed.

'What the fuck has she been saying?'

'Who?'

'Eve, of course.'

'Is it true?'

'Fucking hell! Rumours, that's all.'

'Spread by Eve Wirrel?' Jessie asked incredulously.

'I'm not an idiot, I know Verity courted the press, and Eve had an exhibition on at the time. Call me a cynical bastard, but it was a lot of hot air, no doubt thought up by Verity.'

'Headline hunting?'

'Headline whore,' said P.J. angrily.

'You shouldn't say such things about your wife.'

'You didn't know her.'

'And you couldn't control her.'

'No?' he said lightly. 'Did *you* read anything about their "affair" in the press?'

'No. But I wouldn't.'

'Too smart for that shit, aren't you, Detective Inspector.'

Jessie wouldn't rise to the bait.

'How do you manage to control the press?'

'I have a certain amount of clout in that department.'

'And Verity – did you have a certain amount of clout with her?'

'What's this all about?' asked P.J. sharply. 'Okay, I admit it, I didn't want the story breaking. Is that so hard to understand?'

'But it wasn't true,' said Jessie. 'You said they weren't sleeping with each other.'

'For a copper, you're very naïve. Since when did the truth matter? Look, Verity was many things, but she wasn't a lesbian, or bi. She was a missionary girl. She moaned in the right places, groaned in the right places and lit a fag when she was through.'

Only for you, thought Jessie. Verity Shore may have been many things, but not a missionary girl. The evidence in the house in Barnes was enough to make her suspect that P.J. had got his wife wrong; Craig's statement had clinched it. For Craig, Verity was a siren. A goddess. A dream

183

come true. He had got the best of Verity because he had given her what she wanted. Unconditional love. All she ever got from her husband was conditions. His and Bernie's conditions.

'What about Eve, was she bisexual?'

'Why don't you ask her? She got a lot of joy from humiliating men, so it's possible.'

'I thought you didn't know her personally.'

'Just look at her art,' said P.J. quickly.

'Why did you want to control the story?'

'The boys, of course. Don't you think they'd had enough bullying in the playground, without "lezzie boy" to add to the litany of insults? Gay is good as long as it stays behind the safety of the TV glass. Don't be fooled, we still live in a homophobic world. Gay-bashing is sport in many areas, despite the television awards.'

Jessie paced her office. How far would P. J. Dean go to protect those kids? To keep them. Had his crusade to save his errant wife's children gone too far? And who, she wondered, was saving whom?

'Will you please tell me what's going on?' said P.J.

'I don't like control freaks.'

'What the fuck is that supposed to mean? Come on, Jessie . . .'

'Don't Jessie me.'

'What has she been saying? She obviously didn't like me, the "*objet d'art*" is proof of that. Look, I wasn't a bad husband,' he said, 'just the wrong one. Eve is a nasty piece of self-publicising –'

'She's dead.'

No response.

'Murdered.'

Still no response.

'P.J. . . . ?'

'How?'

'Can't say at present.'

'Is it linked? To Verity?'

'Possibly.'

'Craig was here, you know. He hasn't left the house –'

'I don't think for one minute that Craig killed Eve. Nor Verity, for that matter.'

'I'd hate to think what you'd do to a guilty man.'

'I told you on the bridge what I do to the guilty.'

Jessie heard P.J. breathing down the phone. His breath was getting shorter.

'I'm sorry,' he said very quietly. 'I fucked up.'

'With Eve?'

'With Craig. Jesus, I never thought . . .'

'Craig is a lovely young man. He needs as much care as the boys. If not more.'

'You think I don't care for –'

'It's not about what I think, P.J., it's about what you know. Verity swore him to secrecy about that house. Keeping his word must have nearly killed him.'

'But he went there, on the Friday night, only he couldn't get in. If he'd told us before . . .'

'He wasn't to know.'

'I realise that. I just can't believe he knew where she was. I can't believe he was sneaking drink into her room!' His voice was beginning to crack under the strain. Anger. The control freak had lost control.

'It isn't *his* fault,' said Jessie. It's yours. For turning a blind eye. It was so obvious that Craig was in love with Verity. In a way that only a seventeen-year-old can be. She was a sex symbol. She drank vodka in the bath with him, danced for him, swam naked with him, made love to him. The boy would have done anything she asked.

P.J. sobbed loudly, suddenly. The sound startled Jessie. 'I can't think. I don't know what to think about. I know Craig won't get out of bed, I know he won't eat, I know I feel like shit . . .' His voice cracked. 'I should have kept those letters, I should have taken them seriously. I let her down, I let them all down. You're right, I'm a useless bastard. No one, Jesus Christ, no one deserves to die like that. I mean, God, what were they thinking? She couldn't swim, for fuck's sake. I worry about the boys . . . Jesus, I think about how she died, and I . . . Sorry. Pull yourself together.' He inhaled deeply. 'Thanks, Jessie – I mean, Inspector. I know you've only tried to help. I'm sorry I didn't tell you about Eve before, but there was nothing to tell, it wasn't relevant. I'm sorry, so sorry . . .'

The line went dead. Jessie wondered whether that little performance had been put on purely for her.

In the open-plan office the enemy were huddled like cattle around a feeder. Mark and his boys.

'What's going on?' asked Jessie.

Silence. A newspaper was spread open on the table. Jessie could see the double Ds from where she stood.

'What's going on?' she said into Fry's ear.

'Some ex-con has whipped up a storm about the Verity Shore murder.'

'Who?'

'That ex-gangster who's always parading himself as a crime expert on telly – Ray St Giles. He went for the jugular on this one.'

'Oh shit.' Jessie took the feature from her colleague. She speed-read it. 'Did anyone see it, the programme?'

'It's on at three in the afternoon on some shitty cable channel. No one saw it.'

Mark Ward kept quiet.

'Someone did – this paper is calling for his resignation. And there was I thinking that Verity Shore had fewer fans than us lot. Someone go to the press office and see if it got mentioned anywhere else.' No one moved. Trudi came in. 'Thought you might want to know, Ray St Giles is on *AM Today*, now, defending his actions.' There was a stampede to the TV room.

* * *

Ray St Giles was spread over the orange sofa, looking very sure of himself. 'I wasn't saying anything, I was not being judgemental, I was simply interviewing the guests.'

'But Verity Shore isn't around to defend herself against Danny Knight's allegations, or the allegations of any of your other guests,' said the presenter. She looked nervous in her lilac blouse.

'Look, sweetheart, everyone knows the kind of woman Verity Shore was. You think my guests were wrong, *you* tell me: why was she famous?'

The presenter tried to come back with a diplomatic retort. It fell flat. 'A very talented actress?'

'Acting what, though? I used to know a lot of women in the East End who did what Verity Shore did, only less successfully. They'd spend night after night down alleyways, in cars, in the nick. We revile one kind, yet we hero-worship another. Come on, isn't that a bit hypocritical? If she was an actress, I'm the pope.'

'He's not pulling any punches, is he?' said Fry.

That's the second time someone has called Verity Shore a whore, thought Jessie. The interviewer looked nervous in front of the compact, energetic man, her Plasticine face shining under the studio lights. 'Is it true that you've been temporarily suspended from your programme?'

St Giles sat back in his chair and grinned, flashing his chipped teeth like a hallmark. Labouring his cockney accent for the mid-morning viewers of England, he said, 'They were angry immediately after the show went out, but letters and calls came flooding in, commending our honesty. People are fed up with the endless PR spin, the self-promoting nobodies, people we have wrongly lauded as stars. Look, I'm not getting at anyone who can do their job, who deserves the adoration and the celebrity perks, but everybody from postmen to bank managers gets judged on performance ratings, so why shouldn't these celebrities be? Due to huge public response, the cable company back-tracked. Now we're on at six.' St Giles winked at the camera. 'Tune in tomorrow night for an intimate look at the late Eve Wirrel.' The camera angle changed abruptly.

'Shit! Shit! I don't believe he said that. Did he just say –'

The door opened. Kay Akosa filled the frame. That was all Jessie needed.

'You told me you couldn't confirm it was Miss Wirrel.'

'I couldn't when you asked me. Her parents hadn't got to the hospital, she hadn't been formally ID'd. Would you have preferred we risk it and have Eve Wirrel calling up from a hotel in Barbados threatening to sue? Not to mention putting her parents, family and friends through unnecessary anguish.'

'Well, you'd better make a statement and you had better make it good. Are you aware of the battle we have on our hands with the press? Do you realise how incompetent you look?'

'No, but we do,' said Mark as he left the room chuckling.

Jessie followed him out.

'Where do you think you're going?' Kay Akosa shouted after her.

'Church,' she replied, turning her minidisk on and drowning out Mark's snide retort.

~

Eve Wirrel had converted a church into a house-cum-studio. A council decision that still had the locals smarting. They couldn't build so much as a rabbit hutch in this over-protected area of suburbia, but Eve Wirrel, she had a licence to do exactly as she pleased.

Allegedly a Catholic, Wirrel had claimed that her work was spiritual. She'd hinted at visions and voices, and insisted that she was merely a vessel for a greater being's expression. It was a good take, less anarchic than her predecessors. Being the daughter of a baronet, the anarchic take wouldn't have held much water. Jessie pushed the high arched door open, expecting another den of iniquity. She was surprised when the glossy pages of *Architectural Digest* leapt up and licked her face.

'Very tasteful,' said Burrows, walking towards her.

'I've been looking for you. Ray St Giles has nailed Verity and blown the Eve Wirrel story.'

'I know. Fry called.'

'He's fucking loving this.'

'Don't be too hard –'

Jessie put up her hand. She didn't want to hear it.

The kitchen stretched the length of the nave: thirty foot of zinc atop two-foot-deep drawer units. Brushed steel rods lay in regimented lines, making the kitchen seem to stretch on and on, as far as the eye could see. Jessie ran a finger along it. Dust.

'Not a bad surface to freebase off,' said Burrows.

'I didn't know Wirrel was a druggie.'

Burrows shrugged. 'She was a media babe, hung out with the flash-bulb faces, went to red-carpet functions and was an experimental artist to boot. I'd say the odds were quite low.'

'Very poetic,' said Jessie, looking in the fridge. Cans of Guinness. Cheddar. Uneaten tofu. Half a pack of bacon, going green. Mixed messages. She opened the freezer. Next to an empty ice tray were three plastic phials. The sort of thing the doctor gave you to pee in. They were labelled. Jessie took one out and handed it to Burrows.

Initials. Height in feet. Eye colour and race. 'Well, well, well – looks like Eve Wirrel has been paying the sperm bank a visit.'

'They don't give it to you to take away,' corrected Jessie.

'I'll take your word for it.'

'Just bag them, Burrows.'

The cupboards were well stocked with unusable items. Fish paste. Date honey. Black-eyed beans, split. Jessie crossed the aisle to the sitting area on the left. She noticed a half-drunk cup of cold tea. 'Get fingerprints on this. Found any hate mail, death threats?'

'Nothing like that. In fact, it's just a typical posh bird's pad,' said Burrows. 'Sofa looks sat in, dog-eared mags, telly page is open. Whatever she was doing in the park, I'd say she was coming back.'

Jessie looked around her. 'Thought she was, at any rate. Bedroom?'

'In the crypt.'

'Should've known,' said Jessie. 'Anything of interest?'

'She wasn't a girl who restricted her experimentation to the canvas. This way.'

Jessie followed Burrows down a curved stone stairwell. The treads had been smoothed to the softness of soapstone by the soles of bat-winged priests. The bed was a four-poster without the canopy. Each post was the thickness of a horse's leg and engraved with entwined angels rising ever upwards. The swirling pattern tricked the eye into believing they were actually floating up to heaven.

'She slept with the angels,' said Jessie.

'The dead, you mean. Isn't this where they kept the skeletons? She was certainly into some kinky shit.' Burrows lifted the lid on a heavy teak chest. 'A Quality Street assortment of delectable sexual sweets.'

'Burrows, what has got into you? You're going all wordy on me.'

'Dunno, must be all this creative air.' He pulled out a sharp-toothed clamp. 'It's got my juices flowing.'

The bed was neatly made. Egyptian white cotton. Above it was a black-and-white photograph of Eve chained up by her wrists, her arms pulled taut above her head. Her feet dangling inches off the ground. More mixed messages.

'Strip those sheets and send them to the lab.' Jessie examined the portrait. 'Where is the studio?'

'Upstairs gallery section,' said Burrows, holding up a cat-o'-nine-tails.

'Is there a strap-on in there?'

'You know you can't be taking evidence away, boss.'

'Too close to the wind, Burrows. Way too close.'

'Sorry.'

'Is there anything in the studio?'

Burrows smiled. 'A lot of headless naked men.'

Jessie waited for him to explain.

'In charcoal. Pretty crap, actually, for a million-dollar earner.'

Jessie stood on the thirty-foot landing. The division between the choir balconies had been knocked through, and now they formed a mezzanine above the nave. A regiment of gothic-style leaded windows ran the length of the upper walls, flooding the studio with diffused light. There was plenty of space to paint and a big cushioned area for the models to display their wares. The back wall was decorated with pictures, postcards, photographs, paint charts, swatches of material, book covers, wallpaper, words. Every inch was covered with images. Jessie looked through the pile of nude drawings. All men. All headless. Handless. Footless. Verity Shore. Verity Shore. Verity Shore.

'How was I supposed to know that Eve Wirrel didn't paint heads, hands or feet?'

'I'm not with you, guv.'

'I want to find every last one of those men.'

'How?'

'I don't fucking know. Look in her phone book. Ring her agent, gallery – there must be some kind of artist model agency. Do I have to wipe your arse as well?'

Burrows looked hurt.

'Sorry,' she said. 'I don't like playing catch-up.'

Jessie retraced her steps through the old church and out into the garden. Graveyard. Resting place for bones. Eve, sleeping with skeletons. A skeleton. Verity Shore. That *was* personal. Everything pointed back to Verity. It was a two-way thing. If only she'd known where to look. But she had known. She'd even been offered binoculars to get a clearer view. Someone had details. Intimate details. They were familiar. Or familial?

While the police machinery carried on harvesting Eve Wirrel's life, Jessie gazed up at the church tower. Rumours. Secrets. Celebrities were like icebergs. Too much was hidden below the surface. She walked around the circumference of the church. Paced it out. Rumours and secrets. She stared back up at the church. It looked as if the mezzanine inside should be twenty foot longer. There was no access to the bell tower either. Could it be that this exhibitionist also had something to hide?

Jessie returned to the gallery and stared at the heavily decorated wall with its confusion of colour and images. She looked back down at the sleek zinc kitchen, then back to the giant pinboard. Starting at one end, she began tapping the wall; it was stud partition. She lifted a few flaps of paper and material, pressing, feeling, tapping as she went. Three-quarters of the way along, she found what she was looking for. A concealed door. A gentle press to a photograph of a golden Labrador and the hinged entrance popped open. You couldn't see the join behind the keepsakes. There was no door handle. This was supposed to stay hidden. Kept safe.

She entered the dark room behind the board. The temperature dropped. There were no windows. No filtered sunlight to warm the place up. Jessie reached inside her bag and pulled out the torch. She switched it on and aimed the narrow beam of light straight ahead. A naked man was nailed to a cross, his penis grotesquely engorged. A blank space where his head should have been. His hands and feet were missing too. Jessie found the light switch. Garish halogen lights beamed down from above. It was a painting, about seven feet by ten, and it wasn't finished. Around the crucified man, Eve Wirrel had painted writhing naked bodies in various hues of red. Magenta. Ochre. Crimson. Scarlet. Ruby. Burgundy. Cherry. They were all twisted and they were all men. The unfinished ones were initialled in pencil. It looked like a horrific colour-by-letters. Jessie thought of the phials in the freezer. Since Eve Wirrel's body had been discovered, Jessie had ordered all the artist's back catalogues. Nothing was as good, or as disturbing as this. Eve had titled it in thick, bleeding letters: 'All Men Are Rapists'. Jessie's eye moved back to the well-endowed centrepiece. It too was initialled.

'Jesus Christ,' whispered Jessie to herself. She thought about the woman in the morgue; the mortician had used a circular saw to cut through Eve Wirrel's skull so the pathologist could get to her brain. The epicentre of her creative genius. It would have been weighed with all her other vital organs and, when they were done, the whole lot would have been thrown back in and sewn up. Why did Eve Wirrel hide her work? Was she afraid she would be copied? Or was she afraid she'd be caught? Was this a clue to the next victim? Or not. An ingenious plot, or a wild-goose chase?

P. J. Dean's number appeared on her mobile. Jessie switched it to answering machine. Too many mixed messages. She needed to step back.

*　　*　　*

In the pub, she plied her team with whatever they wanted. Gin. Whiskey. Vodka. Lager. Bitter. Mild. It was all blotting paper to her.

～

Mark pushed open the door of the pub in Victoria. Neville Gray was sitting in a corner. He was the assistant director of the child and family unit that covered Bethnal Green. He'd worked in social services as long as Mark had been in the police force, they went back years. They'd worked a case together in the late seventies. Mark had put a man away who had abused his daughter, his grand-daughter and niece. Incest. Neville got the girls out before the police went in. It had been a good joint effort. They'd been drinking buddies ever since. After the first pint and the habitual pleasantries, Mark got down to business. Neville remembered the Raymond Giles case but was unaware Ray had got himself on television.

'That's a fine way to repay a con, give him a fucking chat show.'

'The mind boggles,' said Mark. 'The man he shot had two kids, Clare and Frank. Both came to you, but someone over there thought it best to change their names. The paper trail on Frank dries up, there and then. Thought you could do some digging around for me. See where he went. All we have is a date of birth.'

'Was he a protection witness against St Giles?'

'Nope. The kid was three. Go figure.'

'Interesting. What about the dad, Trevor? What was his game?'

Mark tore open a packet of crisps and lay them out on the table. 'Normal bloke, by all accounts. I've got a DS going over their lives with a tooth-comb. You know what the East End is like. Parts of it haven't changed. Memories go way back; if he was up to no good, we'll find out.'

'Okay, I'll see what I can do.'

'Do you think it will be classified?'

'No doubt about it. I can't think of one good reason why those kids had to be split up or have their names changed.'

'I know it's a lot to ask, but will you let me know, even if it's classified?'

Neville smiled. 'I'll do more than that.'

'How?'

The grey-haired man tapped his nose with nicotine-stained fingers. 'We have ways and means. Give me a week.'

'Good man yourself,' said Mark, standing up to get his round in. Old ways. Old rules. They worked for him.

~

The woman paid the driver of the black taxi and, close to tears, pulled two heavy suitcases out of the back. Her kids were crying. It felt like they'd been crying since they left the villa in the Canaries to get a last-minute flight at three in the morning. The kids were tired. It wasn't their fault. She was shattered.

'No tip?' asked the burly driver.

The woman burst into tears as she crouched back inside the cab to retrieve her children. The sight of their mother crying shocked them into silence. She slammed the door shut and received a throat full of black diesel fumes in response. She looked up and down the street nervously.

'Come on, kids, quietly, not a word.'

She pulled the suitcases up the old stone steps of the house. Her husband loved this house. She hated it, it was too old, unmanageable and had too many stairs. But she didn't live there, so what did it matter? The front door was not double-locked. This worried her more than the endless unanswered phone calls she'd made from Tenerife. She hurried the kids inside and closed the door. She was safe. No one had seen her. Only a few lights were on in the street. Most people were still asleep.

'Where are we?' asked her son.

'Stay here,' she said. 'Don't make a sound and don't touch anything.'

She'd been worried about an alarm, but there didn't seem to be one. She walked to the bottom of the narrow staircase and looked up the uneven, displaced treads.

'Cary?' she called quietly.

'Is Dad here?' asked her son.

She turned on him. 'Shh. We don't know who

is here. He's Cary, remember, when we're not at home.'

The boy frowned. He was angry and he didn't understand. Nor did she any more.

'Cary! It's me, Lorna! Are you here?'

She took a step up. It creaked solemnly in the silence. She truly hated this house. It smelled funny. The kids watched her walk up the first flight of stairs, move across the landing and take the next flight. The girl started to cry.

'Mummy!'

'Shh, sweetheart, I'm right here.'

Lorna pushed each door to each small, pokey room. None of the fires was lit, but dusty ash sat in the grates of some of them. Cary had been here. Living like a camp Edwardian gentleman with his leather-bound books and prompt serving of tea. It was all an act, he said. The viewers liked it. It paid for the lovely new house in Leeds. But at what cost, thought Lorna, staring at her husband's unmade bed. He hadn't called her for three days. He hadn't joined them in Tenerife for their secret holiday, *en famille*. So she had broken one of the golden rules and called him. But there had been no answer from his mobile or this house. She'd even called work, only to be told he was away on holiday with friends. Friends! Friends! His wife and children, you mean, she wanted to shout at the pious receptionist. It was a stupid cover story. Now she had no one to turn to.

'Mummy!' screamed her daughter.

'Coming, love, coming.'

They sat in the kitchen of the empty house, their tanned faces suddenly pale and worried.

'It smells funny in here,' said her son.

Lorna looked at the cellar door. Cary had told her it was unsafe. The ancient foundations needed underpinning or something. She'd never been down there. She'd never wanted to.

'It's coming from there,' said her son, pointing to the door. He was right. She knew he was right. But she simply couldn't move.

Lorna wedged the door open with a pan and felt along the damp wall for a switch. She couldn't find one. She pointed the torch down the steps and gingerly began to descend into the darkness. The smell became more pronounced the deeper she went. She had given the kids colouring books, but she could hear from the silence that they weren't playing.

'You all right, Mum?' asked her son.

'Yes sweetheart, I'm fine.'

She was far from fine. She was terrified. Had Cary fallen down the stairs? Would she find him dead, with a broken neck? She aimed the torch at the floor and millimetre by millimetre the beam of light etched into the darkness. She was afraid of what the shadows held in store for her, but the fear of what that slow-moving puddle of light might illuminate was somehow even worse. That smell did not signal good news. The stone became wood. Boards. An open trap door. A hole in the ground. Rope. Ropes descending into the fetid pit. She knew immediately it was a septic tank; there had been one on her parents' farm. She shone the beam of light downwards and examined the rough, warm surface of the tank's contents. She saw the underside of a shoe. She screamed and dropped the torch. It fell into the human faeces and sank, right next to her husband.

～

Jessie slowed the bike down over Putney Bridge and watched the mist rise off the water and eddy like a jet engine's exhaust. A few boats were already on the river, pulling hard in unison, fighting the river's strength. She turned the bike on to the slip road and glided to a stop. She parked the bike, pulled her helmet off, ruffled her flattened hair and went in search of some oarsmen.

The digger had made holes all over the lawn of the smuggler's house in Barnes; the drill had done the same in the cement to the foundations. They had found nothing. There had once been tunnels, but they had long been blocked up. Jessie had pored over sewage maps, utility maps, telecommunications maps and water board maps, but had found nothing. The secret tunnels had remained just that. She had also sent a team to follow the tunnel that emerged near where Verity's bones had been found. It looped into a maze of underground systems, but so far nothing that led to the house in Barnes.

She was beginning to think there was another route, a more direct but dangerous route: the river itself. Had someone left the jetty at the bottom of the garden and braved the water to float with the tide downstream, hidden by the canopy of branches along the river's edge, to place Verity's bones in the stinking mud? Jessie had returned to the river today to find out. The first two boathouses she came to were locked up. Securely. The third was open. Jessie peered inside; as her eyes became accustomed to the darkness, she could see the outline of sleek rowing boats floating up each wall. She ran her hand down an expensive fibreglass hull and felt its potential force ripping through the Thames. A rowing boat. A mode of transport that made no noise and left no imprint.

'Can I help you?'

A man stood in the doorway, his legs splayed, holding a dripping hose in his left hand. Despite the cold, he wore only a pair of lycra rowing shorts and black Wellington boots. Jessie tilted her head to one side. His muscles were so well defined she began to list them in her head: triceps, biceps, pectorals, abdominal, periformas, adductors, quads . . . She exhaled softly, and lifted her head. The appraisal had taken less than a second.

'Detective Inspector Driver – may I ask you some questions?'

'Sure.' His manner was easy. He dropped the

hose and grabbed a DURC sweatshirt from inside one of the boats cantilevered to the wall.

'Nick Elliot,' he said, extending a hand. Jessie shook it. Hard. He wasn't the only one with biceps.

'Coffee?' She nodded. 'You want to know if a boat has been stolen?'

'Has one?'

'No.' He pierced the foil on a new jar of instant coffee with a spoon.

'Borrowed?'

'No. This is expensive equipment, we keep it under tight security. But by all means ask around, though I doubt anyone would use the kind of boats we have here.'

'For what?'

'Dumping a body.' He looked over his shoulder at her. 'Sugar?'

Very cute. 'And milk, if you have it.'

He passed her a cup then stood alongside her, looking back out to the river. 'You couldn't safely transport something like that in one of these.' She could smell the sweat on his skin. 'Much more likely they'd use a Zodiac.'

'Too noisy.'

'Maybe. But we're under the flight path here. Wouldn't the sound of a two-litre engine be drowned out by the jets?'

'Not at night.'

'What about a punt, the type you see at regattas?'

'Sorry, I'm not a regatta kind of girl,' said Jessie.

Nick looked at Jessie's leather trousers and helmet. 'Pity . . .'

She waited.

'. . . then you'd know that they're wide, not like the sculling boats. They have a flat end to stand on, and the underside slopes. It would be perfect.'

'You seem to have given this a great deal of thought.'

'Major topic of conversation since the girls found it. It's a small community down here, we all know each other very well.'

Two more equally well-defined men in track-suits appeared. One tall, one shorter.

'Not again, Nick. How many times do we have to tell you? No pulling in the boathouse.'

'Leave those undergraduates alone. They're supposed to be training.'

'Least she's human,' said the shorter one.

They guffawed at their own comic genius.

'Well, partly,' said Jessie. She held out her badge. 'I'm a police officer.'

'A detective inspector,' added Nick.

'Shit. I mean, sorry.'

'She came about the body,' said Nick.

The boys laughed again. Jessie could only hope it was out of nervousness.

'Are you really a copper? You don't look like one.' The shorter one was trying to flirt. He wasn't as good at it as Nick.

She stepped closer to them. 'Why, you worried

about the lump of black you've got stashed away in your locker?'

The shorter rower choked. The taller one shrank. Jessie turned back to Nick. 'Is there some kind of association the boat clubs belong to that would have listings of boatyards and sales?'

'Sure, I'll get you the number.'

Jessie followed him through to the back.

'Sorry about the lads.'

'Don't worry about it. I've got three brothers, all older. There isn't a great deal I haven't heard or seen.' She took the piece of paper from him. 'If you remember anything else, call this number. You've been really helpful, thanks.'

'Why don't you stay for another cup of coffee? It's a beautiful morning.'

It was tempting. She hadn't sat down and talked to a normal person for days. Weeks. She downed the rest of her coffee and held out the empty mug. 'Okay.' He was returning to the kettle when her pager buzzed. She pulled it out and read the text message: CARY CONRAD. GAMES SHOW HOST. FOUND DEAD AT HOME. PLS RESPOND ASAP. She picked up her helmet and started to run.

'Sorry,' she called over her shoulder. 'Occupational hazard.'

'Well, you know where I am if . . .'

The three boys watched her go.

'Lara Croft,' said Nick.

'Meets the Terminator.'

'Meets the Wicked Witch of the West.'

'She wasn't a witch,' said Nick.

'Oh yeah, then how the hell did she know about my hash?'

~

Tarek drove Ray's BMW to the American Car Wash. Ray offered no explanation for the fact that he had to use one key to open the door and another to start the ignition. Obviously one or other of the mechanisms had been replaced. Which implied one thing to Tarek. Stolen. Reformed character? Was everybody blind, or did they just enjoy telling their friends they'd met an East End *gangsta*. It didn't matter that he was a murderer, he had a gold necklace, a sharp suit, and a ring with his name on it. Tarek stepped out of the car and told the attendant what he wanted. Wheel wash? Tarek glanced down at the aluminium spokes. The car was encrusted with mud. His boss must have been on a foray into the country. That, or he'd been dumping bodies. Quite frankly, nothing would surprise him.

'The whole works,' said Tarek. 'Hot wax, the lot. I'll be over the road, having a coffee.'

He didn't mind Ray's little errands. They used to entail waiting around in some forgotten corner of London for a man in a black leather jacket and soft-soled shoes. Brown envelopes. Information. Power. That had stopped when Alistair Gunner turned up. Now it was Alistair who met all the soft-soled men. Ray St Giles, daytime television's own J. Edgar Hoover. Richard and Judy had better look out. Now that he'd seen the files, Tarek knew where Ray was going with this.

Tarek ordered a coffee and opened the newspaper. *The Times* had a feature about St Giles' show on Verity Shore. Reading it, he experienced the same feeling of disquiet that had crawled through him when he'd first heard the identification of the body on the Thames. St Giles had been compiling a file on the 'celebrity' since she had refused to go on his show. He'd been mad when 'the little tart' refused. Ranted about how she thought she was too good for him, but he knew a few things about her and he wasn't going to stop until he had her begging to be allowed on his show. St Giles wanted a big, fat slice of Oprah's world. And Tarek was beginning to believe that he would do anything to get it. The *News of the World* would call what St Giles had a 'dossier'. Ray called these files his chips. To play on the roulette table of celebrity. The prize was fame and fortune. The best the losers could hope for was obscurity. Ray St Giles was not a man for whom obscurity was an option. Tarek had listened to him drunkenly boast about his first fights in the boxing ring at the age of seven, of discovering a natural affinity with violence that was spotted by the local debt collectors. He'd always wanted to be somebody. The really frightening thing with St Giles was that most men of his ilk fabricated the lion's share of their stories, but, with Ray, you knew the lion's share was what he kept quiet. Even when drunk, he was never out of control. One suspicious death and Ray was closer to realising his dream. Verity Shore's death was very convenient. A convenient death was the same as an altered car lock to Tarek. Something was not right.

The car was shining in a brief shaft of sunlight. The boot was open and one of the attendants was hoovering inside. Its contents were piled to the left of him: a plastic petrol container; a can of oil; a spade; a cardboard box; one golf shoe, left foot. Tarek returned to the box. Curiosity was going to get him into trouble, he knew that, but he couldn't help himself. He lifted the lid. Inside was a head. It actually made him jump. Only two days ago Ray had been on about finding Verity Shore's head. He was determined to be the one that found it. But this was a glass head. Hollow. Or had been. Tarek lifted it up. It took a few moments to work out what was inside it. When he did, he nearly dropped it. It was shit. Human shit by the looks of it. Tarek didn't need to see the signature to know who the artist was. Ray's new project.

∼

Five boys. All born on the same day. All sharing the same fate: Social Services. Clare stared at their names. She couldn't believe it. Five names. Five possibilities. Five leads, when she'd only ever had one. Hope. She'd written each one out. Black marker pen. White card. Keep it simple. Because it was bound to get messy. She'd taken down her drawings from the kitchen wall and tacked up the five names in their place. Under each one was the information DI Ward had given her. What care homes the boys had gone to, the names and addresses of their foster parents, the other homes, the other foster parents. Backwards and forwards, to and fro, up and down, forwards and backwards, as confused little boys became angry young men. Three had police records. One had been sent to a youth offenders' unit. Not a great advertisement for children's homes. There were no current addresses for any of them. Only one had been officially adopted, and there was no current address for him on file.

Any of them could be Frank, but, as DI Ward had been at pains to point out, maybe none of them was. She unfolded the photograph of Frank on the day of the funeral. Looking so solemn. She didn't want to be reminded of the day, just his face. She couldn't remember a photographer being at the graveyard, but then she didn't remember much about the day. Except the sheer look of horror on her mother's face when her father was lowered into the ground. Veronica Mills had fallen to her knees and clawed at the soil. She and Frank had stared at their mother – helpless. Hopeless. Somebody else had to help her up. Those dirt smudges on her mother's knees had taunted Clare from the back of the wardrobe. Somebody else had to cut her down.

～

The desk sergeant buzzed Jessie's desk. There was someone to see her. Jessie walked past Niaz, who held a phone to his ear with one hand and waved a piece of paper at her with the other. He cupped his hand over the mouthpiece. 'We are still interviewing artists' models and checking the boatyards' records. All individual sales paid for by cash within the last six months. What news of Cary Conrad?'

'I've arranged a meeting with the investigating officer. Could you organise a river search? Burrows can help you with the paperwork.'

'You expect to find the head?' queried Niaz.

'No. The head is lying dormant, but I have a sinking feeling it will turn up somewhere. No, I want the river searched for a boat. Sinking it would have been easier than pulling it out of the water and taking it away by trailer. One person couldn't carry it out.'

'With all due respect, ma'am, you don't even know if the remains were transported by boat. It wasn't long ago we were searching tunnels and digging up the house in Barnes to find a link.'

'I know. I was supposed to do that. It was supposed to delay me. And it has. But I'm back on course. It has to be a boat.'

Niaz was not convinced, she could tell from the way his olive eyes retreated into his narrow skull.

'If you can think of another mode of transport that could get those remains on to the mud, make no noise and leave no mark, tell me.'

He remained silent.

'I've got to go, someone is waiting for me.'

Jessie buzzed herself out and saw Maggie sitting in the waiting room.

'Oh, hi.'

Maggie beamed at her. 'Were you expecting someone else? Someone slightly more famous, perhaps?'

'No.'

'Liar! You licked your lips.'

Jessie swore silently at her as the ears of several PCs honed in on them.

'Come on, Clouseau,' said Maggie, 'I'm taking you for a coffee. I have news.'

'Don't tell me Denise van Outen has died in a freak yachting accident and you're up for the *Big Breakfast*.'

'Jesus, you're behind the times. She left the show ages ago. Anyway, you shouldn't be saying such things, what with the current mood of the nation.'

'What mood?'

Maggie took Jessie's arm and they walked out of the station, through the car park and to the café that Jones liked so much. Jessie wondered whether Maggie had dropped in just to see the jaws drop. PCs all around them followed them with their eyes.

'You've got to start reading the tabloids, honey. Ray St Giles, the new man of the people, has gone to the press with a dire warning to all those untalented wannabes out there. Honestly, I'm off to buy pepper spray immediately.'

'What are you talking about? And, anyway, you're talented.'

'A little slow on the uptake there, Jessie, but I'll let it pass.'

'You're joking, right?'

'No. Because of Ray St Giles, bookies are taking odds on who will be next.'

'What?'

'Everyone knows she was dipped in acid, that she was ID'd by her tits and that she had no head. Brainless, big-titted blonde is decapitated and left spread-eagled on the mud – this is no accidental overdose. Next comes Eve Wirrel – it's too poetic for words. And now Cary Conrad –'

'What have you heard about him?'

Maggie smiled. 'So it *is* true.'

Jessie put her finger to her lips. Maggie winked. 'Are you working on it?'

'Not directly, but I'm in the loop. A DCI Harris is in charge. Sounds nice on the phone. I'm meeting up with him as soon as the autopsy is done. And, Maggie, accidental death cannot be ruled out. Not a word of this to anyone.'

'What happened to him?'

Jessie sighed.

'You don't trust me?'

'Of course I trust you. The thing is, no one really knows what happened. Yet.' That wasn't true. The game-show host had drowned in his own shit. How he got there was what DCI Harris was trying to find out.

'It is quite thrilling though, isn't it?' said Maggie. 'You should take a walk down Oxford Street, Jess. The masses are jubilant, it's like a Royal Wedding out there.'

'Who have the bookies got down on the list?'

'Where do you want me to start?' said Maggie dramatically. 'All members of male, female and mixed manufactured bands, especially the ones that look pretty and mime to cover versions; the whole plethora of Barbie-doll presenters; It girls; those awful posh titled boys; any former wild child; most footballers' wives; models who've decided to be anything other than models – all the usual bollocks.'

All Jessie could do was shake her head in dismay.

'What is really worrying people is if they're not on the list. No one from *Hollyoaks* or *Big Brother* made it, for instance. Understandably, they're gutted. They are below z-list – z minus. Which, as we know, doesn't exist, and if they don't exist in the media, they don't exist at all. Oh, what shall those poor, untalented exhibitionists do now?'

'I can't believe I'm having this conversation. They would prefer to be thought of as a potential murder victim than not at all.'

'I think there is some jostling to be the favourite, the Red Rum of the z-minus creatures.'

'How does shit like this spread so fast?'

'Think of Jill Dando – people have been expecting this.'

'You are sick.' They ordered drinks.

'It doesn't take a genius to work it out and any gaps in the press, Ray St Giles has filled. He must have a spy in your department,' said Maggie.

'I'm going to have to have words with the personable Mr St Giles.'

'Careful, he isn't a nice piece of work.' They took a seat in the window. 'You don't want to know what my boss offered me to get you to do an interview.'

'You're joking. How do they know you even know me?'

'The film party. Sweetheart, you are a great-looking girl in tight leather pants. People saw you talking to Dame Henrietta Cadell, a woman known for her love of violent ends. A few days later you're on national TV leading the most exciting murder investigation this world has seen since O. J. Simpson did a runner with the LAPD in hot pursuit. People in television are paid vast sums of money to notice things like that.'

'No one knows if the deaths are linked, or, as I said, if Cary Conrad's death is suspicious.'

'Drowned in his own shit – that's not suspicious?'

Jessie's mouth dropped open. 'How do you know this?'

Maggie tapped the side of her nose. 'I, too, have my sources. Anyway, the powers that be want you on the box, with your pouty lips and irritatingly high cheekbones and wash'n'go hair. Quite frankly, I'm getting a little pissed off.'

'What did you tell them?'

'For *Watchdog*, I said I'd bring your head on a plate.'

Jessie laughed. Maggie fished a folded piece of paper from her jacket pocket. 'Instead of hating you, which by rights I should, I've come here with gifts from the Orient.' She waved the piece of paper at Jessie. 'Guess what it is.'

'Jeffrey Archer's DNA.'

'Better. The direct line to the showbiz editor of the *News of the World*. Sweetheart, he is a goldmine, a veritable fountain of knowledge. I met him last night at a party and thought he might come in useful. You're not going to get the information you need ploughing through endless *Hello!* magazines. You want the unprintable stuff. Trust me on this, I know my people.'

Jessie took the piece of paper.

'Right, I've got to go, there's a producer I need to give a blow job to at twelve. Keep your fingers crossed, this would be a big break.' Maggie smiled. 'Love you, see you later – and ring that bloke.'

Jessie called out after her: 'I'll give him what I know in exchange for his dossier on you.'

Maggie turned first, smiled later.

'Joking,' said Jessie. 'Hey, Maggie, did you ever

get another threatening letter?'

'Oh, hon, you don't have to worry about me. I can look after myself.'

'Can I have it?'

Maggie blew her a kiss. 'You worry too much.'

~

Jessie turned the bike into a run-down TV studio car park. The security man on the gate pointed to her destination; she knocked on the door of the Portakabin and went in without waiting. Ray St Giles was sitting in a large leather swivel chair behind a desk.

'What the fuck –'

'Police,' said Jessie. 'I'd like a word.'

'Jesus Christ, I'm busy. Can't it wait?'

Jessie looked at the heels sticking out from under the desk. 'Perhaps she should have a tea break.' Ray St Giles didn't move, the feet retracted under the desk. 'Now,' said Jessie, raising her voice.

'Go on then, fuck off,' said Ray, pushing his chair back to let the girl crawl out. She couldn't have been more than nineteen. The door closed behind her.

'Habit I picked up in the nick,' said Ray, standing up and zipping his fly. 'Hey, I know you. You're that detective off the telly. Looking for an expert to appear with you on *Crime Watch*?' He smiled, revealing his now familiar crooked teeth.

'You'll have to get them capped for Hollywood,' said Jessie.

'I was thinking gold, meself.'

'Good choice of colourway,' said Jessie, walking slowly round the cabin.

'You come here alone, Inspector?'

She turned to look at him. 'You, Mr St Giles, are causing me a bit of bother.'

'I'm sorry to hear that.' He smiled broadly. 'I like to help the police any way I can.'

'We've had the switchboard jammed with calls from media darlings who are demanding police protection. As if we don't have enough to worry about when the American stars come over to grace theatreland with their presence.'

'I'm sorry, but I don't see how I can help you.'

'They seem to think they are the targets of a hate campaign.'

'Sweetheart, I'm only telling the public what the police already know,' said Ray.

'You are creating panic, and panic doesn't help my job.'

Ray tapped out a cigarette and lit it. He blew smoke rings at her and shrugged.

'I had an agreement with the press to keep certain details out of the public eye until a later date.'

'I'm not the press.'

'Where did you get your information, Mr St Giles?'

He smiled. 'You can't keep good gossip quiet in this town, Inspector. If Verity Shore could have, she would have filed the story herself.'

'She has children.'

'Wrong. She had accessories.'

'You don't like her type, then?'

'Armed robbers make for strong moral fibre compared to the likes of her.'

'Water finds its own level, Mr *Saint* Giles.'

'An affectation I added when I became a free man. It sort of has a nice ring about it when the audience start chanting.'

'They chant, do they?'

'They will.' He smiled again, passing his icy blue eyes over her taut, fit figure. 'Is there anything else I can do for you, *Detective Inspector*?'

He didn't scare her. 'Don't go whipping up a storm, Mr St Giles. You'll give yourself a motive.'

He stepped towards her. Jessie stood her ground. 'Don't go handing out threats like that, Detective Inspector, or you might just give me one.'

'I am trying to catch a killer,' she said.

He took her hand, lifted it to his mouth and kissed it. 'And I am trying to put on a show.'

~

Clare Mills stood on the raised flagstone doorstep and clutched her bouquet of flowers. Irene had provided her with her history, her antecedence. She wanted to tell Irene the good news first.

'Hi, Clare. Come in. I've made a cake.'

'We might have found Frank!' She blurted it out. 'Well, not me, Mark – DI Ward. In Sunderland. He's agreed to meet me. DI Ward is driving me there tomorrow. He has no birth certificate. This is the first real possibility. He's white. Like me.'

Irene was not smiling. 'That's um . . .'

'Oh, I hope, I hope it is. Please be pleased.'

'I just don't want you getting your hopes up too high, Clare. You know what happened last time.'

'This is different. DI Ward has been so kind, really. I didn't like him at first, but gosh he's . . .' She took a bite of lemon cake. 'You should meet him, he's about your age.'

'Think I'm a bit old for match-making.'

'Rubbish, you look great. You and Mum were always the prettiest round here. I remember you both getting dressed up for Saturday night, looking a million dollars. I showed Mark all the photos you gave me, he was dead impressed.'

'That's personal stuff, Clare, I told you that.'

'Sorry. But he said it could help.'

'No, Clare. I'm sorry. They'll just manhandle them and get fingerprints all over them. Treat them with no respect. Don't do that again, Clare – promise. Don't tell them private things. Your mother wouldn't like it. They were proud, your parents. Proud and honest. I don't like the idea of . . .' Irene pulled Clare into her arms. 'Sorry, love, I've been working too hard.'

Clare inhaled the smell of Elnett hairspray and shampoo. It was too painful for Irene, dwelling on the past. All that waste had wounded her in some ways more than it had Clare. Irene had lost her best friend of twenty years, she had a bosom-full of memories. They'd shared clothes, boyfriends, secrets. When Veronica's mother had deserted her, she'd moved in with Irene's family. That sort of devotion was rare at the best of times; where they grew up, it was extinct. Irene said she didn't want some man taking her away from all that was hers. Her hair salon. The house in which she was born. Her friends. Her memories. It had been their playground, stomping ground, coming-of-age ground. And the ground in which Veronica, her greatest friend, was buried. Her past. What Clare missed was an imaginary past. She knew that. Her memories were vague, ethereal, dream-like. Except the day of her dad's funeral, of course. That had always happened yesterday.

'They've opened a noodle bar two shops down from the salon,' said Irene. 'I swear, we'll be next. Someone will make me an offer I can't refuse and I'll retire. Travel. I always meant to travel.'

'Maybe Frank and I could come with you?'

Irene smiled in that way of hers, with sad eyes. 'Maybe,' she said.

Tarek walked down Shoreditch High Street towards his flat. An *Evening Standard* seller barked from outside the train station:

'EVE WIRREL DIES FOR ART! EVE WIRREL DIES FOR ART! POLICE GET IT WRONG!'

Tarek handed over thirty-five pence. Sat down on a bench and read:

The body of Eve Wirrel was found in Richmond Park by a man out running with his dog. Following so quickly on the death of Verity Shore, the police immediately treated her death as suspicious. They withheld vital information from the press and cleared the site where she died before allowing reporters in. However, we can now exclusively reveal that Eve Wirrel did in fact, DIE FOR ART.

Internationally renowned photographer, Anton Flame, a close friend and confidant of the artist, was summoned to Richmond Park by Eve Wirrel herself. She had told him where to find her and what to do. Unfortunately, her body was discovered by an unwitting member of the public who immediately called the police.

Anton Flame explains: 'It was beautiful really. Each of her limbs pointed to four giant oaks on which she had spelt out the word DECOMPOSITION. Sadly the police decided to treat it like a crime scene and not a canvas, and began to do unspeakable things to the body. They had no respect for her, for what she stood for and what she was trying to do for the modern art movement. I am completely traumatised.'

Wirrel shot to fame with her controversial installation 'A Particularly Heavy Week', featuring seven pairs of soiled knickers, displayed at the Tate Modern. The police have yet to confirm whether she is the second

victim in a series of terrible murders that have
struck at the heart of
the nation's celebrities or
another of her headline-
grabbing 'installations'.

~

'Bastard!' Jessie threw the paper down on her desk. 'Can we sue?'

'No. He didn't print a photo. But the article goes on to list the photographer's artistic credits and mentions a website.'

'Don't tell me there are photos!'

''Fraid so,' said Fry. 'The PC searched him, I was there, but the conniving twat must have put the film down his trousers. Quite apt, I suppose, considering who the stiff was. Anyway, the pictures are on the website, fan-extremis.com. For a price, you can download them.'

'I don't bloody believe it. Why didn't you show this to me yesterday, when the bloody paper came out?'

'Sorry. Thought you'd have seen it.'

'Can we stop it?'

'Not quickly enough, no. You might want to get online. The photos have been seriously doctored.'

'First St Giles and now this little bastard!'

'What's the deal with the game-show host?' asked DC Fry, in a tone so ingratiating it made Jessie want to hurl him across the room.

She turned to him. 'Tell Mark to come and ask me himself.'

Fry opened his mouth to protest as Trudi walked in. 'DI Driver, there's a young man to see you. I've put him in Jones' office.'

'Hang on, Trudi, I've got –'

'This is important and I don't think his nerve will hold for long.'

Jessie opened the door to Jones' redundant office. A handsome man of medium build was strapping on a shoulder pack. As Trudi had warned, he was doing a good impression of someone preparing to take flight.

'You going somewhere?' asked Jessie.

He looked around the office nervously. His hair was slicked back, he wore designer clothes but he looked scared. Jessie leant against the desk. 'Sit down,' she said gently. 'What can I do for you?'

He fell into the chair but remained silent.

'You told Trudi you had information about the deaths of Verity Shore and Eve Wirrel.'

He nodded. 'Can I talk to you in confidence?' He sounded well educated. Intelligent. But still scared.

'Well, that depends on what you are about to tell me. I'm not a priest, we sort of do the opposite with confessions here. But if you're scared or need protecting because of what you know, then I can help you.'

'I work for Ray St Giles.'

Jessie leant forward. 'Go on . . .'

'He hated Verity Shore for not going on his show. She refused to be a guest and he started

224

digging around to find some real dirt on her. And he did. I don't know what, but he was suddenly very full of himself. Did you see the job he did on her?'

'No, but I heard about it.'

'We worked round the clock to get that show together. He already had the information, all we needed to organise were the logistics. He knew about that house in Barnes – don't ask me how, but he did.'

'Do you have proof?'

'I copied these, from the files. He keeps them locked up, but I recently worked out where he hides the key.'

Jessie flicked through the information St Giles had compiled. There were pictures of Verity Shore meeting a man by a brick wall. She was handing over money. It could have been any drug-swap down any back alley, disused courtyard or empty car park. Jessie guessed Verity arranged to meet her dealer when she was out on her shopping sprees.

'Is it the house in Barnes?' asked Tarek.

She doubted it. Though there was a high garden wall, there would be no reason to make the swap outside, and Ray would have had to have been inside the house to get the picture. There was detailed information about Verity's antics at home with the boys, which according to Tarek's notes included Verity screeching around the house naked, threatening to pour boiling water over herself.

There was another photograph; black-and-white, like the rest. This time it was Verity Shore checking into a hotel with an older man who was clearly not P. J. Dean.

'Who's this?' Jessie asked, pointing to the man.

'No idea,' said Tarek.

'He looks familiar,' said Jessie.

'Well, she wasn't likely to shag any old bloke. He's probably somebody important.'

Jessie couldn't blame Verity for seeking solace elsewhere, but she also understood why P.J. had pushed his ruthlessly ambitious wife away. They should never have got together. Jessie knew from watching her brother and sister-in-law that making a marriage work was a full-time occupation. Verity and P.J. didn't even do it part-time. Here was yet more evidence that Verity was sleeping around. Could P.J. really be the only one who didn't know?

'Who gave Ray all this information?' she asked, holding up the file.

'Danny Knight, before he had his fifteen seconds on the programme. Ray made him out to be a blood-sucking arsehole. Mr Knight is furious, keeps ringing up saying Ray ruined his credibility and harmed his chances of landing a book deal.'

'Serves him right,' said Jessie.

'Mr Knight should watch out. Ray has a sidekick with a penchant for extracting information from people and then enforcing their silence. They all underestimate Ray. Don't make the same mistake.'

'What would happen if he thought you'd talked to me?'

Tarek didn't have to reply. The look in his eyes told her everything.

'We'll get copies, then you'd better get these back before Ray misses them.' Jessie looked Tarek in the eye. 'You should leave your job.'

'I'm working on it.'

'Will you be all right going back?'

'I think so. What will you do?'

'Well, Tarek, I need a little more than this. The police have to be very careful with people like Ray St Giles. Very careful.'

'You think I've got this wrong, watch tonight's show. He's doing a programme on Eve Wirrel.'

'I know. I saw his performance on the breakfast show yesterday,' said Jessie.

Tarek stood up and walked to the window, then he turned back to her. 'Yes, but how long has she been dead? He had one of her installations in the back of his car, in a box. It isn't there any more.'

'Proof?'

'I took a photo with the car-wash attendant holding up that day's paper, and I can bring you more. If that'll make you believe me.' Tarek handed over the picture. 'I had it blown up.'

Jessie looked up at him. 'Is that . . . ?'

'Nice, isn't it? Guess what it's called.'

Jessie waited. If it had anything to do with Cary Conrad, she'd never forgive herself.

'"Shit for Brains".' He laughed. 'Can you believe

227

it? She actually gets money for this.'

A lot of money, thought Jessie. More than the cable company could pay its presenters, if their offices were anything to go by.

'You know I went to see your boss about this already?'

'Did you?' He sounded surprised.

'Wasn't it you? In the car park, keeping a low profile. All bundled up in a cap and brown leather jacket.'

'Oh, no, you're talking about Alistair Gunner. He's Ray's research assistant. The one with the penchant for extracting information. He's certainly on the payroll, if you know what I mean. I'm sure they met in prison, which has done nothing to change either of them. Rumour is, Ray got away with many more killings than he went down for. And Alistair looks like a GBH man.'

Jessie's response was noncommittal.

'If you don't believe me, watch the Eve Wirrel programme. Then tell me Ray isn't the one gaining from all of this. Ambition is as good a motive as any. It's all about money in the end.'

'You really don't like your boss, do you?'

'He's a racist, murdering, chauvinist bully and, trust me, if *that* was my motive for coming to see you, I'd be in here all the time.'

~

The senior investigating officer, DCI Harris, was a man close to his fifties, with sparkling blue eyes and the manner of an East End lad on the make. Jessie liked him immediately, not least because he had bothered to inform her personally that Cary Conrad was dead. Though the body had been discovered on his patch, he wanted to form a joint investigation following the recent deaths of Verity Shore and Eve Wirrel. Such collaboration was rare in a field where statistics kept departments separate.

Jessie walked up the uneven stone steps of the listed house and was immediately taken to the basement. She didn't need long down there. They retreated to the living room and sat on a velvet sofa surrounded by reproductions of pre-Raphaelite paintings.

'The woman who called us turned out to be his missus,' said Harris. 'Cary Conrad kept her and the kids hidden from his public. Bloody disgrace, if you ask me. Thought his fans wouldn't like him if he didn't come across all camp and queer. The mind boggles.'

Jessie nodded while she looked through the autopsy report on Cary Conrad.

'Ever watch his show?'

'No.'

'*Supermarket Sweep* sort of thing, apparently. The housewives love him.'

'Sir, you know that Verity Shore and Eve Wirrel both had a major artery cut. But not Conrad.'

'Yeah, but like Eve Wirrel, there is no trace of

another person and no forced entry. This could easily have been made to look like a kinky game gone wrong or suicide, and he is a celebrity.'

She'd told Harris about the painting hidden behind Eve Wirrel's wall and he'd shown her another secret door, a trap door. Into the underbelly of fame.

'Eve Wirrel was drugged. Conrad's bloodwork is clear,' said Jessie.

'So was Verity Shore's, wasn't it?'

'I wouldn't say clear, more like addled. But you're right, there was nothing that would have put her out like Eve Wirrel.'

'Because only Eve Wirrel died in a public place. She had to be kept quiet. And there are burns on Conrad's wrists and ankles, suggesting he struggled for at least a few minutes.' Jessie thought of the black-and-white picture above Eve's bed.

'My guess is,' continued Harris, 'Cary Conrad didn't usually get that close.'

It was an unimaginable way to die. 'How's his wife?' asked Jessie.

'Beside herself, naturally. Thinks her husband has been murdered.'

'Any history of fetishism?'

'No. But, as I'm sure you know, the spouse is always the last to find out. Not that I'm speaking from experience, mind.'

'I'll have to take your word for it, sir.'

'So what do you think?'

'Let's compare notes, but I should tell you, I

230

have very little at the moment.'

'Now, now, Driver, don't say that. I hear you are a woman of exceptional talents.' It took Jessie several seconds to realise he wasn't being sarcastic.

'So, are we a team, DI Driver?' Harris held out his hand. Jessie took it. 'Good, because I am sure these deaths are linked.'

Jessie pulled out the photograph that she had taken from Tarek. It was the Eve Wirrel head. Harris frowned. 'Is that . . . ?'

'Yes. Another choice offering from Eve Wirrel. I didn't know she worked with human faeces until today.'

'Another link?'

Jessie shrugged. 'It's possible. We're still looking for Verity Shore's head. But I think we should keep this information to ourselves.'

'Too right, or we'll have a panic on our hands. Every bit-part actor from *The Bill* will be begging for protection. You know those types – Jesus, do they have an inflated sense of their own importance!'

~

Ray St Giles smiles for the cameras, his pale blue eyes glistening in the spotlights. 'Good evening and welcome to *Today with Ray*. Eve Wirrel, the daughter of Sir Edward and Lady Fitz-Williams – landed gentry, ladies and gentlemen –' he winks, then continues: 'is dead. The art world, usually a dour bunch, are split down the middle. Did she take her own life or did someone take it for her? Do they mourn the loss of this young talent or celebrate her bravery? You know me, audience, I'm a fairly straight-down-the-line kinda guy and, the thing is, I don't have a clue what these art buffs have been talking about. We did a poll down the local shopping centre and it turns out that not a lot of you get it either. We showed people pictures of well-known contemporary pieces to get a feel of what the nation thinks about all this modern art.'

The face of Ray St Giles splits into a thousand squares and melts away. The Bluewater Shopping Centre appears on the screen.

'Here in the studio, we have replicas of the pieces of art we were showing to the shoppers.'

The first offering – a mannequin with a female top half and male bottom half and a stack of raw beef on its head – is greeted with a collective groan from the audience. Next comes a fish bowl. The preserved goldfish are stuck to the outside. There is a giant cotton reel and a tiny button, a grey canvas with an off-centre orange square painted on it. There are others, but the real eye-catcher is the seven pairs of soiled Y-fronts.

St Giles smiles at the camera. 'We couldn't get the female staff to give up their own possessions, but our dedicated technical lads were all willing, with promises of many beers after the show, to donate their own masterpieces for the sake of art.

This is the Ray St Giles version of "A Particularly Heavy Week" by the late, great, Eve Wirrel . . .'

Jessie watched the footage of the shoppers: some grimaced, others laughed, one man berated the waste of tax-payers' money and one pretty young girl eloquently denounced the lottery as a poor man's tax which was being spent on wealthy men's excesses.

'Actress,' said Tarek, who had returned to the station to watch the programme with Jessie. 'Notice, no sign of Shit for Brains? You think this is bad,' he said, seeing her face, 'wait for the next bit.'

St Giles is introducing an 'expert'. A Mr Bloomberg.

'Mr Bloomberg, please explain to us mere mortals the importance of these works which sold collectively for £7.2 million, £4 million of which came from the National Lottery.'

'Well, first and foremost, we must conclude that their importance is being demonstrated by you, right now, in the very fact that you are debating them on national television. Art of this calibre is indefatigable. It lends balance and purpose to a sometimes naïve world. It reflects this naïvety, yet at the same time repels it.'

'Yes, Mr Bloomberg, but what does that *mean*?'

A titter escapes from the audience.

'It means that these pieces reflect us, society.'

'Because we are naïve?'

'Sometimes?' Mr Bloomberg smiles. He is being enigmatic. The scholars like that.

St Giles walks up to the mannequin. 'So, what the artist is saying here is that if we eat beef we may turn into a lady-boy?'

'Ha, ha, ha, ha, haaaaaa. No. Of course not.'

'So what then?'

'Jez Tamoikay, the creator of the original, takes everyday objects and belittles them through an action. You have to look back over his work to fully comprehend where he is going. This piece is proclaiming that promiscuity, the routine and non-sensical coupling of male and female bodies, will produce a germ in society that consumes as well as nourishes the growing fascination with sex. In this case, the germ is beef, its sickness reflected in the capitalist, anti-environmental world of the franchised fast-food chain and, of course, human vCJD. It is not clear where he lays the blame, only that it is cause and effect.'

'Oh,' says St Giles. 'I see now. Thank you, Mr Bloomberg, for explaining that so clearly. And what of Eve Wirrel's work?'

'She liked to shock.'

'And?'

'Well, as a nation we are renowned for our reserve, our predisposition to shy away from all that is considered overt, demonstrative, explicit. Yet we scour the tabloids for titbits and tantalising tales. I think she was merely playing on that.'

'So rumours that she was a talentless exhibitionist are unfounded?'

'Absolutely. No one can deny that her mind was
a creative nucleus and her talent as an artist was
the vessel for such thinking.'

Ray frowns. 'Eve Wirrel. Did she jump or was
she pushed? After the break, meet our next guest,
Eve's old art teacher. Perhaps she can shed some
light on the creative nucleus that was Eve Wirrel.'

'Where does he find these people?' said Jessie, mut-
ing the TV for the commercial break. It was habit.
She did it at home. If television companies jacked
up the volume for adverts, she would rebel by mut-
ing them. Volume control was key.

'He hasn't even shown any remorse that the
woman is dead.'

'That's because he doesn't care, so long as he
gets noticed. He knew how she had died before
the press did, I'm telling you, he knew.'

'How does he get all this information?' asked
Jessie.

Tarek shrugged. 'If you follow someone long
enough, you'll discover their weaknesses. If Ray
isn't behind this, then who is? A madman? A
grieved starlet? It's too contrived for that.'

Jessie turned to Niaz. 'What do you think?'

'He is very chippy, isn't he? He resents everyone who has become any form of public figure.
But he is ignorant and our killer is clever. He made
a barbed comment about Eve's parents, but

everyone knows that anyone with the name Fitz is no more than the descendant of an illegitimate offspring of the king. Hardly something to be proud of. These murders are graphic but subtle, too subtle for the likes of Ray St Giles.'

'Don't be fooled, he got two masters degrees and a doctorate while in the nick. One of those was in social history, the other was in mathematics. He isn't the thick thug you think he is. I told you, don't underestimate him,' said Tarek.

Burrows knocked on the door. 'Can I have a word?'

Jessie left Tarek and Niaz watching the television.

'Who's that?' asked Burrows. Jessie explained Tarek's fears and told him about the dossiers St Giles had on Verity Shore and Eve Wirrel. It was possible Cary Conrad was in the files too, Tarek had only glimpsed them and couldn't remember. Burrows dismissed her theory. 'He's spent nine years in the nick, why would he want to go back there?'

'Because maybe he doesn't think he will. You and I both know that we cannot put an accurate time on either of the deaths. We have no witnesses, no real motive, it would be hard to prove anything beyond reasonable doubt right now. These killings are all about planning. Tarek says St Giles has information on people, and he's certainly had the time to plan. Nine years of educating himself and learning every trick in the book.'

'But why, boss?'

She didn't know why, she couldn't even imagine why, and that was the weakness in her argument.

'Do you want to know what the boys think?' asked Burrows. Jessie nodded. 'Forget Cary Conrad. He drowned in his own shit, we've seen worse fetishes than that.'

'His death reflects a vice, like the others, and he kept his wife hidden. She was the secret. And then there are the properties. All listed buildings.'

'Come on, ma'am. If you manipulate anything enough, it will fit the profile.'

'The sperm-bank joke I can handle, the strap-on even, but that I find insulting.'

Burrows was not in an apologetic mood. 'I spoke to a mate who works for Harris. They're going through Conrad's computer, and they must be pretty sure they'll find something otherwise they wouldn't go to that expense. His private secretary, a bloke, seems to have gone on extended leave and forgotten to leave a forwarding address. Cary Conrad is confusing the issue. The issue is P. J. Dean. It's the only answer. In fact, we were wondering why you hadn't brought him in.'

Jessie crossed her arms and looked away.

'He's got the money,' said Burrows. 'And his drug addict, money-spending wife was shagging Eve Wirrel. Public humiliation was on the cards, and possibly the loss of those boys you say he cares so much about.'

Jessie looked at Burrows. 'I hear you – I do – but I don't think he did it.'

'Then why not bring him in?'

'I'd rather get a court order and have a look at Ray St Giles' files.'

'You're not serious . . .'

The door to the office opened. It was Niaz. 'Ray's on again,' he said.

'We have to talk about this, ma'am.'

Niaz remained in the doorway.

'Later,' pleaded Burrows.

Jessie looked over her shoulder. 'I'm doing *Crime Watch*. We'll talk tomorrow.'

Then she returned to the TV and watched as Ray St Giles tore Eve Wirrel apart.

~

Brown nylon carpet crackled against her sensible, rubber-soled shoes. Every brushed-aluminium door handle was the perfect conductor for the electricity she was gathering as she followed the neat little arse of the production assistant. Another spark erupted from the end of her finger.

'Nervous?' asked the twenty-year-old TV doll clutching a clipboard.

Crime Watch. Live audience. Nick Ross. 'No,' said Jessie. I'm *fucking* nervous. I'm so fucking nervous I'm generating wattage.

'Wait here, I'll come and get you when they're ready. You can watch the programme in here, but keep the volume down.' Jessie took a pair of high-heeled boots out of her bag. The TV doll looked her up and down. 'It is detective inspector, isn't it?'

Jessie's eyes narrowed. 'That's what it says on my badge.'

The girl bounced out of the room, taking her customised combat trousers and pink trainers with her. Was Jessie getting older or was everyone getting younger? Cockier? And better dressed? Jessie ran her fingers through her hair, it was sticky with the make-up artist's hairspray. She changed into the boots that would lift her to the commanding height of 5'11" and waited, trying to remember to breathe. Eventually she was shown on to the set. Foreign only in its familiarity. Nick Ross was summing up Eve Wirrel's murder. As promised, he had not mentioned Verity Shore or Cary Conrad; Jessie didn't want to fan Ray St Giles' fire. '. . . And here is Detective Inspector Driver from West End Central CID.'

'Good evening. Eve Wirrel went to Richmond Park some time last Wednesday, we believe with her killer. They ate a rudimentary picnic, hidden in which was the drug Rohypnol. Having fallen unconscious, Eve was left in the Isabella Plantation to die. We want to hear from anyone who was in the park who may have seen her. And we would also like to talk to a cyclist who was in the area early on Friday, October 11th, at around six a.m.'

'You have a map to show the viewers where she may have been?'

'Yes.' Jessie turned to the board behind her, then remembered that this wasn't a briefing room and turned back. She stood like a weather girl, pointing out Eve's house, where she was found, and the routes victim and murderer might have taken.

'You also want to talk to any models that posed for her.'

'Eve was working on a collection of drawings of men when she died. We are asking those we have not yet contacted to call the number at the bottom of the screen – in confidence, of course – so we can eliminate them from our enquiries.'

'So, to recap,' said the presenter, 'if you were in Richmond Park on Wednesday the fifteenth, or have modelled for the artist, please call this number. Now, over to Fiona for an update –'

'Going to camera two,' said the voice in Jessie's ear. 'Five, four, three, two, one. You're off air.'

Nick Ross turned to Jessie. 'Very good. If you weren't a copper, I'd worry about my job.' He smiled and turned away. The TV doll appeared from behind a mess of wires and cameras and beckoned her over. Jessie breathed a sigh of relief. She could go home and shake alone.

Maggie jumped up from the low sofa in the reception area of the BBC building and hugged her.

'You were brilliant! Really, you came across so calm, so Poirot.'

Jessie peeled the identity sticker off her leather jacket and screwed it up between her fingers. 'You're sweet for coming. Take me somewhere and get me very pissed now.'

'You didn't look nervous at all. That Nick Ross couldn't take his eyes off you. Honestly, you'll be after my job next.'

'Not enough entrails in your line of work,' said Jessie as they were bundled through the revolving door and out into the purple-tinted London night sky. 'I want martinis and I want many.'

'Let's go to Claridge's, live it up a little. After all, it's your second TV appearance in a week. We'll get some sucker businessman to pay – with all that studio make-up and the tight suit, you could be a professional.'

'Why do I know you're not talking about a lawyer or a doctor –'

'Or a copper. Jessie Driver, a fucking detective inspector, on the telly, solving murders like she said she would. I can't believe you've done it, can you?'

'No,' said Jessie honestly, as she hailed a cab. She hadn't done anything yet.

The heads of blood-red roses filled the low, square vases, the leather seat swallowed her and the candles reflected a thousand flames in the cut-glass deco mirrors that hung on the wall. A skinny waiter arrived with the second round of vodka martinis.

'I'm only just beginning to feel normal,' said

Jessie, lifting the glass to her lips with a steady hand. 'I don't know how you do that every day and live. It's terrifying.'

'From the girl who'd wrestle an axe-wielding homicidal maniac to the floor. Cheers. Now don't look round, but there is a man at the bar who keeps looking over, and after surreptitiously studying him I am reluctant to report that it is you he is ogling like a bloodhound and not me or my L'Oreal hair.'

'I thought you were over that?'

'Only temporarily. Wait until I'm really famous – I'll make sure Joshua Cadell never types a word again. As for his mother, she makes me look like an amateur. She only went and used all the information about my new programme on France to get herself in it. She called up the producer and told him it was my idea, so I can't even be pissed off. She's a pro. I'll be stuck with them both for a week.'

'Don't you think it's weird, that Joshua goes everywhere with his mother?'

'If you're only ever going to be known as one thing, you may as well get used to it and cash in.'

'Which is?'

'Dame Henrietta Cadell's son. Oh my God, he's coming over.'

'Who?'

'The man from the bar.'

Jessie mouthed the word 'no' but it was too late. Maggie gave him her TV personality smile and reeled him in.

'Look, I'm very sorry to disturb you, I don't normally do this but, um . . .' He looked at Jessie. 'Did I just see you on *Crime Watch*?'

'Yes, you did,' said Maggie.

'Thought so. That's so weird, you look exactly the same.'

'Incredible, isn't it?' said Maggie maliciously. The man did not seem to notice.

'It's an amazing case. I mean, it's huge.'

Jessie took a protracted sip of martini and nearly choked.

'Policemen don't normally look like you,' he said.

'Except in Bangkok,' said Maggie. Jessie kicked her.

'My mates won't believe this. We were in the office watching you. I mean, you know, *Crime Watch* . . . Well, it's good to see it, just in case. Anyway, could I have your autograph?'

Maggie spat out her drink and howled with laughter. 'Autograph! Autograph – Jesus, I would have been less shocked if you'd asked her for a quick one in the gents. Sorry, my friend doesn't give autographs.' She turned to Jessie: 'Do you?'

Jessie shook her head then looked at the now crimson man. 'Sorry. It's police procedure.'

He backed off. 'Of course, sorry. Good luck, I hope you catch him.'

'Who?'

'The Z-list Killer.'

'The who?'

'Oh, there are some gags, you know, going around the internet. Anyway, sorry to disturb you. Bye.'

'Bye,' said Jessie. 'The Z-list Killer – I mean, really.'

'I told you,' said Maggie dramatically. 'It's gripping the nation.' She watched the man return to the bar. 'I can't believe it. He didn't even recognise me.'

~

Irene stood on the breezeblock and banged on the door.

'Clare! Open up! I know you're in there!'

A window opened further down the passageway. 'Oi, do you mind! Some people are trying to sleep.'

'Sorry. I'm worried about Clare. Have you seen her?'

'You the filth?'

'Do I look like the frigging police?'

'Some copper came round. We haven't seen her since. We was thinking she'd been arrested.'

'Clare? Don't be thick.'

'Well then, why hasn't she been in to see the old lady next door but one? Relies on Clare, that woman does.'

'You could do it.'

'Not my business, darling.' The man pulled his fat head back inside the window. Irene knelt at the letter box. 'Clare, sweetheart, it's me, Irene. Open the door.' She rummaged in her large, soft leather handbag. 'Right, I'm calling the police. Nine, nine, n—'

Clare appeared in the doorframe at the end of the short hallway. Irene had known that if she was still breathing she wouldn't want anyone wasting the emergency services on her. Clare felt very strongly about that. She wasn't to know that Irene didn't even have a mobile phone.

'That's right, love, open the door.'

Clare opened the door.

'Jesus, love, what's happened?'

'Frank's dead.'

'What?' Irene pushed the stationary Clare back inside and closed the door, put an arm round her and led her to the sitting room. A video of an early Ray St Giles' show was playing silently on the telly. Irene ignored it. There was a solitary dent on the seat cushion. Clare returned to exactly the same spot, sinking lower than she had before. Irene noticed a layer of dust on the faux-mahogany side table. More on the windowsill. Dust eddied in the shaft of light, it was the only thing that moved – that and St Giles, silent on the screen. Time had stopped for Clare Mills. 'I'll make us some tea and you can tell me what's happened.'

Irene poured a hefty amount of whiskey in the tea, added several spoonsful of sugar and brought a duvet back with her. She prised Clare's elbows off her knees and put the duvet over them instead. Clare held the mug with two hands. Unsteady. Childish.

'I'm going to turn this off, sweetheart. It's not helping.'

'He killed my family, Irene. That man killed my family, and there he is, laughing at me.' She looked up at Irene. 'He should have killed me too.'

'Don't talk like that.'

'Why not? He left me here, clinging on to the hope that I would find Frank, and now I know he is dead. What was it all for? Those years of being strong. Pretending I could cope.'

'Tell me about Frank. What happened?'

'That policeman came. He was ever so upset, worried he'd given me too much hope. We went to Sunderland, see, met a man. He was ever so nice. We both did DNA tests. Course he isn't my brother. Frank is dead. I have been fooling myself for too long.'

'So, wait, the policeman didn't tell you he was dead? You don't know for definite?'

'I know –' she pointed to her chest – 'in here. He's dead. 'Cause if he wasn't, we'd have found each other.'

'Sweetheart, he probably doesn't know he had a sister. He may be a completely different person to you.'

'No, Irene. I am a good person. Mum and Dad, they were good people. Frank would have been good too. No one can find him.' She stood up and walked to the kitchen. The five names, written in black marker pen on white card, were still up on the wall.

She ripped the first one off the wall. 'Stewart – returned to mother, aged six.'

She grabbed the second. 'Prison. He was born in Ireland.'

The third. 'Clive. Living in Sunderland, parents unknown, no DNA match.'

The fourth. 'This poor blighter killed himself. Illegitimate son of a priest and a prostitute.'

The last, fifth and final. 'Gareth Blake. Died aged four. Caught some disease a year after being taken into care. Could have been Frank, I suppose. Never traced his parents. But Frank was a healthy boy when they took him. Care was an evil place, but they didn't like us to die on them, looked bad. Meant people came checking. We were always taken to a doctor at any sign of a cough. They wanted us nice and healthy for their dirty ways.'

Irene put her arm round Clare's thin shoulders. 'I'm so sorry. I should have taken you in myself.'

Clare turned to her. 'Both of us?'

'Of course. That's what I meant. I should have taken you both in.'

'Thanks, Irene, you've been a good friend. Mum was lucky to have you.'

~

Her team may have thought she was mad, but the magistrate was easier to convince: he had given her the search warrant straight away. Ray St Giles opened the door for Jessie. The team she had hand-picked for the job – Burrows, Fry, and another PC – stood behind her. Ray St Giles smiled.

'Back so soon, Detective Inspector?'

'I have a warrant to search these premises,' Jessie stated. Ray St Giles did not take the papers she proffered him.

'Look, luv, I know bent coppers, and you aren't one of them. I don't need to go over your paper-work, do I? Wouldn't mind going –'

'That's enough, Giles,' said Burrows, stepping forward.

'St Giles to you.'

'I don't think so.'

Jessie began to direct her team through the series of interconnecting Portakabins that made up the St Giles empire. It wasn't much. Thin blue nylon carpet. A punctured soundproof ceiling on a grid of weak metal rods. Cheap office furniture. The whole thing vibrated with the footfalls of searching policemen. She knew exactly where to look, of course, but played out the 'search', open-ing every drawer and cupboard until she reached the filing cabinet that Tarek had told her about. It was locked. As she knew it would be.

'Keys, please,' said Jessie.

Ray St Giles threw them at her. She caught them left-handed. He smirked. It made her feel stupid. She knew what she was going to find in that cabinet from the look on his face. She opened it. Nothing.

'Rather big piece of furniture to keep in these, well, let's be honest, fairly cramped offices.'

'You're right. I've been on to the company to move it. We've no need for it in here. Having said that, I'm not planning on being in these offices long.'

'Who works here?'

Ray St Giles shook his head. 'Okay, Detective Inspector, if you want to go through that charade. I have a production assistant called Tarek Khan, a good boy, a hard worker. You'd like him, Driver. I have a research assistant, a lad called Alistair Gunner. He's new. Prepared to work for shit just to be in TV, but, hey, that's not my problem. There are others – the receptionist, the secretaries, the make-up girls – but they don't come down here much.'

Jessie remembered the girl on her knees. 'Can't imagine why.'

There wasn't much point, but she carried on searching the premises until she had looked from wall to pre-fab wall. Still nothing. Ray St Giles had known she was coming. It made her worried for Tarek. She wondered where he was.

The window glass was protected by a wire mesh. Outside, a slender man stood in the courtyard. He turned away when he saw Jessie looking.

'Make you feel at home, does it, Mr St Giles?' She nodded towards the window-guard.

'I have served my time, Detective Inspector. Are

you so short of evidence that you have to start harassing old-timers?'

'Just routine enquiries.'

'Routine, my arse. Go away, DI Driver. Go back to your desk and your theories and start again. Bad girl, you go to the bottom of the class. I expected more from you.'

Jessie bristled. 'The cable company can't afford to pay you much, can they?'

Ray picked up a cigarette and lit it.

'You've got a nice house, though. North London, too. It must be worth, what, a million now?' said Jessie, one eye on the lad skulking in the courtyard.

Ray St Giles walked over to where Jessie stood and put a hand firmly in the middle of her back. He pushed her away from the window, a steady, firm push, that directed her to the door. Burrows moved in.

'Down, boy,' said Ray St Giles. 'No need to get heavy, but I think we have concluded our business here, haven't we?'

Jessie nodded for the men to move out of the room.

'You haven't asked me why I'm here,' said Jessie, feeling Ray's hand conduct uncomfortable heat through her leather jacket.

He put his mouth next to her ear. 'I don't have to,' whispered St Giles.

Jessie turned to face him, but Ray put his index finger up to her mouth. 'I care about my career,

DI Driver. I care about it very much. People protect the things they care about. I suggest you do the same.'

'Are you threatening me?'

Ray laughed. 'You've been reading too many of those gangster books. Threatening you, that's very old hat. No, just offering you some career advice. What are you, thirty-two, thirty-three? You must be ambitious. Wouldn't want a harassment charge against your name, would you? Death to a copper, that is, in these oh-so-sensitive times.' He showed her the door and began to close it. She watched him through the narrowing gap. 'Then again, Detective . . .' he said, as the door closed and the flimsy aluminium frame shuddered.

Burrows put his hand on her shoulder. She jumped.

'News from Niaz. He's found your boat.'

Jessie took her bike. It was quicker, and this she wanted to see. At last the much-criticised search of the river had revealed the first solid clue for two, possibly three murders. She had been wrong about the tunnels. They were a red herring. One that had successfully sent her down into dank, disused burrows while the answer lay, like Verity, on the mud all along. But not on the same shore. The opposite shore. That was clever. Jessie never thought the murderer would cross the river. It seemed too dangerous. She'd only been searching the south side. But now, thinking about it, with nothing suspicious on board, how risky was it to cross to the other side, if you weren't afraid of the river itself?

The boat was a punt. Like the rower Nick Elliot had said it would be. It had a flat stern and a shallow draw. Perfect for slipping up and down the mud flats. Jessie reached the river just as the crane was lifting the boat out. Silt-laden water ran through a gaping hole that had been punched in its base. The evidence had been scuttled. Laid to rest in the deeper channel between the north bank and the Richmond Eyot. Hundreds of people walked along this stretch of the river at low tide. The murderer's footprints would have merged with the rest until the next high tide brushed the bank smooth again. Richmond. A nice touch. It wasn't a riddle. It was a reminder.

P. J. Dean wouldn't have gone through all this just to get rid of an errant wife. These murders had the hallmarks of a more sinister motive. If P.J. had wanted Verity dead, all he had to do was give her an overdose. Even if Eve was a thorn in his side, she would be hard pushed to tarnish his good name. Yes, he had strange domestic arrangements, but what famous musician didn't? It wasn't enough to make him a murderer. Not of this calibre. This had been planned. For months, maybe years. So who? Who resented Verity Shore's, Eve Wirrel's and Cary Conrad's celebrity status enough to kill? What could their deaths achieve?

The crane swung the boat round and began to

lower it over the waiting tow-truck. It spat brown water at the on-lookers. There was paint on the side of it. A name. Jessie got closer. The remnants of a name, in green letters. T/T: Tender To . . . The rest had been scratched out. Jessie was determined to find out which larger vessel this boat had belonged to. Who had bought it? Who had sold it? Who had made it, and when? She gave her list of requests to the forensic team and returned to her bike. At last she had something to tell Jones. She'd have to give him the bad news too: Ray St Giles was on to them.

Jessie was spread over the sofa like margarine. It had been a lousy week. Ray St Giles was on her case and the boat was proving hard to trace. They had found evidence in the house in Barnes, even extracted DNA and traced it to known drug dealers. Two were behind bars at the time of the murder and one was abroad. They had several other, unidentified strands of DNA, but nothing that matched evidence picked up at the wood, the church, or Cary Conrad's house.

Maggie came in with a plate of Marmite on toast and two cups of tea. 'It wasn't as bad as I thought it was going to be,' she said, feeding Jessie. 'Henrietta is a dominating old cow, but Joshua isn't bad, once you get to know him.'

'Hm . . .'

'If only his mother didn't suffocate him. She suffocates everyone – it's all about her, her, her. Everyone conveniently forgot it was supposed to be my show. I tell you, she's a bitch. I soon found a way to piss her off, though.'

'What did you do?' asked Jessie, spilling crumbs down her front.

'Flirted with her son, of course. It was quite hilarious to watch. Any time I went anywhere near him, she would appear in a puff of Opium. She has everyone eating out of her hand as if she were royalty, but the truth is she's just some wizened old woman with an Oedipus complex.' Maggie shuddered. 'Joshua has quite a reputation with the women, so I don't think the feeling is mutual.'

'Is there a Mr Cadell?'

'Oh yes, Christopher, he used to be a documentary-maker until he was eclipsed by his wife. Henrietta says he is very busy, no one knows in what though. They are still together, but rumour is he also likes the ladies. Poor old Henrietta, looks like she keeps getting left out. No wonder she writes such gruesome books about sex and murder. All historically accurate, of course,' she mimicked. 'She told me that Ray St Giles murdered more people than he went down for.'

Jessie sat up. She'd heard those words before.

'That got your attention. Henrietta said that he murdered two women, prostitutes, who worked in his club. She's been doing research on it. She wants

254

to know how a man like that gets his own show. She absolutely hates him.'

'She's not alone.' Jessie rubbed her eyes. 'If she hates him so much, why go on his show?'

'Oh, she didn't decide she hated him until afterwards. It was a chance to promote the book, so she took it. You would have thought a woman that famous didn't have to worry about sales, but no, she and her entourage go around the country to bookshops, radio stations – she does the works. I've always told you, success is no accident.'

Jessie lay back down on the sofa. Ray St Giles and two prostitutes. Well, that changed things. Maybe he'd had them killed, maybe he was still having people killed, maybe there was a history between Gunner and St Giles . . .

Maggie hit Jessie's leg. 'Wake up, we're going out.'

Jessie groaned. Maggie stood up. 'Come on, get your arse in gear. You're not getting out of this one. We've got something to celebrate.'

Jessie raised a tired eyebrow.

'That job I was up for. I got it!'

Jessie sat up in a spurt of energy. 'Well done. I said you were fabulous.'

Maggie smiled. 'Thank God we spent all those evenings in, practising on bananas. No, Jessie, don't lie down again . . .'

'Okay, okay, give me . . .' a few moments, I'll get myself sorted right now, I'm . . . Shit! It's my brother's birthday, must call him.

'Give you what?' Maggie stood over her.

'What?'

'You're doing that thing again, drifting off in mid-sentence.'

'Oh, sorry. I'm knackered. Everyone thinks I should arrest P. J. Dean, bring him in for questioning.'

'You can't do that. Women around the world will be up in arms.'

Jessie sat up. 'Maggie, you won't tell –'

'My lips are sealed. As always. Peel yourself out of those obscenely tight leather trousers, get in the bath, then let's go and party.'

'Put so delicately, how could I resist?' Jessie heaved herself off the sofa and went to the phone. 'Get ready to sing,' she said to Maggie. 'It's Colin's birthday.'

'Hello?'

Jessie prodded Maggie and they began to sing Happy Birthday. Badly.

'What an aria,' said Colin.

'Have you had a nice day?'

'Great. The girls brought me sugary lukewarm coffee and soggy toast at five thirty this morning.'

'Oh, sweet.'

'Yes. Adorable. How's Bill?'

'Amazing, as always. Working in dire conditions with more good nature than is actually human. We're thinking of going down the Nile on his next break – what do you think?'

'I think you'd better discuss it with my wife.

Why don't you come up for the weekend? The kids would love to see you.'

'I can't. Sorry.'

'They want a word, let them down gently.'

'JESSSEEEEE,' came the two shrieking voices down the line. 'We're making a tepee in the garden with Dad's old shirts,' said Charlotte.

'That's a wigwam, if you didn't know,' said Ellie.

Moving over to the window, she asked them both in turn what they had given their dad for his birthday. Ellie, the older, was in the middle of describing the Bob the Builder sweatshirt she had chosen for Colin when Jessie pulled the curtain back absentmindedly. Something on the street made her jump. Not something, somebody. Watching.

'Talk to Maggie,' she said, thrusting the phone into Maggie's hand and running to her bedroom. Without turning the light on, she looked out of the window again. Nothing. She looked up and down the street. No one. Her eyes were playing tricks on her. It was Ray St Giles. He'd got her spooked. Exactly as he wanted her to be. Damn him and his liquid eyes.

Maggie was holding up a stunning black dress with spaghetti diamanté straps when Jessie returned to the sitting room.

'Bloody hell,' said Jessie. Maggie turned it round. It had no back and one big label. 'Armani? Did you get a pay rise?'

'Sort of. I like to think of it as a bonus.' She grinned wickedly. 'I went on a photo shoot for *Glamour* magazine – girls on the box, that sort of thing. Anyway, this amazing article of clothing happened to fall into my bag.'

'Maggie . . .'

'Honestly, I've no idea how it got there. I think you should wear it.'

'Me?'

'Come on, P. J. Dean might be there.'

'I doubt it. His wife was recently dipped in acid, he probably isn't in a party mood.'

'From what I hear, that marriage was a sham. Like everything else these days. Now come on, don't be a spoilsport.'

'I can't, that's stolen property.'

'Please get over yourself and put it on.'

Jessie couldn't resist. 'What about you?'

'Funny thing that, some other stuff fell into my bag.' Maggie held up a white leather trouser suit.

'Ouch.'

'It calls for vodka,' said Maggie. 'And if anyone asks, your sugar daddy dressed us.'

When they left the flat an hour later, Jessie scanned the street in both directions. There was no one in sight. Nevertheless, before climbing into their waiting taxi, she did a quick sprint to the tree where she thought she had seen someone. On the pavement was a barely smoked white-tipped cigarette, half of which was squashed flat against the York stone. Using a plastic food bag from her handbag, she picked it up and wrapped it. Instinct and polythene bags. These were the tools of her trade and she never left home without them.

~

Tarek locked the door of the Portakabin and pulled his jacket closer around him. He'd stayed late organising job interviews for himself once the others had gone. Ray had been cheerful all day, the Eve Wirrel show had been a hit. The phones were beginning to ring with legitimate stories of 'stars' behaving atrociously, erratically, obscenely. The gloves were off. These people couldn't hide any more. Tarek hoped the police would move quickly, otherwise Ray would become too big to stop.

For some reason, Alistair didn't seem to be enjoying Ray's meteoric rise. He never smiled. In fact, he seemed even more withdrawn. He had hung around the office until an hour ago. Tarek was fast becoming more nervous of Alistair than he was of Ray. Avoiding the rain-filled potholes, he walked through the car park and pushed the chicken wire gate open. The new job couldn't come fast enough. Tarek was hungry, he decided to stop for a kebab before walking home. It was hours past dinner time.

~

The French fashion house L'Epoch had tented over Bedford Square. Jessie stood back as the flashbulbs popped for Maggie. It was always a freakish moment, Jessie thought, the sudden activity, the rush of men with enlarged lenses, jabbing and straining against the flimsy barrier between them and their catch. Who was preying on whom, Jessie was never sure.

'Maggie! Maggie, over here! Maggie! Lovely . . .'

Jessie watched her flatmate pose and smile, flick her long thick hair and lift her chin. She counted to five and watched Maggie move. It was always five. Maggie said there was a threat of overshoot if you stayed for longer. They destroyed the ones who wanted it at any cost.

They handed in their invites and immediately got caught in a bottleneck. Like cattle to the slaughter, skinny women and men in Gucci rolled their eyes and dug in their heels as they fought the push of the crowd. No one wanted to be first into the empty tent. The guests and the staff eyed each other across the expanse of seagrass. Maggie grabbed Jessie's hand.

'Stop fiddling with that dress, you look great. Don't let go of me and don't catch anyone's eye. If we break through now, we'll be first to the bar.'

They ducked through the madding crowd and hobbled in the direction of the bar. A barman handed them shot glasses suspended in crucibles of crushed ice. They saluted each other, and threw the flavoured vodka down their throats.

'Watch them come,' said Maggie, looking back as the jostling pack of guests suddenly split apart and spread like tentacles towards the various bars. 'Sheep.'

Jessie needed more vodka. 'Another one?'

'Absolutely,' said Maggie, her eyes scanning the room. Suddenly she turned her back on the room. 'Shit!'

'What? Who is it?'

'Cosima Broome. Let's get out of here.'

'Too late, she's coming over.'

The girl was surrounded by a horde of inbred men, all vying for her attention, pecking at her like feeding chickens. Maggie decided to make a run for it just as Cosima looked over in their direction. Their eyes locked for a second and both froze. Then, like a DVD resuming play, without a flicker, Cosima turned back to the men and Maggie bolted into the open arms of Dame Henrietta Cadell. No one had noticed. Except Jessie. She was trained to notice things like that. Not so dissimilar to the gossip-mongers, she thought, following her flatmate across a world of riches safely protected under a twinkling night sky. Artificial, like everything beneath it.

The celebrated queen of literati greeted Maggie with a barbed comment about her 'getting around', but Maggie smiled through the insult. Jessie wondered what would happen if someone stood up to the old trout. Told her a few home truths about her disgraceful lack of manners, her terrible lack of taste and her general disregard for anyone other than herself. She'd probably wither, like all good bullies.

'You don't like her, do you?'

Jessie turned round, startled.

'I'm Josh. We met at the film party.'

'Sorry, I was miles away,' said Jessie.

'It's okay, I don't mind. She's an acquired taste, I suppose.'

'Honestly, I was thinking about . . .' She paused. 'She is a bit overbearing, I suppose.'

Joshua smiled. It completely changed his face. 'Honesty! A rare commodity in these parts.'

'Well, thankfully, I don't inhabit these parts.'

'No. You've wandered a little off your patch, Detective Inspector.'

Jessie was taken aback. Her professional title always jarred in social environments. She looked over to Maggie; the girl was incapable of keeping her mouth shut.

'I saw your press conference.'

'Oh. Well, I –'

'Sorry, I didn't mean to embarrass you. It's just that I'm impressed. Models, actresses, presenters, I meet many of those, all dull, self-obsessed, ineffectual women who talk only about themselves. When I first saw you, I thought there was something different about you. Now I know why. God, I'm gushing. Sorry.'

Jessie suppressed a smile. 'Most people run a mile.'

'That's only because they are intimidated.'

'You think? I always thought it was a guilty conscience.'

'Probably a bit of both.'

'But not you?'

'I'm not intimidated by women. I've known they were the superior race since I was two. And as for a guilty conscience, it's true, I did overfeed my goldfish to see if they would explode.'

'Did they?'

'No. Very disappointing.'

Jessie felt the effects of the vodka radiate through her. She relaxed as Joshua pointed out the people around them. The diminutive pop stars, the unattractive models, the stick-thin actresses. Wherever they looked, gorgeous women were accompanied by balding grey-haired men.

'Old impresarios, club owners, criminals, gun runners,' explained Joshua.

Jessie took a lump of brie off a passing tray.

'True love every time,' he said, winking. Jessie smiled, then regretted it. Maggie was suddenly standing beside them. Between them.

'What are you two getting so cosy about?'

Joshua looked at Jessie and smiled gently.

'We are laughing at those hideous models, the ones with the inverted chests,' he said.

'There is probably a nice stash of rock cocaine in their rhinestone-encrusted baguettes,' said Maggie, putting her hand on Joshua's arm.

'I'm off duty,' Jessie replied, stepping back.

'Does that mean you don't have a set of those plastic handcuffs in your bag?' asked Maggie slyly.

'Not that off duty.'

'Didn't think so.' Maggie laughed. 'I'm sure most of the men in this tent would hand over their dealer's number just to be arrested by you looking like that. Don't you think, Joshua?'

He looked flustered.

'I leave that up to the narcs. I'm strictly a murder girl me,' said Jessie.

'Darling, there isn't room for two murder experts, and I'm afraid I got there first.'

The three of them turned and watched Henrietta move like a carnival float across the floor. 'You two fighting over my son already? And it's so early.' Henrietta Cadell rubbed a bejewelled hand up Joshua's long, lean back. Maggie winked at Jessie. Mothers and only sons. A lethal combination.

'Mother, I –'

'Joshua, dear, they don't seem to stock any Grey Goose behind the bar and I'm simply not going to drink that cheap Eastern European rocket fuel. Would you be a darling and run to the car and ask the driver to go and find some?'

'What about a glass of champagne?'

'If I wanted champagne, Joshua, I wouldn't have come all the way over here and asked you to get me the vodka, would I?'

'Sorry, I'll go now,' said Joshua. He began to walk away.

'I'll keep you company,' said Maggie, smiling broadly at Henrietta.

'That's a shame. I wanted to talk to you about an idea my agent has had. We're looking for a presenter . . .'

Maggie stepped back. 'Oh.'

'Run along, Joshua,' said Henrietta.

Run along? Didn't Henrietta realise her son was out of shorts? 'If you're going to talk shop,' said Jessie impulsively, 'I may as well go with him.' Joshua tried to hide it, but Jessie could tell he was pleased. They walked out of the marquee together, leaving Maggie and Henrietta staring after them.

~

Alistair prised himself off the brick wall and stepped silently out of the shadow. He followed Tarek down the street and watched him turn left on to the main road. After four hundred yards, Tarek stopped at the pedestrian crossing and waited for the lights to change. Alistair stepped back under the awning of a newsagent's as Tarek looked left and right. When Tarek crossed, Alistair slipped between the slow-moving cars. He was walking parallel to Tarek now. Tarek always walked home. It took an hour, but it saved him money. Alistair knew the route well. He'd followed him three times before. In a few minutes he would leave the busy road and turn right down an alley-way that led to the back of an estate. By weaving

265

through the bicycle-proof railings, he would cut through the estate, descend into a labyrinth of sub-ways and be lost from sight and sound.

Cracking his knuckles, Alistair increased his pace. At the railings he veered off left, then broke into a run, opened the door of a nearby block of flats, ran up a flight of stairs and along the length of the corridor. He could see Tarek below him, cut back across the courtyard to the subway entrance. He pushed on, through another doorway, down another flight of stairs and across a deserted playground. Jumping a low fence, he ran on past a shuttered-up parade of shops and emerged on the busy road the other side. Alistair ducked around the late-night traffic and descended the shallow concrete steps of the subway into darkness. The light he had broken the night before had not been fixed. He pressed himself into an alcove that reeked of urine, gripped the cold steel bar, and waited for the echo of Tarek's footsteps.

~

The silver Mercedes S500 limo was parked out-side the gates. Jessie and Joshua had to pass the photographers again, but after a cursory glance the paparazzi went back to their cigarettes and notebooks. Jessie and Joshua were not worthy of a shot. Joshua didn't seem to notice, but Jessie knew the reaction would have been different if his mother had escorted him. She was about to ask him about it when he tapped a uniformed driver on the shoulder.

'Aren't you freezing?' asked Joshua.

The driver looked at the car nervously. 'I was having a cigarette,' he said. Jessie instinctively looked at the driver's empty hands then the ground. There was no butt on the ground. The driver kept glancing at the tinted windows of the car.

'It doesn't bother me, but Mother would like you to go and fetch her some Grey Goose. Do you mind?'

'Now?'

'Afraid so.'

'Right. I'll bring it in, no need for you to wait.'

'Okay.'

The driver remained on the pavement. So did Joshua. The driver looked back at the car. So did Joshua. Jessie had heard it too. Someone was in the car.

'Fucking hell!' spat Joshua. 'Not again.'

The driver opened his mouth then closed it.

'Jesus Christ, there are photographers all over this place!'

'I'm sorry, sir.'

Jessie stepped back. She didn't want to watch Joshua discipline the driver. A man twice his age.

'It's not your fault,' said Joshua. 'Just get them out of here. Who is it?'

The driver shrugged. Joshua seemed to deflate. As he turned back to Jessie, the door of the car opened. A be-suited trouser leg stepped on to the pavement. Joshua moved like a cat.

'Get back in the car. You too. Jesus, at least have the decency to try and be discreet, if not for Henrietta, for yourself.' Joshua slammed the door shut and indicated for the driver to go quickly. 'Don't let them return together.' The driver nodded. 'And don't forget the vodka.'

He rejoined Jessie on the pavement and they watched the car glide effortlessly away.

'I'm very sorry you had to witness that,' said Joshua.

So was Jessie. The man who had partially emerged from the car was the man she had pulled off the girl in the corridor of the film premiere party. Worse still, he was the same man that Verity Shore had checked into a hotel with. Christopher Cadell. She was right, she had seen him somewhere before.

'My father has a penchant for young women. He seems to get a kick out of humiliating my mother. So you see, she may be a discourteous, over-bearing nightmare, but she is a miserable, discourteous, over-bearing nightmare. She only has me. I suppose that's why I put up with her. I need a drink.'

Jessie couldn't move. Joshua turned back.

'Sorry, it's always a bit shocking the first time you notice the crack in the façade. I don't mean to be rude, but I'm very grateful it was you who witnessed that and not Maggie. I'm afraid your flatmate would use it to her advantage. You won't tell her, will you? Mother is very protective of her good name.'

A good name that had just been added to a very short list of suspects. 'No,' said Jessie. 'I won't tell Maggie.'

~

Something made Tarek stop halfway through the subway and listen. He couldn't hear the footsteps behind him any more, but now he thought he could hear something up ahead in the gloom. Local thugs out to catch themselves a bit of sport? If he'd learnt anything working for Ray St Giles it was that routine could get you killed. From tomorrow he'd start taking the bus, maybe get a bike.

~

Jessie left Joshua to sort out his mother's drink and walked back into the party. How much humiliation would Dame Henrietta Cadell take? Anonymous blondes were one thing, but Verity Shore . . . That was a kick in the teeth. Both P. J. Dean and the historian had good reason for wanting to keep that information quiet. Did Henrietta Cadell have as much weight with the press as P.J., or would she resort to more mediaeval methods? Jessie was sorry she had begun to get on with Joshua.

Maggie was no longer with Henrietta's crowd. She was on her own by a table, scrabbling around in a bag. Jessie's bag. Maggie pulled out Jessie's phone and put it to her ear. Despite running, Jessie couldn't get to her flatmate in time.

'Detective Inspector Driver's phone.'

Jessie saw Maggie's mouth drop open and she began to frantically search the room. Jessie waved and kept on running.

'It's P. J. Dean! He says he needs you.'

Jessie snatched the phone. The music was loud and the reception was not good.

'They left her head in a box!'

'What?'

'Some fucking bastard left a box by the gate with her head in it! You said I could go home, so I brought the kids back this evening.'

'I said wait till I'd spoken to Uniform.' Jessie was trying not to shout as she ran out of the tent.

'The kids were unsettled enough.'

'Are you sure –'

'I don't know! I heard a noise. I'm feeling a little paranoid at the moment about the boys. Maybe it's the drugs I used to take, or maybe it's because my wife was DIPPED IN ACID!'

'Calm down, you'll wake the boys.'

'I mean, what kind of cunt would do a thing like that? What if Paul had found it? He'd be in a loony bin. It makes me feel sick thinking about it.'

'Someone knows you're home.'

'No shit! That pig's blood somebody threw at the gate, and all the other fucking things – those letters, death threats . . . What if they weren't cranks? What if this really is about Verity and me and Eve –'

'What do you mean, you and Eve?'

'What if they're after the boys? Help me, please. If anything happened to them . . . Jesus, I'm going out of my mind. Whoever's doing this is fucking sick!'

'Calm down. I'll come and get you.'

'I'm not taking the boys back to that safe house. Some car keeps driving past during the night. They know. Somehow they know. I've had stuff through the letter box.'

'Why didn't you tell me?'

'Because I don't want to live like this. Scared all the fucking time.' He was crying. Jessie could hear it down the phone.

'P.J., I need you to do a few things. Do you trust me?'

Jessie heard his breath whistle down the phone. 'Yes. Jesus Christ –'

'Stop it. Get the boys out of bed, throw some jeans and sweatshirts into a bag – enough for a week or so, warm clothes. I'll be with you in half an hour.'

'Sorry, didn't mean to lose it.'

'It's okay. I'm coming.'

She put her phone back in her bag and waved at Maggie to come and join her.

'Not a word to anyone, Maggie.'

'My lips are sealed. Are you going?'

Protect what you care about, said Ray St Giles. 'I have to. Those boys could be in serious danger.'

Joshua walked towards her. A bottle of Grey Goose in his hand. 'Where are you going?' he asked, looking at her coat.

'I'm sorry.'

He whispered in her ear. 'I embarrassed you –'

'It was nothing to do with that. But I have to go.'

He looked at her rather desperately. 'Can I call you?'

Yes. No. 'Give your number to Maggie.'

Maggie slipped her arm through Joshua's. 'Don't worry,' she said. 'I'll look after him.'

It was too dark. Too dark and too quiet. Tarek stopped for the second time. He was nearly at the end of the long subway. One more corner, a flight of shallow stairs, and he would be back out into the world of the living. Underfoot he felt the broken glass. He looked up to the curved roof of the subway and stared into the gloom where the fizzing orange light should have been. A sabotaged light was the same as a convenient death, the same as an altered lock. Something was not right. He would never know exactly what made him turn and run, but, as he did so, he could have sworn he felt something swoop past his ear.

Jessie watched the patrol car move off, taking the skull with it. Only one other vehicle had been by, an empty mini cab. It was almost dawn; those who were going home had gone and those who weren't would wait until the morning smacked them in the face. Jessie walked up the granite driveway to the house. She followed the noise past Eve Wirrel's installation to the kitchen.

'Hi, Jessie, we're packing provisions. Sausage rolls, cheese slices, and jam tarts, because you like them,' said Paul, dressed in jeans and a sweatshirt.

'Where are we going?' asked Ty.

'On a road trip,' said Jessie.

'Let me take your coat.'

'Thanks.'

Her thick cashmere coat slid over her shoulders and she remembered a moment too late that she was still in the backless Armani dress. She turned to P.J. to explain and caught his eyes sweeping back up to meet hers.

'Wow!' said Ty. 'Someone's cut a hole in your dress.'

Jessie laughed.

P.J. looked delighted.

'I think it's pretty,' said Paul.

'So do I,' said P.J.

'Can I see the sparkly bits?' said Ty.

'Of course you can. Come here, I'll lift you up.'

Paul and P.J. watched Ty walk slowly over to Jessie. He looked pensive for a while, then stretched out his arms. Jessie lifted the five-year-old with ease.

'Like stars,' he said, then lay his head on her shoulder and closed his eyes. Paul giggled.

'Why don't you put that tea in a flask, and we'll set off now,' said Jessie quietly.

P.J. nodded, but continued to look at Ty.

'Amazing.' He looked at her, a grateful smile on his face. 'Can you manage?' he asked.

'Easy. But I might need a sweatshirt for the journey.'

'Paul, go to my room, find some clothes for Jessie and bring them down.'

'What about Mummy's?'

'I wouldn't want Ty to wake up and see me in your mother's clothes. He might get a bit spooked.'

Paul nodded seriously. 'Good thinking, Batman.' Then he ran out.

'Sorry I rang you in the middle of a party. Hope I didn't interrupt anything.'

'No. Nothing at all. I was on my way home anyway . . . Where are Craig and Bernie?'

'In a hotel. Craig didn't want to come back here. They have nothing to do with this.'

'You'll have to let me be the judge of that.'

'Are you a good judge?'

Maybe not, she thought. 'I'm not judgemental, if that's what you mean. It was me who told you about Craig and Verity, remember. I told you he'd need looking after.'

'You were right.'

'So that should answer your question.'

Ty squirmed in Jessie's arms, opened his eyes once, looked at Jessie, then closed them again.

'It's quite a long drive,' whispered Jessie, 'so of your fleet of cars, you should pick the most comfy. And it'll need to be one that can take the odd bumpy road.'

'So not the Porsche?' P.J. whispered back.

Jessie shook her head.

'Aston Martin?'

'Now you're showing off.'

He smiled. It was nice to see. 'I know, the Bentley Turbo.'

'Vulgar. Truly vulgar.'

'Don't worry, I've got just the vehicle.' He laughed softly, then looked at her. 'I am so grateful you are here. I don't think I've been so terrified in my life.' He stepped towards her.

She was glad she had Ty in her arms. A buffer zone. 'We should get going.'

Jessie was curled up in the enormous seat of the Hummer. The NavSat was leading P.J. ever northwards, while she retreated into herself. The boys had watched ten minutes of *Toy Story* on the DVD system, then fallen asleep. She had been trying to follow suit, but every jolt of the car reminded her who she was with and where she was taking him.

'I know I'm prickly,' said P.J.

Jessie kept her eyes closed.

'Bernie and Craig, they mean a lot to me. I guess

I'm over-protective.' He paused. 'They're like family. Bernie's been through a lot. We lived on a rough estate in outer Manchester. It was shit, especially for girls. At least we had football, rugby . . . She was my sister's best friend.'

Jessie opened her eyes but didn't move.

'My sister drowned.'

Jessie waited.

'It happened a long time ago, but it still feels like yesterday. No one talks about her and the press know better than to mention her in a piece. Julie was thirteen when she died; she and Bernie were playing by the estuary. My sister waded out a bit too far and was pulled out by the tide, unfortunately she –'

'– couldn't swim,' said Jessie quietly.

He looked at her briefly. 'How did you know?'

Jessie sat up. 'You said it once, when you were upset. I thought you might have been talking about Bernie.'

'Bernie couldn't swim either. She's still terrified of water. I offered her lessons but she refused. I don't blame her.'

Jessie thought of the punt in the river and the pool at P.J.'s house. Phobias had made convincing alibis before.

'What happened?'

'Bernie ran to get help, but by the time we got there my sister had disappeared. I looked for hours. Until I was blue from the cold. They never found the body. Bernie became a surrogate sister to me.

She was all I had. My family weren't very . . .' He rubbed his face. 'We lost touch for a few years. I went to America and things took off for me. When we met again, she needed a job to support Craig, I needed a housekeeper, and she was prepared to do the work. She is proud, despite everything.'

'And what does she think of Craig and Verity?'

'She's upset, but not for the reasons you'd think. She's not angry with Craig, he's a kid still, and as you said, he is very, very upset. I've sent them to a retreat in the Swiss mountains.'

'You said they were at a hotel.'

'It is a hotel. It's just there are people there he can talk to. It's sort of like a bereavement centre with activities and therapy.'

'In Switzerland! They shouldn't have left the country, P.J., and you know it. We are in the middle of a murder investigation here.'

'I'm sorry. I was trying to look after them, that's all. You can't possibly think that Bernie is involved. I know her, she couldn't have done those things, and neither could Craig.'

'Verity was sleeping with her son. A seventeen-year-old boy. Two years older than Bernie was when she got pregnant.'

'That has got nothing to do with it,' he said angrily.

'How can you be so sure?'

'Because I know her better than I know myself. She no more killed Verity than Ty did. Bernie is a sweet, loving, caring, beautiful woman who is so good, she puts the rest of us to shame.'

Jessie wanted to know how deep these feelings went. Did P.J. really love her like a sister, or was there more to it? She suspected there was. 'What is the history between you two?'

'I've just told you. Isn't that enough?'

'I think you're holding something back from me.'

'That's it!'

'You want to tell me about Craig's father?'

He stared at her, then turned back to the road ahead. 'We need petrol,' he said, and turned off the motorway. P.J. jumped out of the car, lit a Marlboro Light and, hunched against the cold, walked away.

A giant blood-orange sun hovered above Lake Ullswater. The bare barks of Scotch pine trees glowed pink under a canopy of deep forest green. Shards of orange flashed across the gun-metal grey water as the sun rose on another day. Jessie stood on the deck of the timber house and watched fluttering sails of wooden-hulled boats creep towards the centre of the lake. She listened to the clatter of spoons in bowls from the kitchen as her brother and sister-in-law fed an unfamiliar tribe. Her nieces, she knew, would rise to the occasion. Take care of these two, small patients of the modern world that she had brought into theirs. She looked down at P.J.'s jeans and sweatshirt, now three hundred miles away from the threat of decapitated heads, acid, insane obsession, and septic tanks. It wasn't the children she was worried about. Infidelity plagued her. Verity Shore's with Christopher Cadell.

'Jessieeeeee,' called Charlotte. She was dragging P.J. and the boys on to the deck. The girls were excited. The men looked lost.

'We're going to show them our tepee,' said Ellie.

'That's a wigwam,' said Charlotte.

Jessie smiled. 'You'd better find the boys some boots then.'

The boys snaked around P.J.'s legs.

'We've got bows and arrows,' said Charlotte. 'We can be Indians.' She took Ty's hand. 'I'm going to show you all our secret places.' Ty allowed himself to be led away.

'Go with your brother,' said P.J., pushing Paul gently.

'We'll come and find you in half an hour or so,' shouted Jessie as she led P.J. back into the house.

'What about the lake?' said P.J.

'Don't worry, they know not to go near the water unless they have lifejackets,' said Colin.

P.J. looked worried. Colin passed him a steaming cup of coffee. 'I'd be more concerned about the girls taking them up trees than going near the water.'

'Too much of the Driver genes,' said Kate.

'Jessie was exactly the same,' said Colin. 'No fear.'

'Is this supposed to make me feel better?' said

P.J., straining to watch the children as they disappeared into the woodland that backed on to the garden. A jumble of trees waiting to come to life as soon as their backs were turned.

'Sit down,' said Colin. 'Your children are safe. Otherwise Jessie wouldn't have brought you all the way up here. We'll get the boat going later and take them on the lake, there are some great rocks to climb in the next bay.'

'Oh God, I'm too urban for this.'

'You'll get over it,' said Colin. 'So tell me, why did Jessie bring you up here?'

Kate coughed. 'Jessie, more porridge?'

~

Mark Ward walked through the archway that led to the Woolwich Cemetery. The cloudless night had left the ground hard with frost. The death certificate said Gareth Blake's short life had ended on April 11th, 1979. It was a destitute place. Crumbling under the weight of desertion. A place for the poor and forgotten. Or were they just lost, as Clare had said on that long and fruitless journey to Sunderland? He thought of Clare, walking up and down the pathways, reading every gravestone until she found her parents. Always on the look out for a Frank Mills. Waiting to stumble across his final resting place. He'd been a healthy boy, she'd said.

Gareth Blake had been healthy too. Right up

until his sudden death of pneumonia. It had been bugging him. The child had never previously been ill. In fact, according to the records, he was a perfect child. In care, wasn't that an oxymoron? No temper tantrums. No need to discipline. No psychiatry records. Almost as if he wasn't there. Until his sudden death. Mark found the year: 1979. He began to walk slowly along the line of graves: January 2nd, January 29th, February 9th, April 11th. Gareth Blake. RIP. He knelt down and brushed the dead leaves away. They crumbled at his touch. Ashes to ashes. Dust to dust. Could have been Frank, he supposed. Now they'd never know.

~

The spiked shells of fallen beechnuts cracked beneath their feet as Jessie and P.J. picked their way through the wood.

'Your brother and sister-in-law are charming,' said P.J. 'Do you all come from up here?'

'No. They moved after they were married. Kate is a sommelier. One of the best in the business. Her father owned wineries, she picked up the trade. Now they sell to private clients and hotels. She's a bit of a superstar, really.'

'None of the others married?'

'God, no. Imagine trying to compete with Kate.'

'Or you.'

'Me?'

'Well, look at you –'

Jessie heard a twig snap to the left of them. She pointed.

'Hey, boys!' shouted P.J.

'Shh, don't let them know we're coming. We'll be ambushed and it'll all be over in seconds. Here, have this –' Jessie picked up a boomerang-shaped stick.

'What for?'

'It's your gun, of course. We're the cowboys.'

'We are?'

'A little imagination, please.'

P.J. put himself in a manly stance. Jessie giggled. 'You look constipated.'

He tipped an imaginary hat. 'Why, thank you, ma'am.'

'Don't you play games with the boys?'

He immediately came out of his sheriff pose. 'Yeah. Playstation.'

'What about Craig? Did you play with him when he was younger?'

P.J. looked uncomfortable. 'Not really.'

'Well, you're in for a shock. Here you have to make your own games.'

P.J. put his hands on his hips. 'You are really quite annoying.'

'My brothers would agree.'

'Colin tells me you climb mountains.'

'It's a psychological flaw, reaching the same peaks as they can.'

'Which mountains?'

'Kilimanjaro.'

'No?' said P.J. mockingly.

'Mont Blanc. On skis.'

'Now you're showing off.'

'The Eiger.'

'That's vulgar, Jessie Driver, truly vulgar.'

'Touché,' said Jessie.

'Attack! Attack!'

'What?' P.J. whirled round.

'Oops, I think we've been found.'

P.J. and Jessie stood back to back. Four children streaked across the glade chanting Indian war cries. They had put bird feathers in their hair and Ty was wearing an old Hiawatha wig.

'Throw down your weapons,' shouted Ellie.

'What weapons?' whispered P.J.

'The gun.'

P.J. dutifully obeyed.

'Now you are our prisoners, you have to do exactly what we tell you.'

'What do you want?'

'We are hungry. You must go to the rich farmer's house and steal Coca-Cola and flapjacks and chocolate crispies.'

'I can make those,' said Paul.

'Can you?' asked Charlotte, impressed, lowering her stick.

'Let's go and make some now,' said Ellie.

'Yeah!' said Ty and Charlotte.

'How about a whole picnic to take on the boat?' said Jessie.

'An Indian picnic,' said Charlotte.

'Yeah!'

'Are you sure you want to do this?' said P.J., crouching down by Paul.

'It's okay,' he said. 'I'm not sad.'

The four of them dropped their weapons and ran howling back to the house. P.J. turned to Jessie. 'That was a lucky escape.'

'You have no idea. I've been caught by those two before, they can think up unimaginable things for their captives to do.'

She was about to walk away, when P.J. grabbed her arm. She turned back. His hand slid down her forearm and held on to her hand.

'What?' she said, trying to keep the nervousness out of her voice and the panic out of her head.

'There is something I'd like to do.'

He pulled her nearer. I really must stop this, thought Jessie. He put his arms round her and squeezed her tight. 'Thank you,' he mumbled into her neck. 'Thank you for letting me bring the boys here.'

The goose pimples spread like falling dominoes down Jessie's arms, but she kept them resolutely by her sides.

The kids – cold, wet and happy from a long day of unimaginable freedom – were put in the bath by Kate. P.J. glowed. Jessie kept forgetting why they were there. But then Saturday prime-time television pulled her three hundred miles southward and threw her back in the Thames, the stinking mud, the fizzing bones. It was Ray St Giles. Jessie closed the door of the den and stared at the television.

'You know him?' asked P.J.

Jessie didn't answer.

Colin examined the television page. '*Confessions of a Celebrity* with Ray St Giles. You don't want to watch this, do you, Jess?'

'How low will this man sink?' It was P.J. and he too was staring hard at the picture.

'They've got a girl on. I think she was in a band, went solo and, well, here she is.' Colin turned up the volume.

'. . . I don't want to be next, do I? I mean, if there is some madman loose. So I thought I'd confess, then I might not be on his list.'

'On whose list?' asked St Giles, as if he didn't know what she was referring to.

'The Z-list Killer.'

The audience burst into applause. At last a killer who wasn't going after their daughters, wives, sisters. It was only a matter of time before they started hunting through the pages of *OK* and *Hello!* for the next victim. Whereupon Mr St Giles would undoubtedly be ready with a piece of revealing footage and a best man speech for the victim. Was this the new strain of reality TV?

'So, you've been in the music business for seven years, a successful band member and now with a platinum-selling solo record behind you. What is it you want to confess?'

The camera swung round to zoom in on the singer.

'She can't sing,' said P.J.

Colin and Jessie looked at him.

'I'm telling you – had her in the studio. Verity could sing better than her, and Verity couldn't sing at all.'

The girl was still chewing her lip. Afraid.

'Come on, tell old Ray.'

'I can't sing,' she whispered.

The audience gasped. Genuinely shocked.

'Stupid fuckers,' said P.J.

'Language,' said Colin, out of habit.

'Sorry, but surely they knew. There is a reason why these people don't sing live.'

'My voice is electronically adjusted by a computer. I am contractually forbidden to sing live. Anywhere. Not even in the bath at home, in case one of the staff hear.'

'That must be terrible, living a lie.'

'God he's a creepy bastard,' said P.J.

'Language,' said Colin.

'Why do you say that?' asked Jessie.

'He tried to get Verity and me on his cable show, said he had information. Blackmailing fu—. Sorry.'

'What happened?'

'I called his bluff.'

'And?'

'And Verity died. Ray St Giles aired the programme but left me out of it. I had the lawyers on to him by then, but he nailed Verity. After everything

I did to keep her out of the press, that little swine goes and blurts it all anyway. And as for that back-stabbing, money-grabbing Danny Knight – I could kill him.' He was staring at the TV. Colin and Jessie exchanged glances.

'Turn it off,' said Jessie.

'Saturday-night prime time. The man is going to be bigger than Noel Edmonds.'

'How does he have such a hold on people?' asked Jessie, of no one in particular.

'He probably has video footage of her actor husband doing nose-up off some blonde's thigh. They've decided to sacrifice her career to save his. Hers was pretty much over, anyway.'

'Nose-up?' asked Colin, confused.

'Cocaine,' explained Jessie.

'That's horrid.'

'No, that's life,' said P.J.

'Not my life,' insisted Jessie's brother.

'No,' said P.J. 'But it's mine.'

'What did he have on you, P.J.?'

'Nothing. It was Verity. She'd been seen in a hotel with some man. I don't know who, so don't ask. I didn't bother to find out.'

But Jessie knew who. Dame Henrietta Cadell's husband. A woman who, according to her son, liked her reputation just as it was. Not that dissimilar to P. J. Dean.

'I'd better leave you to it,' said Colin, retreating.

'Why did you tell me the affairs were nothing more than rumours?'

'Most of them were,' said P.J.

'I have quite a lot of evidence to the contrary. And you are beginning to look like the jealous husband.'

P.J. laughed spitefully. 'Jealous? Of Verity? Come on, she was pitiful. The only stupid thing I have done is to try to protect her. Ray St Giles knew everything about her: he knew about Eve, he knew Verity was high, he knew everything that Danny Knight knew. It was an open secret. I should never have bothered.'

'So it was true – Eve and Verity?'

P.J. nodded his head silently as he watched St Giles prance around the stage. The audience was just beginning to chant his name when P.J. reached for the remote control.

'St Giles.'

'St Giles.'

'St Giles.'

~

Mark Ward had been sitting outside 7 Elwood Lane for two and a half hours when finally he saw a woman in her mid-fifties walk down the street. From the bulge under her mac, Mark guessed she was carrying money under there. A lot of money it seemed by the way she walked. Fast. With her shoulders raised and her eyes searching the street. He sunk low in his car and waited; he didn't want to startle her. He had done his research on Irene. She was actually more than the owner of a salon. She was the owner of several. Quite an empire she'd built up along Commercial Road. She let them all, bar one. The one she began in. The one she went to every day and served the same women she'd been serving for years.

He waited until she'd been in the house for ten minutes, then he rang the bell.

'Who is it?'

'Detective Inspector Ward. I'd like to talk to you about Clare Mills.'

'Badge, please.' The copper letter-box cover popped open and a bony hand emerged. Mark handed over the wallet.

'Stand back a bit, so I can get a proper look at you.'

Mark took two steps back and wished everyone was as conscientious as this lady. But then not many people had as much to protect as this lady.

'What colour is Clare's kitchen?'

'Excuse me?'

'Look, anyone can fake ID these days, so answer the question or you'll be conducting your interview from the pavement.'

'Yellow.'

'Job?'

'Road sweeper.'

'All right, Detective, you can come in now.' A chain slid back and the door opened. 'Serve the local community and make a pot of tea,' said Irene. 'I've been on my feet all day and I'm knackered.'

* * *

289

Mark walked through to the living room with the tea on a tray. He'd even put some biscuits on a plate. Enlightened self-interest. He was starving.

'Blimey, I said make tea, not make yourself at home.'

'I thought you looked like a lady who'd want things done properly.'

'Well, you thought wrong.'

Mark poured the tea and sat back on a chair opposite her. Irene had her shoes off and her feet stretched out in front of her on the sofa. She had good legs. Even now.

'What can you tell me about Clare's parents?'

'Nothing that you don't already know. I'm sure Clare has told you everything.'

'Now I'd like you to tell me the rest. Stuff only friends talk about.'

'Like?'

'Like how was her marriage?'

'Like marriage.'

'Clare seems to think it was blessed.'

'That's her prerogative.'

'So it wasn't?'

'What marriages do you know round here that are blessed?'

'Why did it take them so long to have Frank?'

'Look, Detective, why do you want to dig up all this stuff now? They're dead and buried, and Clare can believe what she wants to believe. Give the girl that, at least.'

'You are saying there were problems.'

'I'm saying leave it be.'

'I think that belief is killing her. She can't move on.'

'Better the devil you know.'

'So you reckon the truth could kill her?'

'Perhaps. What is truth, except what you perceive it to be?' Irene rubbed a bunion absently. 'Don't look at me like that. I'm not stupid, and good sense tells me that if Clare has come to the conclusion that Frank is dead, well then, it's for the best. Wouldn't you agree?'

'I know you're not stupid. Quite a little empire you've built up around here.'

'What the hell has that got to do with anything?'

'It means I've been doing my research.'

Irene didn't say anything. Mark shifted in his seat. This was not going to be easy. Irene wasn't some old pushover. She'd been burying secrets all her life. But he needed answers and only she had them.

'Clare doesn't know that you signed her and her brother over to the social services, does she? She doesn't know that Veronica had given you power of attorney in case of her death.'

Irene didn't move.

'Clare maintains that her mother didn't know what she was doing when she hung herself on the day of Trevor's funeral. Seems an extraordinary coincidence that she'd signed the relevant papers two days before.'

Irene still did not move.

'Come on, Irene. What was Veronica so frightened of? What was she hiding?'

'Where did you get that information?'

'Never mind what I know, what do *you* know about Frank? I found a grave this morning. Gareth Blake. Born the same day as Frank Mills. That name mean anything to you, Gareth Blake?'

'No.' Irene leant forward to put her cup and saucer on the glass-topped coffee table.

'Ray St Giles?'

China clattered, Irene looked up. She recovered quickly.

'What do you think? He murdered Trevor. He was a tyrant in these parts until they locked him up. Harassing shopkeepers, preying on young girls, fixing the races –'

'Young girls like you.'

Irene didn't say anything.

'Like Clare's mum?'

'Yeah, girls *like* us.'

'Trevor was out of work for a long time. Must have been tough with no money. Clare showed me the photos you gave her. Looking a million dollars – her words. How was that then, if Trevor wasn't earning anything?'

'We worked. In my salon. Well, what became my salon.'

'Clare told me you started by sweeping up and making tea. Would have been around the time those photos were taken. Veronica had a kid, a husband. You telling me your measly wages paid for those fur coats and jewellery?'

'It was all costume.'

'I don't believe you. I think you knew Raymond's mob, went down the clubs, picked up a few perks, drinks, the odd present. Just the way you both looked would have been enough. I should know, I'm from the same era. But your mate Veronica got in deeper, didn't she? Started sleeping with one of the bad boys. Who was it, Irene?'

Irene wiped her eyes. 'This is no good. If you know what those times were like, then leave them be. Veronica is nothing but dust, Clare is living, let her be. This would kill her.'

'So I'm right?'

She wasn't going to give him the satisfaction.

'Who was she sleeping with?'

'I'm tired of all this.'

'Who was it, Irene?'

She continued to stare into the void of the blank television screen. 'Tell me, please.'

He heard the electronic pop of the television as it came to life. He glanced at Irene. She had the remote control in her hand, she was staring at the screen.

'Irene, talk to me.'

The programme was coming to an end. The audience were chanting. Mark sat up.

'St Giles.'

'St Giles.'

'St Giles.'

Mark turned his head, looked at Irene, his

mouth open. The chanting continued. Her eyes slid sideways to meet his, then returned to the television set. She lowered her head and began to weep. Mark moved across the room and put his arm around her shoulders.

~

Jessie watched P.J. and Colin through the glass door. A bottle of Bechevelle 1966 stood open next to them. P.J. was chopping cucumber for the salad. He looked as though he'd been there all his life. Above her head the stars peeked out of the darkening sky. She was reluctant to pass on the good news she'd just received from Jones, but she slid the door back and stepped from the deck into the steamy kitchen.

'Good news,' she said, trying to sound convincing. 'It's safe for you to go home. The skull was a fake. Left by two fourteen-year-old fans. One of the girls' fathers is an osteopath. Apparently they got the information from a website called fanextremis.com. It's anonymous. Impossible to trace who posted it on the net. Sorry.'

'*Fans* left a skull?' Colin looked perturbed.

'Some people are so fanatical they'd shoot you,' said P.J. drily.

'Unbelievable,' said Colin.

'It's my fault. I should have checked the box,' she said.

Jones had made it perfectly clear on the phone

what he thought she should do now.

'It means you can go home,' said Jessie, looking at P.J. He continued to slice the cucumber. 'There is no threat to the boys, or you. It's safe to go home.'

'You can't go,' said Colin. 'We want to say thanks for taking the girls off our hands all day. We had a great afternoon, and the –'

Jessie held up her hand. 'Thanks, Colin, we get the picture.'

'Besides, it's late, you didn't get any sleep last night, you need feeding and a long sleep. Tomorrow is Sunday and it would be uncivilised not to stay for lunch.'

'But –'

'The boys are already in bed, and they couldn't leave without saying goodbye to the girls. Plus, dinner would be ruined and the wine will go to waste. In a nutshell, you're staying put.'

'The trouble is –'

Colin interrupted again. 'Jessie, do you really need to drive back to London tonight?' He threw some herbs into the pan and gave it a stir. Stubbornness ran in the family.

'She's not planning on going anywhere.' P.J. lowered the knife and looked at Jessie. 'Are you?'

It was true. She could stay. The thought of a long car journey was unappealing. The thought of P.J. leaving without her was disturbing. The thought of Jones' disapproval didn't help.

'I'll go and get the boys,' said P.J.

'Don't be ridiculous. It would be dangerous for you to drive – you've had a drink, you haven't slept and it's a long journey. As a policewoman, Jessie should forbid you to go.'

'How much have you drunk?' asked Jessie.

'Two bottles of beer and half a glass of wine, not counting the wine at lunch.'

'A big glass, not half,' said Colin. 'He can't drive. You are both staying.'

~

Mark realised that Irene was a woman too tired not to talk.

'It's been hell, all this time, Clare despising that man. If she ever found out . . .' Irene looked at Mark. 'Who do you think has been making sure she never finds Frank? Me. I've spent my life sending her in the opposite direction because I'm telling you, something terrible would happen if she found out. I've dreaded it all my life.'

'What happened, Irene? What happened to Veronica, why did she kill herself?'

Irene slumped back into the sofa. 'If I tell you, will you scupper this investigation?'

'I can't do that, but I'll make sure I keep what I find from Clare.'

'Veronica felt so guilty. She loved Ray, or she thought she did at first, it was exciting and Trevor, bless him, he was a good man, but . . . Well, you can imagine. Ray fell hard. Veronica sort of did that to men. Then Veronica got pregnant with Frank. Trevor, of course, was over the moon. His miracle baby.'

'Why didn't she leave? Take the kids.'

'Ray didn't want Clare. He was mad about Veronica, but proud, so he didn't want Clare. Well, Veronica wouldn't leave her, wouldn't split those kids up. She came from a terrible family, full of hatred; she'd been deserted, completely deserted, by them. That's how she ended up living with my family. She wasn't going to do that to her kids. And then those two women disappeared. Prostitutes – no one gave a damn back then. Police arrested some trucker for it. He was up to his neck in all sorts of stuff anyway and the murders stuck. But Veronica had seen those women at Ray's club. They'd stolen a lot of money off him. Ray was furious with those two birds. Next thing we know, they're dead. That man is violent, not a normal violence. The sort of violence that takes time to thaw. He doesn't explode. It's slow and calculated.

'Well, after that Veronica was terrified. He kept professing undying love. Then Trevor got shot. That gun going off was no accident. Ray killed Trevor in cold blood. He knew the route Trevor would take home after the job interview. Ray assumed he'd get away with it. He assumed Veronica would go with him, but she wouldn't leave Trevor's side. She was terrified. Ray wanted to leave the country with her and Frank. But she

297

was safe in that hospital. I had the kids. Veronica knew even Ray wouldn't brave the hospital. Eventually he was arrested. Tip-off, apparently. Not from me, mind.'

'All this time, Clare has been looking for Ray's son.'

Irene nodded, blew her nose and lay back against the sofa.

'Does Ray have Frank?'

Irene shrugged. 'Never felt the urge to call him up and ask him. Probably. He's covered up more than that. What difference would it make now, anyway? Clare thinks Frank is dead. Can't we just leave it at that?'

Mark brought a flask out of his inside jacket pocket and handed it to Irene. She took a slug. Then another. 'No blood is better than bad blood, that's what Veronica used to say. No blood is better than bad blood.'

~

P.J. joined Jessie on the deck. A third bottle had been opened, Jessie felt cocooned in red wine. They leant over the wooden railing and stared at the reflection of the Milky Way on the oil-slick surface of Ullswater. Floating icing sugar. The low, round hoot of an owl on the hunt passed close by. P.J. looked up at the sheer half-moon and pointed. 'The sea of tranquillity. It seems closer here.'

She nudged him. 'Are all your lyrics as cheesy as that?'

'Haven't you ever listened to them?'

Jessie laughed. 'Careful, your ego is showing.'

He leant closer to her. 'You're right about this place,' he said. 'It is magical. I'd like to stay, watch the boys grow up carefree like Charlotte and Ellie. I don't want them to be like the other children of famous people. Do any of them turn out normal? What's in store for Rocco Ritchie, Anaïs Gallagher, Brooklyn Beckham? They won't be like Charlotte and Ellie, of that I'm certain.'

'I feel a monologue coming on. Would you like a pen and paper?'

He grabbed her. 'No. Shh, I'm being profound. People used to become famous as an unfortunate by-product of fulfilling their dreams –'

'Oh dear –'

'Now fame is the dream. It requires massive ambition and self-belief, you have to be stronger than the next. It's the plate tectonics of fame. Thin, flat layers get pushed into the mass of molten lava, insignificant against the force of a huge mountain of presence. But however high the peaks are, the troughs are deeper. The unseen underbelly of fame and power is insecurity and neurosis. Does that make a good parent? Absolutely not.'

'I think you're drunk, P.J.'

'I'm being serious. I'll tell you a horrible secret. I refused to sleep with Verity without a condom. I didn't trust her. I would have divorced her if it wasn't for Paul and Ty. You're right about that, the thought of them being dragged off to another man, another house, another unstable life was too much. Couldn't anyone take responsibility? These boys are people. Not commodities.'

Jessie straightened up. He was being serious. Deadly serious. 'Is that why you moved into Verity's ex-husband's house?'

'You don't miss a trick, do you?'

Jessie didn't say anything. She'd seen enough 'at home' photos of Verity Shore and her respective men to know the details of all her soft furnishings.

'Verity wanted it that way. I was against it at first, but she was right, the boys didn't want to move again, and they don't want to move now.'

He turned to her, slid his hand over hers. She didn't pull it away. 'I've made some terrible mistakes with my family, terrible, unforgivable mistakes. I'm not going to make them with Paul and Ty.'

'Is that why you don't speak to your father?'

He nodded.

'Why you missed your mother's funeral?'

'Yes.'

'Is this to do with your sister drowning?'

'In a way, I suppose.'

'And why you are so determined to take care of the boys, someone else's sons?'

'Yes.'

'And Bernie?'

'Of course Bernie! I trust you, Jessie. I want to tell you things no one knows. I don't want you to

300

be suspicious of me, I don't want to lie, but there are things I have sworn not to say to a living soul. Do you understand? After all these years, I just can't.'

Jessie frowned.

'You know, anyway, don't you? That is why you think so badly of me. I see it in your face.'

He was wrong. The doubt in her face was for herself only. But she had begun to suspect why P.J. had acted the way he had. It was watching him on the boat with the boys during the day, the things he said, things he referred to. She was beginning to think that there had been a relationship with Bernie, a long time ago, after his sister drowned. Understandable in the circumstances. The product was Craig. But he had left her, a pregnant fifteen-year-old, and gone to the States. He returned a pop star and never went home again. Whether it was youthfulness or recklessness, he had missed out on all of Craig's childhood and deserted his dead sister's best friend. He had behaved abominably and he couldn't make it up to Craig, and he probably couldn't truly make it up to Bernie either, though he cared and paid for them now. All P.J. could do was make sure it didn't happen again. To Paul and Ty. That was why he was so protective. That explained why he stuck it out with Verity Shore.

'I didn't kill Verity. I am desperate to prove that to you, so desperate I will betray the trust of the one person in the world who actually loves me and who I love back, properly, like family should.'

P.J. was gripping her hand.

'If Craig is your son, P.J., people might think it gives you a motive. That you and Bernie wanted Verity out of the way to play happy families. Do you understand that? Eve and Verity were lovers, lovers tell each other things, so then you had to deal with Eve.'

'I would have thought it was quite obvious to you that I'm not in love with Bernie. And if I'm not in love with Bernie, there is no motive. So go ahead. Ask.'

'Is he your son?'

P.J. blinked at her. His eyes filled with tears. The door to the balcony slid open and Kate and Colin spilled out laughing. 'Oops, sorry, didn't know you were out here. Have a glass of this brandy – we're celebrating! Kate just told me. She's pregnant!'

Jessie pulled away from P.J., who cheered loudly. Only Jessie heard his voice breaking and knew he was cheering to hide his own anguish.

Jessie hugged Kate. 'I'm so happy for you both.'

'To Kate,' said Colin, raising his glass. 'The best woman in the world.'

P.J. raised his glass and eyes to the moon. He downed the brandy and held out his glass for more.

~

Mark Ward walked slowly down the well-trodden corridor of the police station. There was a light on under Jones' door. Jones was probably the only person in the world he wanted to talk to. He knocked.

'Hello, sir, what are you doing here at this time of night?'

'Seems I've become DI Driver's dogsbody.'

Mark smiled. 'You and me both.'

'Women. It's a revolution we aren't going to end.'

'How are you feeling?'

'Still a bit feeble, but much better on the whole. Got a nice scar, do you want to see it?'

'No thanks, don't want to give myself nightmares. Wouldn't mind a nightcap, though. Care to join me? There's something I'd like to talk to you about.'

'If it's a bitching session about Jess –'

'No, guv, it's more important than that.'

They walked side by side along the corridor. Tired men and women came off shift and tired men and women arrived. A night-cleaner slapped a mop on to the vinyl floor and began to move the dirt around in mind-numbing circles. Jones pushed open the exit door and received a blast of cold air. They walked silently across the road into the pub.

'I want to talk to Ray St Giles, I want to bring him in.'

'Not you as well. Is this some shit between you and –'

'He was having an affair with Veronica. She

303

killed herself to stop that fact coming out. There is no trace of the boy, so Ray must have him.'

'No.'

'No what?'

'You can't go bursting in there unless you know. Unless you are sure. Jessie did, and it isn't looking good. He's smart, he'll screw you.'

'What the fuck was Jessie doing?'

'Had a tip that he was involved in these recent murders.'

'Bollocks he is! From who?'

'An insider.'

'Fine. Get her over here, we'll put a call through together, co-ordinate. Sort of thing that makes you happy.'

Jones rubbed his face. Mark picked up on it instantly. 'Where is she?' Jones was not an untruthful man, but if he answered that question, Jessie's career would be all but over.

'Sir?'

'Out of town.'

Mark chuckled. 'In the middle of a murder investigation? Come on, where is she?'

Jones didn't reply.

'She's up to something, isn't she? Oh no, it hasn't got anything to do with that pop singer bloke. Fry told me she'd been giving him the softly-softly approach.'

'Leave it, Mark.'

'Fucking hell –'

'I said leave it.'

Mark placed his glass down with careful precision. 'So let me get this straight: I can't question a murdering bastard who possibly stole a kid from social services, nor can I get to Jessie's insider because she is busy getting familiar with the bloke who should, if she could do her job, be the prime fucking suspect.' He sat back. 'Oh, guv, good work. Bet you're glad you gave her the promotion, eh?'

~

Jessie woke up hot and confused. She heard a stifled cry, but in the darkness she couldn't tell where it was coming from. Outside or inside. Animal or human. Man or boy. Jessie sat up and opened her eyes and ears to the night. She heard the noise again. It was human. Male. Child. And he wanted his mother. Jessie threw back the fat feathered eiderdown and padded across to the door. The curtains in the corridor weren't drawn: shadows from the trees outside slid across the wall, the moonlight picked out the round white face of Ty, standing stock-still in the middle of the passageway. He was staring straight at Jessie.

'Mummy?'

'It's okay, Ty. It's Jessie, I'm here . . .' She crouched down to his eye-level and pushed the sodden hair from his face. He didn't move for a second. Jessie thought the boy might still be asleep, but suddenly he lurched forward and threw his soft arms round her neck.

'I had a bad dream.'

'It's okay now.' Jessie could feel his wet cheeks on her neck. She held him tight and rocked him gently. 'It's okay,' she said, as visions of bleached bones danced in her head. After a few moments Ty's muscles slackened and his breathing evened out. Taking their combined weight in her legs, she slowly lifted him up and carried him back to her room. She fetched the torch from her bag and put it in Ty's small hand. 'Now you'll know where you are,' she said.

There was a rustle of blankets and the squeak of mattress springs.

'I couldn't find the light switch,' said Paul in the dark. 'I heard him crying, but I couldn't find the light switch.'

Jessie held Ty in one arm and felt along the wall. When the light went on, Ty lifted his head off her shoulder and looked at Jessie with enormous, disappointed eyes.

'I thought . . .' Ty's voice trailed off. Jessie knew what he thought. He thought his mother was carrying him to bed. The light had dispelled that dream. Night-time could do that, it could trick you. It was a beautiful, malicious trick because it was so real.

Jessie told them a story until both their chests rose and fell in a gentle rhythm. She waited quietly. Neither boy moved. Ty still clutched her torch in his hand. She left it there, dimmed the light, and quietly opened the bedroom door. She jumped when she saw P.J. standing in a jumper and boxer shorts.

'Sorry, didn't mean to frighten you. I saw the light on and wondered if they were okay.'

He was whispering, she lowered her voice to match his. 'They're fine. Ty had a bad dream.'

'Was he in the hallway? I often find Paul and Ty standing on the landing at the top of the stairs. Ty sleepwalks and Paul goes and finds him.'

Jessie crossed her arms in front of her. Her vest and shorts seemed to have shrunk.

'So what was going to happen in your story?'

Jessie opened her mouth. 'You sneak! You listened.'

'I didn't want to disturb you. You seemed to be doing such a good job of calming them down. Thanks.'

'I've given Ty my torch in case he wakes up again.'

'You didn't bring a bag, but you managed to bring a torch?'

'I'm a police officer, there are some things I always bring along, just in case.'

'Even to parties?'

'Especially to parties.'

They were walking back to her room. 'What else do you always bring along?'

She put her hand on the door knob. 'Handcuffs.'

'What else?'

'Plastic freezer bags, a Bic biro, some Tampax

and lip gloss. That's about it.'

He was inches from her. She didn't move.

'We should finish that conversation,' said P.J.

'Not now,' she said. Too dangerous.

'Please.'

He followed her into her room. This was bad, but somehow she couldn't bring herself to stop it. P. J. Dean didn't kill his wife. Anyone could see that. Surely?

He ran his hand down her arm. 'You have such incredible skin.'

'Please, don't. I can't do this,' she said.

'What can I do to persuade you that I'm not involved in this? All I want is a bit of normality, something secure.'

'You think I'm normal?'

'No, I think you're exceptional.'

'You don't even know me.'

'You make up stories, you play cowboys and Indians in the woods and you eat disgusting jam tarts to make a boy feel better about himself. I may as well admit that the backless dress in which you looked incredible may have had some impact, but not as much as the sight of you in water-proofs and wellies today on the lake. I know that much, Jessie Driver, and I know I'd like to know much more. What I don't know is how to con-vince you that I'm worth knowing too. Give me a chance.'

She stared at him. Was she so intoxicated by those green eyes that she couldn't see sense?

'I know what you want to know, Jessie. So ask me the question, and I'll give a straight yes or no answer. But don't ask me to explain. Not yet. I'm already breaking my word as it is.'

Her eyes were so accustomed to the dark she could see the worry line embedded between his eyebrows. His eyes had darkened to the colour of a stormy sea. Jessie didn't want an answer. Not then. The truth was, she didn't want to think about Verity Shore or the life of any public figure. She wanted a moment for herself. Didn't she have that right? P.J. pulled her closer. He put his hand through her hair, ran it down the back of her neck, over her jaw. Murder victims had one right left to them, to have their murderer caught. Until that happened, she didn't deserve a moment.

'Are you Craig's father?'

His thumb rested on her lower lip. He pressed it slightly then pulled his hand back. He looked right at her, inches away, she could feel his breath on her.

'No. I am not Craig's father and I am not, and never have been, in love with Bernie.'

He pulled her towards him and then she closed her mind and let her senses take over.

~

At six thirty Jessie woke up in bed alone. Her mind was racing and her conscience was cloudy. In the kitchen she made some peppermint tea and stood at the big glass wall looking out over the water.

'Hey, sis.'

'Hey, Colin. What are you doing up so early?'

'Those kids have shot my body clock to pieces, thought I'd go on a run. You exhausted them yesterday, they're all still asleep.'

'The loop?'

'Yeah, you coming?' She nodded. Run. Run away. And don't think.

The loop was a five-mile run along the water's edge, up a hill, then across the brow of the surrounding hills where the view was breathtaking and the world was yours. Bill liked to run. Terry liked to jog to music. And Colin liked to talk. Which they did, all the way round, except for up the hill, where they just heaved and spat in turn. She told him about Ty waking up in the middle of the night. She didn't tell him anything else. By the time they got home, sweaty, hot and jubilant, Colin had run the guilt out of her. They kicked off their running shoes, unsteady on their legs, exhaling puffs of air. Jessie bent over to touch her toes and saw the headline of the *News of the World* upside down at her feet.

JAMI ATTACKED
QUICK-THINKING STARLET
FOILS Z-LIST KILLER

Jessie stood up too quickly, the blood drained from her head and she lurched forward.

Pop sensation Jami has suffered a horrific attack in her own home. The ordeal started when Jami put the key in the front door of her beautiful Chelsea townhouse. A masked man grabbed her round the mouth and throat.

'I felt something cold against my neck and I thought, this is it, I'm going to die.'

Jessie shook her head. There was a picture of Jami's bruised face. Another of a broken china clock.

Next the cold-blooded killer forced her inside and proceeded to strangle her. 'As my life flashed past me, all I could think of was my family, friends and fans. Just then I heard my grandmother's voice shouting at me, "The clock, the clock!" She'd left it to me in her will, it was on the hall table. I was on the verge of blacking out, but she gave me the strength to pick it up . . .'

Jessie put the paper down. 'This is bollocks. The killer has never left a mark before. Why start now?'

'Why would she lie?'

'Oh, Colin, bless you. I've met her, she is some piece of work, she would do anything to get a headline. She's manufactured this, and she's not going to get away with it. This time I'm going to get her on wasting police time, when I've finished with her, she'll wish she never left her fucking tap-dancing class.'

Colin let the swear word slide. 'Does this mean you won't stay for lunch?'

'I shouldn't have stayed for dinner.'

'But you're glad you did?'

Jessie smiled. 'Yes, I'm glad I did.'

He poked Jessie in the ribs. 'Thought you might be.'

'What are you talking about?'

'Let's just say too much red wine makes me sleep badly.'

Jessie's stomach lurched. 'I told you, I found Ty in the corridor . . .' She retreated into the kitchen and started running the cold tap.

'Yes, you told me about Ty, you told me about the story, but you didn't tell me about –'

'Shh,' said Jessie, turning the tap off. 'I think that's my phone.' She followed the noise to the sitting room, where her phone lay charging on a side table. It was Jones. He must have seen the Sunday papers.

'I tried you at home,' said Jones, sounding terse.

'I'm still at my brother's house. It was too late to leave last night, they'd already cooked supper. I'm coming back today.' She didn't want to feel guilty, she was entitled to a break. But she did feel guilty. She hadn't come away for a break.

'Tell me Mr Dean and his children did not stay with you.'

She could have lied. They hadn't, after all, stayed with *her*. They'd stayed with her brother and sister-in-law.

'Jesus, Jessie, this is too complicated a case for you to –'

'It's all right, sir. I've got it under control.'

'Got *what* under control, Detective?'

She thought about him touching her. Him leaning forward. Pressing his face against hers. His hands moving over her skin.

'I'll be in first thing tomorrow morning,' she said.

'I want you in earlier than that.'

'Do you want me to do something about Jami Talbot?'

'What about Jami Talbot?'

'You haven't seen the papers?'

'Not yet.'

'That's not why you called?'

'No, Jessie, I called because you asked me to discover who Craig's father was. Or do you already know the answer?'

Jessie's chest hollowed, remembering last night's close conversation in the dark. 'Yes, I do.'

'I still trust your judgement, Jessie, and I'm sure P.J.'s explanation was convincing, but right now I'm focusing on Craig.'

'Craig?'

'I agree that it doesn't make P.J. more or less of a suspect. The set-up probably suited him quite well. I guess that P.J. is more concerned with the younger boys than Craig.'

'I'm sorry, sir, I'm not with you.'

'Craig wants that kind of attention for himself.

Think about it. He had a key to the house on the river, he's implied that he was sleeping with Verity, he says he was trying to help her, but Verity isn't alive to corroborate any of that. What if he isn't the brooding love-sick teenager? What if it's part of the act, and his trips up and down the drainpipe weren't to help Verity but to harm her?'

'Why?'

'Why? I would've thought that was perfectly obvious. Verity stood in the way of his mother and father. Craig wanted his family back together again, out in the open, like normal people. With Verity dead, Craig could have a proper dad, not just one on paper. Anyone can get hold of a birth certificate. Craig has probably known for years, or maybe Bernie told him – either way, it's natural for a boy to want to know who his father is. P.J. wasn't going to solve the situation. A divorce meant losing the boys, so Craig took charge. He's young, I know, but he has an obsessive personality. It takes one to plan a murder like this. Time and money and opportunity, he had all three and he knew Eve Wirrel. She was the perfect way to take the limelight off the family. She even lived on his cycle route. You must agree, the fact that Craig is P. J. Dean's son changes things?' Jones waited for Jessie to respond. 'Jessie, are you still there?'

There was still no response from Jessie.

'Jessie, I know you like the boy, but put your personal feelings aside. No more special treatment for that family, not even P. J. Dean – especially not

P. J. Dean. He got a fifteen-year-old girl pregnant. It's no different from the shit we have to deal with day in, day out. Dress it up, dress it down, it's still the same old shit. Jessie? Hello, can you hear me? Jessie? Damn these mobile phones.'

Jessie threw her dress and high heels in a bag, left P.J.'s clothes with Colin and was racing past the cooling towers of Sheffield when P.J. appeared, crumpled and disorientated, for breakfast at ten.

Taking a deep breath, Jessie pushed open the door to the incident room. Her team were waiting for her, alert, expectant. The room smelt of caffeine and gossip. For a split second conversation stopped, mouths hung open, then everyone moved at once, trying to resume an air of normality and failing. Attack, the best form of defence.

'I know that you're all thinking P. J. Dean is involved in these murders. And you may be right. It is now common knowledge that he and Bernie have the motive, the means and, if it weren't for a watertight alibi, he'd be our number one suspect.' Someone put their hand up. Jessie ignored it. 'However,' she said loudly, 'there are aspects of Verity's death that could be seen as clues pointing to Eve Wirrel.' Group puzzlement. 'Firstly, the remains of Verity Shore were found below a stretch of bank frequented by an art club. Secondly, the body had no hands, head or feet, the extremities that Eve Wirrel never painted. There were rumours of a lesbian affair between the two women. Both women were bled to death. Bled dry. Like the public have been by them. It could be a message. As irresponsible as it was of me to move P. J. Dean and his stepchildren to another safe house, it would be equally irresponsible of us not to look into the clues left at the scene of Eve Wirrel's death. So, we keep our minds open. This is what I want you to do.' She pointed to a DC. 'Search the internet for any information on Richmond. The name, the park, the area, the Isabella Plantation especially. We now know that Eve Wirrel was bisexual, let's find out who else she saw. I'm told it's a long list. Remember, despite her anarchic protestations, she was the daughter of a baronet. Examine all avenues.'

'What about the Cary Conrad investigation?'

'I'm on top of that.'

'And what about P. J. Dean?' asked Burrows.

'You on top of that too?' said Fry, grinning.

Jessie didn't miss a beat. 'We bring him in for questioning.' Reaction oscillated through her audience.

'I'll get on to it right away,' said Burrows.

Jessie poured herself a glass of water and drank it, drowning out the nausea.

'Any forensics on that boat?'

'Niaz is still investigating that.'

'Taking a bit of a punt, aren't you, boss?'

Jessie had an overwhelming desire to slap Fry

across the face. But rising to him would only make it worse. 'I want every single photograph of Verity Shore in one pile, Eve Wirrel in another, and Cary Conrad a third, I want the parties they went to and the guest lists of those parties entered into a computer. Cross-reference them. Are you getting my drift?'

'Yes,' said Fry. 'You're looking for a serial killer who is culling celebrities he or she doesn't think deserve their status.' His voice dripped with sarcasm.

'It's a possibility.'

'But not a probability.'

'No, Fry. Probability is what has got the Force into the mess it's in today.' Tense laughter scattered through the room. 'And you can tell DI Ward I said that.' Jessie picked up her notes and left the room. Bastards.

Burrows caught up with her on the way to her office. 'Dean won't be back until tomorrow. He wants to know if you can go to his house for the interview. Apparently his housekeeper isn't there and he doesn't want to bring the boys here.'

'No.' She carried on walking. 'He's taking the piss.'

'He implied we would sneak to the press, guv. He doesn't want the boys to be scared by the cameras.'

'What about using a nanny?'

'He doesn't want to leave the kids with a stranger.'

'How very convenient.' She was too angry to think effectively.

'What do you want to do, boss? If he isn't under arrest, we can't force him to come here.'

'Send a WPC and social services there tomorrow. Jones can interview him.'

'Won't he be expecting you to give him a going over, ma'am?'

Jessie stopped walking and looked at Burrows. 'I thought those children were in danger,' she said. 'Someone had left a skull at their gate. It wasn't public information, Burrows. What was I supposed to think?'

Burrows shrugged. 'Hey, I'm not passing judgement.'

'Like hell you're not.'

'All right, boss, I'm sorry about the facetious comment.'

Jessie suddenly felt as if she'd been in a boxing ring. 'I made a mistake,' she said quietly.

Burrows spoke in a soft, consoling tone. 'Yes, you did. Don't make another. If you hide from this now, Mark and his lot will eat you for breakfast. You're right, it could have been Verity's skull. Continue to put that message across. And for God's sake, don't act like you can't face P. J. Dean.' Jessie closed her eyes, embarrassed but grateful that a lower-ranking officer was putting her straight. 'Go to the house, boss. There are bound to be a few things you need to look at again. I'll bring Dean back here.'

She looked at Burrows. 'I'm sorry I let you down.'

'You haven't. Yet.'

Jessie closed the door of her office and leant against it. She'd done herself years of harm by falling for the neatly orchestrated package that is P. J. Dean. The spin. The fluff. The image. He'd lied to her, that was all she could think about. He'd lied to her in the middle of the night, and as a result she'd –

'Hard weekend?'

Jessie swung round. Mark sat in her chair, his feet on her desk, his arms stretched out behind his head. Jessie stared at the sweat patches on his shirt. He was loving this.

'What are you doing in here?'

'You have to do something for me.'

Jessie laughed sarcastically. 'Good thing you didn't join the diplomatic corps.'

'I always wanted to be a groupie, actually.' He smiled, baring yellow teeth and a gloating mind. 'And you are in no position to refuse, since it was you who stormed in on St Giles and got him all rankled.'

'I had reason to –'

'I don't give a shit, Driver. Because of you I can't go and speak to the leech myself. Your snitch – I need to talk to him.'

'This is my case. Jones has no right telling you.'

Mark shrugged. 'First of all, this isn't to do with your case. Second of all, don't be so sure it will be your case for much longer.'

Jessie swallowed her furious retort and kept her arms firmly by her sides. Her brothers had taught her how to fight. Mark wouldn't stand a chance. The idea of him flat on the floor with a broken nose was too tempting. He must have read it on her face because he pushed himself back against the wall. 'Still, I'm not really interested in your extracurricular activities. It's Ray St Giles I'm interested in. Trust me, I wouldn't ask for your help unless it was absolutely necessary. We can't all go running off with pop stars, some of us have real cases to solve. Some of us actually care about the victims –'

'Get to the fucking point.'

'Oh dear, lovers' tiff, was it?'

'Simply a natural response to bores. So, if you wouldn't mind . . .'

He sat up. 'Fine. Ray St Giles was fucking Veronica Mills. It went on for years – five years. Eventually she got pregnant and gave birth to Frank. Poor sad Trevor Mills had no idea, thought the baby was a miracle. Some fucking miracle. Anyway, Ray was a man possessed. He wanted Veronica and Frank for himself. He expected Veronica to leave her daughter behind with Trevor. But Veronica wouldn't leave Clare. Then Trevor got shot. Veronica couldn't live with the guilt and what the truth would do to her children, so she hung herself.'

The strength in Jessie's legs left her. She sat down abruptly. 'Bloody hell.'

'This guy who works for St Giles, call him, find out if there is a St Giles junior lurking about. A prodigy. A son and heir. You didn't come across one by any chance, did you?'

'No.'

'Didn't come across much, did you?'

The fight left her. Poor Clare. She leant over and picked up the phone on her desk. 'So that's why social services changed the names of those children. It was to protect them, after all.'

'Not necessarily. No one except Irene knew that Frank was Ray's son.'

'But if no one knew, why change the names?'

Mark Ward tapped the side of his head three times. 'Now you're catching on.'

~

'Come on in, Tarek. You've been avoiding me.' Ray St Giles pulled out a chair.

'Things have been busy since your meteoric rise.'

Ray smiled to himself. 'Flattery. That's good. Clever. But you're not as clever as you think, are you, Tarek my boy? Always been told I shouldn't trust your type.'

Tarek stood up. It was time to leave. Alistair pushed him back down again. He was strong for a thin guy.

'Did you really believe I was involved with these murders? Don't you think I spent enough time in the fucking clink? Eh? And even if I were involved, do you think I'd be so stupid as to leave files lying around for a nosy little rat to read?'

'Why are you so sure it was me?'

Ray clicked his fingers. Alistair swiped the back of his hand across Tarek's face.

'Alistair wouldn't betray me. That's how I know.'

And finally it dawned on Tarek. Alistair Gunner was not any old creep. He was Ray St Giles' creep.

'Information, boy. That's all I had. It turns out Alistair is an exceptional researcher, got a real knack for it. Anyway, the point is, I know you went to that copper. Nice tight arse she's got, don't you think?'

Alistair gripped Tarek's shoulder harder.

'I can almost understand why. Perhaps it did look strange, all that info on Verity Shore and the rest.' He spread his arms wide. 'But I didn't know someone was going to kill the stupid whore. I just wanted her on the show. Remember what I said to you? No more fat birds bleating on about their unfaithful boyfriends. She was this close to coming on, that Verity Shore, then she fucking died. It would have been fatuous, don't you think, not to use the information we had? Especially since Danny Knight knew before anyone else. It was news, Tarek. It was stuff people deserved to know about. They were being conned.'

He walked round the desk and leant close to Tarek's face. 'I could defend myself, if I had to. Find alibis, jump through the hoops. But I don't want to. Look around you. This new office is just the beginning. I would be very unhappy if your misplaced sense of civic duty got those lovely headlines we've had recently turned against me. You do understand, don't you?'

Tarek's mobile started to ring. He looked at the name. He began to sweat.

'Answer it, then. You're not a prisoner.'

'Hello, Karima,' he said in a stilted voice.

'You can't talk,' said Jessie.

'I'm in a meeting.'

'One question. Has Ray got a son?'

'Possibly. What time?'

'Aged about twenty-eight?'

'About that. I'll be there.'

'Ring me later with a name?'

'Is Muhammad coming?'

'Muhammad?' asked Jessie.

'No. That's a pity.'

'Muhammad . . . Ali?' It rolled off her tongue unconsciously.

'Perfect.'

'Ali?'

'A bit longer than that, we're still at work.'

'Alistair? Alistair Gunner?'

'Yes, sure. Got to go. See you later then.'

'The research assistant?'

'Bye.' He pressed 'end'.

Ray smiled. 'That's nice. Good to keep to your own. So? Do we understand each other?'

Tarek nodded.

'Right. Now fuck off and make me some coffee. I'm going for a piss.'

Tarek stood up and faced Alistair. The family resemblance was not obvious. But it was there. In the eyes. It explained everything. Why Alistair stuck so close to Ray. Why the closet conversations. Why he had access to Ray's personal files.

'I suggest you look for another job,' said Alistair. 'Can't have you ruining plans.'

'Like father, like son –'

Alistair hit him low, fast and hard. Tarek doubled over and fell to the floor.

'Go. If you know what's good for you.'

~

Mark and Jessie stared at each other. The idea that Frank had been by Ray St Giles' side all along was monumentally depressing. Could all that goodness be swallowed up by one man?

'Are there any records of a son visiting him in prison? This Alistair Gunner?'

'No. Raymond wasn't one for visitors, apparently.'

'Seems odd, doesn't it, that he didn't have his son visit him after he'd gone through so much trouble to get him? And why Gunner? Why not St Giles?'

'Because Ray stole him from some bent arsehole in the social services, that's why.'

'So why change Clare's name?'

'Obvious. To muddy the water. Let's face it, it worked. It's taken twenty-five years to unravel this mess. I don't like this either. I don't want to break Clare's heart, but the truth is Ray St Giles stole a kid.'

'His kid.'

'That's not the point.'

'Isn't it? Isn't that exactly the point? Whether Veronica liked it or not, Ray St Giles had rights over that boy. And who looked after him?'

'For a moment I forgot I was talking to a bleeding-heart school girl.'

'Drop it, Mark. This is more important. What are you going to do?'

'Haul him in. Send him down. Everyone goes home happy. You got any better suggestions?'

'Yes. Find out more. You don't hide a child.'

'Why not? Invisible people are very useful. And I've been hearing that our new-found voice of the people isn't quite the rehabilitated fellow he wants us to think he is.'

'Don't start a war with St Giles.'

'You started the war, remember.'

'He could still be involved in these murders. Especially since we now know he has a faithful ally. Why don't we organise some surveillance? Then we –'

Mark stood up. '*We? We* won't do anything. I'm sick of you, Driver. Don't try and pin the murders on St Giles when you know perfectly well your boyfriend did it.'

325

'I resent that.'

'I don't give a fuck,' he said, reaching for the door.

'Clearly. But what about Clare?'

'Tough shit. It's time she grew up. Clare wanted Ray back behind bars. I'll be doing that for her.'

'At what cost?'

'Not as much as gallivanting round the country-side with P. J. Dean has cost you. I know about your brother's safe house. So get off your high horse, Driver. You don't carry much weight around here any more. Lost your sheen, haven't you, girl?' He closed the door, leaving her to suffer in silence.

Jessie didn't move for half an hour. She'd lost a great deal more than her self-respect by believing P. J. Dean.

Niaz knocked and stuck his head round the door. She looked up. 'Tell me you've found out who bought the boat.'

'Sorry. But I will.' Jessie didn't have a tenth of his confidence. 'I do have the lab results back on those cigarettes you sent in. Don't worry, it was just a coincidence they were the same brand.'

'Niaz, have you got mind-reading skills I should know about? X-ray vision?'

'Well, you are wearing the wrong bra size.'

'Niaz!'

'It's true, ma'am. Most women do. You prob-ably wear a 36B, but you have a very narrow back, so you should be wearing a 32D. Maybe C.'

Jessie held out her hand. 'Those lab results, please? Then I'd like to see the back of you for ten minutes until my anger subsides.'

'You're smiling on the inside, ma'am.'

She looked down at the lab results. 'Out.'

'*Time Out*, actually.'

'What?'

'*Time Out*,' he said, holding up the magazine. 'It purports to keep people up to date –'

'Thank you. I know what it is.'

'A gallery on Davies Street is showing a retrospective of Eve Wirrel's work. Including, it is rumoured, some previously unseen pieces.' He held up the advert.

'Aren't we supposed to have all her unseen work?'

'Quite. I thought you might like to escape the whispering gallery for an art gallery. You never know what you might find.'

'Niaz, are you sure there isn't a genie tucked inside your uniform?'

He smiled, tapped his head and pulled the door closed behind him. Niaz Ahmet gave her tremendous strength. There was something quite magical about him. Jessie examined the evidence from the cigarettes. The first white-tipped Marlboro Light had been partially smoked outside her house by a woman called Frances Leonard. She was forty-three and had a small list of petty crimes to her name. Predominantly shoplifting. Woolworths seemed a particular favourite. She hadn't been active for three years. Jessie wouldn't have thought anything of it, except Frances Leonard lived in Acton. So she wouldn't be out walking her dog or stretching her legs in Paddington at ten o'clock on a Friday night.

The second cigarette had been smoked by P. J. Dean. She'd seen him take three or four drags, then stub it out lengthways under his foot. He'd done the same thing with every cigarette he smoked over the weekend. It was a very particular way of smoking. The lab concurred that the two cigarettes had been stubbed out in exactly the same way and the brand was identical. The similarities stopped there. Jessie wasn't so sure. She called Acton police station and instructed them to pay Frances Leonard a visit. It was probably a waste of time, but she wanted to throw the net wide. Wide enough to include Dame Henrietta Cadell, her philandering husband and her put-upon son. Jessie called in a WPC and told her to find everything there was to know about the Cadells. Galvanised, she was ready now for a chat with DC Fry.

She found him in the lunch queue and beckoned him over. He swaggered as he followed her into the deserted corridor.

'Ma'am, I never knew you felt –'

'Shut the fuck up, Fry. I have an offer to put to you, one you will not refuse. You will report back to me on everything DI Ward does with St Giles, or get a transfer.'

He raised a challenging eyebrow. 'On what grounds?'

'Insubordination and spying.'

'But you're asking me to spy.'

'Only after you volunteered for the job, Fry.'

'I didn't,' he protested.

'Yes, you did – to DI Ward. Now it works both ways or not at all. You got me?'

Fry didn't speak.

'There's a vacancy in Traffic, Fry. You want me to put your name forward?'

'You wouldn't do that.'

'Watch me.' She began to dial a number on her mobile phone, talking as she punched in the numbers. 'Due to strains in his personal life, DC Fry has requested a transfer to Traffic. He needs a lighter load to save his relationship. Oh yes, I quite agree, too many policemen end up alone.' She looked at him. 'It's ringing . . .'

'Okay, okay, I'll do it. Jesus, you're making me into a snitch.'

'You were already a snitch, Fry. I'm just making the most of your natural flair for the job. Everything, Fry, verbatim, or it's Traffic. You read me?'

'Like a porn mag, boss.'

~

The short ride through Mayfair was not enough to ease her addled brain. She needed to open up the throttle, eat up the miles, scare herself with speed. Even then, Jessie wondered if it would be enough to erase the feel of P.J.'s skin and the look in her colleagues' eyes.

She scanned the address Niaz had given her and headed north along Davies Street. Galleries and designer home stores, where you bought other people's taste and their idea of 'good' art. The glass-fronted gallery was shrouded in a huge white sheet with one small hole cut out in the middle. It looked like a marriage sheet for the devout. Jessie chose not to peer through it and rang the bell instead. A portly man with porthole glasses to match bounced towards her on the balls of his feet. She could smell his pomade as soon as he opened the door.

'I'm afraid, madam, the private view isn't until tomorrow evening. Nothing is on display yet.'

She held out her identity badge.

'Oh,' he said, and took two bounces back.

Standing in the perfectly proportioned white room, dressed in thick rubber-soled boots and leathers, Jessie couldn't decide whether she looked incongruous or installed.

'It will be very tasteful,' said the gentleman with the porthole glasses. 'Very tasteful.'

'I have reason to believe that you are intending to display a previously unseen piece by the late artist.'

The man was beginning to sweat. Niaz's information was correct.

'I'd like to see it, please.'

The man looked heartbroken.

'And then I'd like to know where you got it from.'

Jessie followed him through to the back of the gallery and down some stairs to a room where pictures and photographs were arranged and numbered. 'We don't take them up until the day,' the man said. 'This is like our rehearsal room, if you like.' Jessie wasn't interested. She'd examined the back catalogue of Eve Wirrel's work. She'd seen too many disfigured sexual organs and blurred heads. Now that she knew why Eve Wirrel painted the way she did, they no longer held any interest. No wonder the artist threw herself at the installation bandwagon. Dirty underwear, used condoms and now . . . The man opened the door of a free-standing family-sized freezer.

'They're all there,' he said.

Except three, thought Jessie. The three back in the lab. The three they had found in Eve's own fridge. Eve Wirrel's private sperm bank. Neatly labelled. In matching phials.

'We have a cooling tray being delivered. Square. For upstairs. It will be central to the whole show,' said the man, desperation clawing at his throat.

'How many are there?' asked Jessie, looking at the rows of surgical containers.

'Four hundred and sixty-three,' he said, sounding exhausted at the thought of it. 'It's called "A Life's Work". Get it? "A Life's Work". That's why it's so central, because we are showing her life's –'

Jessie held up her hand. She got the point.

'Where did you get these?'

He seemed to shrink before her. Perhaps it was the freakish atmosphere, or his palpable nervousness, but he was beginning to resemble Penfold. Jessie relented.

'I know this is a major coup for you. I understand that the gallery will make a lot of money. But Eve Wirrel was given Rohypnol, stripped bare and left to bleed to death, alone. Her murderer made a mockery of her art. This –' she pointed to the contents of the freezer – 'cannot be done tastefully. The DNA of the murderer may be in there. You still want to display it?'

He looked at his well-polished shoes.

'It's evidence,' she said. 'And I think you know that.' He nodded as she began to make the arrangements.

Jessie swung her leg over her bike, forced the foam of the helmet down over her head and clipped the strap into place. The police van had arrived and another harvest of Eve Wirrel's life had begun. She did not yet know whether 'A Life's Work' included any female deposits, or if Eve kept that aspect separate, secret, not for commercial consumption. If that was the case, it was women who held the key to Eve Wirrel. Men she had en masse, but they were meaningless. Mocked. Like the 'Average Week'. A message of solidarity to Verity, perhaps.

332

P.J. had said himself he used condoms with his own wife because he didn't trust her.

As the first tray of phials was carried out, the curator followed woefully behind. He was checking each phial against a list. Jessie took the list from him. He'd listed the phials chronologically. She ran her finger down until she came to what she was looking for. She took a sharp intake of breath. Three letters. Her worst fears. Jessie looked back at Eve's 'Life's Work' and wondered which one in that frozen still-life was P.J.D.

Jessie turned on her minidisk, jacked up the volume and steered the bike through the backstreets towards Park Lane. She needed the speed, to open the throttle. Get some air in her lungs before they imploded. The traffic was slow so she edged her way through the stationary cars with one foot hovering inches off the ground. Once on Park Lane, the lights were generous to her, green all the way. She caught an amber at the entrance to Marble Arch and skirted around into the park. The long, straight road lay flat and enticing in front of her. She kicked the bike into gear and pulled the throttle towards her, changing up quickly, making the bike bite faster and faster. For a blissful few moments the speedometer hit sixty-five. She saw a group of tourists up ahead on the left and knew instinctively they would step out on to the road without looking. It was a park, they didn't expect traffic and had forgotten it came from their right. Jessie reluctantly squeezed the brakes. Nothing happened. She squeezed again. She changed down a gear, the bike roared in complaint, the speedometer dropped but not enough. The first woman stepped into the road just metres ahead of her. Jessie sounded her horn and shouted. A car was coming towards her on the opposite side of the road. The woman, shocked, ran to the central reservation. A second followed. The others scattered. Jessie couldn't risk it; at fifty miles an hour she aimed the bike up the thick pavement, gave herself a jolt, steadied the bike, changed down a gear and raced through the ancient oak trees. The grass was wet, the bike was slipping and there were people shouting at her. She changed gear again. She aimed the bike towards an empty stretch of grass, hit a muddy patch and fell into a sideways skid. There was nothing she could do to stop the bike from toppling. If she put out her leg it would break. If the bike landed on her, it would break and burn. Jessie pulled the key out and threw herself backwards. She rolled four times before coming to a stop in time to see the bike, her precious Virago, hit a tree and come to a clattering halt. The American tourists came running. Jessie pulled off her helmet and checked herself for injuries. Pain came later, after the shock had died down.

'Are you okay?' asked one woman.

Jessie burst into tears.

Harris showed Jessie to a table. 'Are you all right? I heard about the accident.'

'News travels fast.'

'Bad news travels fast,' said Harris. They were in a coffee shop near Cary Conrad's house. 'In my youth these sort of conversations were had over a pint, not a cappuccino.'

'You sound like Mark Ward.'

'I know your fellow DI. His own worst enemy, that one, but he isn't as bad as he comes across.'

'It wasn't an accident,' said Jessie suddenly. Accidentally. 'I was going fast, I admit, but my brakes failed because someone had greased the wheel rims with lubricating oil.'

'Not Mark –'

'No, of course not Mark. Sorry, I shouldn't have said anything.'

'You haven't told anyone? Jones?'

Jessie shook her head.

'Who do you think did it, then?'

Pick a card. Any card. 'I don't know,' said Jessie. She couldn't even bring herself to think about the options.

'Know thine enemy, Driver – a vital rule, if you are going to survive this game.'

'Thanks, that thought did come to me while I was upside down at thirty miles an hour, somersaulting my way through Hyde Park.'

'Any injuries?'

'No. I learnt how to roll on a skydiving course with my brothers. Never thought it would come in useful.'

'Action girl.'

'Obviously not.' She stuck a spoon in her over-priced steamed cow's milk. 'Harris, what would you say to having this conversation the old way, over a pint and a large whiskey?'

Harris chose a table in the corner, away from the daytime drinkers and the clutter of men in suits. He had photos of an obscene nature. Definitely not images to be seen over coffee and a poppyseed muffin. On Cary Conrad's home computer they had found, encrypted, a number of extraordinary images. They found others that had been looked at and then deleted. Even those images had left their mark on the computer's memory.

'Seems you were right about the fetishism.'

Jessie could not believe her eyes. Cary Conrad was lying beneath the Perspex bowl of a boxed-in toilet while an unknown accomplice defecated on his face. From the angle of the photograph, Jessie could see this seemed to be bringing Conrad enormous pleasure. Jessie turned the photo over.

'It explains why he purchased that old, unmodernised house. No doubt delighted the council had stuck a grade one listing on it. He couldn't change it. He told his friends it was like living in a museum – not that he had many friends. I believe his wife knew nothing of this, though you can never tell how blind people are prepared to be.'

Jessie didn't need to imagine what that felt like.

'It's incredible what people do behind their spouse's back,' said Harris. 'I'm beginning to think this isn't what we thought, the third victim. Conrad's just a sad man caught in the act. Not suicide, mind. It was damp down there, the knots could have slipped. Except –'

'He needed someone to lower him in.'

'Precisely.'

'What about this missing private secretary?'

'He was due leave. No one knows what the arrangement was between him and Conrad. He's travelling somewhere in Asia. We're tracking him down.'

All someone needed was the information. Jessie explained that Verity Shore's house was also listed. As was the church that Eve Wirrel managed to alter from the inside. It was a cobweb-thin link, but it was a link. They were all celebrities and somehow their deaths had exposed the area of their lives the camera never saw and the papers never printed.

'Any forensics in the house?' asked Jessie wishfully.

'Nothing. Clean as a whistle. What about yours?'

'Nothing. Not a mark. Invisible, even to CCTV.'

'If this person is going to kill all the famous

people with peculiar habits, there won't be many left.'

'Perhaps that's the point. Except, Cary Conrad didn't bleed to death like the other two.'

'You don't think drowning in your own faeces is enough of a point?'

Jessie couldn't help it. She started laughing. Harris joined in. It was simply too revolting to comprehend. Humour and draught lager, safer ground.

~

A crowd of people had gathered at the top of the stairs. Mark Ward was bringing in his big catch. Raymond St Giles. Mark showed the compact and angry TV personality into an interview room. When Fry knocked on the door to interview room two, Mark gave him a suspicious look but let him stay.

'I want a fucking lawyer. Do you know what this will do to my reputation if it gets out? I'm a reformed fucking character, and this is police harassment.'

'We just want to talk to you about the death of Trevor Mills.'

'Who?'

'The man you served nine years for killing.'

'Oh, that Trevor Mills. What about him? He's dead, isn't he?'

'Yes, Ray, along with his wife, Veronica.'

'My friends call me Ray. You can call me Mr St Giles. What is it you really want? Tickets to the show? I can arrange that, front row and all. Bet that's what's galling you, eh? You don't like the thought of me becoming a star. Well, get used to it, boys. I'm on a trajectory that you cannot curtail.' Ray looked around the room. 'Any words you lot don't understand, I'll explain. All you need is a good teacher. I had a great one in the nick, taught me a lot.'

'Remorse, Ray, did they teach you that?'

Ray tapped out a cigarette. He pulled a Dunhill lighter from his pocket and lit it. A few long drags and he dropped the partially smoked cigarette in the plastic cup. It fizzed in the cold tea.

'Just tell me what the fuck this is about.'

'Do you feel remorse for Trevor Mills?'

Ray didn't respond.

'What about his wife, Veronica? Beside herself, she was. Hung herself from the wardrobe. Heard she got about a bit. Never understood why she topped herself, if she had so many men waiting in the background. Unless they were all married. Perhaps she was on the game. She always had lovely clothes. She was probably overcome with . . .' Mark Ward paused, watching Ray's knuckles whiten, '. . . remorse. What do you think, Ray? If an old whore can feel remorse there may even be a chance for you. You've gone very quiet, Ray. Are you feeling all right?'

Ray's eyes turned to ice. Fry felt the coldness of

his stare as he looked at every single face in turn. When it came to his turn, Fry looked at his feet.

'Is there anything else?' Ray said in a soft, hard voice. 'Only I've got a lunch at the Dorchester. An old pal of mine has written his memoirs, two hundred grand for the book rights. Sorry.' He rose to leave, sliding his packet of fags and lighter off the table in one swoop.

'How's your son?' Mark asked when Ray had reached the door.

Ray turned back. It was a full minute before he spoke again. 'Fine, thank you. How's yours? Oh yeah, forgot – you don't have any kids.'

'How kind of you to remember.'

'It's my job to remember who's who in the police force. Wouldn't have complained so much if that lovely DI Driver had brought me in. Wouldn't mind doing a few rounds in the ring with her. She boxes, did you know that? Very sexy. Must be hard, Ward, having a peer half your age who looks that good. Perhaps she'll have an accident on that bike she loves so much, then you'll be free of her. You'd like that, wouldn't you, Ward?' His eyes still navigated the room, taking in the opposition. 'How long you been DI now? Twelve years, isn't it? That's a pity. And no kids.'

'Does he look like his mother or you?'

'Who?'

'Your boy. Not really a boy any more. What is he – twenty-eight?'

Ray didn't move.

'Pity he didn't get more of his mother's genes. She was attractive, that's why all the lads liked her.'

'What the fuck do you want with Alistair's mother, eh?'

'Alistair? Oh, sorry, Ray, must have got you confused. I was talking about Frank.'

Ray St Giles' eyes paled. 'Who's Frank?' he asked. A little too late.

'You don't know? Perhaps we should talk to Alistair about it instead.'

'Leave him alone. I'll get my lawyers on you if you so much as fucking look at him.'

'Doesn't he know you killed his mother?'

'That's it, I'm leaving.'

'How did you find him, Ray?'

Ray had one hand on the doorknob.

'Probably best he didn't know his slut of a mother,' said Mark.

The knuckles whitened.

'Still, every family has the odd skeleton. It all comes out in the end. The press would love a story like this, especially since your new-found fame. Bet Alistair wouldn't mind knowing the truth either.'

'Alistair's mother is dead.'

'Yes, Ray, we know that. Your trigger-happy handiwork did that for her. Funny how even slags can stick by their old men.'

Ray carried on, ignoring Mark's taunts. 'She died three years ago from cancer. Her name was Alice Gunner, she worked in one of my clubs, earning money for medical college.'

'Yes, Ray, I've read the beautifully constructed birth certificate. Another useful little sideline, wasn't it, documentation? Ray St Giles father, Alice Gunner mother, gave birth to beautiful baby boy called Alistair at St Mary's Hospital, Reading. Very nice piece of work.'

'That is the truth.' He spat the words.

'Really? Funny Alice and Alistair never lived in the area. What did you do? Set her up somewhere nice in the country while you did your time?' Mark looked at Ray. 'We know everything.'

'Is that right?'

'Yes. Stealing babies is a crime, Mr St Giles, even if the child's mother was a slag.'

Ray took a step towards Mark. 'I know where you are getting this information from and it will stop.'

'You go near –' Mark stopped himself.

Ray laughed. 'You have nothing. And now, thanks to your splendid incompetence, I have everything. You should have done your homework before you called the likes of me in. I'm a professional when it comes to gleaning information.' He looked around the room once more. 'Look it up, if you don't understand.' Then he left.

'Shit,' said Mark.

'You'd better warn Irene,' said Fry.

'He's playing with us. Frank is Alistair, of course he bloody is.'

'Still, just in case, you'd better warn Irene.'

Mark looked at him. 'One fucking word of this

342

to Driver and I'll have you transferred to Traffic.'

Fry knew then he'd tell Driver everything that had happened. Verbatim. 'Too late,' said Fry. 'DI Driver's already put me in for the job. You two aren't as different as you think.'

~

Jessie walked through the revolving doors of the Pall Mall club and stepped back in time. Everything from the wooden panelling to the reverent hush emanated old money. Men sat in high-backed leather chairs reading the *Financial Times* while sipping pink gin. It was not yet twelve.

She was informed that Christopher Cadell was waiting for her in the visitors' bar. The one place women were allowed. Jessie found him in a corner. A waiter was removing an empty crystal glass and replacing it with a full one. As Mr Cadell lifted it to his lips he noticed her approach and rose to introduce himself. Jessie wondered whether it was nerves or alcohol that made him quiver. According to the information from the WPC, Christopher Cadell had been a social alcoholic for years. His career as a documentary maker had floundered as a result, though he blamed short-sighted superiors rather than inebriation for his downfall. Fortunately, his wife had become increasingly wealthy and he had retreated to his club safe in the knowledge that Henrietta would pick up the bill. Divorce was not an option. This Jessie knew was because the Dame set great store by reputation. They had now been unhappily married for thirty-nine years. Joshua, who arrived after six years, had obviously not made it any better. Jessie was still working out how to bring up the subject of infidelity and murder when Cadell leant forward in his chair and spoke.

'No doubt you want to ask me about the dead girl.'

'Verity Shore?'

'Yes. Verity.' He said the name as though he hadn't spoken it before.

'You were having an affair with her when she died?'

'No. It was over. At my age these things don't last long.'

'How did you meet her?'

'Through my wife. She hated Verity, thought she was stupid. Henrietta doesn't like stupid people, she finds it insulting they breathe the same air as she does.' Christopher took a sip of gin and tonic. Then another. He was handsome, or had been. The spider's web of broken blood vessels criss-crossed his cheeks and nose. He was shorter than Joshua and had brown eyes. So did Henrietta. Jessie wondered where Joshua's dark blue eyes had come from.

'Mr Cadell, how did you know that I was here about Verity Shore?'

'If that dreadful man on television knew, I rather thought the police would soon enough.'

'Is that why Henrietta went on the show, because he was blackmailing you?'

'Nothing as dramatic as that. Though of course she'll never let me forget it. You would have thought this was the first time she'd ever done anything she considered beneath her to promote a book.'

'Why didn't you come forward?' asked Jessie.

'It's not for me to do your job, is it?'

He seemed completely unfazed by her arrival. 'We've met before, Mr Cadell. At the film premiere party, in the corridor by the ladies.'

'Did we? I can't remember.' He closed his eyes for a moment. 'I've been to so many.'

'Did Ray St Giles tell Henrietta about Verity?'

He smiled meanly. 'There would be no sport in it, if she didn't know.'

'So you told her?'

He shrugged. 'Not exactly, but she does like checking the credit-card bills. What else would I have been doing on Monday afternoons in Dukes Hotel?'

'Mr Cadell, Verity Shore was killed by someone who knew what she was really like. A lover, or perhaps the lover's aggrieved wife.'

'Henrietta? Aggrieved?' He spat when he laughed. 'You've got the wrong wife. All she cares about is her position and her precious son.'

'*Her* son?'

Christopher looked muddled for a moment, then clicked his finger and ordered another double Bombay Gin and tonic.

'Is that why you flaunt your affairs, Mr Cadell?'

'There is something you should understand about my wife, Inspector. When she puts her mind to something, whatever it is, she always gets it.'

'And your wife wanted a child.'

'More than anything. She couldn't understand why she could succeed where others had failed but couldn't do what millions of women did every day. It drove her mad. When she discovered it wasn't her fault, she was over the moon. It was my fault, you see, not hers. She was still perfect.'

'So she had an affair?'

Christopher Cadell spun the ice round the glass before sucking the last of the gin out of it. 'If it had been that, I might have understood. But it wasn't, it was an exercise. She fucked her way around the intelligentsia until she got pregnant. Obviously that was less degrading than a visit to the IVF clinic.'

So Joshua was all hers. Henrietta didn't even have to pretend to share him.

'But not for you?'

'What do you think?'

She had humiliated him. So now he humiliated her.

'She always wanted more,' said Christopher, staring into his empty glass. 'Joshua was never going to criticise her. He would never rave about her one minute, then slate her the next. He had to love her. She made pretty sure of that.'

'What do you mean, Mr Cadell?'

Christopher picked up the wine list and scanned it. Finally he looked up. 'I think a bottle of claret, don't you? Just to wash a sandwich down.'

'What did you mean about Henrietta and Joshua?'

'Didn't you come here to talk about that woman?'

'Yes.'

'Well.' He snapped the wine list shut. 'I know when she died, and I was here. The club will verify that.'

Jessie sat back in her chair. 'You seem to know more than we do. Because of the state of the body, we can't tell exactly when she died. Thank you for your alibi, but it isn't quite enough. There is still the motive.'

'What motive? She was just some silly girl. I'm sorry she died, but it really has nothing to do with us. Henrietta and I play a nasty little game, but it is only with each other. No one else gets hurt.'

'That isn't true, I'm afraid, Mr Cadell. What do you think it does to Joshua to see his father drunk, feeling up women, humiliating his mother?'

'Joshua doesn't give a shit. You think his mother would miss the opportunity of telling him how ineffectual his father really is? He's known for years. So, as I said, this is merely a nasty little game between us. It's kept us going for years.'

'Mr Cadell, did you know Eve Wirrel?'

He shook his head. 'And neither did Joshua.'

'Joshua?'

Christopher stood up. 'My table is ready. Sorry, but women aren't allowed in the dining room.'

~

Jessie pulled up outside the familiar green gates and pressed the button. P.J.'s disembodied voice reverberated through the speaker.

'Jessie, thanks for coming, this really means –'

'Can we come in?'

'Of course.'

The gate buzzed, clicked and began to move. She looked in the rear-view mirror. A woman from social services and a WPC occupied the rear seat. Burrows and a PC were in the car behind. This was an ambush. She was the Trojan horse. She wasn't here for him. She was here because of something Christopher Cadell had said. Monday afternoons. Tarek's photo of Christopher and Verity was dated. It had been taken four Mondays before Verity died. Jessie had returned to the station and re-checked the security videos. The tape did not show Verity Shore leaving the house on that or any subsequent Monday. That meant one of two things. Either the video had been doctored, or Verity had found another way to sneak out of the house. Jessie was having the tape examined. Meanwhile, she would check out the property again.

P.J. was walking down the black tiled driveway towards her. He looked more crumpled, less sure and more ravaged by sleeplessness. He watched the second car with suspicion, but managed a smile when Jessie got out of the car.

'DC Burrows is here to take you to the station,' said Jessie, before P.J. could even say hello.

'Oh.' He looked at her with his big green eyes; they had dulled to the colour of sage. Doleful. Like his sons.

'DCI Jones will do the interview. You may as well tell him everything, because we'll find out in the end.' She sounded angry. Too angry.

'You couldn't find it in your heart to trust me, could you?' said P.J. quietly.

Jessie wouldn't fall for that soft voice again.

'This way, please.'

'The boys are in the garden out the back, they're making a tepee.' He was looking straight at her. 'That's a wigwam, you know.'

She did know, and it was making her stomach flip. 'DC Burrows is waiting.'

'I should tell them –'

'*I'll* tell them,' she said quickly, holding open the car door.

His eyes narrowed and all softness left his face. She watched him realise that she'd spat out the worm, that he couldn't reel her in any more. The change in him was immediate. Down went the charade and the real beast showed its face.

'Bernie and Craig will be here in a few hours. If I'm not back, tell Bernie to call my lawyer. Presumably you'll know where to send her.'

'Bernie?'

'No. My lawyer.' He pulled himself up to his full height. He was tall. Like his son. 'You don't know everything, Detective Inspector Driver. You just think you do.'

It was a blow. A deep, painful blow, and even after the non-descript Rover pulled out of the driveway, she felt the aftershock radiate through her.

Jessie started in the pool house. She checked the windows in the changing rooms, but they had been sealed shut. There was a fence dividing the property from the neighbours. It wasn't impossible that Verity had climbed over it, but in the photo she was dressed in high heels and a minuscule dress, so it wasn't likely. If she did get out, it had to be easy. Then it dawned on Jessie that maybe Verity hadn't been home at all. Craig had said he was frightened for her when she was away, Danny Knight had told Ray St Giles she was away a lot. Perhaps P.J. had lost control long before Verity died.

She walked back into the house. The Eve Wirrel installation with its two and a half wrinkled condoms made her feel worse. An average week. Not even. Mark had been right, she was no better than a groupie. One in a long line. Jessie walked up the stairs and watched the boys play from the landing. She picked up the binoculars and looked at the fifteen-foot-high brick wall. Verity certainly hadn't climbed that. She looked out over the park to the Isabella Plantation. There was something she wasn't seeing, something she was missing. But what? She returned to Verity's bedroom. She would begin the search again.

~

Jones pulled up a chair opposite P. J. Dean and for a few moments studied the papers in front of him. He was pleased that Jessie had come to her senses, sorry that she had over-estimated the super star. He too had liked P. J. Dean, but he suspected P.J. had been playing God for so long he'd started to believe his own press. Burrows stood a fraction behind Jones and Fry stood at the door. P. J. Dean had requested a private interview. The request had been denied. This was a serious matter. Dean needed to know that.

'I'm not under arrest,' said P. J. Dean.

'No. You can leave at any time. But I wouldn't advise it. Next time – and there will be a next time, Mr Dean – our meeting might attract a little more attention.'

'How do I know whether you can be trusted? I've had coppers squeal to the press before.' Jones studied the room. He could vouch for Burrows. Fry was a different matter.

'Fry, would you mind getting us all some tea before we start?' Jones watched Fry's expression harden. 'We'll wait for you to return before we continue,' he said reassuringly. Jones wanted Fry to know that, if anyone squealed, he would be the number-one suspect, but until that time Jones would give him the benefit of the doubt. Fry left and Jones once more fell into silence. After a few seconds P.J. scraped his chair along the floor and stood up. 'I can't stand this. What the fuck do you lot want with me?'

'Mr Dean, we are trying to find out what happened to your wife. Most people in your position would do anything to help us.'

'Most people aren't in my position.'

'Don't be so sure, Mr Dean. A lot of people are married to someone they don't want to be with.'

P.J. threw him an arrogant look. 'The stakes are a bit higher in this case, don't you think?'

Jones sighed in his enigmatic way. 'Not really, Mr Dean, it's still an unhappy marriage, however many stones there may be on the ring.'

'I've asked you before, call me P.J. Mr Dean is my father and I am not my father.'

Jones looked at Jessie's notes on P.J. There were press-cuttings about P.J. not attending his mother's funeral; many people from the Mancunian suburb had taken umbrage at their local hero turning his back on them. Fame is addictive, even vicariously.

'Please sit down.' Jones waited for P.J. to return to his chair. 'When did you last see your father?'

P.J.'s eyes rose slowly to meet Jones'. Fry returned with the tea. Jones made a point of taking a loud slurp of Fry's brew and replacing the cup on the table. He leant back in his chair.

'Was your father disappointed to find out what

you'd been up to with your sister's best friend?'

P.J. let out a dry laugh, regained control quickly and looked Jones in the eye. 'My sister was dead.'

'I know – drowned. A very bad age for you to lose someone so close.' P.J. clenched his fists and his jaw. He looked ready to explode. 'They never found the body, did they? That must have been quite fascinating for a boy of fifteen.'

'Football, rugby, girls, these things are fascinating. Dragging the estuary day after day for my sister was not what I would call a spectator sport.'

'Your father is your only family now, isn't he?'

'I have the boys.'

'No, P.J., they're not yours. You can't keep them.'

Jones saw the flash of anger. 'You don't know what you're talking about,' P.J. said.

'You've lost so many of your family, your sister, your mother, your father. It's understandable you should want to keep Bernie and Craig close.'

'They are like family to me, only better. They stay because they want to.'

'*Like* family, P.J.?'

'This has nothing to do with Verity's death. Verity was a drug addict, she hung about with mad, bad people. Anyone could have killed her. I didn't.'

'Motive, Mr Dean, that's our problem. No one else has a motive. Only you, and possibly Bernie . . . oh, and thinking about it, Craig too, I suppose. The three of you probably make quite a good team.'

353

P.J. shook his head. 'I'm not staying here to listen to this shit. Ask me the question and I'll tell you the answer, but I am not listening to this shit. Craig is a great boy, Bernie is an amazing woman. As for me, I didn't have much feeling towards Verity either way, certainly not enough to kill her. Trust me, I know anger, I've dealt with hatred, and I haven't killed anyone yet.'

'You can see where I'm going with this, can't you? You, Bernie, Craig . . .'

P.J. stood up. 'Ask me the fucking question!'

Jones looked at the indignant bundle of energy. 'Are you Craig's father?'

'No.'

'It's your name on the birth certificate?'

'Yes.'

'But he's not your child?'

'No.'

'Will you take a paternity test?'

'No.'

Jones threw up his arms. 'Why the hell should I believe you?'

'For the sake of that boy. He doesn't know who his father is. He certainly doesn't think it's me – Bernie put my name down because she thought I wouldn't mind, and I don't, but that is her business. It happened a long time ago and it has nothing, absolutely nothing to do with Verity's death.'

'He has your height, your bone structure,' said Jones.

P.J. leant forward, clenched the table with both

hands. 'I wish I was his father. Truly, I wish to God I was. But I'm not. And not even me, with my God-like status, can change that.'

'You could've adopted him.'

'It was safer Bernie playing the housekeeper. She and Craig are not for public consumption.'

'Safer? For whom?'

P.J. didn't respond.

'Why are you protecting them?'

'I didn't.'

'Didn't?'

'Couldn't.'

'When couldn't you, Mr Dean?'

P.J. pushed the table away from him. 'Stop calling me Mr Dean!'

And suddenly Jones knew. Jessie had got him right all along. He understood why P.J. was so reluctant to talk. Jones had made a mistake, he should have left this to Jessie. She was the girl for the job.

'Burrows, Fry, could you leave us, please?' They looked confused. P.J.'s secret was safe, neither of them had worked it out. Jones showed them to the door and watched them disappear down the corridor. He passed P.J. some tea. 'Drink it,' he said in a voice so soft that P.J. deflated at the lightness of its sound. 'It's all right, P.J. I'm sorry, we did this the wrong way round.'

P.J. frowned. 'What's going on?'

'I see why you didn't want to talk before. You – everyone has a lot to lose.'

P.J. just stared at him.

'You can trust me,' said Jones. 'And Jessie.'

P.J. continued to stare at him.

'Craig isn't your son,' said Jones.

P.J. shook his head.

'He's your brother.'

Jones had seen many men cry, but few with the intensity of P.J. Dean.

~

Jessie was walking into the garden when she heard her phone. Seeing Jones' number made her chest clamp tight. She put the phone to her ear and listened to his rapid voice. The boys had jumped down from the tree and now stood stock-still, watching her.

Jones was talking fast. 'He says he'll do the test, anonymously and in total confidence, but he swears he was in the States on some youth-club music training camp when Craig was conceived. I'm sure it'll all check out. His father had been abusing Bernie since P.J.'s sister drowned. Makes you wonder whether the poor girl drowned by mistake or on purpose. You were right to put your faith in him. He wants to talk to you . . .'

Jones was still talking, but Jessie had stopped listening. Paul had turned away from her. He was halfway to the back of the garden when he turned around and beckoned her to follow him. With the phone still pressed to her ear, Jessie began to walk in the footsteps of a child. She wanted to call Paul back, tell him to forget what he knew, tell him it was over, it was all right, they needn't go any further. But Paul didn't turn around again and Jessie didn't call out.

'P.J. is sorry he didn't tell you straight away. He was protecting Craig. Bernie has been through enough without the scandal being splashed all over the press. She made him swear he wouldn't tell you until she'd had a chance to tell Craig the truth. She was terrified of him finding out another way. Jessie? Jessie? Are you there? God, I hate these things . . .'

She caught up with Paul on the other side of the overgrown border. He was standing with his back to her, facing the high garden wall. Without looking at her, he pulled back the ivy. At first Jessie didn't know what he was showing her. Part of the brick wall. Then slowly Paul clenched his hand into a fist and hit the wall. She reached out to stop him hurting himself, but he didn't graze his knuckles and the dense brickwork did not swallow up the sound of them hitting the wall. Paul knocked again. Three loud knocks. A hollow sound echoed around them. Jessie ran her hand down the smooth surface. It was wood. Painted to look like brick. A cunning little trompe l'oeil. With all the magic of a children's fairy tale, it could make people disappear.

Paul turned and looked at Jessie. She'd never seen such old eyes in a young face. 'Mummy said Heaven was through that door.'

*   *   *

Jessie stood at the wooden door and stared out into Richmond Park. It hadn't taken long to pick the lock. No wonder P.J. had handed over the security tapes so readily. Anyone could leave the Dean residence undetected. He had been so keen to stress how much he liked his weekends at home. He stayed in, he said, because he travelled so much in the week. Was he using the boys as unwitting alibis? Paul said his mother would pick up packages or meet a man at the door. It explained the stash of drugs they had found hidden in the shoe box. The boy would watch her sneak out at night. He would stand on the landing and watch her through his binoculars. The stash could be left at any point in the day, all Verity had to do was wait until the coast was clear. It hadn't only been Craig who had used the garage roof for illicit means. Now Jessie knew how Verity got her drugs in and how she sneaked out during the daytime, when the boys were at school and Bernie was shopping. So why not P.J.? Or Bernie? Or both of them taking turns?

Paul held her hand until he heard the voices. Bernie and Craig were back. Showtime. Craig came into the garden first. He saw daylight through the solid brick wall and stopped in his tracks. He put his hand to his mouth then lowered his head. Bernie's reaction was even stranger, stronger.

'What the hell have you been doing?' She looked at Jessie. 'Did you do this? Anyone could wander in.'

Jessie slowly pushed the door closed. She scraped the metal bolt through its catch.

'What the bloody hell . . . ?'

'Bernie!' admonished Ty.

'Sorry, sweetheart. What's going on? Where's P.J.?'

'At the police station with my boss.'

Bernie looked at Jessie with fear and anger in her eyes. She reached for Craig and kissed his forehead. 'Take the boys inside, they're freezing.'

Craig looked at Paul, then back up to the window of the house. He was a bright boy, cottoning on fast, thought Jessie. Or he'd been well rehearsed. 'I didn't know about that,' said Craig.

'I know,' said Paul.

'Why didn't you tell me? I might have stopped her.'

'I didn't want to get Mum into trouble.'

Jessie listened to the boys talk. Had it been the kids who'd been taking responsibility for Verity? They were the ones who loved her. Different sort of love, but both real and powerful.

'You should have told me,' said Craig. 'She trusted us.'

'All of you, go inside, now. I would like a word with Detective Inspector Driver alone.'

Craig carried Ty in, Paul followed a few feet behind.

'We knew nothing about this,' said Bernie.

'We?'

'P.J. and I. I know he told you – doesn't that

mean anything to you? You know more about my son than he knows himself.' Bernie was crying before the words were fully out. 'That kills me, but P.J. wanted to tell you. I begged him not to. He trusted you, and you sent him to the police station. Well, congratulations. When the story hits the papers I'll be sure to let Craig know you were only doing your job.'

Jessie followed Bernie back out to the lawn. 'How long has this door been here?'

'I don't know.'

'A secret door was put into this garden wall and *you* didn't know?'

Bernie looked as if Jessie had slapped her. 'I don't know what he sees in you,' she hissed. She began to walk back to the house, then turned back. 'All I've tried to do is look after everyone. Don't you dare come into my *family* and point your vicious little finger at me.'

'How far would you go to protect your family from more . . .' Jessie paused, wanting to stop, but unable to, '. . . interference?'

Bernie walked back to her, a look of pure hatred in her eyes. '*Interference?*' She laughed, incredulous. 'Is that what you call it? A forty-year-old man raping a thirteen-year-old girl? That's rape, and it lasted two years. No, make that twenty. It never stops. It's always in here –' Bernie pressed her hand to her head.

'I know you're angry.'

'You don't know the meaning of the word.'

'I know you'd do anything to keep Craig safe.'

'What kind of monster are you? You think I killed those women to protect my son?' Jessie didn't respond. 'No, you think I killed those women to protect P.J., because I'm in love with him.' The sneer in her voice slid through the long shadows and wrapped itself around Jessie's throat. 'Oh dear, Inspector, that's not very professional, is it?'

'What isn't?'

Jessie jumped at the sound of Jones' voice. He and P.J. were looking at the two of them, locked in an angry stance.

'Ask her,' said Bernie. She walked up to P.J. and grabbed his face in her left hand. 'Have you seen a picture of P.J.'s father?' Jessie shook her head. 'Spitting image. Sometimes I look at P.J. and feel sick. Then I have to remember that, if it wasn't for him, we would have been in some sink estate in Manchester. But he believed me, he spent five years looking for us because he knew, deep down, he knew. He knew what his sister had been through. He knew what I'd been through.' Bernie's fingers were leaving white indentations on P.J.'s cheek. 'He confronted his father, and you know what he said? "Well, son, we all have our little ways."'

'I'm sorry, Bernie,' said P.J., with difficulty.

Bernie shook her head. 'No, darlin', you've got nothing to be sorry about. Until Verity got sick, we were happy.' Bernie let go of P.J.'s face and turned back to Jessie. 'You were right about one thing. I should have known that Verity would get to Craig. It's obvious now, but I was spinning too many plates, I didn't see it until it was too late. I caught him coming down that blasted drainpipe one night, and he smelt of her. When I saw you looking at the window box I panicked, got the gardener to plant those chrysanthemums straight away. I was terrified you'd think it was Craig. But you are wrong about everything else and, when you realise that, your apology will not be enough to undo the damage you've done here.'

'Shh.' P.J. put his arm around Bernie then looked at Jessie. 'We really knew nothing about this. Remember, I told you, this house belonged to Verity's second husband. She wanted to stay here.' Jessie could hear the pleading in his voice. 'She must have been using that door for years. Surely you see that?'

Jessie's silence spoke for her.

'How can I prove it to you? Ask Paul if he ever saw me here. Ask Paul now, otherwise you'll think I've got to him.'

'He's been through enough today,' said Jessie.

'What, now you care?' barked Bernie. 'I've ripped out my heart because of you, and now you care!'

'Perhaps we should return tomorrow,' said Jessie.

'Like fuck you will,' said P.J. 'Enough is enough. You know everything. Now I'd like you to leave my house and my family alone.' He was hugging

Bernie to his chest. 'Don't make Paul an excuse to doubt me because it's easier for you that way. You're a big girl, Jessie. Deal with your own mistakes. I didn't lie to you.'

Jessie slowly walked up to him. From her bag she brought a photograph of Eve Wirrel's 'A Life's Work'. Attached to it was a single photograph of the initialled phial. 'Yes, you did.'

P.J. looked at the close-up. 'What the fu—'

'Mum,' said a voice from the garden doors.

'All right, darlin', we're coming.'

Craig stepped into the garden. He was carrying a packing box. 'Mum.'

'What have you got there?'

Craig was looking at P.J. 'It's not her fault.'

P.J. was staring at Jessie. 'Yes it is.'

No one spoke.

'I mean Verity. It wasn't her fault, P.J.' With obvious difficulty, P.J. turned to face him. 'I know who my father is.'

Bernie's knees buckled. P.J. caught her.

'I've known for ages. I'm so sorry about Verity.' He started crying. 'I loved her. It was wrong, I know, but I couldn't help it.' He sobbed. 'My brother's wife. I should have stopped it.'

P.J. left Bernie and ran over to the boy. The box Craig was carrying fell to the floor. 'Shh, Craig, it's my fault, not yours. I should have stopped it. That disgusting man. I knew, Craig, I knew what he was doing.' Bernie was staring at him. He turned back to her. 'God, Bernie, I'm sorry, I didn't want you to leave too, not you as well as my beautiful baby sister, I'm sorry, I'm so sorry.'

Bernie didn't move.

P.J. looked back at Craig. 'I was so happy when I found you – you and Bernie. You were such a great kid, so strong and smart. I was glad you were alive. My brother. Look at you. I don't mind about Verity. At least you made her happy, you should be proud of that . . .'

'I miss her . . .'

'I know, I know.'

Jessie crouched down by the box. She leafed through the contents and looked up at Jones. Hate mail. Death threats. Rabbit's claw. Blood-soaked rags. Many of them signed W.T.

'Where did you get these, Craig?' asked Jessie.

'Leave my boy alone!' shouted Bernie. 'All of you!' Bernie grabbed Craig's arm and pulled him away from P.J.

'He's my son. Mine. Mine, P.J., not yours.'

'I know, Bernie.'

She held a finger up to his face. 'How could you have done nothing?'

'I'm sorry –'

'Sorry! Julie killed herself and you didn't do *anything* . . .'

'Please –'

P.J. reached for her but Bernie brushed him away. She grabbed her son and led him away. 'Just leave us alone.'

P.J. looked over to Jessie. 'I think you should go.'

'May I take these?' said Jessie, holding up the box.

'I don't GIVE A FUCK! Get out of here. Now.'

'P.J., I –'

'Go away.'

Jessie took the box and followed Jones to the front of the house. As they climbed into the car, Ty appeared clutching her black torch.

'Dad says I have to give this back.'

'I'm sorry,' she said through the window as he waved goodbye.

Jones turned on her. 'You pushed too hard, Jessie. What I just witnessed should not have taken place.'

'I was trying to do my job, sir,' she said, feeling shaky and unsure.

'No, Jessie, you were trying to make up for not doing your job professionally in the first place. I'd start driving, if I were you.'

'You heard Bernie, he wanted those kids, he's on the edge.'

'P. J. Dean knew what his father was doing and didn't stop it. Worse, he ran away. He is a man consumed with guilt. That is not the same as a guilty man, and you know it.'

Jessie pulled away from the house. Those sea-green eyes had sucked her in and churned her around like a breaking wave. Muddled and confused, she'd kicked out in every direction. When she surfaced she was far out to sea, alone, in very deep water.

Mark Ward had driven to the village where Alice and Alistair were supposed to have lived with her father. Alice was dead, she couldn't corroborate St Giles' story, but the old man was still alive. Mark had paid the farm cottage a visit, but Mr Gunner wouldn't answer a single question about either his daughter or his grandson. When Mark asked who Alistair's father was, Pete Gunner slammed the door in his face. So he had waited until the old man shuffled out of the house, then let himself in. The kitchen was lime green Formica, the wallpaper a spongeable plastic. It was neat and orderly and smelt of Sunlight lemon washing-up liquid. There was a hatch through to the dining room, which housed a good mahogany table and set of chairs. Mark went quickly and quietly upstairs. There were three bedrooms and a bathroom. The smell of wet wool and sandalwood told him which room was Mr Gunner's. Alice's room had been left untouched since her death. Mark picked up a photograph of a young woman and a baby. It was inscribed on the back. The boy's name, birth date and weight. It was convincing, but it wasn't proof. It could be any baby; Mr and Mrs Gunner weren't necessarily in on the plot. Mark replaced the photograph, but he had to admit to himself that it was looking less and less likely that Alistair was

Frank. There was no sign of Ray St Giles anywhere.

The third room Mark went into was Alistair's. It wasn't the school photos on the wall or the stack of dumbbells in the corner that gave it away, it was the collection of 'gangland' literature so vast that it caused the plywood shelves to droop. Mark picked up a book and flicked through it. Sections had been highlighted with yellow marker pen. He pulled out another and another. Each one the same. The aspect of each book that had held Alistair's interest was the same: his father, Ray St Giles. Here was a boy obsessed. Mark began to jot down the titles and authors, a veritable A–Z of the English underworld. When he'd finished, he opened drawers and examined under the bed. In a cardboard box he found recently posted jiffy bags and stiff A4 envelopes. All addressed to Alistair Gunner. All sent from London. Mark tore one open. A photograph fell out. An older man in a suit, his hand up a blonde woman's skirt. He didn't recognise the man but he knew exactly who the blonde was. She was lying in the morgue. Nothing but bones. There was another: two women kissing. He didn't recognise either of the women. There was one of Ray St Giles shaking hands with John Banner, a well-known East End villain. He grabbed another envelope and ripped it open. Newspaper-cuttings spilled out. Headlines he recognised. Headlines he'd mocked. THE Z-LIST KILLER. EVE WIRREL DIES FOR ART. DYED BLONDE –

Jessie had been right. St Giles was involved. He stood up quickly, stuck the envelopes he'd opened under his arm and ran out to the car. Throwing the envelopes in, he started the engine and spun the car around. He was angry and worried and driving at speed. He didn't see the tractor pull out of the side entrance.

~

Jessie nursed a vodka martini. It was her third. The previous two had done nothing to ease the pain, the humiliation, the sheer ugliness of it all. She had been dazzled by P. J. Dean, no better than the fans rendered speechless by his presence. She might have clung on to Cary Conrad's death as a distraction, but Harris had called. The missing secretary had been found in Northern Thailand. Under questioning, the man had broken down and confessed. He had set Cary up in the position as usual, and left him to it. When he returned two hours later, Cary had drowned. Harris was now leaning towards accidental death. He believed the knots had slipped. It explained the lack of forensics: no forced entry, no struggle. Statistics had won: like Eve and Verity, Cary Conrad had known his killer. The crucial difference was that Cary's death had been an accident, whereas those women had been brutally murdered. Jessie shuddered. It was no way to die.

A whole new dilemma now confronted her. If another body turned up, it lessened the likelihood that P.J. was involved. But it meant that someone else had to die. And she didn't want that to happen. She didn't want P.J. to be guilty either.

Someone tapped her on the shoulder. Jessie turned.

'Hey, ma'am.'

'Hey, Niaz. I'm in the doghouse.'

'Pleasant doghouse,' said Niaz, looking around Claridge's bar.

'I bet you're wishing I'd left you in peace in Putney.'

'No, ma'am.'

'How did you I know I was here?'

Niaz tapped his head. 'My genie, remember.'

'Would you like a drink?'

He shook his head. 'I don't drink. But thank you for the offer. I recommend you order some ginger tea.' Niaz summoned the barman.

'I'm fine on vodka, thanks.'

'No, ma'am, you need a clear head. Ginger will speed the process up.'

Jessie began to protest.

Niaz held up his colossal hand and ordered the tea. 'I found the owner of the boat.'

Jessie straightened.

'It did not belong to Mr Dean, or his house-keeper, or his housekeeper's –'

'Who did it belong to?' Jessie interrupted impatiently.

'Lady F. C. Lennox-Broome, according to the credit card.'

'A woman.' Jessie was perplexed. Almost disappointed.

'We traced the punt to a yard outside Henley. It was bought over the phone by credit card and was picked up by a man with a trailer. It was a present for Lady Felicity's father. A surprise sixtieth birthday present. The credit card transaction was verified. The details have been on my list for some time but, like the boat-yard owner, I had no reason to doubt the validity of the purchase. I'm sorry, ma'am, I've let you down. Perhaps you should have left me where you found me.'

'No, Niaz, you have been a truly great help.' Jessie sighed. 'So, I was wrong. The boat was not the clue.'

'Not necessarily. It doesn't explain how the boat ended up in the Thames.'

'You want me to ask her, this Lady F. C. double-barrel?' Jessie looked at her watch. It was getting late.

'No. According to her flatmate, she is on holiday with a man. Precise location unknown. Name of man, also unknown.'

'You've been busy.'

'I'm doing the job you asked me to do.'

'You think I'm slacking. You think I should call out the cavalry again. You think she is missing? This Lady Felicity C. Lennox-Br—' Jessie felt it, like a bolt of electricity. Knowledge. 'Oh my

God, Niaz. I wasn't wrong, I wasn't bloody wrong. What did the flatmate call her? Not Felicity, I bet.'

'As a matter of fact, no. She called her Cos—'

'—ima. Lady Cosima Broome. Niaz, that boat never had a tender. That was the fucking clue! T.T., the initials stand for the Titled Tart, not "Tender To". Shit!' Jessie stood up abruptly and swayed.

Niaz caught her. 'Perhaps you should have that tea now,' he said.

Jessie called the number of the family estate, Haverbrook Hall, and asked for Cosima.

'Lady Cosima is not at home. May I take a message?'

'Either of her parents?'

'I'm afraid they are with guests at present.'

'Please tell them Detective Inspector Driver would like to speak to them on a matter of extreme urgency.' Jessie waited for three minutes. Either it was a very big house or the upper classes didn't do urgency.

'What's happened?' said a young, female voice. 'Is Cosima in trouble?'

'Who am I speaking to?'

'Viscountess Lennox-Broome.'

The voice didn't match the image. It was unsure, youthful, with a very faint London twang.

'May I ask when you last saw your daughter?'

'My daughter? Oh. Oh no, you're mistaken.

371

Cosima isn't my daughter, she's my stepdaughter and friend. Is she all right?'

'When did you last speak to her?'

'Coral?' barked a loud, rasping voice.

'Geoffrey, it's the police.'

'I'll deal with this,' said the voice.

'But –'

'If my daughter is in trouble, I'll deal with it.' Jessie introduced herself.

'What has she done that you have to call me at home at this hour?'

'I'm sorry to disturb you, but I need to confirm the whereabouts of your daughter. Can you tell me when you last saw her?'

'She is an adult now. I don't keep tracks on her.'

Jessie didn't want to alarm the man, but two women had been killed.

'Her credit cards haven't been used for a couple of days –'

'What the hell are you looking at my daughter's finances for?'

'We believe she may be missing.'

A female voice interrupted. 'She was here the weekend before last.'

'How dare you listen to this conversation! You should be with the guests!'

Coral defied her husband, speaking hurriedly and breathlessly. 'She came for the weekend. My husband was away shooting. We spoke –'

'Get off the line! I'm warning you!'

'Sir, I don't think you understand the seriousness

of this situation. Two women have been killed in London in the last month. I am very worried for Cosima's safety.'

'The guests, Coral! No one likes to be kept hanging around.'

Jessie heard the click.

'If your daughter is in a rehabilitation centre, you can tell me. I need –'

'How dare you insinuate such a thing!'

'It wouldn't be the first time, would it?'

'I don't know where my daughter is. Now, if you will excuse me, I have guests, important guests, who require my attention.'

'But –'

'Good evening, Detective Inspector.'

Niaz insisted on driving her home. He even walked her to the door of the building.

'I'll be fine now,' said Jessie, puzzled by his concern.

'Even so, I'd like to see you to your flat.' Again Jessie started to protest. 'Your crash was no accident. Please. Indulge me.'

Jessie relented. 'Don't tell me – the genie.'

Niaz smiled. 'Actually, it was the man in the garage, when I called up to see if the bike was ready.'

They walked up the two flights of stairs together.

'Is it?'

'Day after tomorrow. They'll deliver it to the station in the afternoon.'

'Good, I can't stand traffic.'

'I'll be on to her travel agent first thing,' said Niaz. 'See if she really is on holiday, what do you think?' But Jessie didn't respond. She was staring at her front door. Someone had daubed it with a cross. In red. Jessie ran her finger through it. Lipstick. She opened the door and returned with a dripping sponge. She looked at Niaz, who was shaking his head.

'Not a word of this to anyone,' said Jessie, scrubbing the smeared red lipstick off her white front door.

Niaz tried to stop her. 'It is a sign. A message.'

'It is not. It's just someone trying to scare me. I don't scare easily.'

'I think you should take this seriously. Do you know what it means?'

'Niaz, this is one piece of trivia you can keep to yourself.'

'It means "bring out the dead". They would put a red cross on doors of infected households during the plague –'

'Stop it. It's nothing. Please, go home, Niaz.'

He hesitated.

'That's an order.'

When Jessie returned from rinsing the sponge, Niaz had gone. She finished wiping the gloss paint surface until it was spotless. She stood back.

'I don't scare easily,' she repeated to herself as she locked and double locked the door.

*   *   *

Jessie knocked on Maggie's door and went in. There was a manic rustle of sheets.

'Oh God, sorry . . .' Jessie retreated quickly as a man dived under Maggie's duvet. Then she tapped on the door again. 'Maggie, can I have a word?'

'Now?' came a strained voice.

'Sorry, it's important.'

Maggie joined her in the sitting room. She was flushed in the face and wrapped in her fake-fur bed throw.

'This had better be good.'

'When did you get back tonight?'

'Jessie, you aren't my moth—'

'Tell me,' said Jessie sternly.

'Ten. Why?'

'There wasn't anything on the door?'

'Like what?'

Obviously not. Even Maggie would notice the mark of a cross in red lipstick. 'Oh, nothing.' She didn't want to scare her.

'You got me out of bed for that?'

Jessie grinned. 'Sorry. Who is it?'

'No one you know,' she said quickly.

Jessie waited.

'Really, just some cameraman.'

'Not your celebrity shag, then?'

'God no, I'll be doing that in a suite at the Metropolitan, darling. Still, I need the practice, so if you don't mind . . . ?'

Maggie swept the faux-fur around her.

'Wait –' said Jessie. 'Cosima Broome, what do you know about her?'

Maggie turned back abruptly. 'Why are you asking me?'

'Because you know her.'

'No I don't.'

'Well, you don't like her. So I presumed –'

'I don't like what she stands for, that's all.'

'So you don't know anything personal about her?'

'No, Jessie. How many more times!'

A little after six in the morning Jessie heard someone struggle with the double lock. She sat up in bed and peered through the curtain to the street below. A few moments later, a man appeared. She would never have known if he hadn't looked up. But he did. Just as he reached the lamppost. Straight at her. It was no cameraman. It was Joshua Cadell. Jessie let go of the curtain and shrank from the window. Maggie never did like competition.

~

Jessie laid everything out in front of her. A photograph of Eve Wirrel's initialled painting. The list of sperm donors from 'A Life's Work'. Every photograph ever taken of the artist since her rise to fame. For a rebel, she certainly liked the unchallenging pages of *Hello!*. Jessie had stuck them up on a pinboard. There was a strange photo of Eve sitting in an impressive art deco fireplace; she was naked and covered in ash. She had assembled a similar board for Verity. Each threatening letter. All the ones signed W.T. Every nude picture. The blood-soaked rag. There was a picture of the sunken boat, a close-up of T.T. She had played with anagrams and puzzles, but the letters and photographs continued to stare blankly back at her. Jessie returned to the threats. They were tangible at least. Forensics hadn't found a single print. The person sending them was a professional. Gloves had been used. Standard office paper that was supplied to millions, and felt-tips that could be bought in every stationer's in the country.

Jessie picked up one of the plastic-shrouded letters. 'You told me you missed me, you told me you'd felt my wet kisses, my salty song, you told me you didn't want to live without me. SO WHAT WENT WRONG?'

'You never waved,' said Niaz.

Jessie turned startled. 'Shit. Don't creep up on me like that.'

'I thought you didn't scare easily,' he said. 'Before you tell me to get out, I want to show you what I found outside your house last night.'

Niaz held up a white-tipped cigarette. Semi-crushed, like the others. 'I'll send it to be tested. Is it Mr Dean or your admirer from Acton, I wonder?'

Jessie looked at the see-through bag. 'Or nothing at all.' She turned back to the death-threats. 'What did you mean, you never waved?'

'I was simply referring to the song you were quoting from.'

'The letter, you mean.'

'No, the song: "You Never Waved". It's one of P. J. Deans', from his first album. A big hit, I believe.'

Jessie held up the plastic folder containing the letter. 'This?'

'It's an adaptation. I suppose the song was about his sister, waving not drowning, a play on the poem. Some demented fool thought he wrote the words for them. I would guess a woman, but you never know these days.'

'So this was written to P.J.?'

'Yes. Who did you think it was written to?'

'Verity Shore. Everything was sent to Verity . . .' Jessie rested her chin in her hand and stared at the evidence. Something was staring back at her. '. . . Everything was sent to Verity, but it was about P.J. He could be the trigger. Niaz, get online, check out this fan-extremis.com. Keep an eye on it, see if anyone gets online with the web name W.T. I know Acton police said they found nothing, but if that fag you found last night was also smoked by Frances Leonard, I think we may be on to something.'

'You think she greased the wheel of the bike?'

'I thought it was Ray St Giles trying to scare me off.'

'It *was* just after you'd gone away with Mr Dean. Maybe you're right, maybe competition triggers her off.'

'Niaz, I didn't –'

He smiled knowingly. 'I know.'

Jessie pulled up a stool and sat on it, reflecting on the possibilities regarding Frances Leonard. 'She's a middle-aged woman, hardly fits the profile of a serial killer.'

'"Probabilities are what got the Force into the mess it is in today." You said that.'

'Did I? How irritating.'

It could be a middle-aged woman. The murders had never been about strength, Jessie had said that from the beginning, when she'd had Bernie in mind. And both Eve and Verity had had relationships with women. If Cosima was next, did that mean P.J. had been with her too?

'Why don't you ask him?' said Niaz, interrupting her thoughts. She frowned at him. 'Simple deduction, ma'am. I'll take this to the lab straight away.' He opened the door to the evidence room. Outside there was a commotion. Jessie followed Niaz and was taken aback by the sight of DC Fry holding a tearful Clare Mills.

'Fry?'

'Thank God you're here.'

'What's happened?'

'Oh, Inspector Driver,' wailed Clare. 'He's dead!'

'Who?'

'And Irene has put the salon up for sale. I can't find her. I think she's leaving, she's going to leave me too, I can't . . .'

Clare was breathing erratically. Jessie looked at Fry nervously. 'What's going on?'

'Give me a sec, I'll fill you in word for word,' he said earnestly.

Jessie paced her office nervously. It took ages for Fry to return. If she hadn't seen the look of fear in his eyes, she would have thought it was a wind-up. Eventually he walked in and closed the door firmly behind him.

'DI Ward was in a car accident,' he said gravely.

'No. He's –' But Clare had already told her. Dead.

'He's in Reading Hospital with concussion. He's shaken, the car is a write-off, but he'll live.'

Jessie frowned. 'So who's dead?'

'Frank Mills. Alistair Gunner is a son from another relationship.'

'How do you know Frank is dead?'

'He's buried in Woolwich Cemetery, under the name Gareth Blake. Has been for twenty-odd years.'

'You've lost me? Who's Gareth Blake?'

'He was born on the same day as Frank Mills, according to DSS records. He came into care aged three, same day that Frank did. He was fit and healthy until he died of pneumonia aged four. A lot of children got ill in care. He was buried in Woolwich Cemetery under the name social services gave him.'

'How do you know all this?'

'Mark called from the hospital. In fact, he said

he'd like to see you. In person. No wind-up, I swear.'

Jessie sat down. 'Poor Clare. So it's over?'

'Not exactly. Ray St Giles said he knew where Ward was getting his information – Irene. Ray said it would stop. Now Irene has disappeared. That's why Clare Mills is here. I only thought it fair to tell her what's been going on.'

'You told her about Ray St Giles?' asked Jessie, startled.

'No. About Gareth Blake. So now she thinks her brother is dead and doesn't know why her friend seems to have vanished. She's freaked out about the salon. It seems it's been the only constant thing in Clare's life.'

'You seem to know a lot about this, Fry.'

'Yeah, well, I came from the same part of town. Let's just say I was going to be putting people behind bars or be behind bars myself. Family support is not a social given, ma'am.'

So he had joined another sort of family, thought Jessie. The police force. Not so very different to the kind of unit the likes of Ray St Giles have to offer. Why did it always come back to Ray St Giles?

'Look, boss, I know I've fucked up in the past, but Clare is very upset, so is Mark. They think Ray might have got to Irene.'

Jessie knew what he was asking. She called Tarek but got no response.

'Send a surveillance team round to St Giles' house. He isn't at the cable company any more.

And, Fry?' He turned. 'Thanks for keeping me up to speed. I appreciate it.'

He smiled and winked. 'Don't get carried away, I'm not all good.'

'Mostly good then,' she replied. 'And make sure Clare doesn't know about St Giles. I don't want to have to cut her down from a wardrobe door.'

Fry looked shocked.

'If we are not very careful, that is where we are heading with this, Fry, I can feel it.'

'I'll keep her here,' said Fry softly.

Jones summoned Jessie to his office. She wondered whether she would have the courage to ask him to do what she could not. Ring P. J. Dean and ask him if he'd also had an extra-marital affair with the Titled Tart. Missing. Now presumed dead.

Jessie found Clare standing alone in the corridor. She was swaying slightly, her narrow frame struggling to cope with the weight of all the news. Jessie led her to the small TV room. Clare said she didn't want to go home. She just wanted to wait. Wait for news. DC Fry was looking for Irene. Jessie was about to leave her when she spoke, quietly, into the cup of tea Jessie had made her.

'I want him exhumed.'

'What?'

'Frank. I want him exhumed.' Clare looked at her with wide, flat eyes. 'Dead or alive, remember?'

Jessie did. Jones had given his word. 'I'll start court proceedings immediately.'

Jessie pushed open the door to Jones' office. He had two cups of fresh coffee and croissants from the café. He smiled kindly. It worried her greatly.

'Hear you've been burning the midnight oil.'

She took the sweet, milky coffee gratefully.

'Have you eaten?'

Had she? She couldn't remember.

'Obviously not. You look starving.'

She bit into the pastry and chewed hungrily. 'Sir, I know you think I've gone off the wall on this, but I'm close. If only I knew how to put the pieces together. I discovered something about Cosima Broome this morning. Her mother was called Penelope Richmond. She went mad and was sent to a home. Her nurse became Cosima's stepmother. More secrets. Richmond. The boat. It was staring me in the face.'

'Cosima Lennox-Broome . . . doesn't spell Richmond to me.'

'No. And I think that is the point. All these clues have been muddying the water. Sending me on a wild-goose chase. But there is another possible link, sir.' She took a deep breath. 'P. J. Dean.'

'Now, Jessie . . .'

She quickly explained about the mystery W.T. 'If only we could find out from him whether he slept –'

'No, Jessie!'

'But, sir, every other murder told me where to look next, if I'd been clever enough. The plantation in the park, the smuggler's house, the punt in the Thames –'

'Absolutely not. No.'

'What if Cosima Broome is lying at the bottom of a lake at her father's house, like the boat was laid to rest in the Thames? She obviously didn't buy the punt herself. Maybe there is a private chapel on the estate, some link with a church. All you have to do is –'

'He is suing you.'

'What?'

'For harassment.'

Jessie dropped the croissant. Her appetite deserted her. She stared back at Jones.

'Sorry, Jessie. Depending on what the lawyers tell us, you may have to be suspended.'

~

Jessie brought Mark Ward some cans of bitter and a book to hide them with. A peace offering. She felt inexplicably nervous walking towards his bed, passing other car-crash victims. The ones who'd been let off lightly. Mark pulled his dressing gown around him to hide the hospital pyjamas. Dignity was difficult in open-plan wards. An impressive bruise covered the left side of his face and his shoulder was strapped up.

'Typical bloody copper,' said Mark. 'No seatbelt.'

Jessie could tell it was difficult for him to speak. 'I hope you like history,' she said, handing over the bag. Mark peered inside. Then looked up smiling. 'Seems you know my tastes quite well.'

'Better than you think, DI Ward.' Jessie sat down on the low, hard visitor's chair and waited for Mark to explain his summons. He looked tired. It was probably shock. He reached out and took three cardboard envelopes from his bedside table, and handed them over to her silently. The first thought that flashed through her mind was bribery. She opened the first one cautiously and pulled out an A4 photograph. She tried to fathom Mark's expression before turning the picture around. It was the same photograph that Tarek had showed her. Verity Shore and Christopher Cadell grabbing each other in a hotel lobby.

'Do you know who it is?'

'Yes,' said Jessie. 'Christopher Cadell, and I've already questioned him. Where did you get this?'

'Alistair Gunner's bedroom. Along with all the rest. Looks like the bloke is obsessed with his father and the murders. Could be one and the same obsession, couldn't it?'

'But it doesn't mean either of them are directly involved. What boy isn't curious about his absent father, more so if he's a notorious gangster? And it's the murders that are making Ray into a household name.'

'Ray St Giles is involved,' said Mark. 'The proof is right in front of your nose.'

Jessie opened the remaining envelopes and slowly flicked through the pictures and cuttings. 'We've got a lead on the person who was sending P. J. Dean hate mail about his wife –'

'Ray killed two women before Trevor Mills was shot. The Met fucked it up and pinned it on some trucker, but it was Ray. He beat the women to death and set them on fire. He's a killer. P. J. Dean is a sappy twat from Manchester. It takes a certain type of person to kill.'

'I don't think he did it, but he could be the trigger.' Jessie looked at the photo of Cary Conrad and grimaced.

'The police said the tractor rolled into the road, they said it was unmanned, a freak accident. What do you think the chances of that are, Driver?'

'Did Ray know you were going to the village?'

'Look at the fucking photos. Ray knows everything. Where do you think Irene is – taking a holiday? She's never missed a day in that salon. Come on, Jessie. Stop hounding lover boy and do something. Jesus, I thought you'd be pleased. You were right: Ray St Giles is in this up to his neck.'

He knew exactly how to turn the knife. What he didn't know was that he couldn't make her feel any worse. She looked him in the eye. 'What do I do about Clare?'

'Exhume the body, take a DNA sample. It will prove they are related. She doesn't have to know that they are not as closely related as she thinks. Everyone goes home happy.'

Jessie got to the last photo. It was of Cosima Broome hugging another woman. 'Shit!'

'What?'

'Lady Cosima Broome. The person who the punt belonged to. She's missing.'

Mark lay back against his pillow. 'She's dead.'

'Fuck.' Jessie stood up.

'Where are you going?'

'To Haverbrook Hall. I think she's there.'

'What about Ray?'

'I'll up the surveillance. You know, Alistair may hate his dad. Ray deserted him. Maybe Alistair would like to see his father put away again. Maybe he can help us.'

'I doubt it. Birds of a feather, and all that.' Mark pulled out the book that Jessie had chosen for him. 'Ray has spent years building up his reputation, he isn't going to let some pipsqueak do-gooder of a son get the better of him.' He flicked the book over. There was a photo of Dame Henrietta Cadell draped over a 1930s pewter fireplace. It was adorned with photos of her precious son.

'Cadell? Any relation to the bloke poking Verity Shore?'

'His wife. He was drunk in his club all weekend.'

'Still, it's a bit weird.'

'What is?'

'Isabella of France.' Jessie stared at him blankly. 'Wasn't Eve Wirrel found dead in the Isabella Plantation?'

'Oh God, this is getting too confusing. They've all slept with each other.'

'Celebrity is very exclusive.'

'I think you mean incestuous,' said Jessie, studying the back cover of Dame Henrietta's biography.

While Jessie waited for Niaz to bring the car round, she called Sally Grimes. Jessie knew that she was asking a lot of the pathologist, but she wanted Sally's eye. Sally wouldn't budge. 'You haven't even got a body yet.'

'She's dead,' said Jessie. 'I know it.'

'Then trust your own judgement.'

'But –'

'Jessie,' she said sternly, 'I haven't told you or pointed out anything to you that you hadn't already seen for yourself. If you come across something strange, call me.'

'If you change your mind,' said Jessie, 'the corpse is at Haverbrook Hall, outside Oxford.'

'It's flu season,' said Sally. 'We've got bodies stacking up as it is.'

'Sure I can't tempt you?'

'Sorry, too many . . .' Sally paused. 'You know.'

Jessie did. Faces to peel back. Lips to lift off. Teeth to remove. Human offal to weigh.

'Good luck,' said Sally before hanging up. 'I hope you find the girl alive.'

The first thing Jessie noticed about Haverbrook Hall was that it had no moat, lake or river running through it. It was a dry plot, high on a hill in Oxfordshire. Little use for a punt. The family had won the land through typically nefarious means, a hodgepodge of illegitimate offspring and royal affairs. Like the Fitz in Fitz-Williams. Jessie did not have a good feeling about this. And then she saw the police. There must have been five local constables standing around. She sent Niaz over to glean a few details.

When she spotted the mortician's estate, Jessie knew for sure that Cosima Broome was dead and probably had been for some time. She cursed herself for being too slow. There were other cars: an old roller, and a silver Audi with a potentially lethal pheasant on the bonnet. She looked back to the house. The front door was open. Jessie decided she couldn't wait. She was making her way through the pillared hall when Niaz caught up with her.

'The body was found in the Wendy house,' he whispered.

'What?'

'A small gazebo-like garden dwelling that accommodates children.'

'The Wendy house?' repeated Jessie.

'There is possibly a Peter Pan connection there.'

'With Cosima?'

'No, with the name. Wendy.'

'What are you talking about, Niaz?'

'Never having to grow up, always being a child.'

389

'Shh.' Jessie heard a clatter of ice on glass and glass on silver. From behind a set of double doors came the sound of a woman sobbing. Jessie knocked gently and pushed the door open. Coral Lennox-Broome looked up at Jessie. Her cheeks were awash with blue-black tears. Her slim frame was dressed in a charcoal cashmere dress, knee-high boots and wide silver bracelets on both wrists. She was an attractive woman. And had probably looked a million dollars until the body was found.

'Who are you?' she sniffed.

'Detective Inspector Driver. We spoke on the phone. I'm very sor—'

'You knew this was going to happen,' the woman said. 'Why didn't you tell me it was serious!?'

'I did try –'

'No you didn't. You didn't tell me what was going on, you didn't say she'd been . . .'

'Been what?'

Coral lifted the crystal tumbler to her mouth and drank. Desperately. The way Christopher Cadell drank.

'I don't think I'm the one who has been keeping things back,' said Jessie calmly. For a second, the woman looked as if she was going to explode in indignant fury. But she collapsed instead.

'You don't know what it's like. I couldn't tell you.'

'Tell me what?'

The door behind her creaked open. Coral shrank from her husband. Jessie introduced herself.

'I'm afraid you were right. She had been in a rehabilitation centre. It didn't work. I find these things difficult to talk about.'

'What happened?'

'She passed out drunk in the Wendy house. It was very cold. Hypothermia, I believe they call it.'

Jessie watched Coral drink the chilled vodka like water.

'It is no secret that Cosima and I didn't have a . . .' He stumbled over the words. 'I never understood her, you see. But I didn't want it to end like this.'

'This may not be Cosima's fault, sir. Those other women I told you about, they were killed because someone knew what was going on behind the scenes.'

'This has nothing to do with those other people! This is my daughter you are talking about. It was an accident.'

'I'd like to see her,' said Jessie.

'The doctor has already done all that. And the police,' said Viscount Lennox-Broome.

'I'd still like to see for myself.' She pointed at the French doors. 'Is this the way to the garden?'

'Yes,' said Coral. 'Follow the path round to the left.' She returned to her drink as soon as the words were out of her mouth.

Jessie put her hand on the door.

'This is a private matter,' the Viscount protested again.

'Not in this century, sir.'

*   *   *

The doctor and local detective were startled to see her. More so when she produced her badge and informed them that she'd had Cosima down on her missing list for some time. The Viscount had obviously failed to tell them about her call. Jessie wondered what he had told them.

Cosima was curled up under a blanket. Jessie could tell from the smell that she had been dead for a couple of days. Stacked up in the corner of the wooden hut was a box of croquet mallets, leaning against the wall were the metal hoops painted white with pointed rusting ends. The layer of dust was several autumns deep. There was no furniture in the hut, just spider webs and the skeleton of a decapitated mouse. Owl's work. The only sign of life in the Wendy house was the pathway in the dust from door to corpse, cleared by the soles of her busy family. All that coming and going merely confirmed Jessie's suspicions. She bent down to peel back the grey woollen blanket. Cosima was naked; there were marks around her wrists and her feet were black and swollen. Her femoral artery, however, had not been cut. Jessie sat back on her knees.

'She'd been drinking heavily,' said the doctor. 'Look at the red wine stains –'

'Are you a pathologist?'

'No.'

'Then how can you be sure?' said Jessie, crouching next to the corpse.

'I am a very –'

She waved him away. 'Yes, I'm sure, a very good friend of the family. What did he tell you? Drugs? That she took drugs. And drank in excess. That she was out of control. Hush it up, there's a good fellow.' The doctor stepped back. 'You think the marks around her wrist were self-inflicted? You think this looks like an accident?'

'She had a history of self-harm, she used to cut herself a lot. I've treated her many times.'

'For what?'

'Cuts, bruises, burns, you name it.'

'And you never questioned that the injuries were *self*-inflicted?'

'Her father wouldn't lie about such . . .' His voice trailed off. 'He is a fine man.'

'What did Cosima say?'

'That she –' he coughed into his handkerchief – 'she deserved it. She hated herself, you see.'

Jessie looked up at him. 'What do you really see here?' She paused. 'And this time, think before you answer.'

'She got drunk, passed out and died of hypothermia.'

'Wrong.'

'Accidental drug overdose.'

'Wrong again.'

'Positional asphyxia?'

'Here?'

'Yes.'

'No, Doctor. Not here.'

'Where, then?' he asked challengingly.

'I don't know. But not in the fucking Wendy house, I know that much.' Jessie stood up.

'She drank. She was out of control,' insisted the doctor.

'I don't think so. Niaz, guard this site and let no one in except me. You, Doctor, will accompany me to the house. There are a few inconsistencies I'd like to clear up.'

'I really should be –'

'I don't remember saying please, *Doctor*.'

He followed her across the saturated lawn, her leather boots slipping on the frictionless blades. She was relieved to get on to the stone path. Either side of the path were beds of purple and blue heather, neatly clipped and well tended. A perfect country house. Jessie returned to the drawing room. Coral was smoking now. Her husband's voice could be heard from behind another oak door.

'Please ask your husband to join us,' said Jessie. The red-rimmed eyes made Coral look more like a rabbit caught in the glare of an oncoming car. A sick rabbit. Sick and scared. Coral returned empty-handed, so Jessie went through to the study, walked up to the telephone, cut him off and returned to the drawing room. He was furious.

'I have had enough of your –'

'Why did you move your daughter's body?' she said.

Coral let out an involuntary squeal.

'You are upsetting my wife,' bellowed the Viscount.

'Not as much as I will, if you don't start telling me the truth.'

'Coral found her this morning. She is very upset.'

Jessie turned to Coral. 'Is that true?'

Coral nodded but didn't speak. She turned the wide silver bangle on her wrist nervously.

'In the Wendy house?'

'Of course in the Wendy house,' he answered for her.

'I'm not talking to you,' said Jessie without looking at the man. 'Viscountess?'

She nodded again. 'Call me Coral.'

'Why did you go to the Wendy house?'

Coral looked at her husband.

'She was taking the dogs for a walk.'

Jessie turned on the older man. 'Stop lying. Your daughter was strung up somewhere. The blood collected in her legs and feet – *anyone* in the profession could have told you that.' She could feel the doctor shrink without even looking at him. 'You can't cover this up. This isn't another little scandal that you can control.'

He didn't pick Jessie up on the use of the word 'another'.

'Cosima has marks on her wrist.'

'My daughter had a history of self-harm. So, for the last time, my wife found her in the Wendy house,' said Geoffrey Lennox-Broome. Slowly and clearly.

'I'll give you one more chance. We are going to

take the body and perform an autopsy. From that we will be able to determine how and in what position she died. I know what the outcome of that investigation will *not* be. It will not be that your daughter died of hypothermia lying on the floor of a disused Wendy house having passed out from ingesting too much alcohol. Then I will come here with an arrest warrant. It is a criminal offence to pervert the course of justice and I don't give a damn what high-powered judges you may think you have in your fraternity, I will not rest until this goes to court.'

'You'll be hearing from my lawyer,' he barked.

'Your daughter was murdered. Here. On this property.'

'My daughter died after a drinking binge in the Wendy house.'

'Why would your daughter crawl naked into a dirty, empty Wendy house in the middle of the night?'

The Viscount looked at his wife with scorn. 'There were a lot of things my daughter did that I didn't understand.'

The door to the drawing room opened. Jessie swung round angrily. Sally Grimes stood in the doorway holding a plastic phial in her hand.

'Sally!' exclaimed Jessie, relieved to see a kindred soul. 'How did you –?'

'I changed my mind.'

'Have you seen the body?'

'Yes. Lady Cosima Lennox-Broome drowned,' said Sally.

'Drowned?' came the simultaneous response.

'Where? There isn't a lake here,' said Jessie.

'Not where. In what.'

'What?'

'I'm sorry to tell you this, sir, but your daughter drowned in alcohol. I used an *in situ* test we do at crash sites. Your daughter's blood-to-alcohol ratio was off the scale.'

Jessie's eyes widened. She knew what that meant.

'It is impossible to drink that much and stay conscious,' said Sally.

'What do you mean?' asked Coral, who was walking towards Sally, her eyes focusing through the vodka, adrenaline-induced clarity.

'She means,' said Jessie, 'that Cosima was force-fed alcohol until it was running through her veins.'

Sally continued, 'That amount of additional liquid to the system would ordinarily have caused her brain to swell, and that in itself would have killed her. But she was cut on the soles of her feet and drained of blood. What little blood she had left in her system would not have been able to carry the oxygen to her brain. She drowned.'

'Sit down, Coral,' said the Viscount firmly.

Jessie kept her eye on the rapidly ageing blonde. 'All you'd need is a plastic tube, a funnel, and a large quantity of alcohol – wine, for instance,' she said, taking hold of Coral's arm as she walked past. 'Oh, and somewhere to tie her up.'

'Get your hands off my wife,' shouted Lennox-Broome.

'Somewhere like a cellar,' said Jessie. 'Imagine how scared she'd have been. Tied up, force-fed . . . She'd have vomited and urinated on herself.' Jessie dropped Coral's arm. 'But you know all this, you found her. Now, I'd like to see your cellar.'

'We don't have a cellar.'

'Yes you do. I saw the windows through the grate in the ground. If you lie to me again, sir, I shall arrest you for obstruction. This is a murder case. Show me your cellar.'

Jessie, Sally and Niaz followed the couple into the subterranean level of the house. The doctor had opted to stay near the drinks cabinet. An earthy, damp corridor stretched out in the darkness, running the full length of the house. The smell of alcohol intermingled with damp and dust. Their footsteps were swallowed whole by the dense stone below their feet. Off the central corridor were skinny archways opening to brick-lined antechambers. Those on the right had dirty windows to the outside world above, those on the left did not. A few naked light bulbs glowed a pale orange, but the brickwork seemed to suck up their weak light as it had absorbed the sound of their footsteps. It was an eerie place, thought Jessie. No place to die.

They checked each antechamber, Jessie pointing her torch into the dark corners and along each curved ceiling. Most were full of wine, row upon row of cold, smoky green bottles. Masonry dust had collected in a thin line along the length of each bottle. Some of the labels had dried up, cracked and fallen away. If Jessie hadn't told the portly man to remain silent, they would have had the full sommelier's tour. This collection of fortified fruit juice was his pride and joy, shame he hadn't shown the same interest in his daughter. They came to the end of the corridor.

'Is that it?' Jessie asked. She remembered the door to Eve Wirrel's secret studio, the door in the garden wall at P. J. Dean's. 'And before you answer me, you should know that I am aware of the existence of a hidden doorway. I don't know where it is, but I will find it. You don't want the police crawling all over your house, do you? Imagine the press.' Jessie touched the wall. 'I estimate the length of this passageway is sixty feet, which takes us just under your library. So which is the switch? *Lady Chatterley's Lover*? *Animal Farm*? *Quatermass and the Pit*? *Lord Jim*? *Death in a White Tie* . . . ? Am I getting warm?'

The Viscount began to walk away from her. 'It was built as a hiding place in case of invasion.'

Jessie told the others to stay where they were and followed his booming voice in the darkness. 'Invasion from whom?'

'The bloody Protestants.'

'And what do you use it for now?'

'Nothing.'

Suddenly she remembered the black-and-white photograph above Eve Wirrel's bed. Chained up,

399

hanging from a hook, feet hovering off the ground. 'You're sure about that?'

The Viscount led her back up the stairs and through the house to the library. He pushed a hidden button and one section of the bookcase swung open to reveal a similar set of stone steps descending into darkness. Jessie pointed her torch downwards and stepped on to the cold smooth surface.

'There is nothing down there,' he said confidently.

Jessie could smell the bleach before she was all the way down the steps. The middle of the floor was damp with disinfectant, darker than the surrounding dust. There was a drainage hole in the floor and hooks in the ceiling.

'We used to hang meat here, before BSE.' Jessie gave him an impenetrable look and began tapping on the walls.

'What the bloody hell are you doing?' he asked.

'This place wouldn't be much good as an escape route if there was no way out.'

'It was a place for the Catholic priest to hide.'

Jessie carried on tapping. 'Sally? Niaz? Can you hear me?' No reply. She turned back to Cosima's incomprehensible father. 'You have destroyed vital evidence by cleaning this place up.' And then it dawned on her. The murderer knew that was what would happen. That was why the registration number had been left on the boat. It was all part of the game. 'The murderer relied on you doing exactly this, knowing that all the evidence would be washed down that drain along with your dirty habits and guilt. Don't you want your daughter's killer caught?'

'I have no idea what you are talking about.'

Jessie heard a noise to her left. The brick wall began to move. Then Coral slipped through the narrow gap to join them. Once inside, she stood and stared at the hooks in the ceiling.

'What the bloody hell do you think you are doing, Coral!?'

'We found Cosima hanging there,' she said quietly.

'We?'

'Shut up, Coral! Shut up now, you stupid girl. You're all the same!'

'Who? Who are all the same, sir? Women?' She turned back to the now shaking woman. 'What were you doing down here, Coral?'

There was a long, tense silence before she answered. 'Looking for Cosima,' she said eventually and started to cry. Jessie went to put her arm around her, but something caught her attention and instead, she gently raised Coral's arm.

'Get off my wife!'

Jessie took hold of the shiny silver bracelet on Coral's wrist and pressed the release mechanism. It sprung open.

'Coral, get away from that woman. We hang meat in here.'

'Meat?'

Coral was limp, her strength had seeped into

the stone floor, along with light and sound and Cosima's blood and vomit. Jessie unclasped the other bracelet and held both wrists up to the thin beam of light. The raw markings stood out angrily on the alabaster skin of her thin wrists.

'What sick sort of punishment do you go in for?'

'I don't know what you are talking about. My wife hurt her wrists riding, the reins gave her a burn – didn't they, darling?'

Jessie lowered Coral's arm into Sally Grimes' hand. Sally examined the injuries.

'Exactly like the ones on Cosima's arms.'

'What have you done with the chains and handcuffs? Where is the tube, the funnel, the wine bottles. What wine was it?' Jessie walked back through the narrow gap. She started reading off the wooden crates. 'La Baunaudine '63 Châteauneuf-du-Pape? St Emilion . . . Rothschild's '52 Claret?' She picked up a bottle from a rack and returned to the room. 'Chateau Lafite '51? It'll all come out in the post-mortem.'

'That bastard poured two crates of vintage Don Perignon down Cosima's throat. Forty-four thousand pounds' worth of champagne!'

'You're the bastard!' shouted Coral. 'Cosima is dead and all you care about is your fucking wine.'

'As opposed to my fucking wife!'

'Niaz, get him out and get forensics down here. We need to find Cosima's car; the murderer probably drove her here in it.' She turned to Coral. 'Tell me you still have whatever you found down here.'

She shook her head. 'He made me burn every-thing.'

'But you didn't, did you?'

She shook her head and sobbed. 'I kept her dress.'

'Good. Where is it?'

Coral was staring at the hooks in the ceiling.

'Coral?'

Coral kept shaking her head, the horror of unknown things passing over her eyes.

Jessie took the woman's shoulders. 'What's been going on here?'

'Sugar and spice and all things nice,' whispered Coral. Then she looked at Jessie. 'Geoffrey doesn't like naughty little girls. Poor Cosima, poor sweet beautiful Cosima . . . I loved her. She wanted those men to love her, but she was just a conquest to them. Her father never loved her. He wanted a boy, of course, so Cosima was punished for merely being alive. Running in the corridor, falling over, eating too slowly, eating too fast. Then she noticed the markings on my wrist and it all came out. I would have killed myself if it wasn't for her. I really loved her and she loved me.'

Jessie pulled out the photograph of Cosima and the woman she now knew was Coral. 'Do you want to tell me about Ray St Giles?'

She shuddered. 'He wanted Cosima on his awful show.'

'What happened?'

'We refused. And now Cosima is dead. You get

403

him, you get the bastard that did this.'

'Can you vouch for your husband?' asked Jessie.

'Unfortunately, yes.'

Jessie led Coral up the stone steps and waited for her to retrieve the dead girl's dress. 'People envied her. Isn't that ironic?'

'Tell me, did Cosima ever receive death threats or hate mail?'

'No, never. Just endless proposals of marriage. She used to laugh at those.'

Coral stared at Cosima's soiled dress: Chloe. 'When I was a nurse, I used to read all the glossy magazines. It looked like such fun – the glamour, the parties, the famous people. But it isn't. It's lonely and destructive and the only thing worse than going on with it, is going back. Obscurity is more feared than loneliness.'

~

Four cars were parked in front of the rusting iron gate of Woolwich Cemetery. It was a few minutes before dawn. South East London was ghostly quiet. Their torchlight picked out the thick, furry weeds growing in clumps around the base of the crumbling brick pillars. Majestic once. But no longer.

Jessie walked alongside Clare Mills in silence. Removing a child from the ground, when that child should have been a man of her age, saddened Jessie. Time stands still for no one. Except the dead. Shovels and spades would bring this boy back to the world of the living, twenty years too late. Jessie put her arm gently on Clare's shoulders as they approached the fizzing portable lights. Three chunky men leant against spades, watching them approach, next to the six foot of earth that had been removed and hidden under a blanket of acid green Astroturf. Jones peered into the hole. The wood had kept well. The coffin was still intact. Jones summoned the four morticians forward. The labourers wouldn't touch it. This little boy had more power dead than alive, thought Jessie, watching the men and their spades withdraw to a respectful distance and light up imported cigarettes. Clare gasped when she saw the coffin.

'It's so small,' she said. And it was. Chillingly small.

'You may want to look away, Clare,' said Jones as the mortician gathered the tools necessary to prise the lid off.

'No. I'm staying here. With Frank.'

Jones gave Jessie a worried look. Jessie took Clare's arm. She was ready to catch Clare when the lid came off and she saw her brother for the first time since she was eight. A genealogist was standing by. The necessary samples would be taken and compared to the samples that Clare had already given the lab. The body would be interred immediately after the samples were taken. Returned to peace everlasting.

Everyone took a step closer when the mortician bent down by the box. They took an involuntary step back when the wood cracked open. He looked up at Clare, Clare nodded, then he lifted the lid off. Everyone stared at the contents of the child's coffin.

Stones. Three large flint stones.

The morticians gasped simultaneously. Jessie continued to stare at the stones in disbelief. Jones tried to pull Clare away, but she fell to her knees and began to pray. 'Thank you, thank you God . . .'

'What's been going on, Inspector?' asked a mortician.

'He's alive,' said Clare, staring into the small box.

Not necessarily, thought Jessie. They didn't even know for sure that Gareth Blake was Frank.

'I want an investigation into this immediately,' said Jones angrily. He didn't like surprises.

'It wasn't my Frank, after all. He's out there somewhere, waiting for me.'

Jessie put her arm through Clare's and pulled her up. She didn't know what the stones meant, but she knew it couldn't be good.

'Don't you agree? This is good, right, Inspector? He's still alive?'

'Clare . . .'

Jones spoke over her. 'We need more information before we can say anything.'

'What do you think happened to Gareth Blake?' The question floated between the gathered crowd. No one answered because no one could think of one good reason why anyone would fake a child's death and bury stones in his place. Clare suddenly sobbed. 'Oh God, no, they took him, didn't they . . .'

'Who took him, Clare?' asked Jones gently.

'They were all evil,' said Clare. 'If they could take Gareth Blake, they could've taken my Frank. They were too young to defend themselves . . .' She pulled herself up to her full height. 'No. I'm not going to think like that. You find him. Like you promised you would.'

Clare started to walk away.

'Let me come with you, Clare. It's still dark.'

'Can I borrow a torch? My mother is buried here. Give me a few minutes, I'll be fine, just . . .'

'I'm sorry, Clare.'

Clare bit the skin around her fingernail. 'Don't be. Bones would have been worse.'

They watched Clare move between the crumbling headstones, her torch picking up the ageing slabs. Flashes of colour were rare; few visitors left flowers here. Jessie leant closer to Jones' ear. 'Ray St Giles. Mark's right, it's the only explanation.'

Jones seemed to be ageing before her eyes. 'Wrong. There is another explanation, but it's too frightening to contemplate.' He straightened himself up. 'Frank and Gareth may be the tip of the iceberg. If there are others, we may have dug up a previously uncovered child-pornography ring. In which case we'll have a great deal more to worry about, because no victim has come forward with a complaint against this department. Which can only mean one thing . . .'

Jessie looked sadly at the three stones. 'They're all dead,' said Jessie.

Perhaps bones would have been better.

Jessie left the small coffin and the large men and followed Clare up the pathway. Daylight had crept up on them stealthily. From the crest of the hill she could see Clare kneel by a marble cross. It gleamed white against the all-pervading grey of the surrounding cemetery. Clare was crying. She held up a dry old bunch of roses, the dirty yellow petals falling from the stems.

'She hasn't been,' said Clare. 'Irene hasn't been. It's the first month she missed, ever.'

'Come on Clare, let's get you home, it's been a difficult morning.'

'But where is she? I can't lose her too, not Irene,' she sobbed.

'These things dig up old memories. She probably needed a break, time to think.'

Clare continued to stare at the dead yellow roses.

'As for you,' continued Jessie, 'most people would have cracked years ago. You're stronger than you think. Impressively so.'

Clare took Jessie's hand. 'Thanks.'

'We are with you all the way.'

'Okay,' said Clare, standing up.

'Come on, let's go and have breakfast some-where. These early starts make me very hungry.'

'Okay,' said Clare again. This time she smiled. It was a small smile. With three stones in it.

~

It wasn't until much later that day that the lab report came back. As Jessie sped along Ealing High Road, she stared at the test result. It was not what she'd been expecting. The IT expert at the station had tracked a web name found to be a frequent user of fan-extremis and other P. J. Dean fan sites. The moniker was WhiteTip: W.T. WhiteTip had then been traced to a number in Acton. Frances Leonard's telephone number. According to the lab test, however, the cigarette found by Niaz outside her flat the night the malevolent cross appeared on her door had been smoked not by Frances Leonard but by P. J. Dean.

As she turned into Frances Leonard's street, Jessie was sorry that she had sent Niaz back to Haverbrook Hall to oversee the sifting of Cosima's belongings. This break was all his. Four police cars pulled up outside the terraced house in Acton. Burrows and Fry went around the back, she and three uniformed officers approached the front. Jessie rang the doorbell. A middle-aged woman with cheap-looking dyed blonde hair opened the door. She stared at Jessie, then smiled.

'P.J. sent an escort,' she said. 'Hang on, let me

get my things. I'm not dressed, I've got a special outfit, you see.'

'Are you Frances Leonard?'

'Of course, but then *you* know that. Come in.' She opened the door wider. In the living room, P. J. Dean saturated the wall space, his music filled the air space and his image bore down from every angle.

'Frances, we need to ask you some questions.'

'Yes, I know. I should have come to you earlier, but I needed him to come and get me. He's waiting, I presume?' Her eyes darted between Jessie and the police officers.

'Frances, do you know who I am?'

'Detective Inspector Driver. I saw you on the telly. I tried to tell you before, but I got scared. I'm such a chicken, really. He gives me so much strength – love is an amazing thing.'

'What did you want to tell me?'

She smiled playfully. 'Spoilsport! Where's P.J.? I should tell him first, don't you think?' Suddenly she squinted and put her hand to her mouth. Her nails were bitten to the quick. 'Is he cross? I hate it when he's cross. Is he cross? Is he? Does he think I should have stopped it sooner? Well, he should have stopped it.'

'Stopped what?'

'Sleeping with those women – that tart.' Frances put her hand to her mouth again. 'Sorry, sorry, sorry, sorry. I shouldn't say that, should I? They're dead. It'll all be okay.'

'Why don't you tell me, and I'll tell P.J. That way he won't be cross with you. He'll be cross with me instead. Then he can just be pleased with you.'

'What about my nice dress?'

'You can still wear that.'

'Okay. I'll go and fetch it. Come with me if you want.' Burrows followed Jessie instinctively. 'Not you. No men. Just her, alone, it's private.'

'Boss . . .'

'It's okay.' Jessie smiled at Frances. 'It's only girls' talk, right?'

'Boss!'

'It's okay, Burrows. Everyone wait here.'

Jessie walked up the creaking, narrow staircase behind Frances, along a dark corridor and through a cheap veneer door. A computer blinked in the corner. She was online to fan-extremis.com. Pictures of Cary Conrad suspended over a vat of excrement filled the screen.

'Oops,' said Frances. 'What a filthy little man. It says here his butler lowered him in. The rope was wet and the knots slipped.' Frances looked at Jessie. 'Not a very nice way to go.'

Jessie stared at the photograph. No wonder the secretary had disappeared. Some tabloids would pay good money for those images. 'That hasn't been proved yet, Frances.'

'It says so – there. Anyway, I thought I'd wear this.' From the closet Frances pulled a black

Armani dress with diamanté straps. 'Do you like it?'

Jessie felt the sweat on her upper lip. She wiped it off with a sleeve. 'Frances, what did you want to tell P.J.?'

'That I saw who killed Verity, of course.'

'You *saw*?'

'Yes. That house in Barnes – she took lovers there. I told him she wasn't good enough, that slut –' Frances suddenly swiped at a photograph over the small Victorian fireplace. It landed at Jessie's feet. It was a picture of Verity Shore cut from a magazine. She was draped over a large pewter mantelpiece in a low-cut dress. Nothing was left to the imagination. Jessie picked it up and stared at it. She'd seen that fireplace before. Back at the station, pinned to a board, was a photograph of Eve Wirrel, doused in ash, sitting in a pewter fireplace. And here was Verity. Standing at the same fireplace. And that was not the only picture she'd seen of the distinctive art deco fireplace . . .

'You think I should have said something sooner? But P.J. didn't, he wanted rid of them. He did, he told me. He wrote them for me you know. All of them.'

'What did you see, in the house at Barnes?'

'A person. On a bike with a big backpack. Hit her over the head. I watched.'

'Man or woman, Frances?'

'Can't tell you all my secrets, can I?'

'Would you recognise this person again?'

'When do I see P.J.?'

'Soon, Frances. Sooner if you come to the station with me.'

'You like him?'

'I'm just doing my job, it isn't personal.'

'I know, I saw you on the telly. You're a detective inspector. Fast-tracked.'

'Frances, have I made you cross?'

'No. You're only doing your job. You'll be cross with me, because I didn't tell.'

Jessie looked from the Armani dress to the woman's dressing table. Frances had been inside more than the house in Barnes. 'Did you paint that cross on my door?'

She shifted from one foot to the other. 'No.'

'Are you sure?'

'I don't lie!' she shouted.

'Boss!'

'It's okay, Burrows. We're fine. Aren't we, Frances?'

She calmed down. 'I came to tell you what I saw. But I was a bit cross when you took him away. I'm sorry about your bike, I'm sorry I got cross. I didn't realise you were trying to save him – us. I'm sorry.'

'It's okay, Frances.'

'Do you like my dress?'

Jessie looked at the sparkling straps. 'Very much. Shall we go?'

'Okay.'

'Can I borrow this photo?'
'Okay.'

Eventually the picture editor at *Hello!* magazine told Jessie what she already knew. The 'at home' with Verity Shore in 1998 and the 'at home' with Eve Wirrel in 2000 were fakes. Neither woman was at her own home. Apparently it happened quite often when stars did not have residences to back up their glamorous image. The magazine paid the home owner a considerable sum of money for the intrusion, said the editor. And their silence, thought Jessie.

The editor-in-chief wouldn't give Jessie the name of the real home owner, but it didn't matter. Jessie already knew. She was looking at her. Dame Henrietta Cadell: author of *Isabella of France*. Jessie walked back to the evidence room very slowly. A terrible feeling was beginning to take hold of her. She picked up the list of initials from Eve Wirrel's collection of bizarre keepsakes and read down it. Towards the end, she found what she was looking for, the phial initialled J.C. She moved to the painting, the giant, grotesque painting, and stared at the well-endowed centrepiece. It wasn't Jesus Christ. It was Joshua Cadell. Henrietta's precious son had slept with Eve Wirrel. Her husband had slept with Verity Shore. Maybe Joshua had, too. He had a reputation, according to Maggie . . .

Maggie! Jessie picked up the phone and dialled her flatmate's number. Jessie knew which Cadell had been with Maggie, she'd seen him herself. Frances was telling the truth, she hadn't painted the red cross on their door. It hadn't even been for Jessie, it had been for Maggie.

'Hey, Jessie, how are you?'

'Has Henrietta Cadell tried to get in touch with you?'

'Um, no.'

'If she does, call me immediately. And do me a favour, do not under any circumstances meet up with her.'

'What's all this about?'

'Promise me, Maggie.'

'Fine, I promise. I'm filming, anyway.'

'And don't see Joshua either.'

'Joshua? Why would I –?'

'I saw him leave the flat, Maggie. Your cameraman, remember?'

'I'm sorry, I didn't realise you liked him so much. I thought you only had eyes for P. J. Dean. It certainly looked that way when you ran out of the party.'

'This is serious, Maggie,' said Jessie firmly. 'Don't see him.'

'It was just a shag. To be honest, he hasn't even called.'

'Good.'

'Good? Jesus, Jessie –'

'I can't explain now. Maggie, please do as I ask.'

'Who made you –'

'MAGGIE!'

'Okay, okay, I'll be good.'

Jessie put the phone down and exhaled loudly. Sometimes she could happily throttle Maggie. As Joshua had said, it was always shocking the first time you saw the crack in the façade. The fault lines were creeping through their friendship. Jessie was so proud of herself for not compromising herself in her job, but she did it all the time with Maggie.

She picked up her bag and leather jacket. She had never abandoned the possibility that a woman had committed the murders. They required mental, not physical, fortitude. Jessie didn't know if Henrietta Cadell had it in her to turn the written word into reality, but she had means, motive and access to all the dead girls. And when it came to mental fortitude, Henrietta wore her intellectual superiority like armour.

~

Irene came from an era of quiet distrust. But now, at last, she had confessed her secret. To someone who, despite their best intentions, would tell. It was a weighty truth that had dominated her life, her work and her relationships. She had loved Veronica dearly. They were family, and that made Veronica's affair with Raymond Giles doubly distressing. They'd been obsessed with each other. She needed him like an addict needs a hit. Even if it killed her. And it did, in the end. She could not stay away from him for ever. She did not possess that sort of strength. Away from the protection of the night nurses and the hospital walls, she would fold like she had so many times before. Irene had always thought that Veronica took her life to save her daughter's. But perhaps Veronica knew that her daughter's life was already ruined and it was guilt that made her climb up on the bedroom chair, hook the dressing-gown cord round her neck and kick her life away.

Frank, as far as Irene was concerned, had fared better. An imprisoned father may be absent, but at least he was consistent. It wasn't a big deal that Ray had been inside, either. Criminality was just a job to them. It put food on the table and heat in the pipes. So now it was time for Frank to do something for his sister. The policeman would talk and, if she didn't do something, Clare would find out. And, like her mother, it would kill her.

Clare could not know her beloved Frank was Ray's son. Irene had no option but to warn Raymond Giles that the police were on to him. And to do that, she was going to bring Frank in on a little secret.

Irene pushed open the door and stepped into Ray St Giles' new deluxe office suite. The young man was standing by a filing cabinet. He slammed the drawer shut and took a menacing step forward. Irene had had enough of menace. Mean men scaring women into submission – she had the victims in her salon all the time. She looked at him and tried to recall the small boy hammering on the window of the car as he was taken away.

'I want to speak to you,' said Irene calmly.

'How did you get in here? No one is –' said Alistair.

'About your mother,' she said softly.

He blinked at her. He had his father's eyes.

'I knew her very well. We used to go to Raymond's clubs. They met there.'

'I don't know what you're talking about.'

Irene smiled sadly. 'I don't suppose you call him Dad, do you? That would give the secret away.'

'The secret?' he repeated quietly.

They stood facing each other. 'Hasn't he told you?'

'No. He doesn't really talk about . . .' he struggled to keep control of his voice '. . . my mother.'

'She was married when they met.'

'Married! Mum was married?'

'They knew it was wrong, they knew they shouldn't fall for each other, but they did. Raymond fell hard. He was in love with your mother. They tried to stop it. She would go back to her husband, swearing never to see Raymond again. Raymond even got together with some young innocent lass, but he was only trying to make your mother jealous. It was too strong, you see.'

The lad was staring at her, a fixed and desperate look in his eyes.

'Didn't your father ever tell you any of this?'

Very slowly Alistair shook his head.

'Do you know why he went to prison?'

He nodded.

'The man he killed was your mother's husband. You have a half-sister. Her name is Clare and she has been searching for you all her life. Don't you remember? Being taken away by social services after your mother . . .' Irene breathed deeply '. . . died.'

He shook his head again.

'Your father found you, and here you are working for him. Not an ideal man for a father, but he must love you. Getting you away from social services can't have been easy. You were lucky. Clare stayed in care. Raymond didn't want her. Her father was dead, so was her mother, she has been alone all this time.'

The young man listened.

'I'm sorry,' said Irene. 'This must be hard for you. But it's harder for Clare. You do understand that she must never find you. If she knew what Raymond had done to her mother . . .'

'It would kill her,' he finished for her.

'Yes. I'm so sorry you had to find out like this.'

He was shaking. 'This lass, you say Ray . . .' he paused, 'my, my *father*, flaunted . . . Do you remember her name?'

'Alice. But she was nothing to him, I promise

you, he just used Alice to stop Veronica going back to Trevor.'

'Veronica,' he said painfully.

Irene smiled sadly. The boy obviously had no memory of his mother. Her friend.

'And did it work?' asked Alistair through gritted teeth.

'Yes. It did. You were born shortly afterwards. Their secret boy. Every opportunity Veronica had, she'd take you to see Raymond. Sometimes they'd meet in a hotel in Southend, but more often she'd take the bus to Woolwich Cemetery. When it rained, they'd hide in the Giles family crypt. Raymond had the key. That was how desperate they were to see each other. He visits her still. Every month. Now, of course, he takes the flowers himself. Being behind bars couldn't stop him leaving those damned yellow roses . . .' Irene faltered. Her voice cracked. 'Yellow. For envy. The man is still jealous. She chose death over him.'

Alistair turned round and leant on Ray's desk to steady himself. His breathing was ragged. Irene wanted to comfort him. She didn't see him reach out for the marble pen holder, and she didn't realise until it was too late that he had twisted his body, gathering up his strength. He spun towards her with alarming speed. Irene didn't even have time to raise her hand to protect herself. The new thick carpet muffled the sound as she fell to the floor.

Jessie pressed the bell of the Regency house until a harassed-looking woman came to the door.

'I need to speak to Dame Henrietta.'

'Who may I say is calling?'

'DI Driver of West End Central CID.' The woman did not move aside. 'May I come in?'

'Sorry, she is writing. I'm not normally supposed to –'

'Is it normal for the police to show up on the doorstep?'

'No.'

'Well then.'

Jessie followed the nervous, retreating woman down an impressive hallway and into a room on the right. The floor was solid walnut, the skirting boards were white, the walls were cream. The large sofas were also rich white, the cushions were jewel-coloured silk and black-and-white sketches by famous artists adorned the walls. Jessie was disappointed, there was no art deco fireplace.

On the ottoman were three of the daily newspapers. Ray St Giles was on the front cover of every single one. 'Ray the Voice of Reason.' 'Ray St Giles – patron saint of the people's pocket!' 'No more rip-offs, says Ray.' His latest coup had been to expose Jami Talbot live on television for the fraud that she was. She had paid some junkie to beat her up and the junkie had found a way to double his money. It seemed there were people who would stop at nothing to reach their goal. But the goal was a mirage. As soon as you reached it, it moved. These people were chasing the spotlight, but the light eluded them. It was a dangerous light. A fool's light. They thought they could bask in it for ever, but in the end it moved on, leaving them in total darkness. Alone. Perhaps where they had always been.

'I know you,' said a blustering voice from the doorway. 'You're the little thing my son was talking to at the L'Epoch party. Jessica? The one with the broken heart.'

'Detective Inspector Driver,' she said, holding out her ID. Henrietta Cadell waved it away, seemingly unimpressed. She picked up a cigarette box and removed a white-tipped Marlboro. Jessie watched the smoke unfurl.

'Those parties are dreadful, aren't they? I couldn't do it if it wasn't for Joshua. My husband hates that sort of thing, poor man. He'd be much happier at home with a good book.'

So the woman was deluded and possessive. No different to Frances Leonard, except that Henrietta Cadell was better packaged. Jessie held out the hardback edition.

'Oh, sweet, you want a dedication?'

'Where was the photo taken?' asked Jessie.

'Here, why?'

'May I see the room?'

'Well, I'm writing at the moment, and I don't

422

like to have my concentration broken.'

'I understand. This won't take long.' Jessie stood up.

'I really must insist that you allow me to return to work. Deadlines, you know.'

'Did you know Verity Shore or Eve Wirrel?'

'No.'

'Are you sure? Your husband said you introduced him to Verity Shore.'

'Very unlikely. I try to avoid people like that.'

'What about Lady Cosima Broome?'

Henrietta laughed. 'The Titled Tart? The only thing that stupid little girl wrote well was a cheque.'

'You know they are all dead?'

Henrietta took a long drag of her cigarette and then flicked the ash. 'Cosima, too?' she enquired, trying to feign concern, and failing.

Jessie nodded.

'And what exactly has that got to do with me?'

Jessie showed her the photographs of the fireplace.

'Oh God, that was ages ago. I needed the money at the time. It isn't easy being the major bread-winner, bringing up a son, and keeping a certain, well, you know, reputation. You don't know what it's like out there. One Duchess of Devonshire and you're all but forgotten.'

'I'd like to see it, please.'

'What? Why?'

'This is a murder investigation. You knew the

deceased. I'm simply crossing off names.'

'I didn't really know them – you don't really know those sort of people, you just kiss them hello occasionally and make an excuse as you move on.'

Jessie slid the photograph of Mr Cadell and Verity Shore in the hotel lobby across the ottoman. 'And your husband, when he isn't sitting at home with a good book, does he also kiss and move on?'

With extraordinary calmness Henrietta slowly screwed her cigarette into the base of a solid silver ashtray. 'You think knowing about my husband's affairs makes you a good detective? *Everyone* knows my husband screws around. Little girls who think he is impressive,' she laughed harshly. 'I really don't know who I feel more sorry for – him for having to pretend that what they talk about is interesting, or them for having to pretend his wrinkly old sterile body is attractive.'

'He told me you liked to use that against him.'

'God, he tried that on you too, did he? That line tends to work best on the stupid and the desperate. Don't tell me, I am the witch for getting pregnant without him. Someone had to do something. It was too awful knowing he was endlessly beating away into a plastic cup only to discover one or two healthy ones. Very difficult to respect a man after that. So, keep your picture, it doesn't even raise my temperature. And the answer is, yes, eventually, he always moves on. Houses like this don't come cheap and he isn't a bedsit sort of man.'

'And Joshua? Did he also kiss and move on?'

Henrietta winced. 'My son has better taste than that. What would a boy of his calibre want with those women?'

'Breathing space, perhaps?'

Henrietta stood up. 'What exactly are you accusing me of?'

'Me? Nothing.'

'I love my son. If there is a crime in that then I give up. The world has become a stupid place.'

'And a violent one.'

'Hardly. We don't even know the meaning of the word.'

'Dame Henrietta, could I see your study, please?'

'You are a very irritating person, aren't you? Ambition and envy are not attractive traits, Detective Inspector Driver.'

'Your study. Now.'

It was a shrine. An altar to Joshua. It wasn't a large room but every available space had a photograph of him on it. They all but drowned out the history books and the beautifully moulded 1930s pewter fireplace. Jessie held up the pictures of Eve Wirrel and Verity Shore. She traced the line of the wall, the fringe of the lamp, the pattern of the club fender. It was the same fireplace. The same room. The same soft furnishings. Verity Shore and Eve Wirrel had been 'at home' with Henrietta Cadell. And Henrietta Cadell had been playing house with her son. Christopher Cadell couldn't compete.

Jessie picked up a photo of Joshua. He was on a beach wearing skimpy swimming trunks. The trunks were wet. The material clung to him suggestively. He had his arms spread out wide and his head thrown back laughing. Joshua Cadell. Eve Wirrel's well-endowed nude. Henrietta took the photo from her. She might not mind her husband fooling around with the likes of Verity Shore, but her son? Her precious son. That was unthinkable. Here was a woman surrounded by literature documenting the barbaric acts of mankind and constant reminders of what she was missing. Could maternal love turn murderous? Could anyone be that jealous of their own flesh and blood?

'Will there be anything else?' Henrietta was holding the door open.

'He lives with you, doesn't he?'

'Downstairs. It's a self-contained flat and he isn't in at the moment.'

'Isn't he a little old to be living with his mother?'

Henrietta wore the same self-satisfied smile Jessie had seen before. 'A pity, I know, that his writing career didn't quite take off as he would have liked. I felt terrible that his novels were turned down – people can be so cruel. I feel guilty, of course. The publishers compared him to me and, well . . . As I said, I feel terrible about it.'

Jessie didn't think so. P. J. Dean had taught her one thing about the world Dame Cadell inhabited. If you were at the top of your profession there was very little you couldn't manipulate to your advantage. Henrietta Cadell didn't want her son to go. A word here, a threat there . . . It was like P.J. controlling the press over his errant wife. Henrietta had stopped her son achieving anything. That was what Christopher had meant when he said his wife had made sure Joshua was always there for her.

'What publishers did Joshua send his work to?' asked Jessie.

'I can't recall,' said Henrietta.

'The subject?'

'Love stories, I'm afraid.'

'Good?'

'A little unbelievable, but yes, of course. He's my son.'

'And he hasn't had a love affair himself?'

'He has rather high standards, I'm pleased to say.'

Jessie handed Henrietta a list of dates. 'Where were you at these times?'

Henrietta folded the page in half and passed it back. 'Have you any idea how busy I am? My PA will be able to tell you, but I do write, I spend great swathes of time in isolation. It's the only way to get the work done. I wouldn't expect the likes of you to understand.'

'I need to see her then.'

'Him, actually. And he isn't here yet.'

'Where can I find him?'

Henrietta folded her arms under her shelf-like breasts.

'Three women are dead. I don't expect to have to ask twice.'

'He won't be in until midday. You are welcome to wait, but I really have to work.'

'Thank you,' said Jessie, a false smile fixed on her face. 'I think I will.'

~

Jessie took herself to a small café to think. The PA had arrived at twelve and shown Jessie the secrets of Henrietta's schedule. Henrietta had been as busy as she claimed around the times that the first two women died. Although she still had no exact time of death for Cosima, Jessie didn't see how Henrietta could have got to Haverbrook Hall and back in time to present a literary award, attend a dinner and visit the Reading Festival. On the other hand, Reading was not far from Haverbrook Hall, and if the murder had taken place at night and she'd had help . . . Jessie sighed out loud. It was all too tenuous, circumstantial. The CPS wouldn't buy it. She wouldn't have bought it. And Henrietta knew it. Jessie didn't have one grain of evidence.

As the barista handed over her takeaway coffee, Jessie's phone rang. She pressed it to her ear.

'DI Driver.'

'Why didn't you tell me?' The voice sounded constrained. Angry. Hurt.

'Clare?' Jessie pushed through the crowd to the street.

'You knew, didn't you? About my mother and that bastard!'

'Clare, where are you? I'll come and get you.'

'You bloody knew, you all bloody knew.'

'Where are you?'

'Never you fucking mind. Stupid, stupid, stupid me! Well, fuck your pity.'

'Clare, let's meet, we'll talk.'

'Too fucking late for that. I'm going to finish this, now, once and for all!'

'Clare?'

Her voice echoed in the silence.

'Clare? Damn!'

Jessie dialled the surveillance team outside St Giles' house. How on earth had Clare found out? Had Fry let it slip? Had she seen a file? Overheard someone discussing the case? The surveillance team seemed uneasy hearing Jessie's voice and it worried her. She wanted to know what was going on. But they couldn't give her an answer. Ray had given his followers the slip walking through a shopping centre. Jessie paced the street angrily.

'He got mobbed, women everywhere. By the time the crowd cleared, he'd disappeared.'

'You idiots, he probably did it on purpose.' Jessie was stuck. There was no point trying to find him, he could be anywhere. The man on the phone was apologising again. Jessie couldn't be bothered to listen to his paltry excuses.

'Find him, and bring him to West End Central.' She was going to get Clare back on the phone, talk some sense to her, calm her down. She'd send Fry to go and get her . . .

'With all due respect, DI Driver, I don't think St Giles was up to no good. He left the house carrying a bunch of yellow roses –' Jessie's coffee fell to the ground and splattered over the pavement.

It took forty minutes to get to Woolwich Cemetery in the car, even with the lights flashing. There was a man leaning a bike against the forlorn gates. Jessie recognised the hunch of the shoulders as she switched the engine off.

'What are you doing here, Mark?'

He turned round. The side of his face was still discoloured from the bruising.

'Clare disappeared from the station. She isn't at home, she hasn't been to work. I couldn't shake this bad feeling, so I checked myself out of hospital. I was hoping she'd be here.'

'Isn't she?'

'No. But there are some fresh flowers, so I guess that means Irene is okay.'

Jessie shook her head and started to run along the cracked, weed-infested pathway to Veronica Mills' grave. 'Irene didn't leave those flowers. Ray did!'

She was running too fast to hear Mark's response. She saw the bright yellow roses lying on the ground in front of the luminous white cross. They were still in their paper. And their dead predecessors were still scattered over the grave. Ray had been interrupted. Jessie moved closer to the cross. Mark panted behind her.

'How could he have left them? He was in the nick.'

'He didn't have to do it himself. He has enough influence to get this done without anyone knowing. Irene must have covered for him, like she always has.'

'Clare knows, doesn't she?'

Jessie didn't reply directly. Instead she pointed to the splash of red blood on the corner of the headstone then put a finger to her lips. There was a rustle in the bordering hedgerow. Someone was watching them. She pointed to her eyes then indicated the spiky hawthorn bushes. Mark nodded and began to walk along the edge. Jessie scanned the big tombstones. Clare must have seen Ray leave the roses; she'd called Jessie because she couldn't believe what she was seeing. St Giles leaving roses on her mother's grave. Jessie tried to imagine the rage Clare would have felt. It would have superseded any fear Clare may have felt for the man. She would have gone for him, no question. Jessie would have done the same. But Ray had been fighting off opposition for years. Jessie was pretty certain it was Clare's blood on the gravestone. Mark walked up beside her.

'Whoever was there, they've scarpered.'

'Well, he didn't have time to move her very far. She must be here somewhere.' They reached the crypts on the brow of the hill and started trying doors. The crypts looked as forgotten as the cemetery; they belonged to a different time, when families stayed in one place, lived, died and were buried together. She approached the last one, saw the name above the door and stopped in her tracks. GILES. Carved in a roman-style script into the crumbling York stone. Jessie reached for the thick steel door. She knew already it would open. The ground had been disturbed and the bolt was drawn. Jessie retrieved the torch from her bag, took a deep breath and pulled the door towards her. The beam of light cut through the inky black space within. Ray's ash-white face and glassy eyes loomed back at her. She dropped the torch.

'Mark! Mark! Come here quick –!'

Jessie scooped the torch up from the musty earth-covered floor and forced herself to look at Ray St Giles. He was semi-naked, tied up against the wooden frame of the shelves upon which his dead family lay. He would be joining them soon if Jessie didn't do something. He was bleeding profusely from a gash in his inner thigh. His femoral artery had been severed. Blood was pouring down his leg on to the dusty floor. He was five foot nine, weighed approximately thirteen stone and he'd be dead in thirty-five minutes. Jessie pointed the torch downward. Clare Mills was balled up on the floor at Ray's feet. She too was unconscious. Bleeding from the head. Jessie thought of Eve Wirrel's painting and wondered whether two worlds could really collide like this.

Mark went straight for Clare. 'She's breathing,' he said. 'She's got a nasty bump on the head.'

Jessie put her bag on the floor. 'Cut?'

'It's a bit sticky, but it's not bleeding badly.'

'I don't mean her head, I mean like that –' she shone the torch on the oozing wound on Ray's thigh. A long, clean, deep incision glistened in the torchlight.

'No.'

'We've got to stem this bleeding,' said Jessie.

'I'll call for back-up.'

'We don't have time. Come here, I need that bottle of whiskey.'

'What whiskey?'

'The one in your pocket. Quick.'

Mark looked bewildered as Jessie accepted the quarter-bottle.

'Get him down, Mark. Make a tourniquet with your tie and pen around the top of his thigh and raise the leg up, above his heart.'

Jessie snapped a Bic biro in half. She pulled out the ink tube and threw it aside. With the torch in her mouth, she dipped the end section of the biro into the whiskey then poured a little over her hands. The flow of blood had slowed because of the tourniquet and the elevation of the leg. Jessie slipped the biro over one end of the exposed artery and with her other hand fed the severed artery down inside the biro.

'Now, gently undo the tourniquet, just enough to keep a fresh blood supply to the leg. That way

433

he might not lose it.' They watched the see-though biro fill with blood.

'It's weeping a bit, but I think it'll work,' said Jessie. 'Okay, now call for back-up.'

'Where the hell did you learn to do that?' said Mark.

'That would be telling.'

'Very impressive,' said Mark. Except this time his lips didn't move.

Jessie turned round in time to see the door close. She threw herself against it, but the person outside was too quick. The door was bolted. She kicked it. The steel jarred against the sole of her foot and reverberated up her leg.

'Stupid kids,' said Mark, not sounding as confident as he'd like.

'That wasn't kids,' said Jessie, watching the sliver of light under the steel door slowly disappear.

'Hey!' shouted Mark, jumping over Clare and hitting the door. 'Hey!'

Jessie was watching their airway disappear.

Mark took out his phone. She didn't need him to tell her there was no signal in the lead-lined mausoleum, his face in the beam told her everything she needed to know. The torch started fading, so she switched it off. 'Damn,' said Jessie. Paul and Ty had run the batteries down and she didn't have any spares.

Mark lit his lighter. 'What happened?'

'Batteries. How's the wound?'

Mark passed the small blue flame over Ray's leg. 'Holding. What the fuck is going on?'

'I don't know. This doesn't fit the pattern,' said Jessie. 'I was so sure it was a mother–son thing, but Joshua wasn't sleeping with Ray St Giles –'

'Ow!' Mark dropped the lighter. 'Shit!' Jessie could hear Mark's breathing shorten. 'I can't find it!' He was scrabbling around in the dust furiously. 'Oh Christ, he moved!'

Jessie crouched down in the darkness. 'Mark,' said Jessie softly. 'Take my hand – here. Now stand up with me. There's plenty of room in here. See, here's the door, I want you to lean against it. Don't move, just breathe slowly.'

Mark's hand was clammy and he was struggling to control his breathing.

'I can't breathe, I can't . . .'

'Yes, you can. In for four, out for six. Keep going.' Jessie slowly let go of his hand.

'Don't leave me. I can't, I can't see . . .'

'It's okay, I'm here. I'm going to pass you the torch. Then you know you have it if you need it.' Jessie pressed the torch into his other hand. He clicked it on, pointed it to the floor. 'There, my lighter.'

Jessie bent down and retrieved it. In the fading light, she looked at Clare. Mark must have moved her as he was frantically searching for the lighter. Her arm was stretched across Ray St Giles' leg, her body was no longer curled up in a ball. Mark clicked the torch off as Jessie stood up again.

'Sorry about that,' said Mark, taking her hand again.

'Claustrophobia is a horrible thing.'

'It isn't that, it's the dark.'

They stood in the echoing blackness holding hands. Total darkness was not something Jessie experienced often. It made her feel very closed-in while at the same time very small.

'We were poor,' said Mark quietly. 'Mum had to work after the old man left. It was a different time, there wasn't the help. She didn't know what to do with me.'

Jessie squeezed his hand.

'It was for my safety,' said Mark. 'I couldn't come to any harm in the closet, but it was so dark and she was away for so long. I . . .'

'It's okay. They'll find us. The surveillance team know about the roses, someone will put it together.'

'Not as fast as you did.'

Jessie smiled in the darkness. 'You're not going soft on me, are you?'

Mark didn't respond.

'Will you be all right? I want to check Ray's wound.'

He handed the torch back and took the lighter. Jessie shone the pale orange light at Ray's leg.

'I think the biro must have slipped,' said Jessie. 'His pulse is barely there. Mark, we're losing him.'

'Him we can afford to lose,' said Mark. 'It's the

three of us I'm worried about.' He passed Jessie the whiskey. She let the stringent blend sit on her tongue until it burned. The darkness in the tomb was overwhelming. Heavy. It bore down on them. She didn't allow herself to think of the cold spreading through her own limbs or the man slowly bleeding to death beside her. She thought instead of Henrietta Cadell, of Joshua and of Clare Mills. She thought long and hard and when she stopped Ray St Giles was dead. She heard the long exhalation. His last breath. She had failed. Her bag of tricks had failed. She couldn't get them out of this and she felt utterly demoralised.

'I should have let you call for back-up –'

Mark put his arm around Jessie. 'This isn't your fault.'

'I should have got Clare out first, I should have known.'

'Known what? We thought Ray was a suspect, not a victim.'

'He isn't.'

'What do you mean?'

'Nothing,' said Jessie, listening to the silence.

'Hey,' said Mark, flicking his lighter on. 'I won't have you falling apart – not the unsinkable Jessie Driver.'

'I've made a cock-up of this, Mark.'

'Rubbish. You've done what detectives are supposed to do: examine every avenue, and never apologise if it's a dead end.'

'I think I can smell burning skin.'

The flame went out, leaving its imprint floating around in front of Jessie's eyes.

'Mark, your mum, was it just the two of you?'

'Yeah.'

'And you never told her you were afraid.'

'How could I? She was doing her best. I was her little man, men are brave, so I put up with it, but took it out on everyone else. I probably still am. Especially on women. It's not easy to trust women after the one who loved you the most locked you in a cupboard and left you in the pitch-black.'

'Is that why you never got married?'

'Oh I got married – to seventy-odd blokes in the Met. And I'm not angry with Ma. She didn't do it to be cruel, she did it to be practical. Even then I knew the difference.'

'And if it had been cruelty?'

'I'd be one of the many fucked-up souls we deal with every day.'

'Mark, do you think there are always extenuating circumstances?'

'No, not always. Some people are born with a black hole where their heart should have been.'

As Jessie shifted her weight, the door behind her and Mark suddenly opened. They fell back squinting at the sudden brightness. A figure was standing over them.

'Clare!'

It was Irene. She ran straight for the bundle on the floor as Jessie and Mark got unsteadily to their feet. And Irene had not come alone. She had brought Fry and he had brought back-up and medical help. Jessie watched her cradle Clare. Irene had a bruise on the side of her face that almost matched Mark's. Jessie wondered if it had anything to do with Irene's recent absence.

Irene looked very briefly at Ray.

'Is he dead?'

'Yes,' said Mark. Jessie didn't begrudge Irene the relief that was palpable on her face. Her nemesis was dead. As Fry carried Clare out, she came round. He lay her on the ground and let Irene hold her and whisper to her reassuringly, keeping her close. Jessie watched the two women as the medical team swarmed the stone crypt. Clare seemed very calm; concussion could do that. What it couldn't do was leave no physical mark. Clare Mills had no bruise.

Jessie had to move fast. She directed her first question to Irene. How had she known they were there? The answer was straightforward enough. The crypt was where Ray used to meet Veronica. It was the first place she thought to look. She knew Clare was missing because she had telephoned the station. When it became known that Jessie and Mark had disappeared and that Ray had last been seen carrying yellow roses, Irene put the pieces together and told DC Fry to meet her at the cemetery. It was a neat explanation, thought Jessie.

'Did you see anything, Clare?'

She shook her head, then frowned. 'I saw him put those roses on her grave. I couldn't believe it, I thought maybe he just happened to be passing, and had seen the flowers, so I rang you and you told me everything I needed to know. Ray and my mother were . . .' Clare shuddered.

'I'm so sorry, love,' sobbed Irene.

Clare clutched Irene's wrist. Jessie noticed the blood on Clare's fingers. 'I saw red. I ran at him screaming, he turned around and hit me.' She touched her head and winced. 'I must have hit my head on something. I managed to get on to my hands and knees. I tried to crawl away. But I couldn't get away quick enough. I remember seeing his feet.' Clare started to cry. 'I thought he was going to kill me. *I* begged *him* for mercy. *Him*. I should have spat in his face. I don't know what happened next.'

'Did you see anyone else?'

Clare frowned again. 'Maybe I saw a man, I can't remember. He'd gone by the time I'd finished talking to you.'

'A man?'

Clare nodded. 'Tall, white skin. Dark hair, I think.'

'Are you sure, Clare?'

Clare stared back at Jessie, then slowly shook her head. 'No, not completely. I was too angry.'

'But you think you did?'

Irene squeezed Clare's hand.

'Yes,' she said quietly. 'He looked like a ghost.'

Jessie returned to the station to see Frances Leonard. She was expecting a woman possessed with rage at having been duped into leaving her shrine. All dressed up and no hero to meet. Instead, Frances was sitting quietly in the corner with her dress folded neatly on her lap.

'You're back,' said Frances, smiling. 'I am so sorry I messed with your bike. When I get angry, I can't seem to control what I'm doing. I didn't mean to hurt you. Will I get into trouble?'

'None of that matters,' said Jessie, pulling up a chair. 'But I do need you to answer those questions now.'

'I know. P.J. told me. He was very kind and explained a lot of things. I have to leave him alone, he has some private things to deal with. But my goodness, it was so nice to talk to him.'

Jessie nodded in a way she hoped was noncommittal. If she imagined P. J. Dean had come to see her, good, now Frances would talk. Jessie needed one question answered very quickly. She pulled out a photograph of Henrietta Cadell and her son and showed it to Frances. Frances nodded.

'Yes,' she said. 'That's him. I saw him.'

So, thought Jessie, she was getting warmer. 'What did you see him do, Frances?'

'He went to the house in Barnes. He was doing it with Verity.'

'That wasn't all though, was it?'

Frances screwed up her face but said nothing.

'Frances, you said you'd seen who *killed* Verity Shore, remember? Someone hit her over the head. Was it him?'

Frances chewed her lip.

'Frances?' said Jessie, getting angry. 'You said –'

'I know, I'm sorry. I did see him once. But I don't know if it was him exactly. He looked different.'

'But it was a man?'

'I think so.'

'You *think*?'

'I'm sorry, I wanted to see P.J. They always lie and say he's coming, and he never does, so why shouldn't I tell lies? But you took me seriously. You really did send P.J. to see me.'

The woman was conveniently using her fantasy to absolve her from the trouble she'd got herself in. 'Frances, I am very angry with you. I thought you were reliable. You've given me nothing to go on. P.J. will be angry with you too. He wants to see the killer caught as much as I do.'

'I did see that man there,' pleaded Frances. 'And the woman. Not in Barnes. At the church in Richmond. She had a big fight with Eve Wirrel.'

'When was this?'

'A few days before she died.'

'Frances, the person who hit Verity, was he tall, like this man?'

'Yes. He had dark hair too.'

Jessie stood up. She explained that the next

442

people to come into the room were there to help her. Frances smiled. She knew, she said, P.J. had told her about them too. Jessie passed the mental health worker as she ran to the yard.

The garage were just delivering her mended bike. They couldn't untie it from the truck quickly enough.

~

Jessie returned to the Cadells' house, she kept her finger on the bell until it was answered by Henrietta herself, then she barged in.

'Where is Joshua?'

'Don't you possess manners?'

'I am moments away from arresting you, I suggest you answer my questions.'

'No one speaks to me like that. If you had any sort of evidence then you would have already arrested me. So please don't insult my intelligence with your vain threats.'

'Why did you argue with Eve Wirrel? Was it because you discovered she was screwing your son? She also painted him naked – it's hanging in the station. Quite a sight it is, too.'

'Knowing that the girl was a jumped-up, talentless exhibitionist is one thing. Killing her is quite another.'

'You said you didn't know her.'

'I don't. I was trying to protect Joshua. She was a headline-hunting whore; Joshua is too sweet, he doesn't see it. She would have gone to the papers and dragged my name through the mud in order to get herself a little exposure. Well, I wasn't having it. Joshua had to be told.'

'Your son has killed four people. Not as sweet as you think.'

'Don't be ridiculous.'

'Where is he?'

'Get out of my house!'

Jessie started to walk along the hallway, tapping the wall beneath the stairs.

'What on earth are you doing?'

'One of the themes of these murders has been secrecy. Hidden doorways, secret tunnels. Very mediaeval, wouldn't you say? Where do you think the murderer would have got an idea like that?'

'I am too busy for this nonsense.'

'When did you separate the basement from the rest of the house, Henrietta?' Jessie ran her hand along the underside of the stair tread. She found a cold copper button and pressed it. A panel in front of her popped open.

'You don't have a search warrant.'

'You let me into your house. We're still in it.' The staircase disappeared into the basement.

'If you take another step, I shall call your superiors.'

'What have you got to hide?'

'Nothing. This is an invasion of privacy and you know it.'

'I am a fast-tracked detective. I'm bound to make some mistakes.'

The basement flat was tidy to the point of disorder. All the pens on the desk were lined up. The books exactly even. The cushions were plump and the carpet had been hoovered in lines. Sitting in an armchair by an unlit but neatly laid fire was Christopher Cadell.

'What the hell are you doing in Joshua's flat?' demanded Henrietta.

Christopher looked at his wife with melancholic eyes and sighed loudly. 'Thinking,' he said.

'Well, get out. You know he doesn't like *you* being down here.'

'No, Henrietta. He doesn't like anyone being down here.' Christopher looked at Jessie. 'Joshua introduced me to Verity. Not my wife.'

'I thought so,' said Jessie. Henrietta was unlikely to grace Verity Shore with a nod, let alone an introduction to her philandering husband.

'Shut up, Christopher. You can't be effectual, but please don't try and be actively destructive.' Henrietta turned to Jessie. 'He has always been jealous of Joshua. It was not my fault he loved me more.'

'Where is he?' asked Jessie, looking at Christopher.

'NOT YOUR FAULT!' shouted Christopher, standing up. 'I could have forgiven the affairs, I could have forgiven you for letting the world know

I wasn't a real man, but telling Josh, when he was just a child. That was unforgivable.'

'Don't be ridiculous. He wanted to know why his daddy didn't love him. He deserved the truth. You aren't his daddy. Joshua understood after that.'

'You have created a monster, Henrietta, and you won't allow yourself to see it.' Christopher turned back to Jessie. 'She would play games with him –'

'Do shut up!'

'She'd tell him horrific tales then put him in places he couldn't get out of. He would scream and shout and finally she would rescue him –'

'Those were just games!'

'The poor boy forgot it was *you* who put him in there –'

'I will divorce you if you say another word. I will make sure you don't get a penny. No more club, no more drink, no more little girls. I will ruin you.'

And there it was, Jessie realised. Henrietta's tell. The closer anyone got to the truth behind the image, the more of a bully Henrietta would become.

'This is a murder investigation, if you don't tell me everything you can about your son, I shall arrest you both for obstruction of justice. That wouldn't look so good on the front pages, would it?'

'I'm calling my lawyer,' said Henrietta finally.

'Well,' said Jessie. 'Now we're getting some-where.' She leant back on Joshua's desk, nudging the mouse by accident and sending the sleeping computer whirring into action. Jessie let her eyes wander over the screensaver.

'Oh no . . .'

'What,' said Henrietta cattily. 'Have you never seen a picture of a naked girl?'

Jessie put her head in her hands. She'd been so stupid. All that time she'd wasted in the cemetery, back at the police station.

'Where is she?' Jessie took a menacing step towards Henrietta.

'Splashed all over some magazine. You have to admit, it is tacky. Let go of me! Didn't you know your flatmate was just another nasty little exhibitionist?'

'I will make sure you never see the light of day unless you tell me now. Where has he taken Maggie?'

'Have you read my wife's books?' said Christopher.

'Shut up,' shouted Henrietta.

'No.'

'You should have,' he said. Just as his son had at the Epoch party. Joshua had been playing with her all along. Christopher directed Jessie to the bookshelf with his eyes. 'She wrote about smuggling in the eighteenth century. There was a famous woman smuggler, as cruel as you like. And then there was the story of the priest hole, and the crippled man who'd been kept in a hole for years. He was the last recusant priest to hang.'

Jessie frantically began to pull out titles by

447

Dame Henrietta Cadell. How could she have been so blind? The Isabella Plantation – it had been screaming at her for days. 'Which one is next?'

Henrietta shook her head. 'You are insane, both of you. My Joshua would never do such a thing. Do you realise how intelligent he is?'

'He could have done anything, been anyone,' said Christopher. 'But you stopped him. You made sure his books didn't get published.'

'How dare you! I've supported him every step of the way. Who do you think gave him the contacts in the first place? Who got him the column?'

'Stop lying. Look what you've done.'

'Me? Me? And where the fuck were you all this time? Drunk. Like you've always been. Well, congratulations. You are just as guilty as me. We're in this together.'

Christopher sunk back into the chair and bowed his head. Henrietta had won. Again. Jessie was close to tears. There were too many books. Too many essays. Joshua had surrounded himself with his mother's heavy-hitting words. They would have bored down on him every day, reminding him how ineffectual he too had become. And yet all around him were those women – Verity, Eve, Cosima and now Maggie. Splashed over the society pages, famous for no reason at all, naked on glossy pages, taunting him. He had lived in his mother's shadow, dependent on her, wary of her, resentful of her, obsessed with her . . .

'Which fucking book is it!' screamed Jessie,

pulling another from the shelf.

Christopher shook his head. Henrietta didn't move. 'This is absolutely insane,' she said, but the certainty had left her voice.

'If she dies, if she fucking dies, I will . . .'

'What? What could you possibly do to someone like me?'

Jessie closed her eyes for a moment as blood roared through her brain. She could feel herself expand with anger. She breathed again, slowly, like she had told Mark to do in the crypt. The crypt had put her off the trail. Joshua wasn't interested in Ray St Giles – of course he wasn't, there wasn't any link, any clue. It hadn't been him standing mysteriously in the cemetery.

Cosima and Maggie had some secret in their past, that was why Maggie was so jumpy around her. What were the other clues, what had she missed?

'The plague,' said Jessie suddenly. 'The plague, you've written something about the plague?'

'No,' said Henrietta.

'Yes,' said Christopher.

Henrietta moved incredibly quickly for a woman her size. But Jessie was faster and she grabbed Henrietta's arm just before she brought the lamp down on her husband's head. Christopher jumped away. 'You can't protect him any more. She is writing about the plague now, how it affected London. She's working on it at the moment. Josh has read it.'

449

'You bastard, he'll never forgive you now.'

'And nor should he,' said Christopher. 'I was too feeble to stop you. I can't forgive myself.' He moved to the other side of the room and opened a drawer in Joshua's desk. 'Moorfields. There was a burial pit. It's still wasteland, right in the middle of the City. Joshua has been there. It's a car park and dealers use it to supply the City boys . . .'

Jessie didn't hear the rest of the lesson. She didn't care if the Cadells ripped each other to shreds. Maggie was dying in a wasteland in the city, surrounded by people too busy to stop, all because Jessie hadn't wanted to see what Clare Mills had done.

The first policeman scrambled to the site radioed what he had found. A black VW beetle was parked next to the wire fence at the very back of the waste-land. Two people were sitting in it. One male. One female. They were talking. Jessie cried with relief. By the time she arrived, they had the car park sur-rounded.

Jessie went in alone, she didn't want to ignite the situation. She pulled the driver's door open. She didn't know who was more surprised to see her. Maggie or Joshua. Joshua disguised it better, though that didn't surprise Jessie.

'Jessie! What are you doing here?' exclaimed Maggie, leaning over the handbrake.

'Joshua, Maggie,' said Jessie, 'would you both

mind stepping out of the car?'

'Hey,' moaned Maggie. 'What's going on?'

'No problem,' said Joshua.

'Come on, we weren't doing anything –' Maggie caught the expression in Jessie's eyes and stopped talking. 'Christ, Barnaby, you're no fun any more.' Maggie's television diction was slipping. Her eyelids kept sliding closed. Joshua followed Jessie's eye to the near-empty bottle jammed between Maggie's legs.

'Oh, don't worry,' slurred Maggie. 'I wasn't doing the driving. It's been one of those days, you don't know what . . .' She stepped out of the car and her legs gave way. The bottle shattered on the ground. Maggie didn't seem to notice. She kept on talking as she slowly sank lower.

'Christ,' she slurred. 'I don't feel so good.' She hauled herself up again and made her way round to the back of the car, where she collapsed to the compressed rubble ground.

'Your friend likes to drink,' said Joshua, emerging from the driver's seat. Jessie did not move. The keys were in the ignition of the car. He was nearer to them than she was.

'She thinks I'll help her career, but I can't. She drinks too much, everyone knows it. She's good, but she won't get on unless she quits. But you know this, don't you? It's difficult telling someone you love to stop, isn't it? Deep down you want their approval more and you know they'll hate you for pointing out their weaknesses. Don't be fooled, the messenger always gets shot. And I suppose you need what she provides – the excitement, the parties, the famous people. Not for you a pint of bitter and a packet of pork scratchings.'

'Joshua Cadell, I am arresting you on suspicion of the murders of Verity Shore, Eve Wirrel, Cosima Broome and the attempted murder of Maggie Hall.'

He raised an eyebrow. 'That's a bit harsh, isn't it? She's killing herself. Don't blame it on me.'

'Maggie Hall will wake up when the Rohypnol in that drink wears off. She will not remember a thing until I tell her that you were going to slice her artery and leave her here to die above this human cesspit.'

Joshua smiled a wolverine smile then chuckled. 'Oh. So even you didn't know about the pills?' Jessie wouldn't fall for the trick. 'Oh, come on,' said Joshua. 'You surely didn't think the sudden mood swings were hormonal? It's been going on under your nose. One minute sitting on the floor in a dark room, the next minute, all smiles. My, how she bounced back from those set-backs.'

Jessie felt a cold sweat creep over her.

'She is dying. Right now. I have your stubbornness on my side. Don't I? The more we wait, the less you have. You are so confident, you aren't even wired. It didn't cross your mind, did it? You are always in control. Let me tell you something, Miss Driver. I would not have had to slit another vein after Cosima died because everyone would have known it was me whether it had my insignia or not. Eventually, all the great artists stop signing their name because their work spells it out for them. Maggie Hall, another tragic victim exposed as the sorry little junkie she was.' Joshua stepped to one side. 'Check her handbag, if you don't believe me about the pills. You think she came here because I asked her to? A lot of pills change hands in this car park. Maggie took too many, that's all. She loves her tranquillisers. Trust me,' he said. 'You won't find a trace of Rohypnol in her bloodwork, and the autopsy report will pronounce liver failure brought on by prescription drug abuse.'

Something in his voice made her believe him. All the way through, Joshua had been pointing out weaknesses. Verity's, P.J.'s, Eve's, the Broome family secret, his own mother's, and now hers. Idiosyncrasies that played straight into his hands. She abandoned her position and moved to the back of the car where Maggie lay, inches from the rear bumper. There is a world of difference between being unconscious and struggling to stay alive. Maggie was blue. Her eyes had rolled to the back of her head and she was frothing at the mouth. Jessie pushed her fingers down Maggie's throat, rolled her on to her side and watched the contents of her flatmate's stomach regurgitate on to the compact earth.

When the engine suddenly burst into life, instinct took over. Jessie dropped Maggie, pulled out her gun and shot once through the rear window without a warning. Then she moved round the right side of the car, kicked the door fully open and stared at the shattered glass on the old leather seat. Joshua was not inside. She screamed for back-up and started to run, frantically searching the other cars. Joshua had always intended to leave this place, the question was how.

Within seconds, police were streaming through the gates, checking every car they passed. Jessie was barking orders: 'Lock the gates!' 'Check under the cars!' 'Find him!' The paramedics arrived and Jessie led them to the Beetle, then watched as they carried Maggie's limp body away from the car and laid her on a stretcher. Maggie was grey. She wasn't breathing.

'What happened?' asked Jessie, moving incessantly around the working paramedics.

'She's choked.'

'Oh my God,' cried Jessie. 'I left her, I . . .' She fell to her knees and began to pray as one of the paramedics ripped open Maggie's shirt and began to pump her heart while the other breathed air into her mouth. The equipment was charged, and everyone stood back as 200 joules of electricity passed through her flatmate's body. Jessie continued to pray as oxygen was manually pumped into Maggie's lungs. The paramedic felt for a pulse, the world shrank and time expanded. Sometimes Jessie thinks she is still on her knees praying to God on a piece of land into which the luckless were thrown.

She would kill Joshua if Maggie died. She would find a way. Somehow. And then the paramedic nodded. He'd found a pulse. They raised the stretcher to its full height and pushed Maggie across the crude, uneven burial ground.

The police, meanwhile, had stopped their frenetic search. Joshua Cadell had disappeared.

From the first moment she had seen him with wisps of mist swirling around his ankles on the morning Verity Shore's remains were discovered, Jessie had sensed that there was something very special about Niaz Ahmet. And she had been right. About that, if nothing else. While the police had searched every car in the place, Niaz had slipped away to the back of the perimeter fence and gone in search of Joshua's getaway vehicle. He knew this piece of wasteland was used by dealers, and he calculated that to transport their illicit goods safely it had to be done at night, when the place was empty. After the gates were locked. The car park was separated from the backs of the surrounding buildings by a high wire fence and a narrow passageway. The wire had been cut several months before. All you needed was to know where and which bits to untwist in order to escape unseen through the back of one of the buildings and out into a rabbit warren of narrow streets that led south to Old Street with its seven subway entrances or east to the sprawling council estate, north to Kings Cross, or east back to Bethnal Green.

Niaz found the bike propped unchained behind some rubbish carts. He removed the bolts that held the wheels in place and loosened the seat. When Joshua jumped on the bike and pushed down on the pedal, the front wheel jammed, the frame lurched forward and the seat dropped six inches, causing temporarily crippling injuries. Under normal circumstances, Niaz would not have been strong enough to overpower Joshua, but with his opponent on the floor, writhing in agony, all he had to do was walk up behind him and swipe him round the head with his standard-issue cosh.

～

Jessie heard the same unmistakable scrape of metal against metal and saw the large brown eye peer out at her. The expression had changed. As Jessie had known it would.

Jones' tenacity had finally paid off: Frank had been found. The trail had led to a Dr John Gurney, who had arranged for wealthy, childless parents who did not fit the adoption rules of the time to have a child from care. At a price, of course. The child in question would have no siblings and no surviving immediate family. Names were changed, records were lost, death certificates were forged. Three stones were buried and one child went on to a new and hopefully happy life. Jones did not discover a paedophile ring, he discovered an eccentric and ageing philanthropist who believed he was rescuing these children from a terrible life in care.

Irene, in her promise to Veronica to keep Frank away from St Giles, had signed him over as Trevor White. White was Trevor's mother's maiden name. That was why two cars had arrived the day after Veronica died.

On paper, little Frank was perfect for Dr Gurney's purposes. A loner. Trevor White became Gareth Blake and Gareth Blake was put to death on paper and reborn as son and heir to a Mr and Mrs Tennant. No one reckoned on Clare and her unceasing tenacity. Irene had always believed she'd failed and that Ray had found Frank and taken him away. She could never have imagined what had really happened. So she clung on to her secret, year in year out, believing that she was protecting Clare from the truth. Now Clare knew the truth, but that wasn't the cause of the bravado in the big brown eye that stared back through the crack in the door.

'Can I come in?'

'It's not a good time.'

Jessie shook her head. 'I want to do this quietly, Clare. Don't make me have to call for back-up. I need to talk to Alistair.'

Clare's eye widened.

'Let her in,' said a voice from inside the flat.

They were sitting around the coffee table sipping whiskey-laden tea: Clare, Alistair, Irene. Irene's bruise was now yellow.

'How did you know Joshua Cadell was killing people, Alistair?'

Three mouths gaped at her like guppies in an aquarium.

'Let's not make this any harder than it has to be,' said Jessie.

'Don't say anything –' said Clare.

'It's okay,' reassured Alistair. 'You said she was smart.' He looked at Jessie. 'I was following the women on Ray's orders. I had no idea what was going to happen.'

'Why didn't you tell us?' asked Jessie. 'You could have stopped those women dying.'

'Honestly,' said Alistair, 'it was only when Cosima died that I knew it was him for sure. I'd seen them leave a party together and drive off. He was dressed like a chauffeur. She was in on the joke – it got her away from some lecherous bloke.'

Jessie folded her arms in front of her.

'How it looks to me, is that you knew Joshua's modus operandi and were waiting until you could kill Ray and make it look like the Z-list Killer had struck again.'

'It wasn't like that,' said Clare.

'It was my fault,' said Irene. 'I thought he was Frank. I went to tell him to warn Ray that the police were nearly at their door. I was terrified Clare was going to find out. I thought Frank would understand. All I did was tell Alistair the reason why his old man had never given a damn about him or his mother. Ray only had eyes for Veronica, he didn't care who he hurt along the way.'

'All those women I'd dug dirt on, I couldn't find

a grain on Ray. I'd never even heard of Veronica and Frank. I thought Trevor had been another gang member. Ray had just used Mum to make Veronica jealous; he didn't give a shit that he'd ruined her life. Or mine. The bastard. He probably would have killed Mum too, if she'd made a fuss, but she took herself back to the country and never got over it. Something in me snapped when Irene told me about Veronica. I hit her, left her unconscious on the floor, and went to the cemetery. Those fucking roses.'

'Me, too. I was there too,' said Clare. 'Everything I told you was true. I was on my knees, I thought he was going to kill me, then this bloke turned up. Ray smiled at him and told him to finish me off. He raised his arm, I prayed to Mum to save me and it worked. Alistair hit Ray on the back of the neck. He went down immediately. We took him to the crypt, Alistair told me everything Irene had told him. Between the two of us, we soon filled in the rest –'

'Clare didn't do anything,' interrupted Alistair. 'It was me – and I don't mind going to prison for it.'

'Alistair –'

'Please, Clare. You're the best thing that's come out of all this shit.'

'I'm not letting you do this alone.'

'Clare, please, we've talked about this.'

'Alistair, if you identify Joshua, I will make a deal that we lower the charge to manslaughter.

You went back to Irene when we showed up, you woke her up and told her to return to the cemetery. You told Irene what to say to Clare. There was no tall, ghostly figure in the cemetery, but you were pointing me in the right direction and that probably saved Maggie Hall's life. I will help you.'

'How did you know?' asked Clare.

'The blood on your fingers,' Jessie replied. 'It wasn't from your head. You never were unconscious. You pushed the biro off Ray's vein.' Clare opened her mouth. 'But I can't prove it and I don't want to. The pathologist found the biro further inside his leg. It could have slipped.'

'I'll tell you –'

'It slipped,' said Alistair. 'This is my fault. I killed Ray.'

'No, it's mine,' said Irene.

'No it isn't,' said Clare. 'It's my mother's, for having the affair with him in the first place.'

'Don't be too harsh on her, Clare,' said Jessie. 'It was your mother who told the police where to find Ray.'

Irene and Clare stared at her in disbelief.

'I traced the phone number. It was the payphone in the hospital. I think she was trying to make amends.' Jessie stood up. 'Alistair, will you come with me? There's someone I need you to identify.'

'I really didn't work it out until Cosima. I wouldn't have let those women die – that would have been the sort of thing he did, and I'm nothing like him.'

'I believe you,' said Jessie.

'He saved me,' said Clare.

'And that will work in his favour as well. What about Tarek? Where is he?'

'Channel Five, I think. I wanted to warn him off. Tarek had used up his lives, Ray was going to get rid of him, permanently, if he made any more trouble. He was going to sue if you came after him again. You would have unwittingly created a hero. Ray St Giles, a hero? It doesn't make sense, does it?'

'No,' said Jessie. 'It doesn't.'

'I'll come and visit,' said Clare as Jessie led Alistair to the door.

'I'd like that. You should both go and meet my granddad, he's practically family now.' Clare hugged him. At last she had a brother. A true blood brother. Veronica had been wrong. Bad blood was better than no blood. Jessie looked at Clare.

'What are you going to do about Frank?'

'I don't know,' said Clare. 'I come with quite a story.'

~

'I deny everything,' said Joshua. 'I had absolutely nothing to do with the crimes you are accusing me of. Ask Maggie if I forced pills down her throat. I didn't.'

'Maggie can't talk at the moment.' She'd had her stomach pumped, her blood washed out with saline, and adrenaline injected into her to keep her blood pressure from dropping again. Initial tests showed no Rohypnol in the blood. But Sally had found traces of many other pharmaceuticals.

'Where is your evidence?'

'We have someone who can place you at the house in Barnes. You left your own evidence with Eve Wirrel, and when Cosima's dress is fully examined, I have no doubt we will find something you left behind there.'

'If the crime is sleeping with Verity and Eve, then you'll have to arrest half of London. Including my dear old dad.'

'You were also seen driving Cosima to Haverbrook Hall the night she died.'

'Come on, Jessie, you can't really think –'

'Don't "Jessie" me.'

'Why not? It worked for P.J.,' said Joshua sharply.

Jessie leant across the table. 'And I myself saw you leaving my flat after you'd slept with Maggie.'

'So? The girls like me.'

'They like your mother. Her status.'

Joshua shrank from her.

'I spoke to your mother's agent this morning. I'm afraid when Henrietta showed your work to him, she told him in no uncertain terms that he was *not* to get you a deal. She ruined your career.'

'That's not true.'

'I'm afraid it is. Just like she used to lock you in dark places on your own, like she used to tell you bloodthirsty stories then make it all better when you had nightmares. Violence and affection are intertwined in your psyche, Joshua.'

'Bullshit! Armchair psychobabble. I'm sure it works great with lesser mortals, but –'

'Your methods were ingenious, but the messages to your mother were obvious once I knew where to look.' Jessie pushed over the four titles: *A Smuggler's Tale; Father Bernard – A Recusant Priest; Isabella of France;* and the manuscript on London's Great Disease. 'Henrietta told you that loyal mothers like her would jump into the burial pits to be with their dead children. More and more bodies would be piled on top of them until they died of suffocation. But you know deep down that her loyalty is only to herself. She won't join you in this pit. She has her reputation to think of.'

'Why? Why would I kill all those women?'

'Because they were famous and you weren't, and it drove you mad. You knew what they were really like, behind the glossy photos and the PR bollocks.'

'No. You're bluffing. I know you.'

'Not as well as you think.' Jessie slowly pulled back her leather jacket and showed him the mini-disk clipped to the inside. 'I lost a good track, recording you.' She pressed 'play' and Joshua's voice filled the room.

'. . . I would not have had to slit another vein after Cosima died because everyone would have known it was me whether it had my insignia or not. Eventually, all the great artists stop signing . . .'

Jessie stopped the machine and looked at Joshua. 'Add it all up, and it's not a bad case against you,' she said.

'I want my mother,' he said.

'She's had to go on a book-signing tour.'

'I want my mother,' Joshua said again, louder.

'Christopher is here. He wants to see you.'

Joshua suddenly stood up and ran to the locked door. 'NO! I WANT MY MOTHER! I WANT MY MOTHER! MOTHER! MOTHER!' He turned back to Jessie. 'She always comes in the end, always . . .'

Jessie took his arm and led him back to the chair. 'We'll get you help.'

'She loves me,' said Joshua. 'She won't be able to cope without me. She needs me, you see. I'm all she has, don't you understand . . . ?'

Jessie softly closed the door as Joshua continued to mumble quiet words to himself.

EPILOGUE

Jessie held the plastic bag containing the white-tipped cigarette found outside her house and continued to stare in disbelief at the typed details on the corresponding report. P. J. Dean. He'd stood outside her house. Why? It was the one thing that didn't add up.

'He probably came to explain the lawsuit.'

Jessie looked up and saw Niaz in the doorway. She smiled, stood up, walked around the desk and gave him a hug.

'You have proved yourself more than worthy of the murder squad. I was wondering if you'd like to remain here? Depending, of course, on the outcome of the Dean investigation. I may not be here myself . . .'

'Ma'am, he isn't going to go through with it.'

She appreciated his confidence but didn't share it. 'It'll mean long hours, Niaz, and exams.'

His head shook on his long neck. 'No matter. My wife won't mind.'

Jessie was horrified. They had been through a whole case together and she didn't even know he was married.

'I'm so sorry, Niaz, I never asked. I'd love to meet her.'

'You will, when I have. And when I do, she'll understand about the long hours. I can feel it.'

She had an overwhelming desire to kiss Niaz. 'Okay, Niaz, I'll talk to Jones straight away.' Jessie looked back at the cigarette. 'You really think he came to explain?'

'Absolutely.'

'How can you be so sure?' Jessie unlocked her filing cabinet and carefully placed the envelope inside.

'Because he is here.'

'Not funny, genie. With that transfer in mind, don't you think you should go to the surprise drinks that Burrows has organised, rather than standing here and taunting me about bloody P. J. Dean,' she said, carefully closing the drawer and locking it.

'Actually, ma'am, he is here. Standing right next to me.'

Jessie looked up. And he was. Niaz retreated, smiling quietly to himself as he was prone to do. Jessie went through a rapid succession of emotions. Embarrassment, guilt, humiliation, but recovered quite well with anger.

'You're suing me. If you want to live, you should leave,' said Jessie.

'It wasn't me, it was the record label – damage limitation bollocks. Anyway, I've put a stop to it.' P.J. pointed to the plastic bag containing the cigarette. 'Mine?'

Jessie nodded.

'I came to explain, but I chickened out,' he said. 'Then I came here, but you've been busy.'

'Here? Did you speak to –'

'Frances Leonard. Yes. Another problem I should have addressed a long time ago. We talked about everything. She isn't mad, she's just lonely. I guess on closer inspection I lost some of that sheen she thought I had.' He paused. 'And she isn't the only one to think less of me now, is she?'

Jessie wouldn't be drawn on that. She tidied her desk and didn't look at him.

'Anyway, I wanted to say sorry. Sorry for what happened in the garden.'

Jessie relented. 'It was my fault.'

'How is that possible when I was the one who lied, I was the one who left Bernie with that man, and I was the one who ignored Verity's misery so I could keep the illusion of a family around me? If I'd told you about Eve earlier, she might still be alive. And I did that for the most unforgivable reason.'

Jessie waited.

'I didn't want you to think badly of me.'

Jessie smiled slightly. 'In retrospect, shagging Eve Wirrel was probably the least of your worries.'

'Yeah, well, that's famous people for you – short

on perspective. Long on selfishness, blind ambition, insecurity, money and misery.'

Jessie tilted her head to one side. She could still see the metal plates shooting volts through Maggie's chest. 'Why do it then?' she asked seriously. 'When it so often ends in tears?'

P.J. leant back against the doorframe. 'To escape, I suppose.'

'And do you?'

'No.' P.J. paused, his green eyes studying her. Jessie stared straight back. 'Unless you're lucky and meet someone who doesn't believe the hype.'

'But, P.J., you are the hype, you created the hype.'

'That is the nature of the beast.'

Jessie shook her head and stood up. 'You know what, I've seen way too much of that beast and, although I'm sure you'd love to talk about yourself for the next few hours, I am very thirsty. I have a pub full of people waiting to surprise *me* on *my* success. I'm probably going to get very pissed, I might even dance on a few tables, cry into my pint. And it is possible that around eleven I'll puke up because I can't remember when I last ate.'

P.J. was smiling at her. It wasn't the reaction she'd expected.

'So, if you don't mind, I'd like to go to the pub.'

'Can I at least help you on your way and buy you a drink?'

Perhaps she should have said no. But she didn't. 'You'd better get in there quick. I'm a popular girl at the moment.'

'That comes as no surprise to me,' said P.J., a smile in his eyes.

'No queue-barging, just because you've been on *Top of the Pops*.'

He saluted. 'Yes, ma'am.'

'Or signing of autographs.'

'Yes, ma'am.'

'And don't expect me to protect you from the lads. They can be brutal.'

'I never expected you to make this easy for me.'

'And the first whiff of a photographer, you will do the decent thing and bugger off.'

'Not necessarily.' P.J. held the door open. 'Come on, your fans await.'

Jessie peeled on her leather jacket. 'Not fans.'

'No. Not fans. Colleagues. People who admire you. People who look up to you. People who respect you because you are good at your job. And the odd hanger-on who would like to cook you cheese on toast some time, drink red wine and play Scrabble.'

'Scrabble?' she mocked.

'Not Scrabble then. Whatever you like doing, anything – just don't write me off yet.'

'I like dancing,' she said, zipping up her jacket.

P.J. lowered his head into his hands and groaned.

'What? You're always prancing about in those videos.'

He looked at her through his fingers. 'I thought you said you'd never listened to my songs?'

'Just doing my job,' said Jessie primly.

'Did you like them?'

She stood opposite him in the narrow doorway. 'Don't change the subject. Can you dance?'

P.J. shook his head slowly from left to right.

'And the videos?'

'Body doubles.'

'I don't believe it. You are a con, Paul John Dean.'

P.J. laughed loudly and took her arm. 'At last,' he said. 'A woman who understands me.'